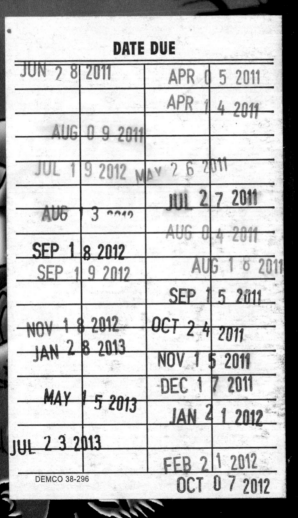

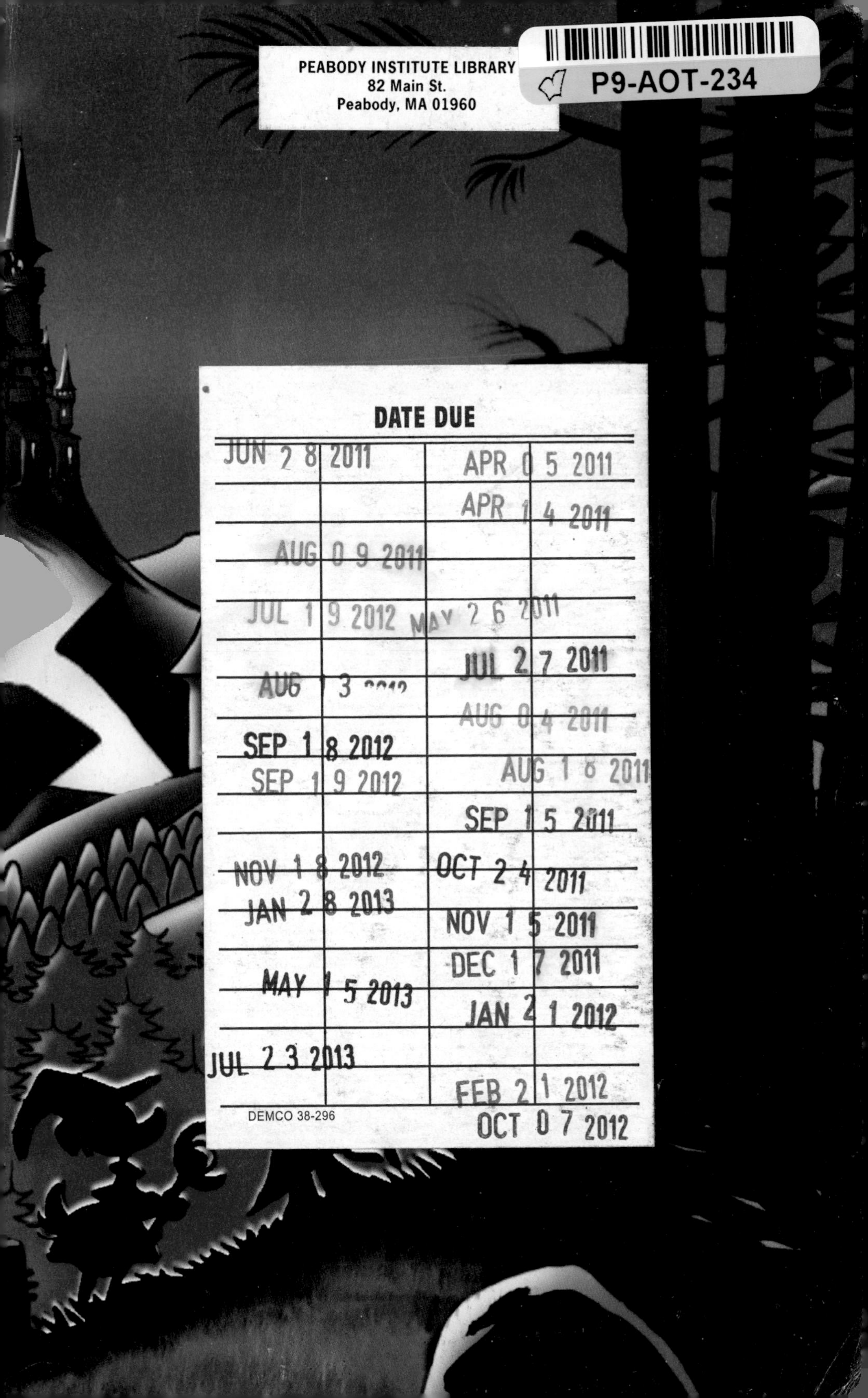

Walt Disney's Wizards of Mickey
Battle for the Crown

Ross Richie - Chief Executive Officer	Bryce Carlson - Managing Editor	Neil Loughrie - Publishing Coordinator
Mark Waid - Chief Creative Officer	Ian Brill - Editor	Travis Beaty - Traffic Coordinator
Matt Gagnon - Editor-in-Chief	Dafna Pleban - Editor	Ivan Salazar - Marketing Assistant
Adam Fortier - VP-New Business	Christopher Burns - Editor	Kate Hayden - Executive Assistant
Wes Harris - VP-Publishing	Christopher Meyer - Editor	Brian Latimer - Lead Graphic Designer
Lance Kreiter - VP-Licensing & Merchandising	Shannon Watters - Assistant Editor	Erika Terriquez - Graphic Designer
Chip Mosher - Marketing Director	Eric Harburn - Assistant Editor	

Office of publication: 6310 San Vicente Blvd Ste 107, Los Angeles, CA 90048-5457.

A catalog record for this book is available from OCLC and on our website www.boom-kids.com on the Librarians page.

For information regarding the CPSIA on this printed material call: 203-595-3636 and provide reference # EAST – 70232

FIRST EDITION: DECEMBER 2010

10 9 8 7 6 5 4 3 2 1

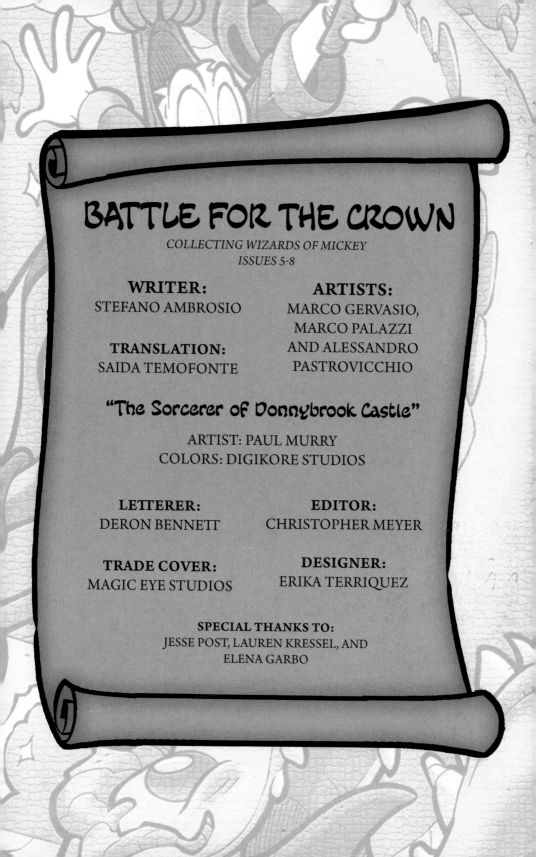

BATTLE FOR THE CROWN

COLLECTING WIZARDS OF MICKEY
ISSUES 5-8

WRITER:
STEFANO AMBROSIO

ARTISTS:
MARCO GERVASIO,
MARCO PALAZZI
AND ALESSANDRO
PASTROVICCHIO

TRANSLATION:
SAIDA TEMOFONTE

"The Sorcerer of Donnybrook Castle"

ARTIST: PAUL MURRY
COLORS: DIGIKORE STUDIOS

LETTERER:
DERON BENNETT

EDITOR:
CHRISTOPHER MEYER

TRADE COVER:
MAGIC EYE STUDIOS

DESIGNER:
ERIKA TERRIQUEZ

SPECIAL THANKS TO:
JESSE POST, LAUREN KRESSEL, AND
ELENA GARBO

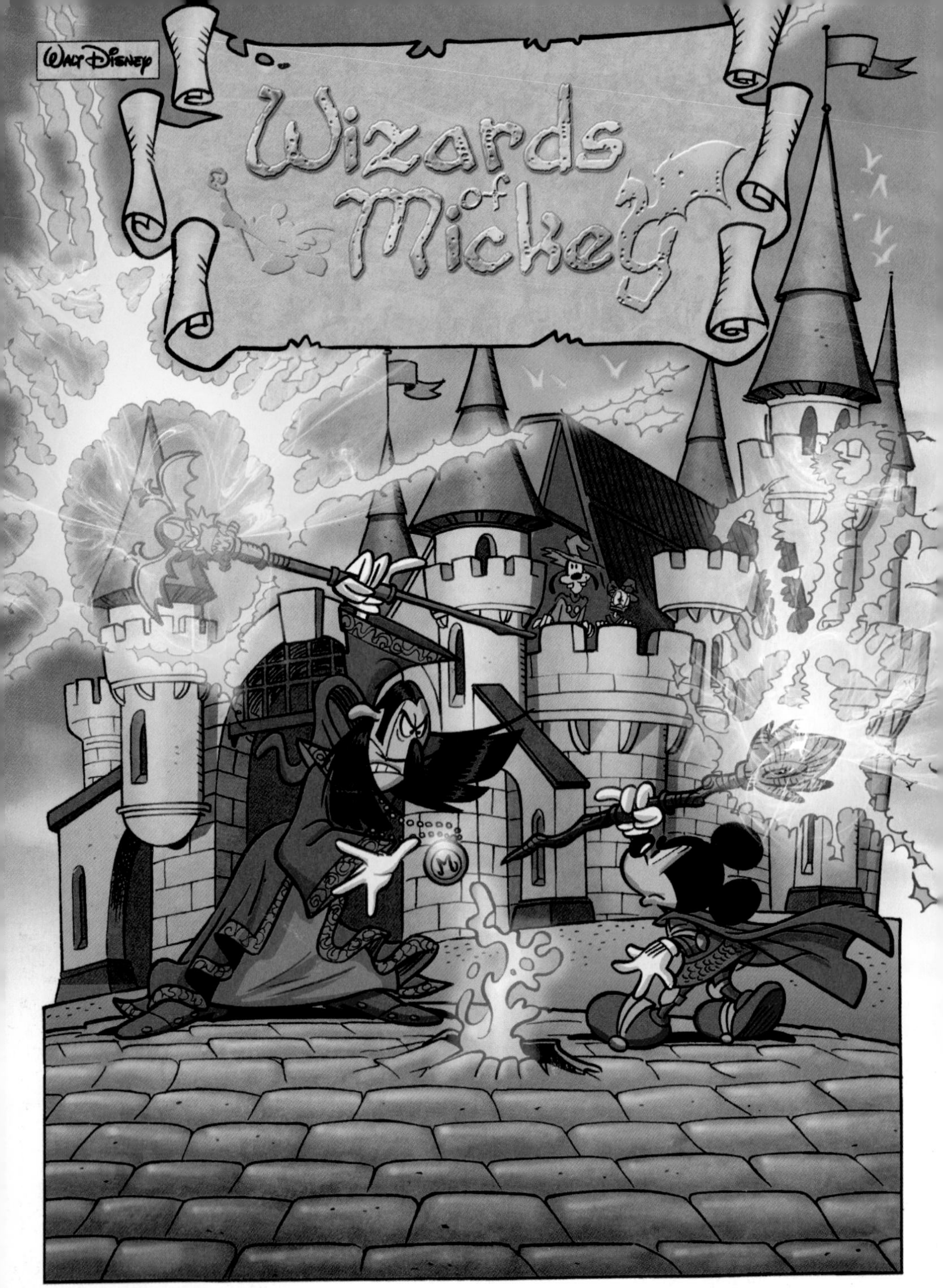
Walt Disney
Wizards of Mickey

Our story so far... Mickey has formed the ***Wizards of Mickey*** with ***Donald*** and ***Goofy*** to enter the great sorcery tournament! Preparing for a match against the ***Tapestry Sorcerers***, they have traveled to the town of Blackburg. There, they've run afoul of ***Peg-Leg Pete*** and the ***Beagle Brothers***, who are scamming money out of the local townsfolk by pretending to be monster hunters! However, a ***real monster*** is headed right for Blackburg — and it's been following the Wizards of Mickey!

EPISODE 8: MONSTER GAMES

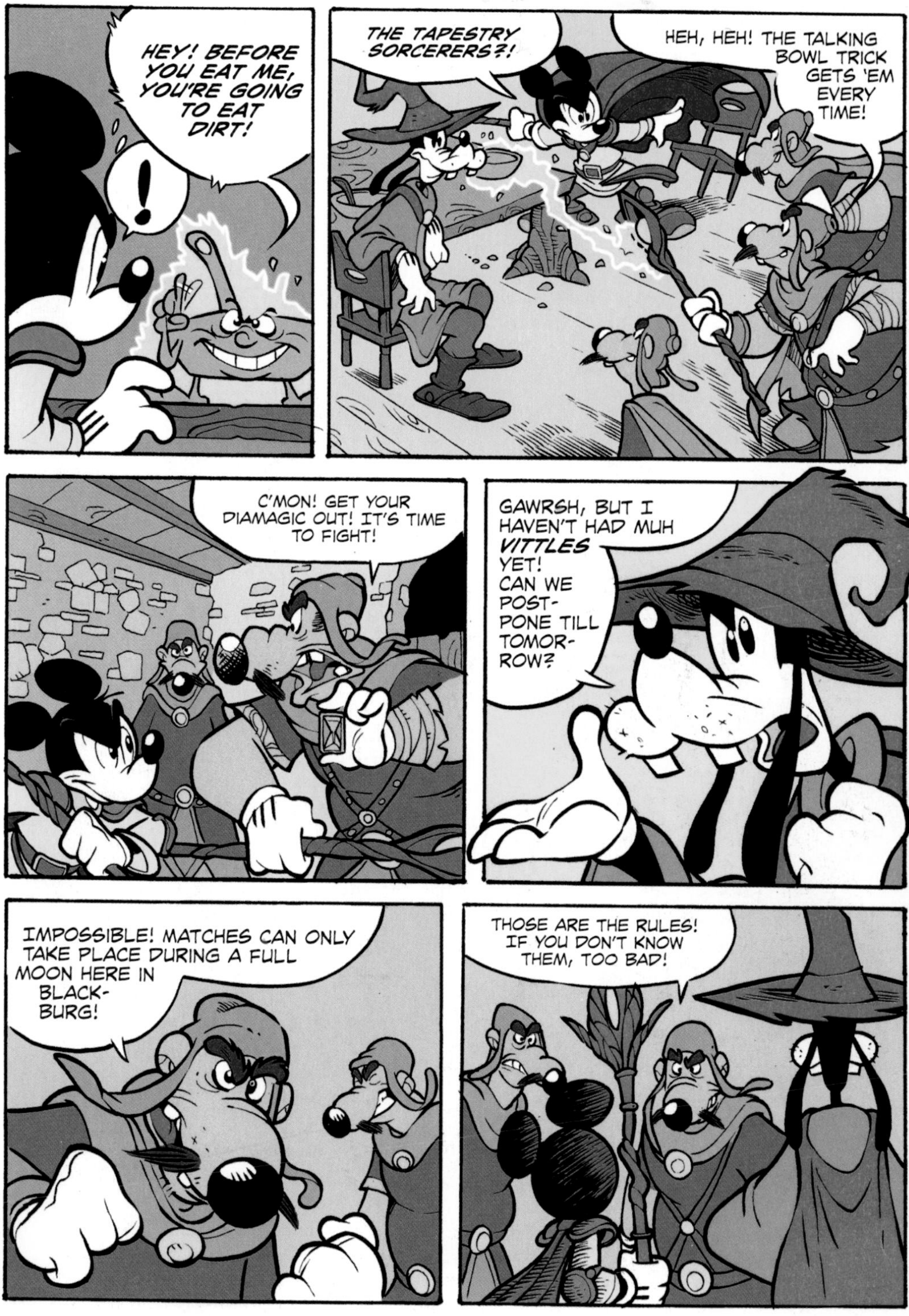
HEY! BEFORE YOU EAT ME, YOU'RE GOING TO EAT DIRT!
!
THE TAPESTRY SORCERERS?!
HEH, HEH! THE TALKING BOWL TRICK GETS 'EM EVERY TIME!
C'MON! GET YOUR DIAMAGIC OUT! IT'S TIME TO FIGHT!
GAWRSH, BUT I HAVEN'T HAD MUH VITTLES YET! CAN WE POST-PONE TILL TOMOR-ROW?
IMPOSSIBLE! MATCHES CAN ONLY TAKE PLACE DURING A FULL MOON HERE IN BLACK-BURG!
THOSE ARE THE RULES! IF YOU DON'T KNOW THEM, TOO BAD!

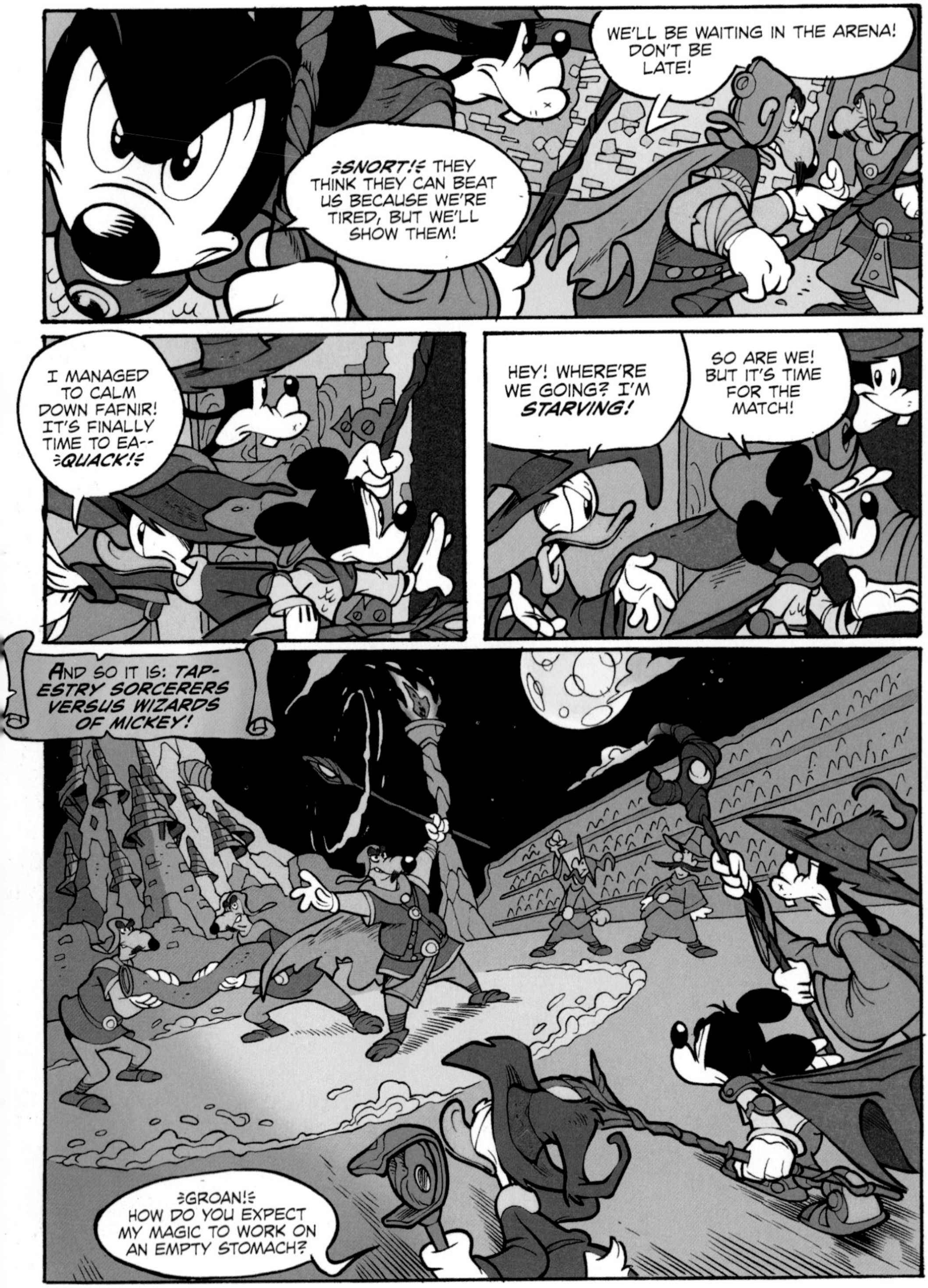

WE'LL BE WAITING IN THE ARENA! DON'T BE LATE!
SNORT! THEY THINK THEY CAN BEAT US BECAUSE WE'RE TIRED, BUT WE'LL SHOW THEM!
I MANAGED TO CALM DOWN FAFNIR! IT'S FINALLY TIME TO EA-- QUACK!
HEY! WHERE'RE WE GOING? I'M STARVING!
SO ARE WE! BUT IT'S TIME FOR THE MATCH!
AND SO IT IS: TAPESTRY SORCERERS VERSUS WIZARDS OF MICKEY!
GROAN! HOW DO YOU EXPECT MY MAGIC TO WORK ON AN EMPTY STOMACH?

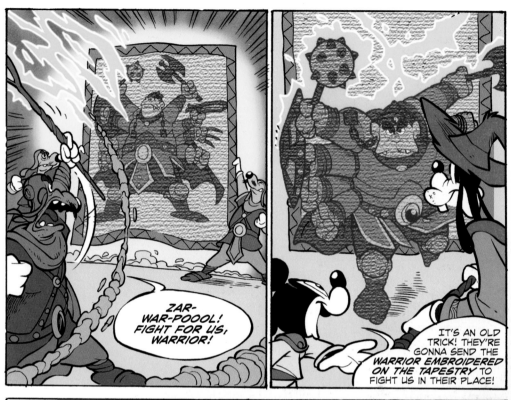

ZAR-WAR-POOOL! FIGHT FOR US, WARRIOR!

IT'S AN OLD TRICK! THEY'RE GONNA SEND THE *WARRIOR EMBROIDERED ON THE TAPESTRY* TO FIGHT US IN THEIR PLACE!

AND WE'LL DEFEAT HIM THE USUAL WAY...BY *UNRAVELING IT LIKE A BALL OF YARN!*

SWOSSSH

ZINC

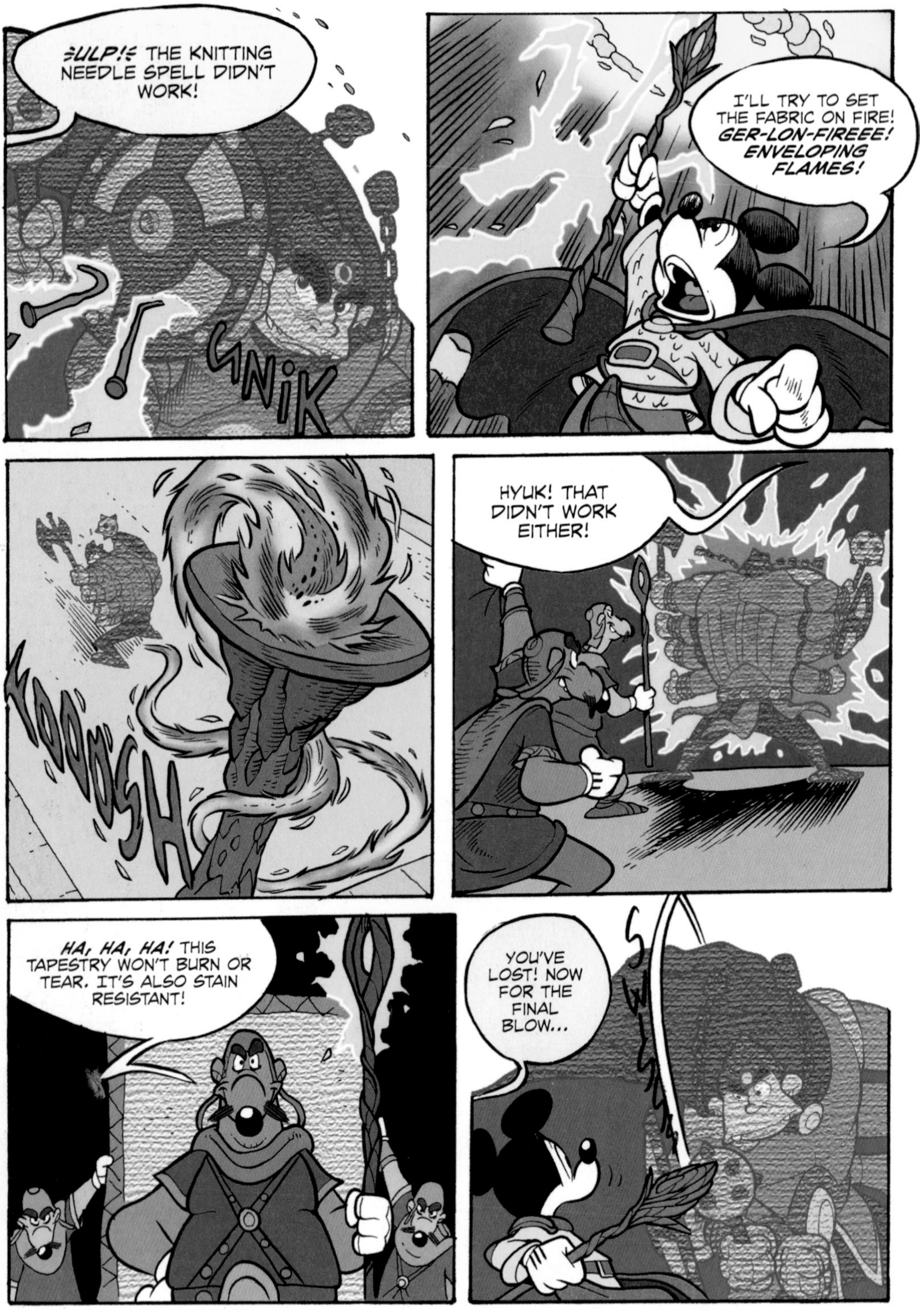
GULP! THE KNITTING NEEDLE SPELL DIDN'T WORK!
UNIK
I'LL TRY TO SET THE FABRIC ON FIRE! GER-LON-FIREEE! ENVELOPING FLAMES!
WOOOSH
HYUK! THAT DIDN'T WORK EITHER!
HA, HA, HA! THIS TAPESTRY WON'T BURN OR TEAR. IT'S ALSO STAIN RESISTANT!
YOU'VE LOST! NOW FOR THE FINAL BLOW...

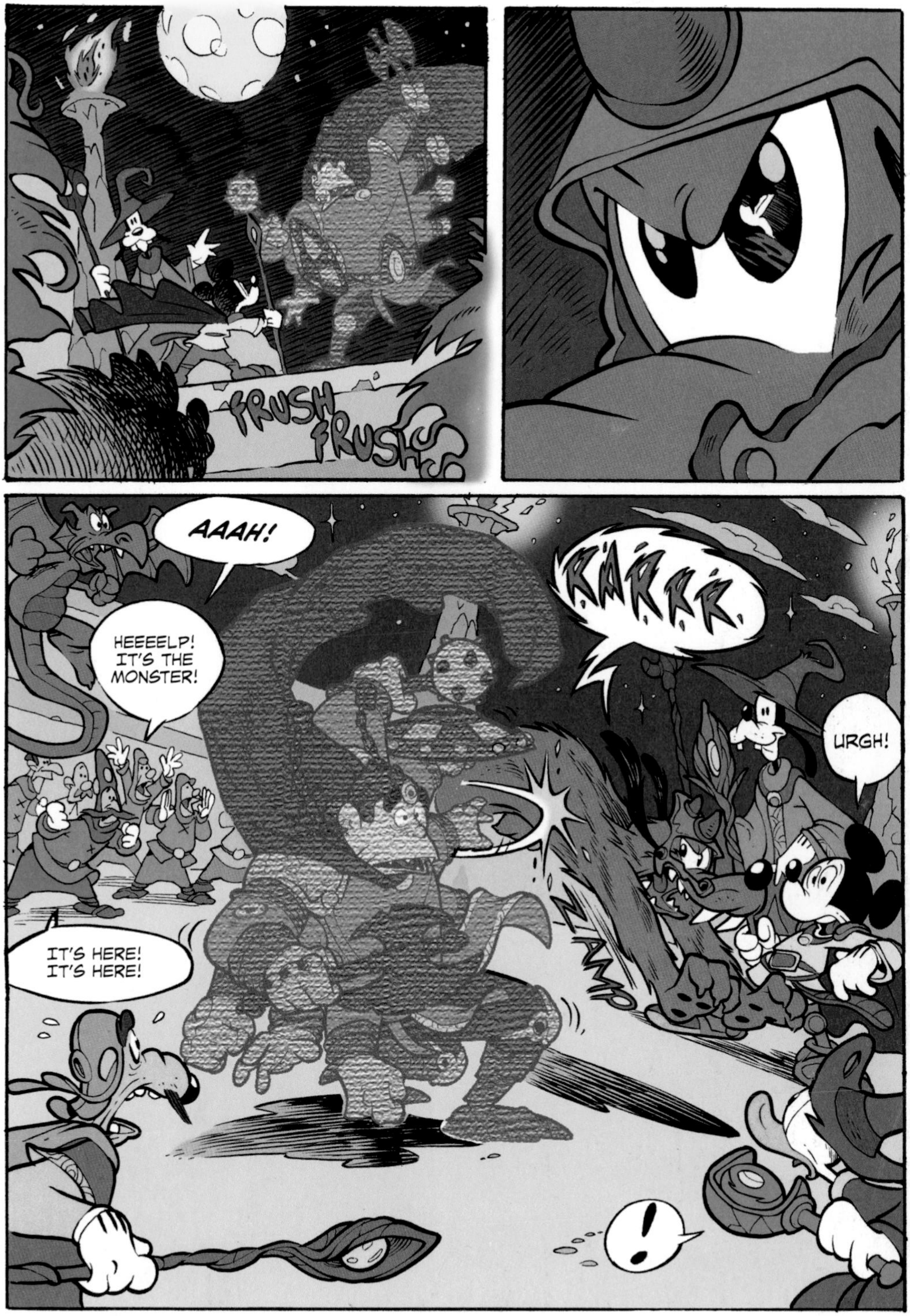
FRUSH
FRUSH
AAAH!
HEEEELP! IT'S THE MONSTER!
RARRR
URGH!
ZLAMP
IT'S HERE! IT'S HERE!
!

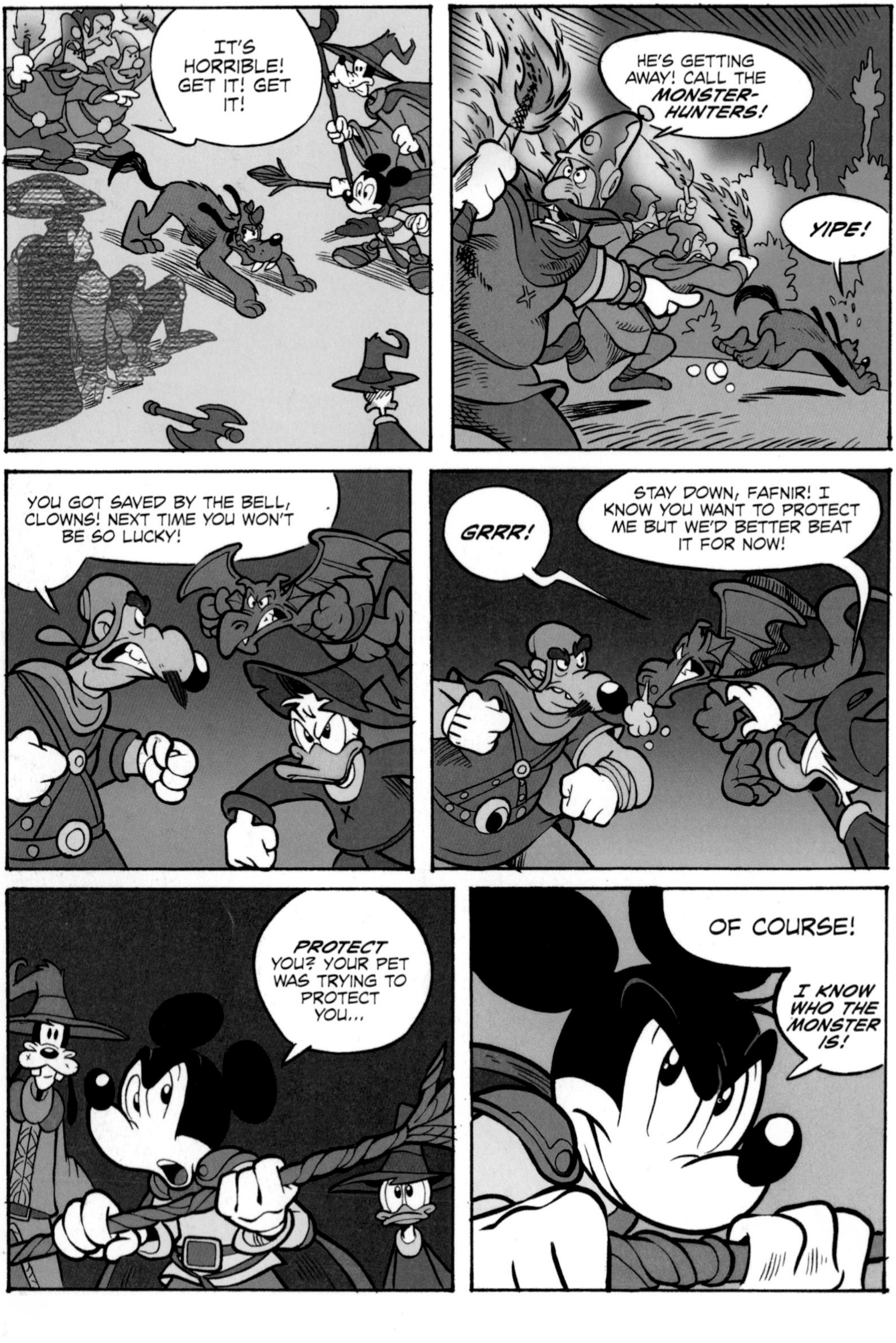
IT'S HORRIBLE! GET IT! GET IT!
HE'S GETTING AWAY! CALL THE MONSTER-HUNTERS!
YIPE!
YOU GOT SAVED BY THE BELL, CLOWNS! NEXT TIME YOU WON'T BE SO LUCKY!
GRRR!
STAY DOWN, FAFNIR! I KNOW YOU WANT TO PROTECT ME BUT WE'D BETTER BEAT IT FOR NOW!
PROTECT YOU? YOUR PET WAS TRYING TO PROTECT YOU...
OF COURSE!
I KNOW WHO THE MONSTER IS!

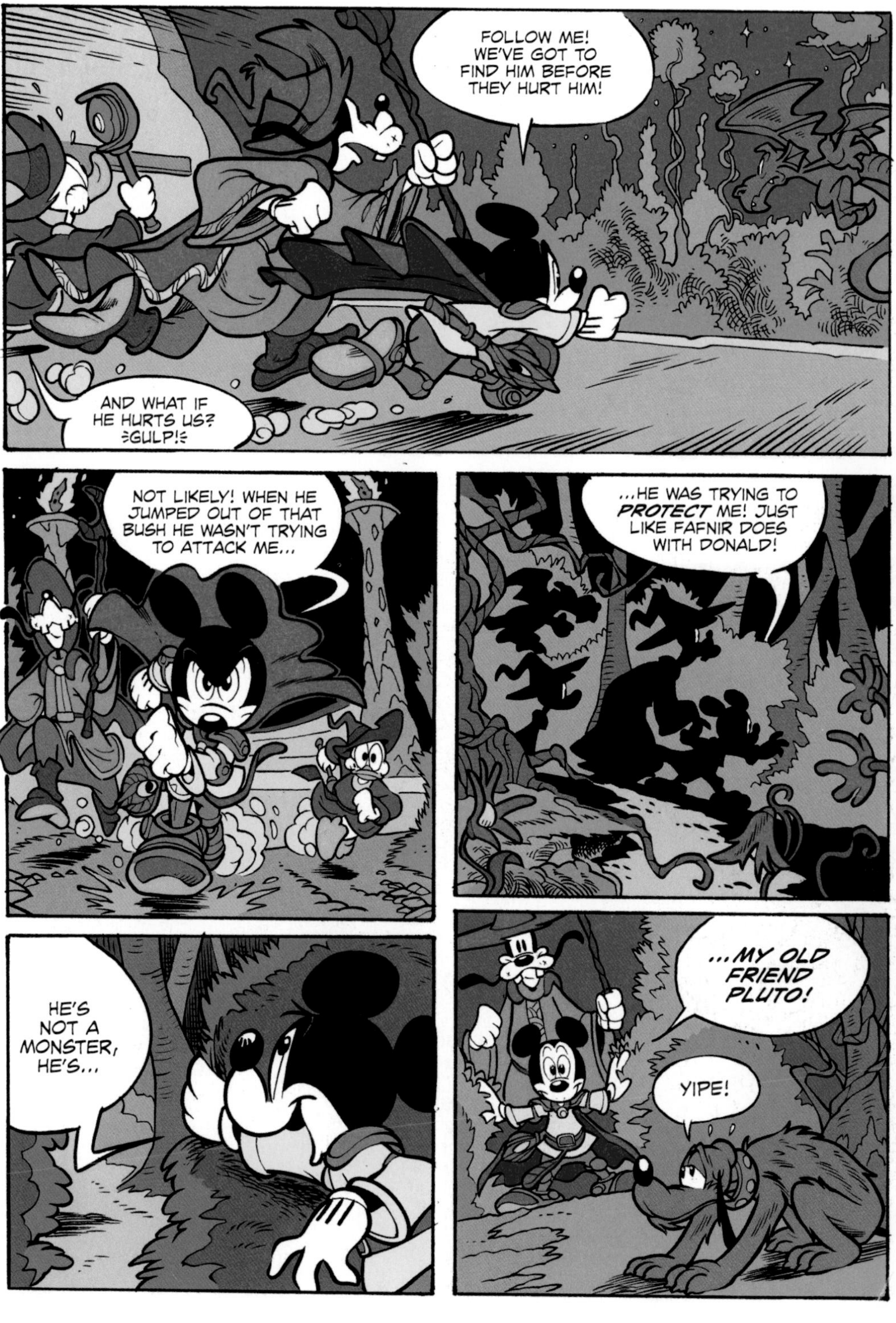
FOLLOW ME! WE'VE GOT TO FIND HIM BEFORE THEY HURT HIM!
AND WHAT IF HE HURTS US? GULP!
NOT LIKELY! WHEN HE JUMPED OUT OF THAT BUSH HE WASN'T TRYING TO ATTACK ME...
...HE WAS TRYING TO PROTECT ME! JUST LIKE FAFNIR DOES WITH DONALD!
HE'S NOT A MONSTER, HE'S...
...MY OLD FRIEND PLUTO!
YIPE!

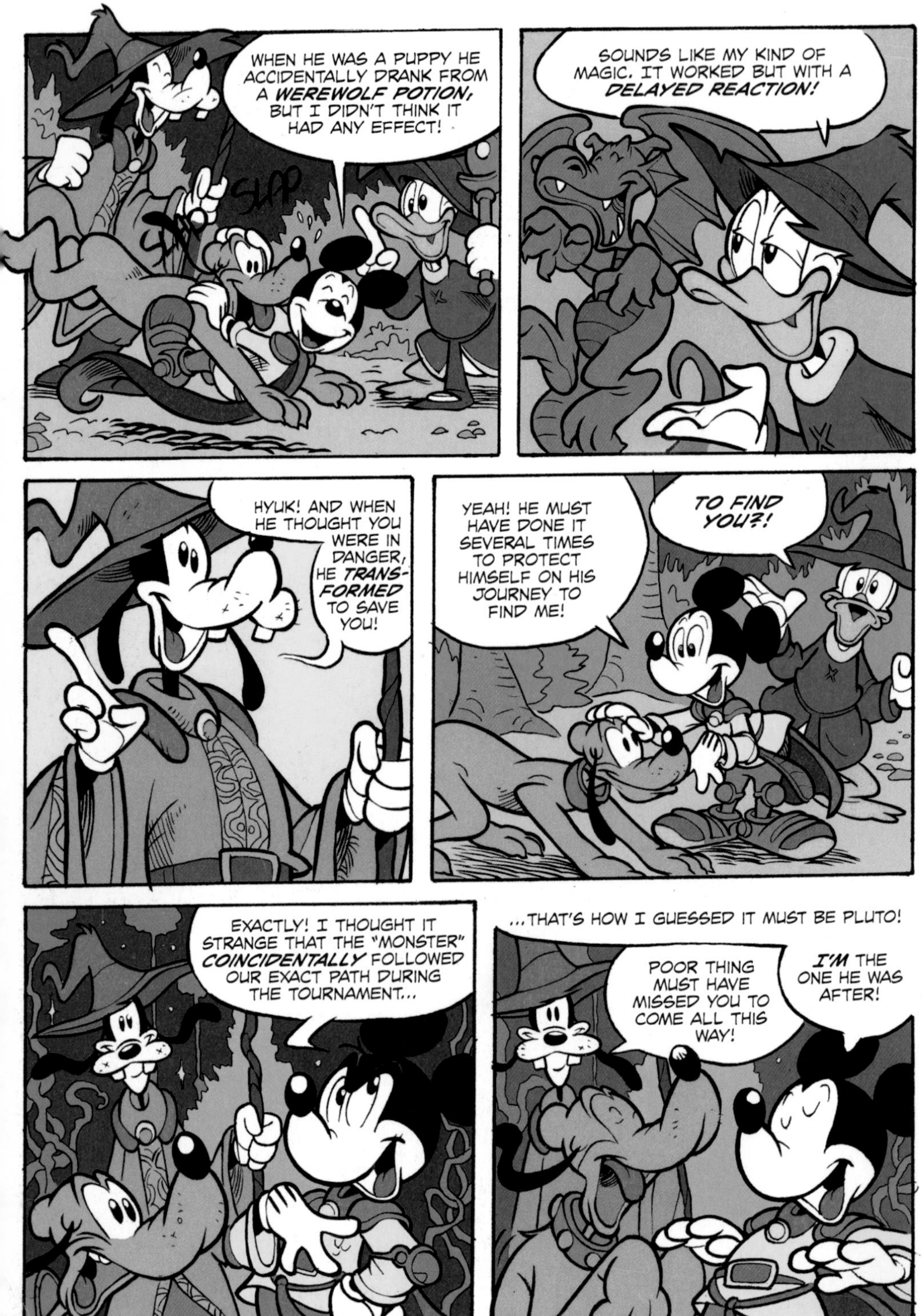
WHEN HE WAS A PUPPY HE ACCIDENTALLY DRANK FROM A WEREWOLF POTION, BUT I DIDN'T THINK IT HAD ANY EFFECT!
SLAP
SLAP
SOUNDS LIKE MY KIND OF MAGIC. IT WORKED BUT WITH A DELAYED REACTION!
HYUK! AND WHEN HE THOUGHT YOU WERE IN DANGER, HE TRANSFORMED TO SAVE YOU!
YEAH! HE MUST HAVE DONE IT SEVERAL TIMES TO PROTECT HIMSELF ON HIS JOURNEY TO FIND ME!
TO FIND YOU?!
EXACTLY! I THOUGHT IT STRANGE THAT THE "MONSTER" COINCIDENTALLY FOLLOWED OUR EXACT PATH DURING THE TOURNAMENT...
...THAT'S HOW I GUESSED IT MUST BE PLUTO!
POOR THING MUST HAVE MISSED YOU TO COME ALL THIS WAY!
I'M THE ONE HE WAS AFTER!

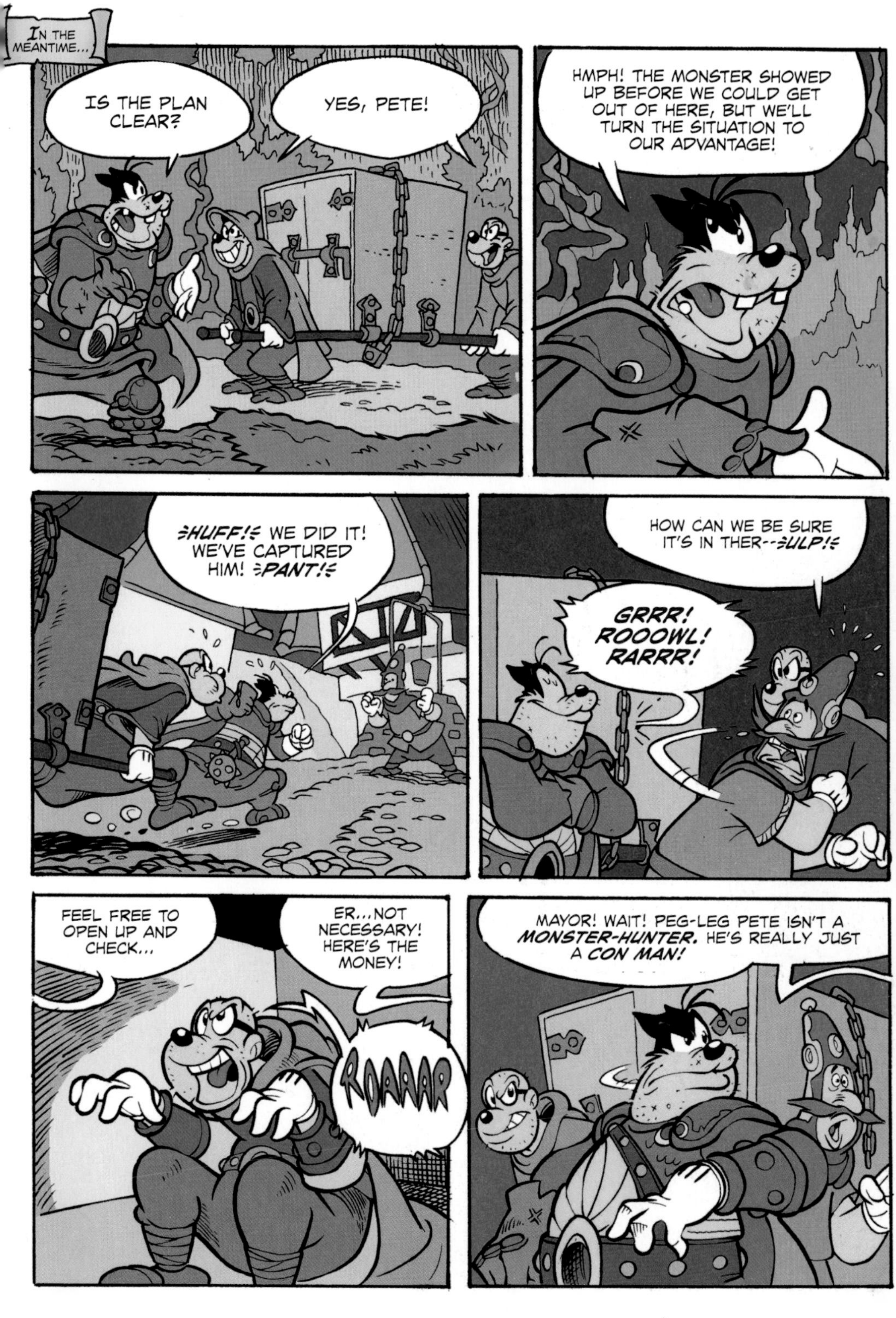
IN THE MEANTIME...
IS THE PLAN CLEAR?
YES, PETE!
HMPH! THE MONSTER SHOWED UP BEFORE WE COULD GET OUT OF HERE, BUT WE'LL TURN THE SITUATION TO OUR ADVANTAGE!
HUFF! WE DID IT! WE'VE CAPTURED HIM! PANT!
HOW CAN WE BE SURE IT'S IN THER--GULP!
GRRR! ROOOWL! RARRR!
FEEL FREE TO OPEN UP AND CHECK...
ER...NOT NECESSARY! HERE'S THE MONEY!
ROAAAR
MAYOR! WAIT! PEG-LEG PETE ISN'T A MONSTER-HUNTER. HE'S REALLY JUST A CON MAN!

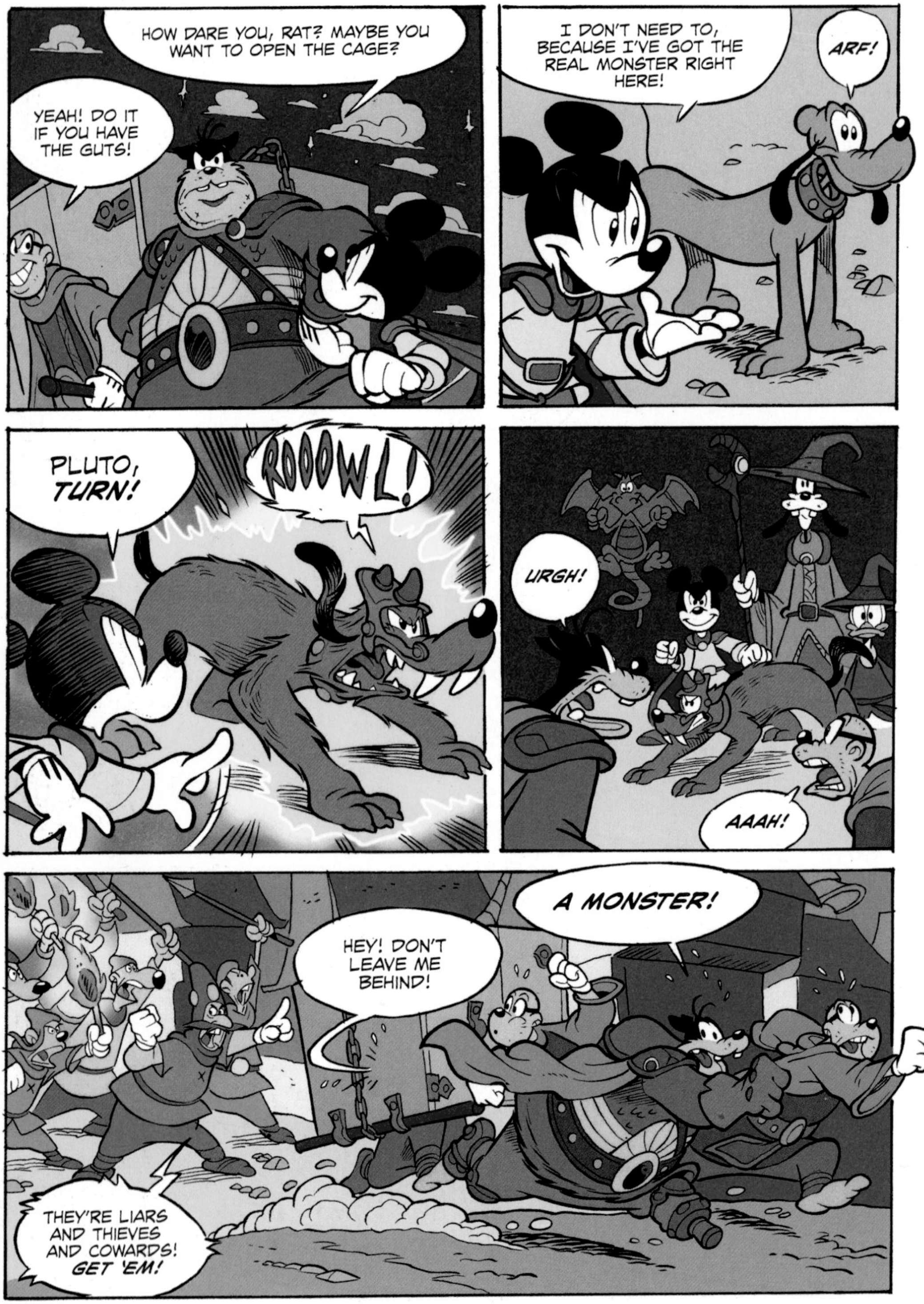
HOW DARE YOU, RAT? MAYBE YOU WANT TO OPEN THE CAGE?
YEAH! DO IT IF YOU HAVE THE GUTS!
I DON'T NEED TO, BECAUSE I'VE GOT THE REAL MONSTER RIGHT HERE!
ARF!
PLUTO, TURN!
ROOOWL!
URGH!
AAAH!
A MONSTER!
HEY! DON'T LEAVE ME BEHIND!
THEY'RE LIARS AND THIEVES AND COWARDS! GET 'EM!

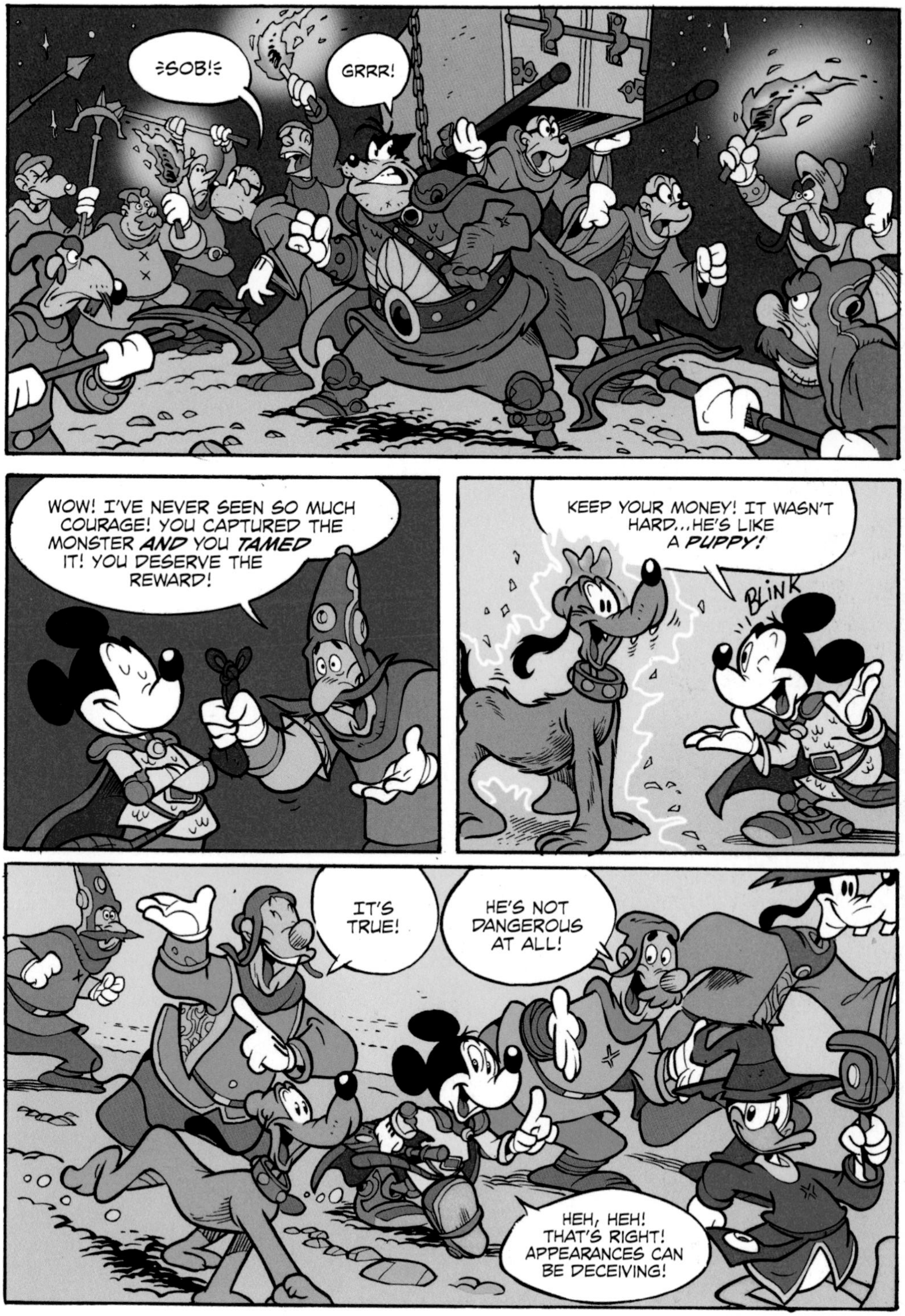

SOB!
GRRR!
WOW! I'VE NEVER SEEN SO MUCH COURAGE! YOU CAPTURED THE MONSTER *AND* YOU *TAMED* IT! YOU DESERVE THE REWARD!
KEEP YOUR MONEY! IT WASN'T HARD... HE'S LIKE A *PUPPY!*
BLINK
IT'S TRUE!
HE'S NOT DANGEROUS AT ALL!
HEH, HEH! THAT'S RIGHT! APPEARANCES CAN BE DECEIVING!

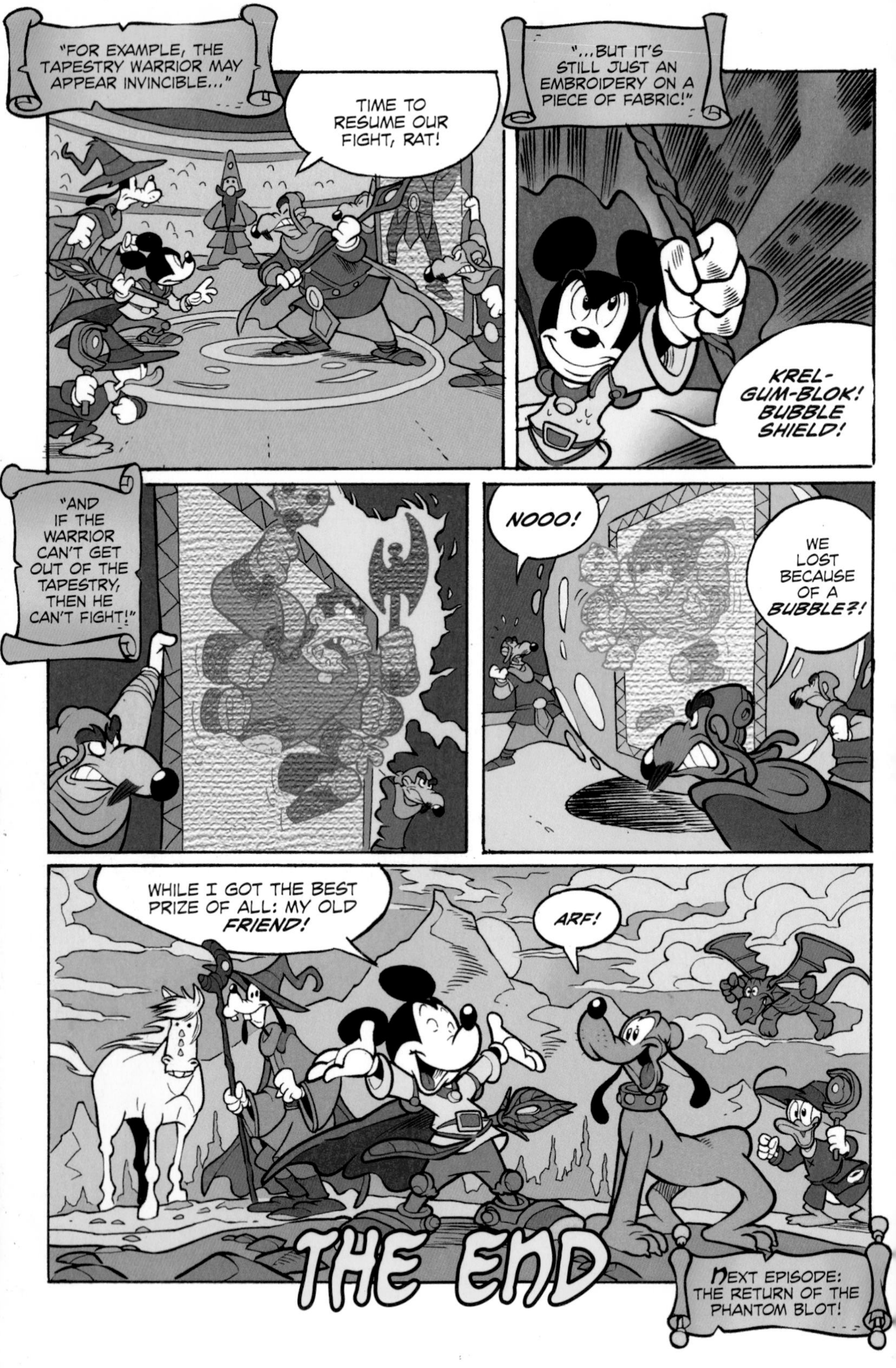
"FOR EXAMPLE, THE TAPESTRY WARRIOR MAY APPEAR INVINCIBLE..."
TIME TO RESUME OUR FIGHT, RAT!
"...BUT IT'S STILL JUST AN EMBROIDERY ON A PIECE OF FABRIC!"
KREL-GUM-BLOK! BUBBLE SHIELD!
"AND IF THE WARRIOR CAN'T GET OUT OF THE TAPESTRY, THEN HE CAN'T FIGHT!"
NOOO!
WE LOST BECAUSE OF A BUBBLE?!
WHILE I GOT THE BEST PRIZE OF ALL: MY OLD FRIEND!
ARF!
THE END
NEXT EPISODE: THE RETURN OF THE PHANTOM BLOT!

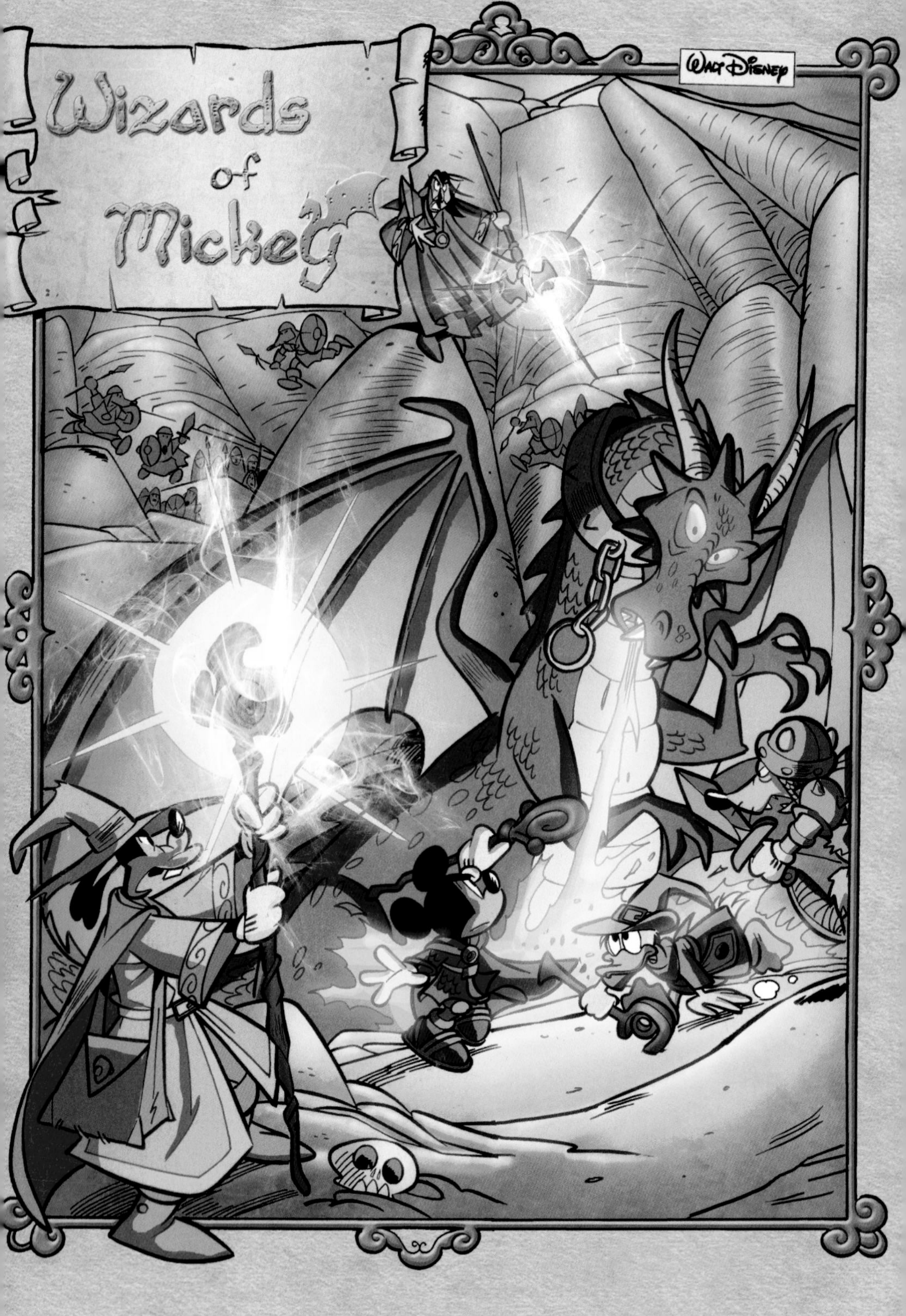
Wizards
of
Mickey
Walt Disney

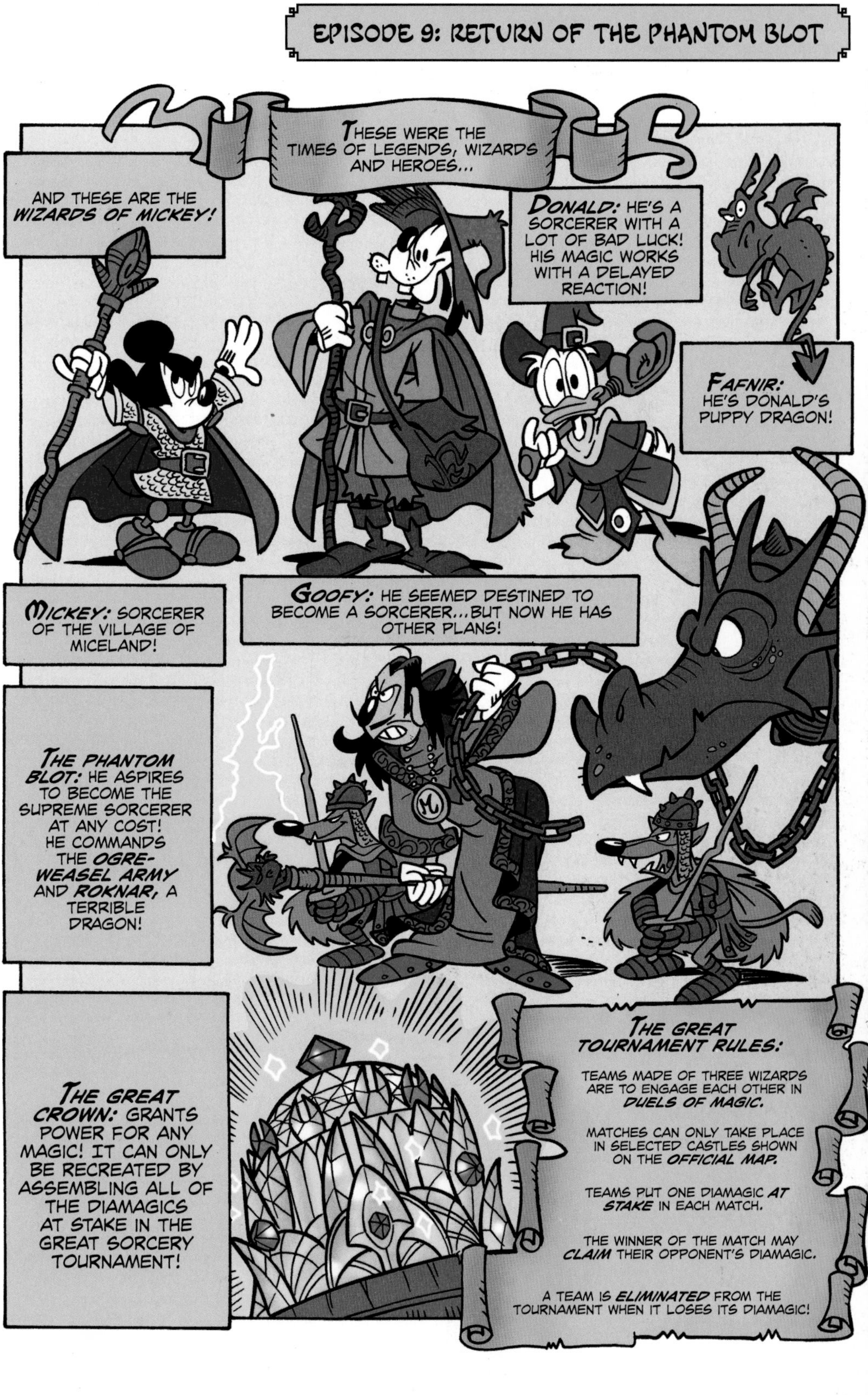
EPISODE 9: RETURN OF THE PHANTOM BLOT
THESE WERE THE TIMES OF LEGENDS, WIZARDS AND HEROES...
AND THESE ARE THE WIZARDS OF MICKEY!
DONALD: HE'S A SORCERER WITH A LOT OF BAD LUCK! HIS MAGIC WORKS WITH A DELAYED REACTION!
FAFNIR: HE'S DONALD'S PUPPY DRAGON!
MICKEY: SORCERER OF THE VILLAGE OF MICELAND!
GOOFY: HE SEEMED DESTINED TO BECOME A SORCERER...BUT NOW HE HAS OTHER PLANS!
THE PHANTOM BLOT: HE ASPIRES TO BECOME THE SUPREME SORCERER AT ANY COST! HE COMMANDS THE OGRE-WEASEL ARMY AND ROKNAR, A TERRIBLE DRAGON!
THE GREAT CROWN: GRANTS POWER FOR ANY MAGIC! IT CAN ONLY BE RECREATED BY ASSEMBLING ALL OF THE DIAMAGICS AT STAKE IN THE GREAT SORCERY TOURNAMENT!
THE GREAT TOURNAMENT RULES:
TEAMS MADE OF THREE WIZARDS ARE TO ENGAGE EACH OTHER IN DUELS OF MAGIC.
MATCHES CAN ONLY TAKE PLACE IN SELECTED CASTLES SHOWN ON THE OFFICIAL MAP.
TEAMS PUT ONE DIAMAGIC AT STAKE IN EACH MATCH.
THE WINNER OF THE MATCH MAY CLAIM THEIR OPPONENT'S DIAMAGIC.
A TEAM IS ELIMINATED FROM THE TOURNAMENT WHEN IT LOSES ITS DIAMAGIC!

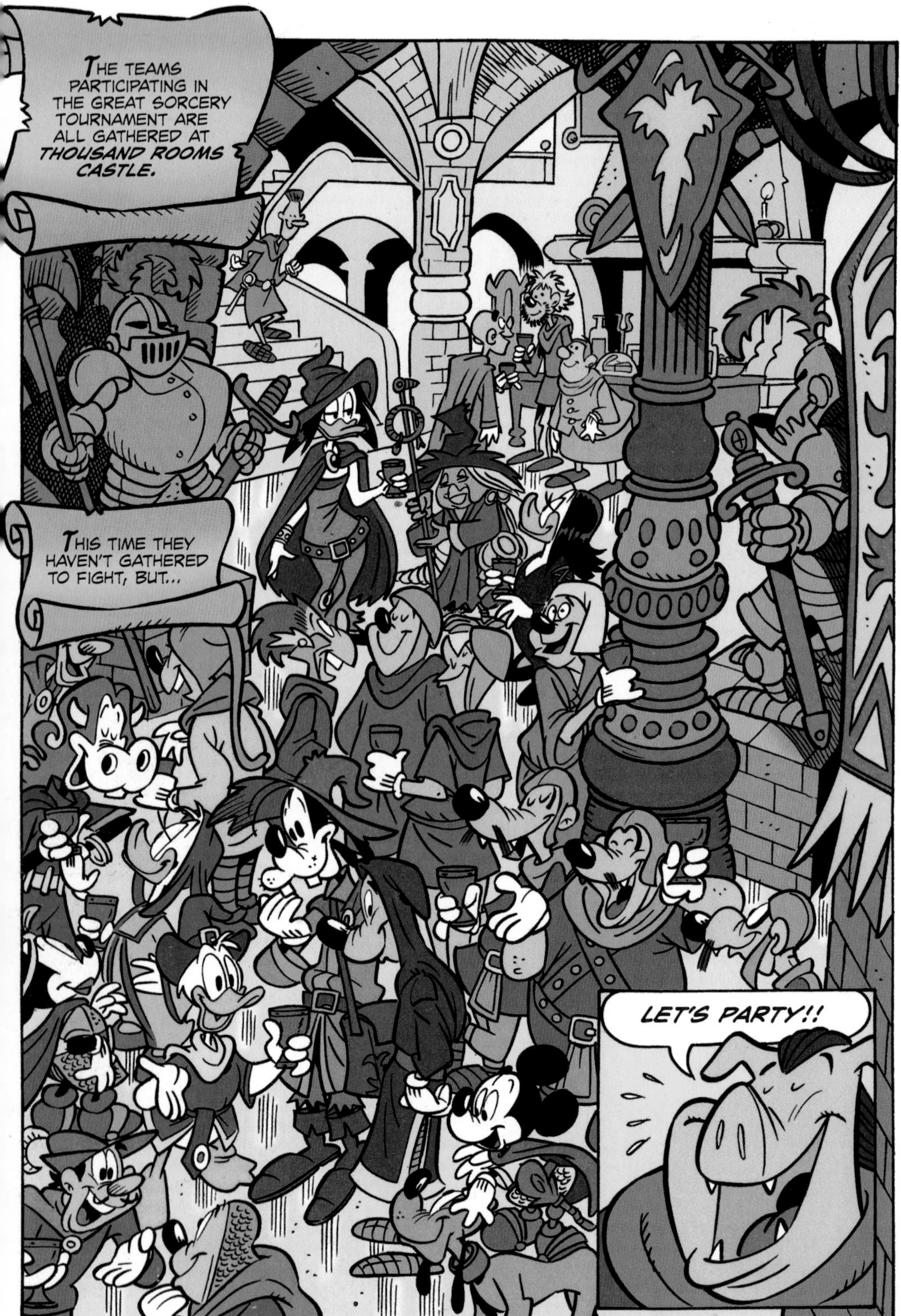
THE TEAMS PARTICIPATING IN THE GREAT SORCERY TOURNAMENT ARE ALL GATHERED AT THOUSAND ROOMS CASTLE.
THIS TIME THEY HAVEN'T GATHERED TO FIGHT, BUT...
LET'S PARTY!!

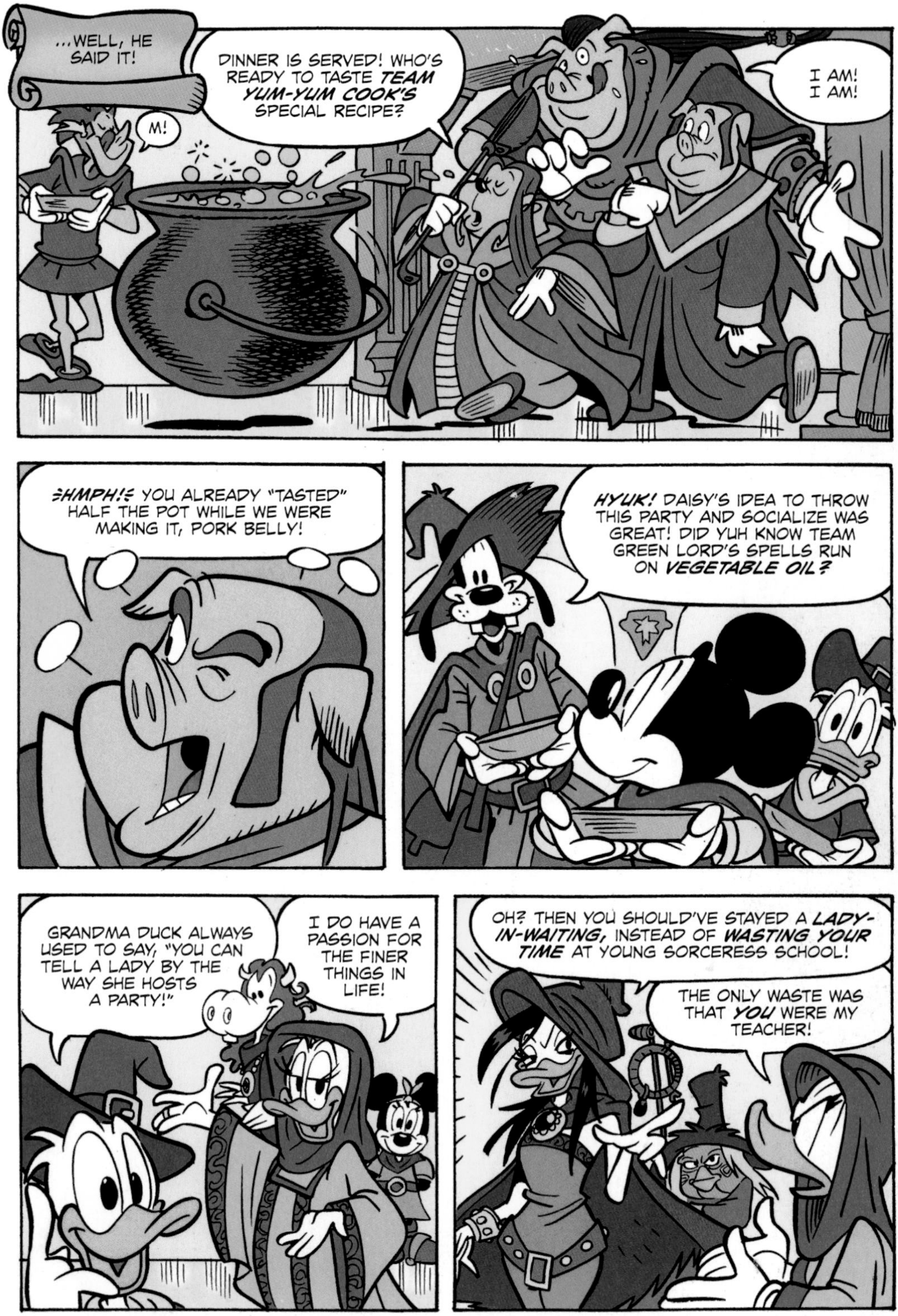
...WELL, HE SAID IT!
M!
DINNER IS SERVED! WHO'S READY TO TASTE TEAM YUM-YUM COOK'S SPECIAL RECIPE?
I AM! I AM!
HMPH! YOU ALREADY "TASTED" HALF THE POT WHILE WE WERE MAKING IT, PORK BELLY!
HYUK! DAISY'S IDEA TO THROW THIS PARTY AND SOCIALIZE WAS GREAT! DID YUH KNOW TEAM GREEN LORD'S SPELLS RUN ON VEGETABLE OIL?
GRANDMA DUCK ALWAYS USED TO SAY, "YOU CAN TELL A LADY BY THE WAY SHE HOSTS A PARTY!"
I DO HAVE A PASSION FOR THE FINER THINGS IN LIFE!
OH? THEN YOU SHOULD'VE STAYED A LADY-IN-WAITING, INSTEAD OF WASTING YOUR TIME AT YOUNG SORCERESS SCHOOL!
THE ONLY WASTE WAS THAT YOU WERE MY TEACHER!

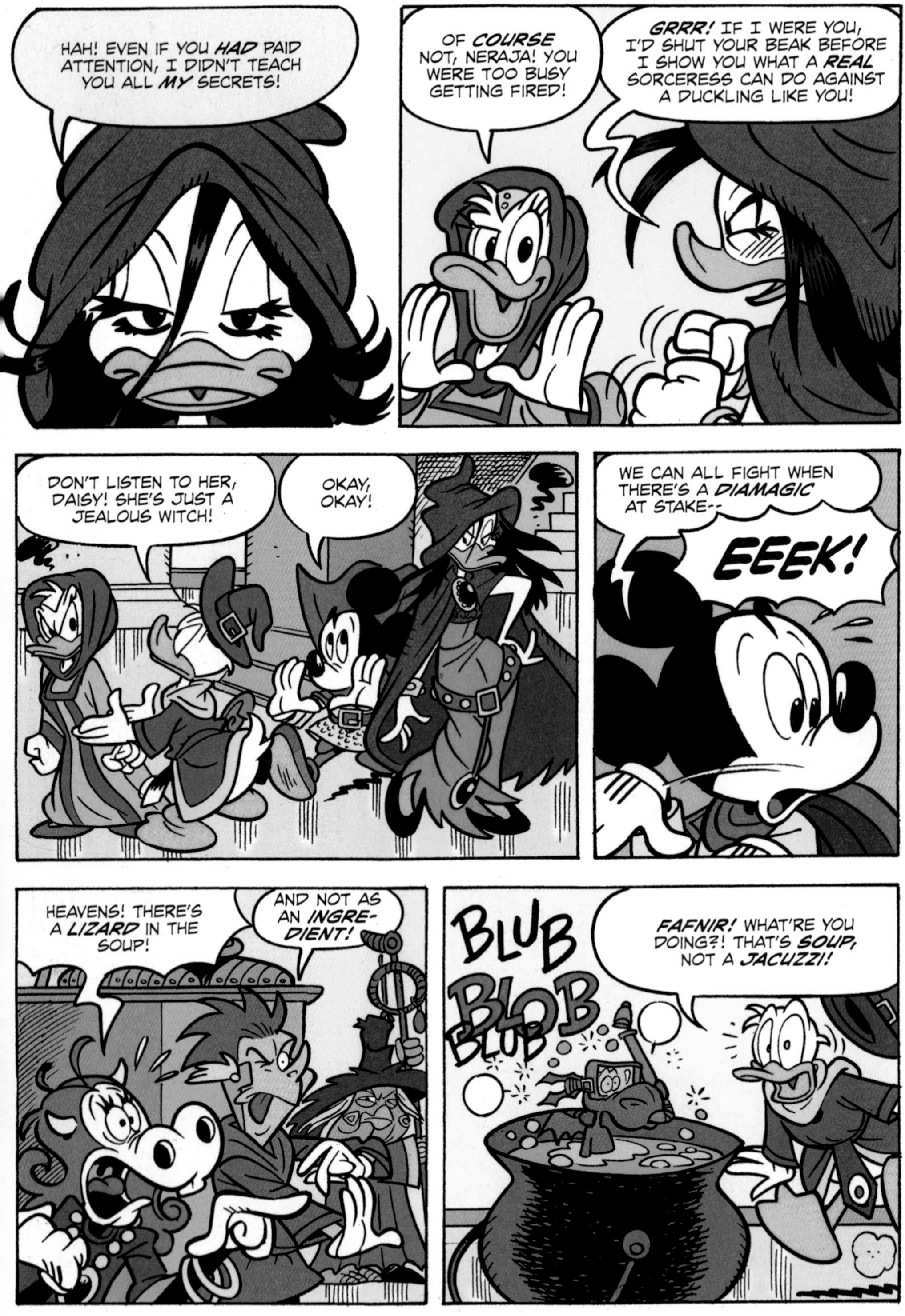
HAH! EVEN IF YOU HAD PAID ATTENTION, I DIDN'T TEACH YOU ALL MY SECRETS!
OF COURSE NOT, NERAJA! YOU WERE TOO BUSY GETTING FIRED!
GRRR! IF I WERE YOU, I'D SHUT YOUR BEAK BEFORE I SHOW YOU WHAT A REAL SORCERESS CAN DO AGAINST A DUCKLING LIKE YOU!
DON'T LISTEN TO HER, DAISY! SHE'S JUST A JEALOUS WITCH!
OKAY, OKAY!
WE CAN ALL FIGHT WHEN THERE'S A DIAMAGIC AT STAKE--
EEEK!
HEAVENS! THERE'S A LIZARD IN THE SOUP!
AND NOT AS AN INGRE-DIENT!
BLUB
BLOB
BLUB
FAFNIR! WHAT'RE YOU DOING?! THAT'S SOUP, NOT A JACUZZI!

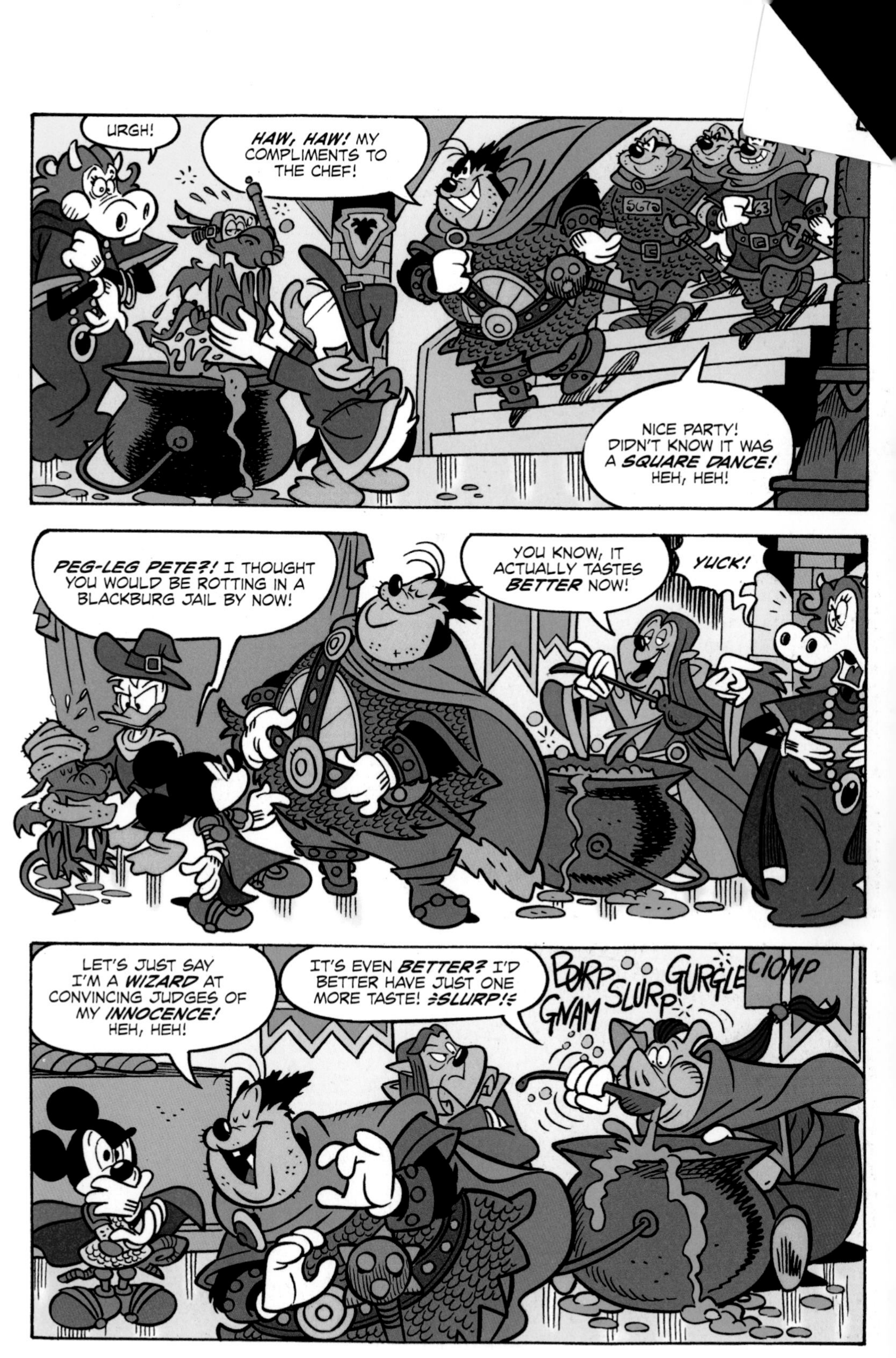
URGH!
HAW, HAW! MY COMPLIMENTS TO THE CHEF!
NICE PARTY! DIDN'T KNOW IT WAS A SQUARE DANCE! HEH, HEH!
PEG-LEG PETE?! I THOUGHT YOU WOULD BE ROTTING IN A BLACKBURG JAIL BY NOW!
YOU KNOW, IT ACTUALLY TASTES BETTER NOW!
YUCK!
LET'S JUST SAY I'M A WIZARD AT CONVINCING JUDGES OF MY INNOCENCE! HEH, HEH!
IT'S EVEN BETTER? I'D BETTER HAVE JUST ONE MORE TASTE! SLURP!
GNAM
SLURP
GURGLE
CIOMP

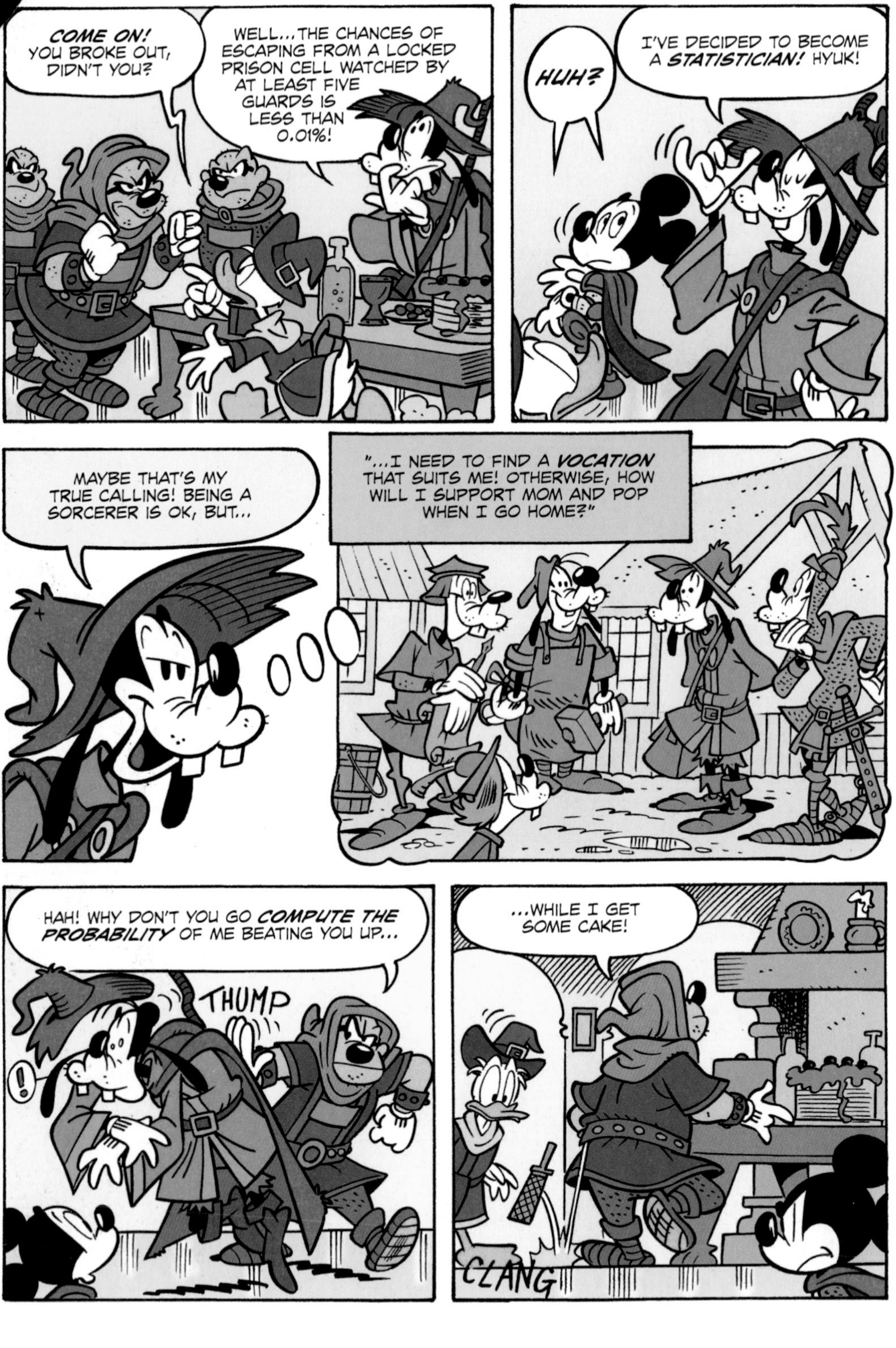
COME ON! YOU BROKE OUT, DIDN'T YOU?
WELL... THE CHANCES OF ESCAPING FROM A LOCKED PRISON CELL WATCHED BY AT LEAST FIVE GUARDS IS LESS THAN 0.01%!
HUH?
I'VE DECIDED TO BECOME A STATISTICIAN! HYUK!
MAYBE THAT'S MY TRUE CALLING! BEING A SORCERER IS OK, BUT...
"...I NEED TO FIND A VOCATION THAT SUITS ME! OTHERWISE, HOW WILL I SUPPORT MOM AND POP WHEN I GO HOME?"
HAH! WHY DON'T YOU GO COMPUTE THE PROBABILITY OF ME BEATING YOU UP...
THUMP
!
...WHILE I GET SOME CAKE!
CLANG

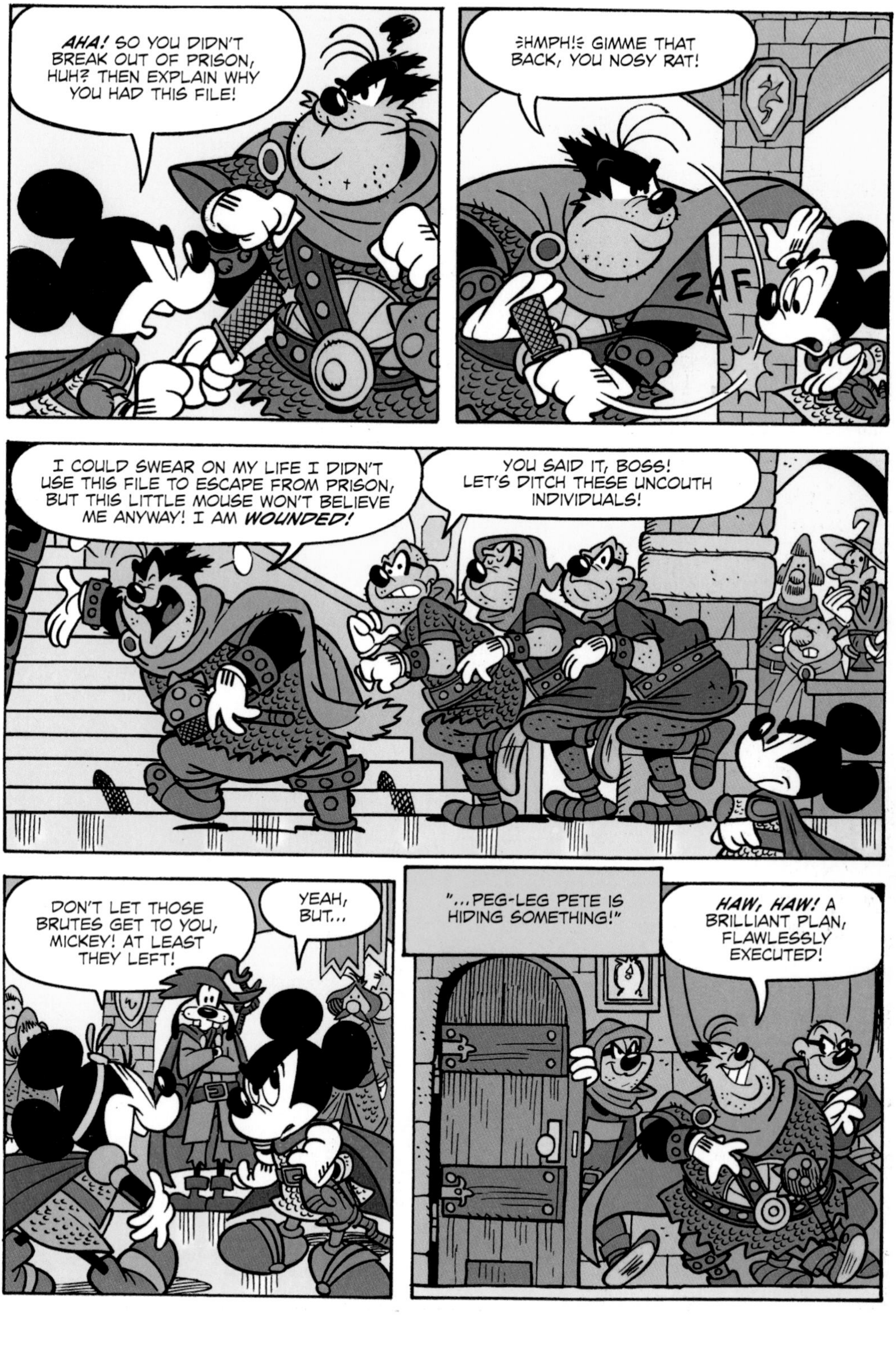

AHA! SO YOU DIDN'T BREAK OUT OF PRISON, HUH? THEN EXPLAIN WHY YOU HAD THIS FILE!
HMPH! GIMME THAT BACK, YOU NOSY RAT!
ZAF
I COULD SWEAR ON MY LIFE I DIDN'T USE THIS FILE TO ESCAPE FROM PRISON, BUT THIS LITTLE MOUSE WON'T BELIEVE ME ANYWAY! I AM WOUNDED!
YOU SAID IT, BOSS! LET'S DITCH THESE UNCOUTH INDIVIDUALS!
DON'T LET THOSE BRUTES GET TO YOU, MICKEY! AT LEAST THEY LEFT!
YEAH, BUT...
"...PEG-LEG PETE IS HIDING SOMETHING!"
HAW, HAW! A BRILLIANT PLAN, FLAWLESSLY EXECUTED!

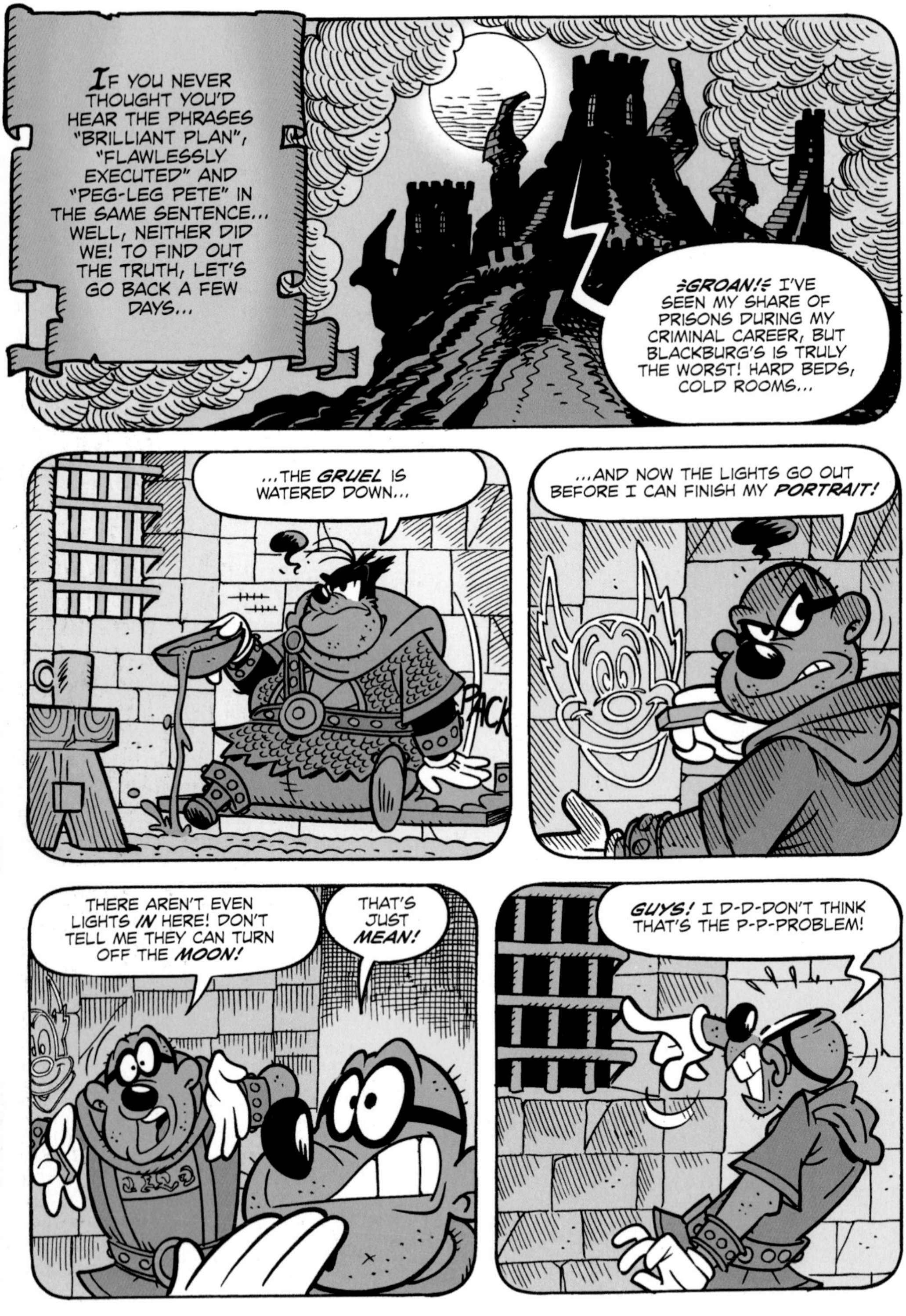
IF YOU NEVER THOUGHT YOU'D HEAR THE PHRASES "BRILLIANT PLAN", "FLAWLESSLY EXECUTED" AND "PEG-LEG PETE" IN THE SAME SENTENCE... WELL, NEITHER DID WE! TO FIND OUT THE TRUTH, LET'S GO BACK A FEW DAYS...
GROAN! I'VE SEEN MY SHARE OF PRISONS DURING MY CRIMINAL CAREER, BUT BLACKBURG'S IS TRULY THE WORST! HARD BEDS, COLD ROOMS...
...THE GRUEL IS WATERED DOWN...
...AND NOW THE LIGHTS GO OUT BEFORE I CAN FINISH MY PORTRAIT!
THERE AREN'T EVEN LIGHTS IN HERE! DON'T TELL ME THEY CAN TURN OFF THE MOON!
THAT'S JUST MEAN!
GUYS! I D-D-DON'T THINK THAT'S THE P-P-PROBLEM!

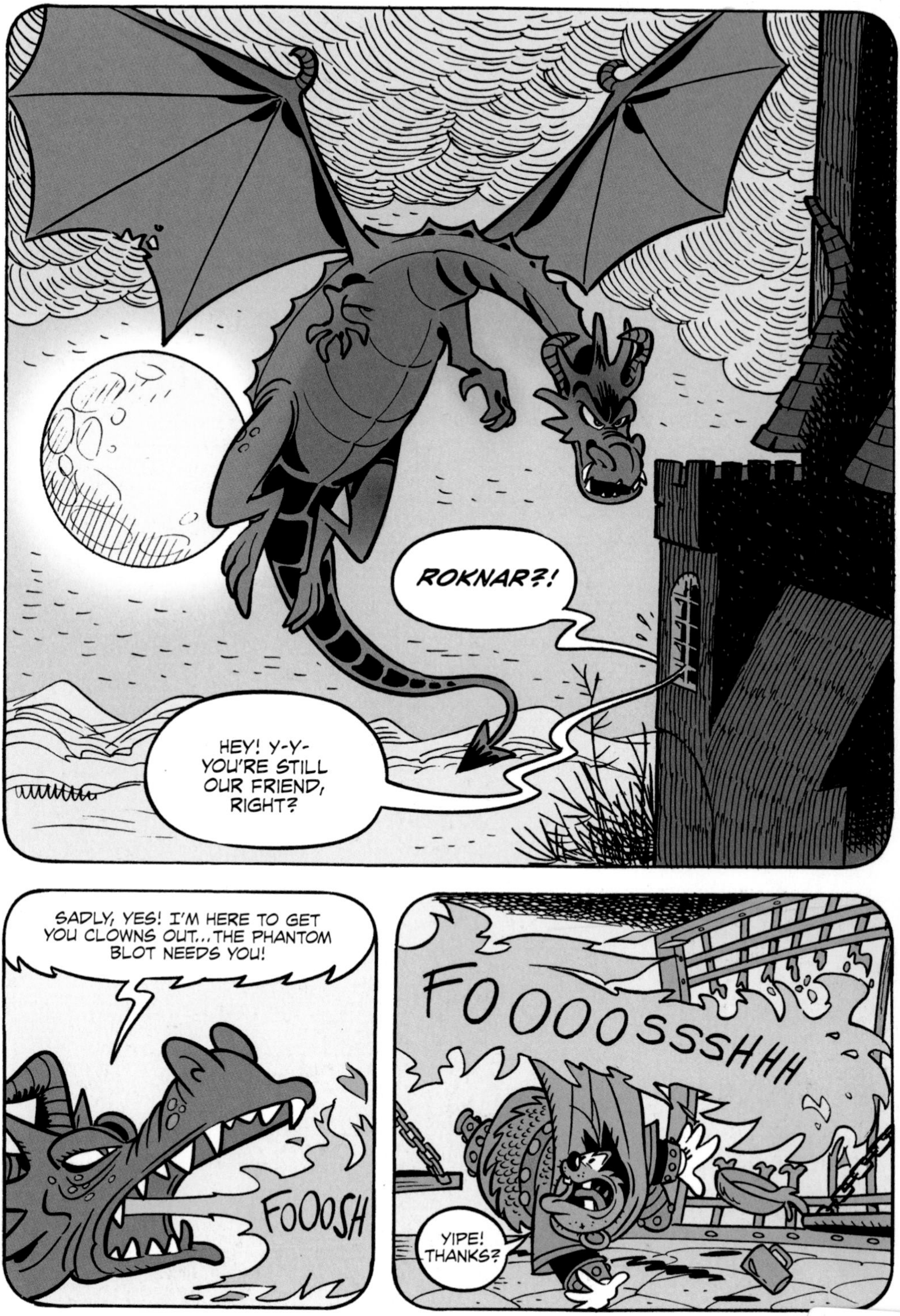
ROKNAR?!
HEY! Y-Y- YOU'RE STILL OUR FRIEND, RIGHT?
SADLY, YES! I'M HERE TO GET YOU CLOWNS OUT... THE PHANTOM BLOT NEEDS YOU!
FOOOSH
FOOOOOSSSSHHH
YIPE! THANKS?

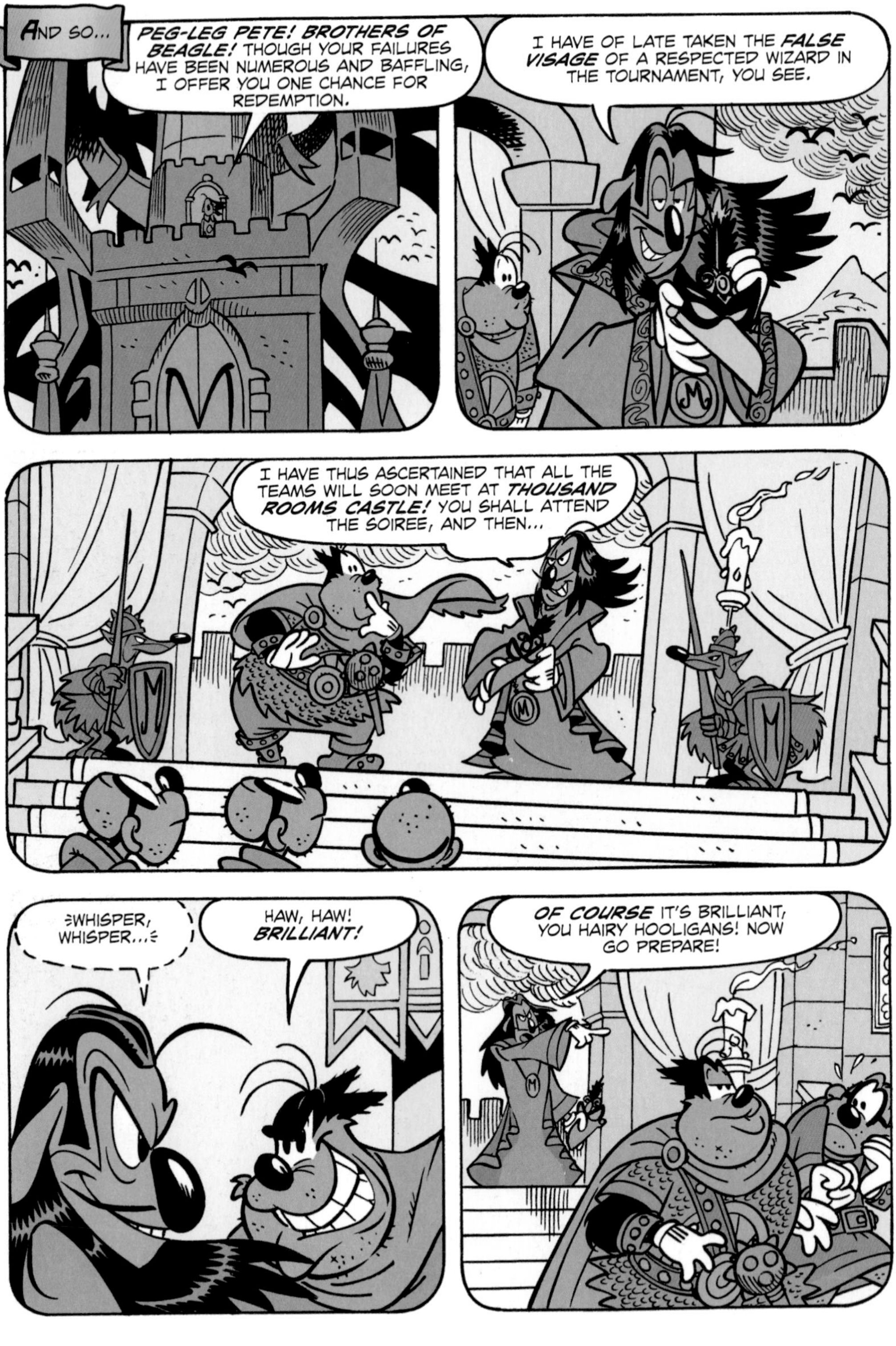
AND SO...
PEG-LEG PETE! BROTHERS OF BEAGLE! THOUGH YOUR FAILURES HAVE BEEN NUMEROUS AND BAFFLING, I OFFER YOU ONE CHANCE FOR REDEMPTION.
I HAVE OF LATE TAKEN THE FALSE VISAGE OF A RESPECTED WIZARD IN THE TOURNAMENT, YOU SEE.
I HAVE THUS ASCERTAINED THAT ALL THE TEAMS WILL SOON MEET AT THOUSAND ROOMS CASTLE! YOU SHALL ATTEND THE SOIREE, AND THEN...
WHISPER, WHISPER...
HAW, HAW! BRILLIANT!
OF COURSE IT'S BRILLIANT, YOU HAIRY HOOLIGANS! NOW GO PREPARE!

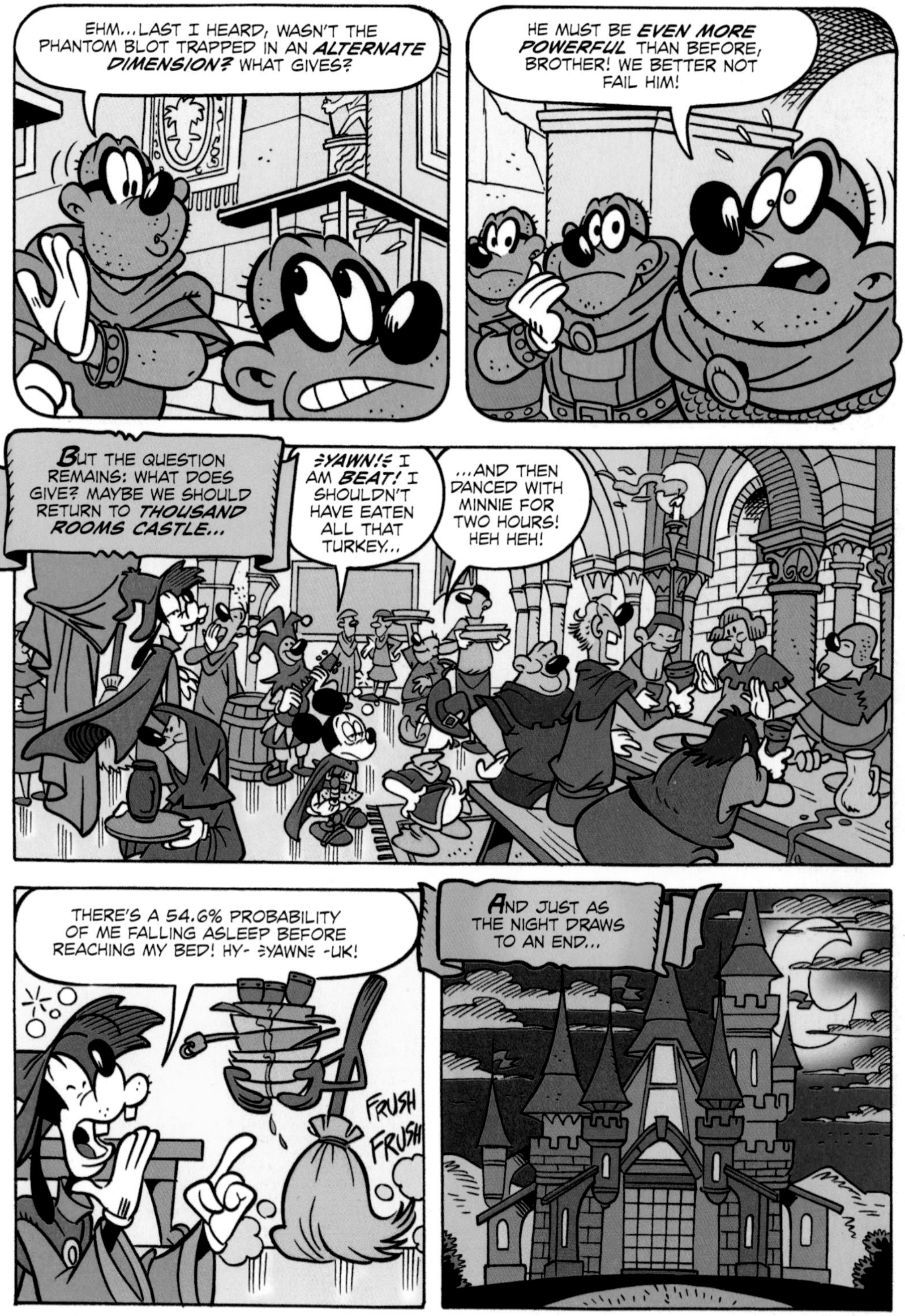
EHM... LAST I HEARD, WASN'T THE PHANTOM BLOT TRAPPED IN AN ALTERNATE DIMENSION? WHAT GIVES?
HE MUST BE EVEN MORE POWERFUL THAN BEFORE, BROTHER! WE BETTER NOT FAIL HIM!
BUT THE QUESTION REMAINS: WHAT DOES GIVE? MAYBE WE SHOULD RETURN TO THOUSAND ROOMS CASTLE...
=YAWN!= I AM BEAT! I SHOULDN'T HAVE EATEN ALL THAT TURKEY...
...AND THEN DANCED WITH MINNIE FOR TWO HOURS! HEH HEH!
THERE'S A 54.6% PROBABILITY OF ME FALLING ASLEEP BEFORE REACHING MY BED! HY- =YAWN= -UK!
FRUSH
FRUSH
AND JUST AS THE NIGHT DRAWS TO AN END...

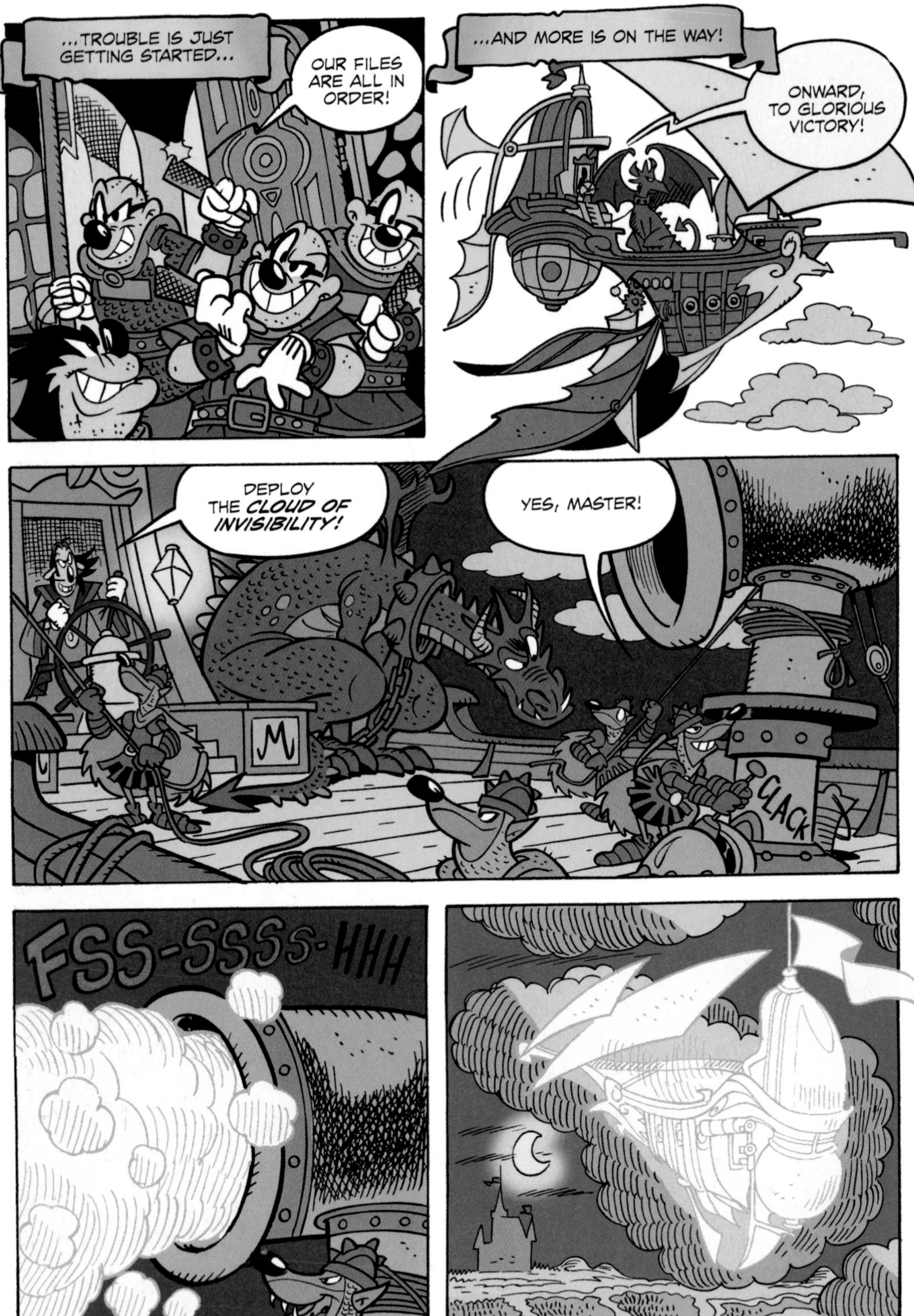
...TROUBLE IS JUST GETTING STARTED...
OUR FILES ARE ALL IN ORDER!
...AND MORE IS ON THE WAY!
ONWARD, TO GLORIOUS VICTORY!
DEPLOY THE *CLOUD OF INVISIBILITY!*
YES, MASTER!
CLACK
FSS-SSSS-HHH

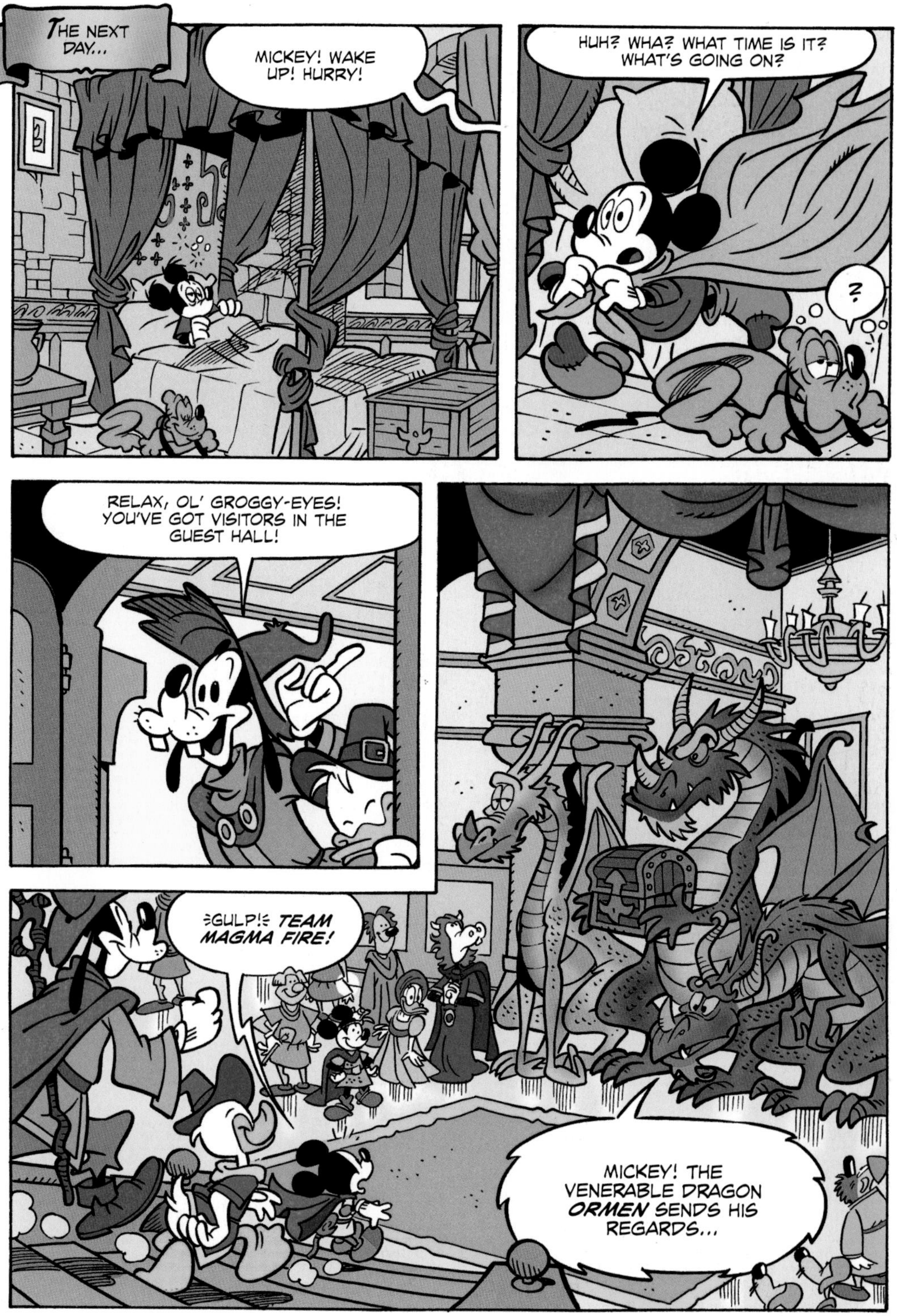
THE NEXT DAY...
MICKEY! WAKE UP! HURRY!
HUH? WHA? WHAT TIME IS IT? WHAT'S GOING ON?
?
RELAX, OL' GROGGY-EYES! YOU'VE GOT VISITORS IN THE GUEST HALL!
GULP! TEAM MAGMA FIRE!
MICKEY! THE VENERABLE DRAGON ORMEN SENDS HIS REGARDS...

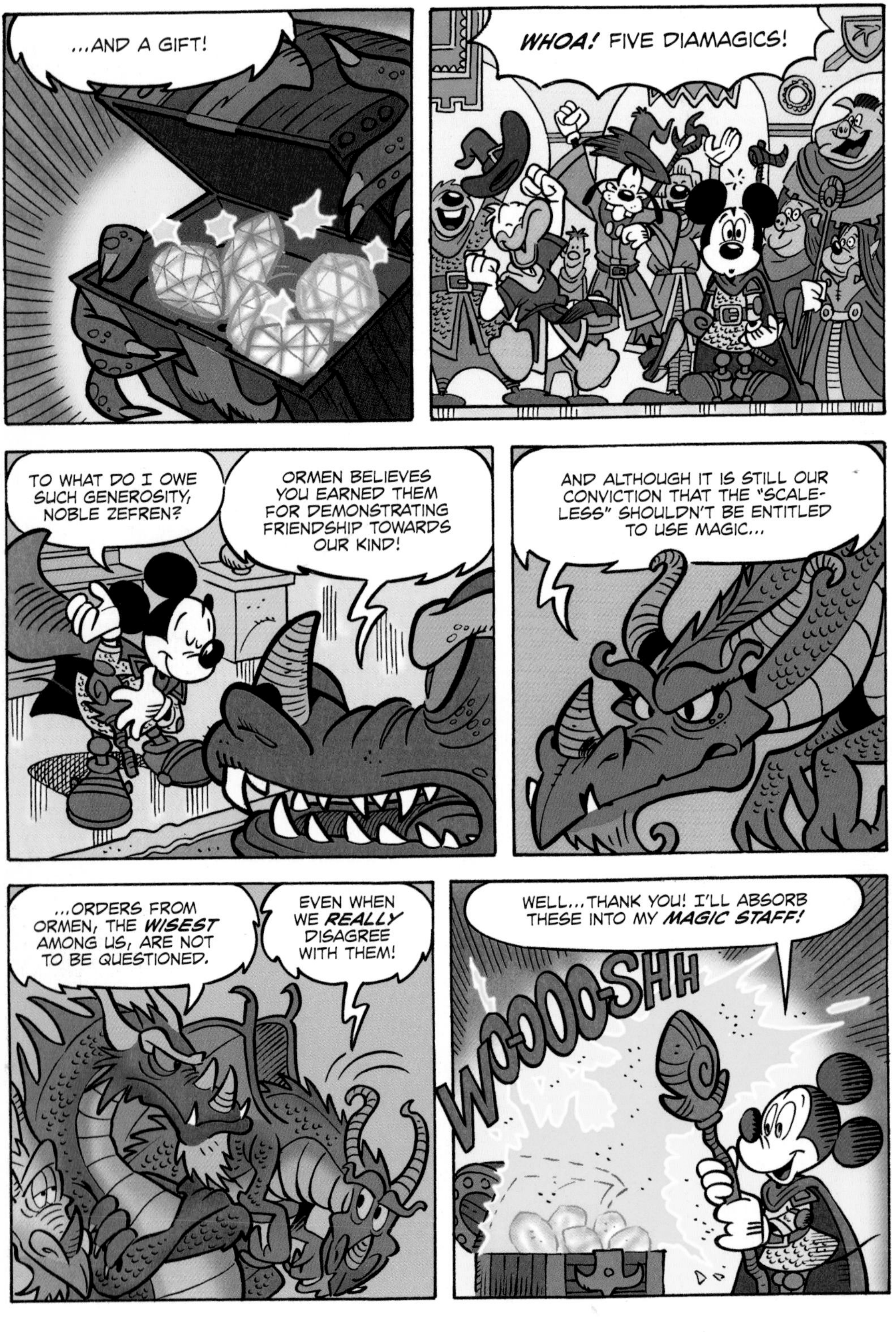
...AND A GIFT!
WHOA! FIVE DIAMAGICS!
TO WHAT DO I OWE SUCH GENEROSITY, NOBLE ZEFREN?
ORMEN BELIEVES YOU EARNED THEM FOR DEMONSTRATING FRIENDSHIP TOWARDS OUR KIND!
AND ALTHOUGH IT IS STILL OUR CONVICTION THAT THE "SCALE-LESS" SHOULDN'T BE ENTITLED TO USE MAGIC...
...ORDERS FROM ORMEN, THE WISEST AMONG US, ARE NOT TO BE QUESTIONED.
EVEN WHEN WE REALLY DISAGREE WITH THEM!
WELL...THANK YOU! I'LL ABSORB THESE INTO MY MAGIC STAFF!
WOOOOO-SHH

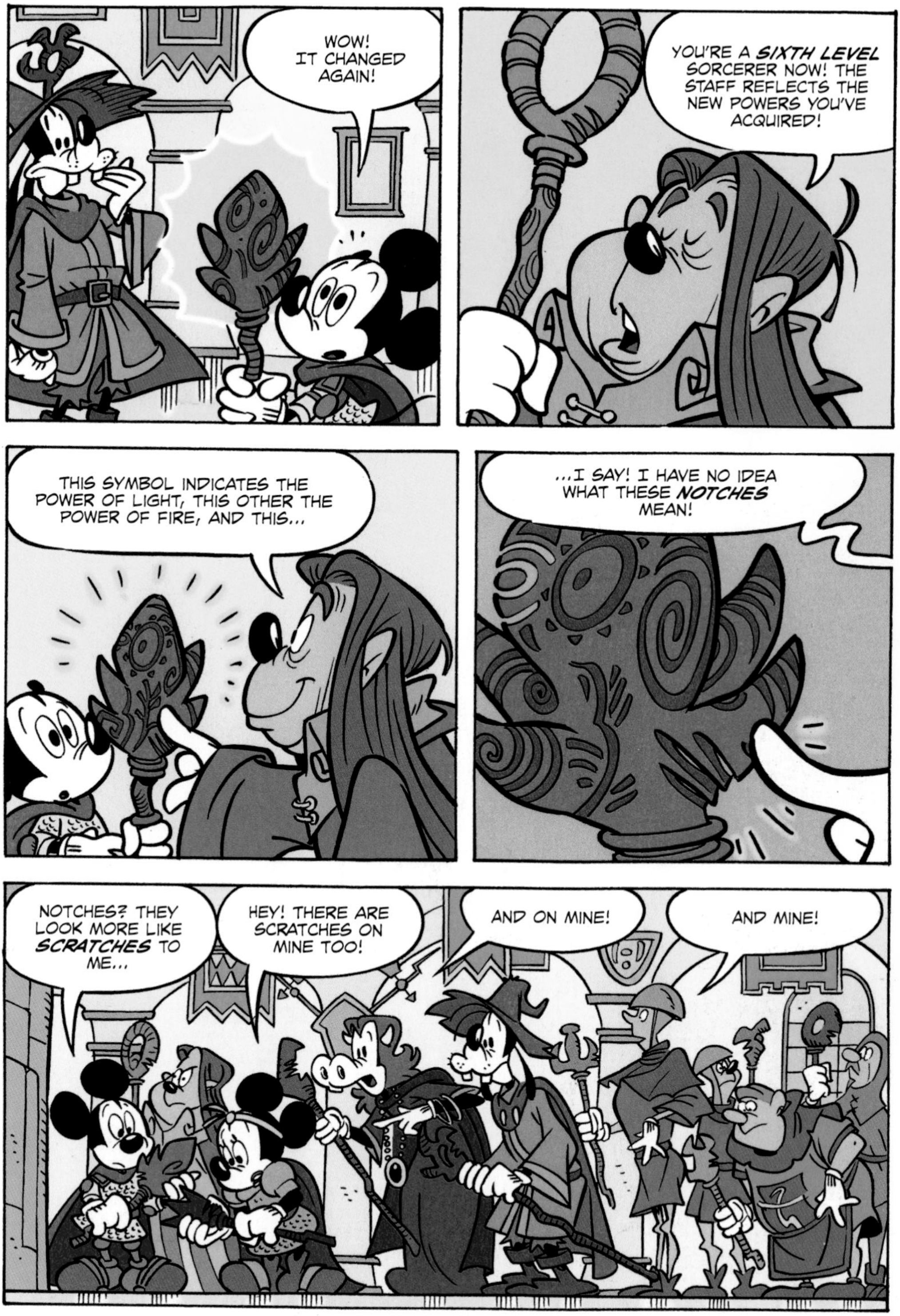
WOW! IT CHANGED AGAIN!
YOU'RE A *SIXTH LEVEL* SORCERER NOW! THE STAFF REFLECTS THE NEW POWERS YOU'VE ACQUIRED!
THIS SYMBOL INDICATES THE POWER OF LIGHT, THIS OTHER THE POWER OF FIRE, AND THIS...
...I SAY! I HAVE NO IDEA WHAT THESE *NOTCHES* MEAN!
NOTCHES? THEY LOOK MORE LIKE *SCRATCHES* TO ME...
HEY! THERE ARE SCRATCHES ON MINE TOO!
AND ON MINE!
AND MINE!

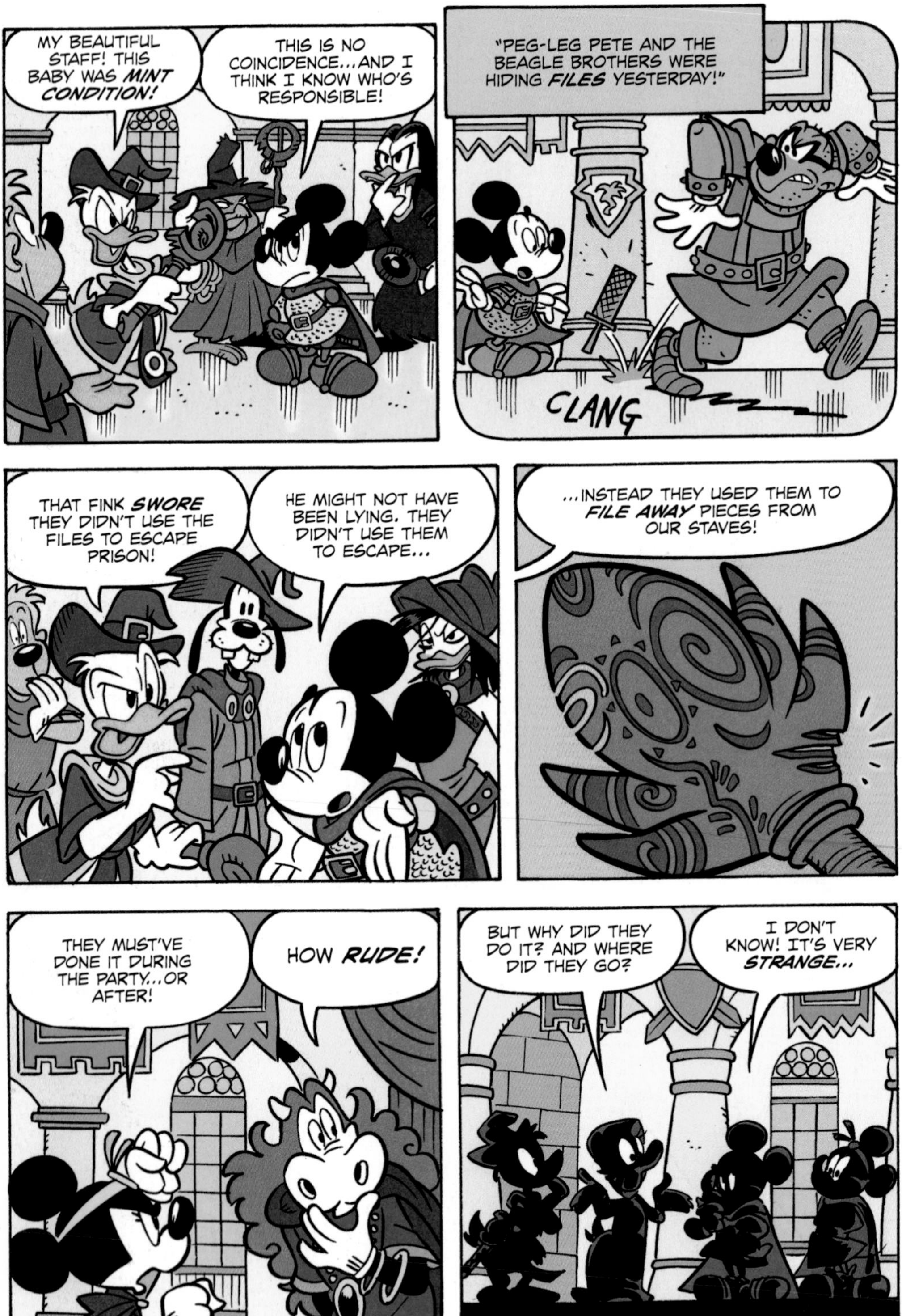
MY BEAUTIFUL STAFF! THIS BABY WAS MINT CONDITION!
THIS IS NO COINCIDENCE...AND I THINK I KNOW WHO'S RESPONSIBLE!
"PEG-LEG PETE AND THE BEAGLE BROTHERS WERE HIDING FILES YESTERDAY!"
CLANG
THAT FINK SWORE THEY DIDN'T USE THE FILES TO ESCAPE PRISON!
HE MIGHT NOT HAVE BEEN LYING. THEY DIDN'T USE THEM TO ESCAPE...
...INSTEAD THEY USED THEM TO FILE AWAY PIECES FROM OUR STAVES!
THEY MUST'VE DONE IT DURING THE PARTY...OR AFTER!
HOW RUDE!
BUT WHY DID THEY DO IT? AND WHERE DID THEY GO?
I DON'T KNOW! IT'S VERY STRANGE...

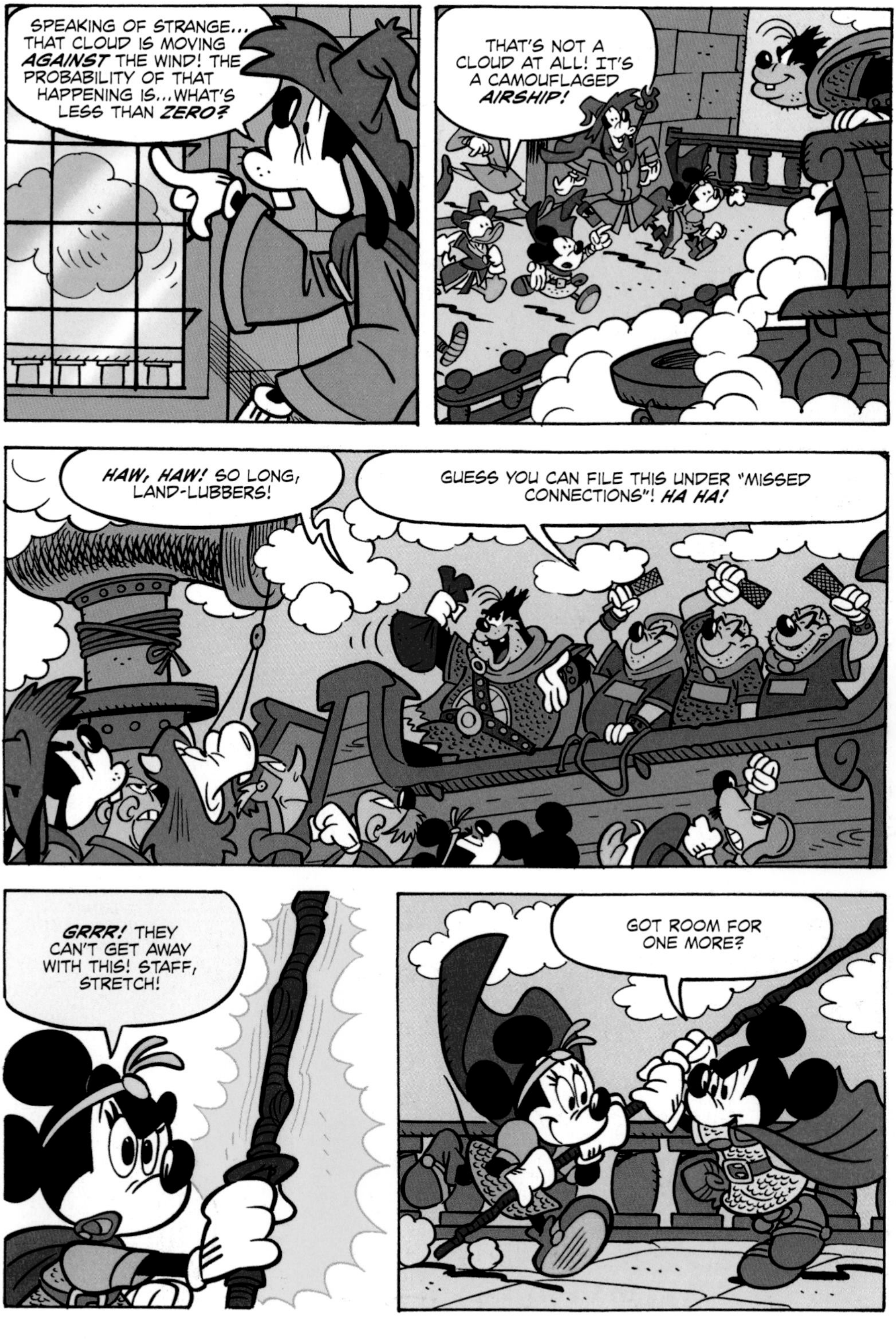
SPEAKING OF STRANGE... THAT CLOUD IS MOVING AGAINST THE WIND! THE PROBABILITY OF THAT HAPPENING IS...WHAT'S LESS THAN ZERO?
THAT'S NOT A CLOUD AT ALL! IT'S A CAMOUFLAGED AIRSHIP!
HAW, HAW! SO LONG, LAND-LUBBERS!
GUESS YOU CAN FILE THIS UNDER "MISSED CONNECTIONS"! HA HA!
GRRR! THEY CAN'T GET AWAY WITH THIS! STAFF, STRETCH!
GOT ROOM FOR ONE MORE?

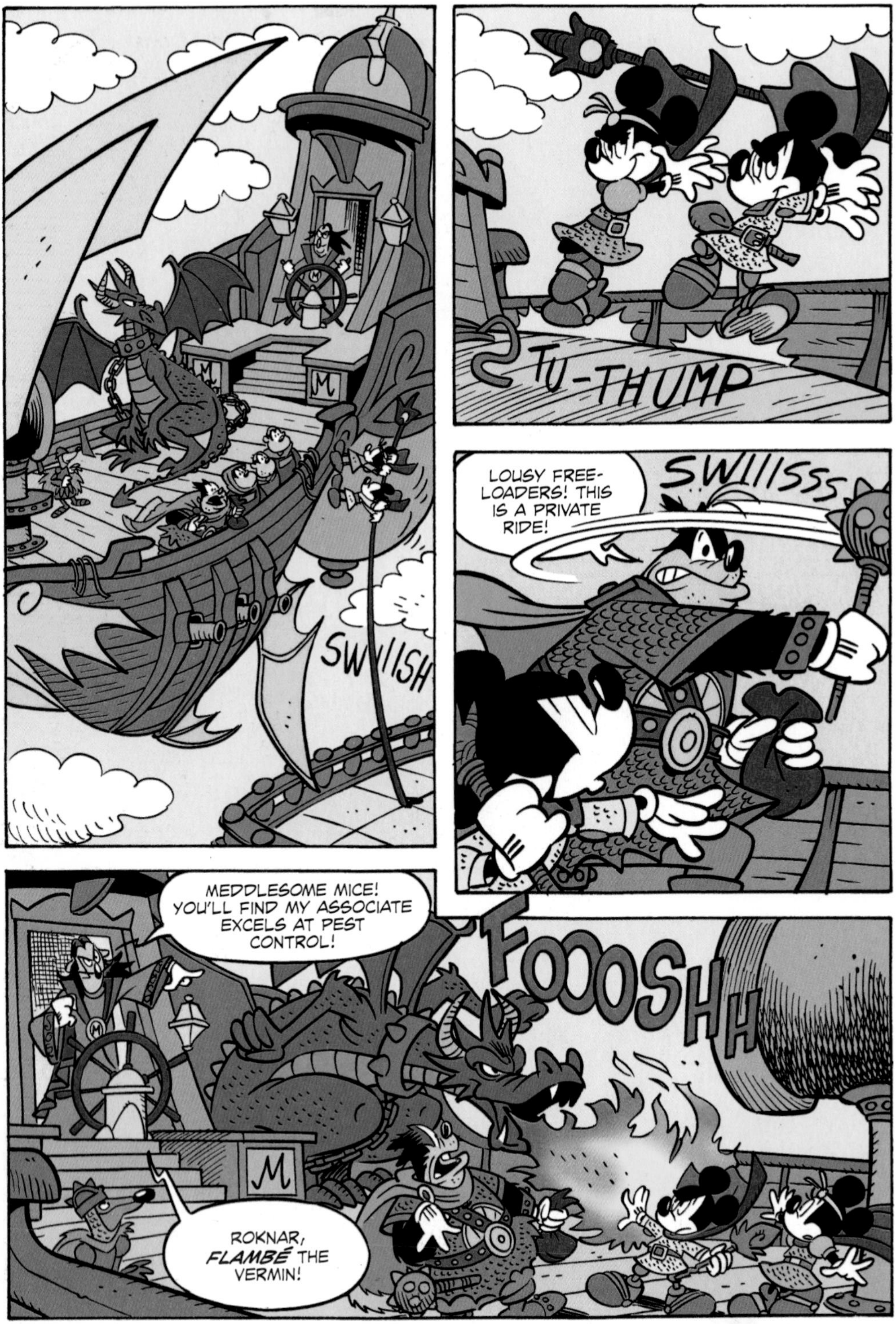
SWIIISH
TU-THUMP
LOUSY FREE-LOADERS! THIS IS A PRIVATE RIDE!
SWIIISSS
MEDDLESOME MICE! YOU'LL FIND MY ASSOCIATE EXCELS AT PEST CONTROL!
FOOOSHH
ROKNAR, *FLAMBÉ* THE VERMIN!

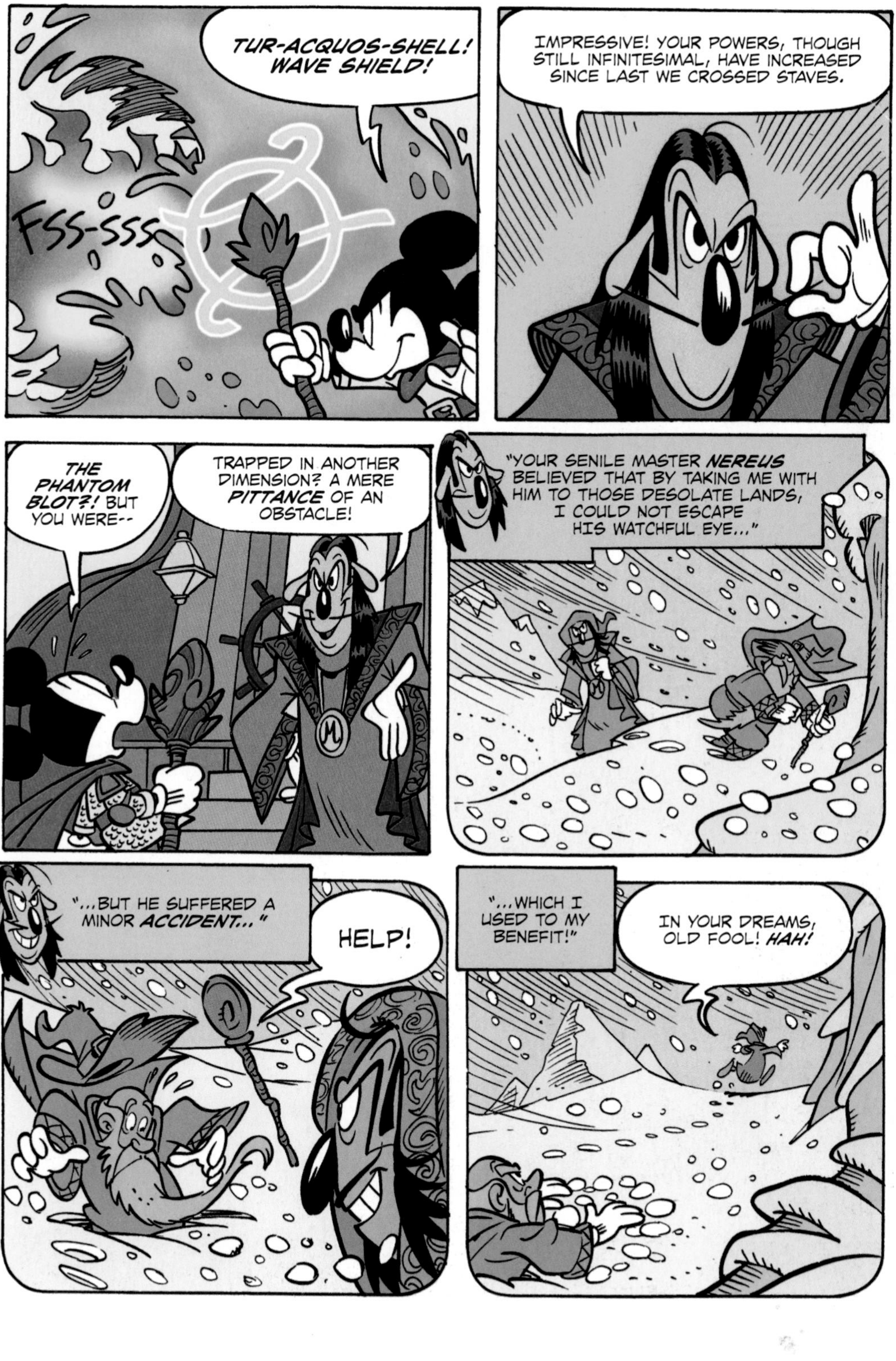
TUR-ACQUOS-SHELL! WAVE SHIELD!
FSS-SSS
IMPRESSIVE! YOUR POWERS, THOUGH STILL INFINITESIMAL, HAVE INCREASED SINCE LAST WE CROSSED STAVES.
THE PHANTOM BLOT?! BUT YOU WERE--
TRAPPED IN ANOTHER DIMENSION? A MERE PITTANCE OF AN OBSTACLE!
"YOUR SENILE MASTER NEREUS BELIEVED THAT BY TAKING ME WITH HIM TO THOSE DESOLATE LANDS, I COULD NOT ESCAPE HIS WATCHFUL EYE..."
"...BUT HE SUFFERED A MINOR ACCIDENT..."
HELP!
"...WHICH I USED TO MY BENEFIT!"
IN YOUR DREAMS, OLD FOOL! HAH!

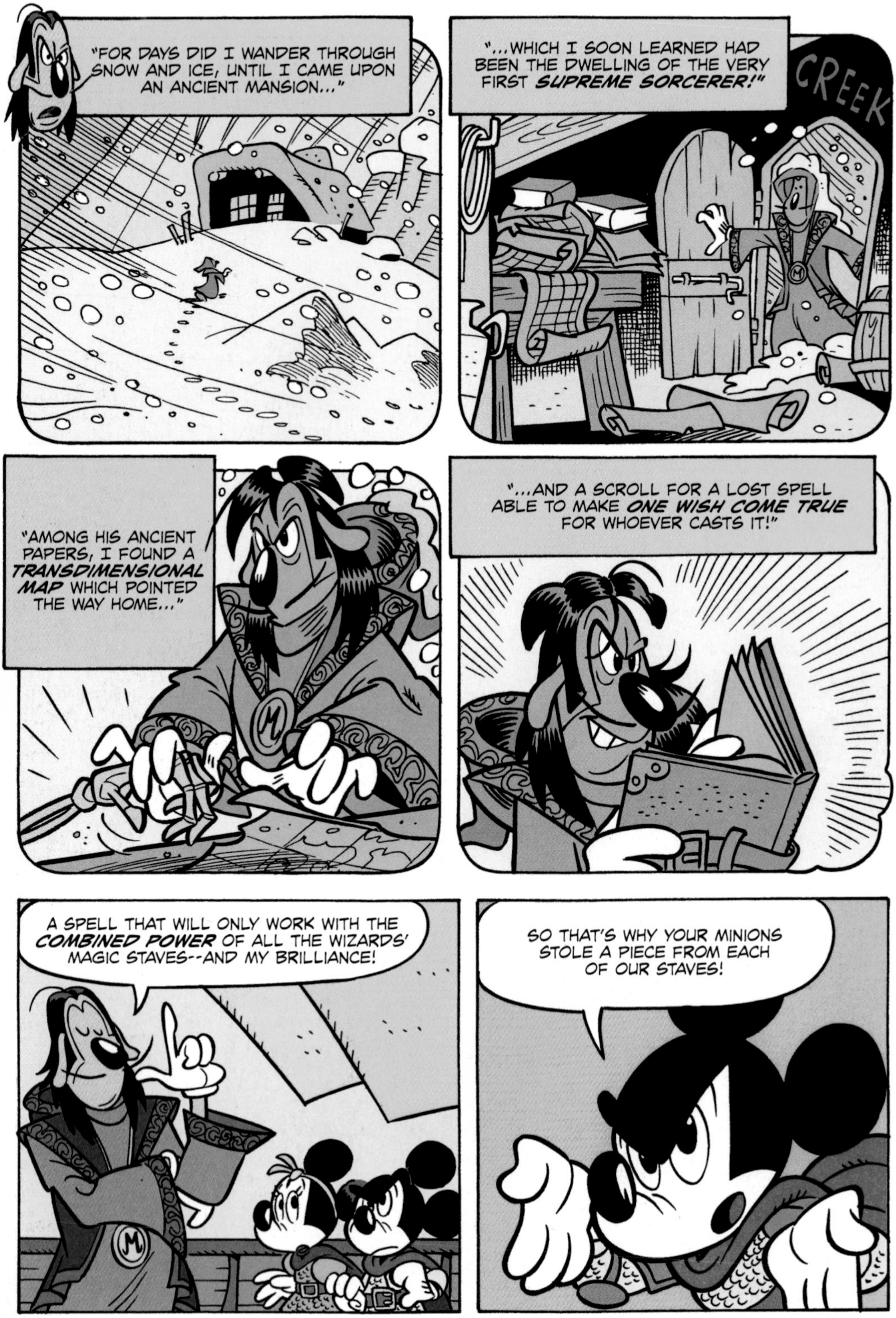
"FOR DAYS DID I WANDER THROUGH SNOW AND ICE, UNTIL I CAME UPON AN ANCIENT MANSION..."
"...WHICH I SOON LEARNED HAD BEEN THE DWELLING OF THE VERY FIRST SUPREME SORCERER!"
CREEK
"AMONG HIS ANCIENT PAPERS, I FOUND A TRANSDIMENSIONAL MAP WHICH POINTED THE WAY HOME..."
"...AND A SCROLL FOR A LOST SPELL ABLE TO MAKE ONE WISH COME TRUE FOR WHOEVER CASTS IT!"
A SPELL THAT WILL ONLY WORK WITH THE COMBINED POWER OF ALL THE WIZARDS' MAGIC STAVES--AND MY BRILLIANCE!
SO THAT'S WHY YOUR MINIONS STOLE A PIECE FROM EACH OF OUR STAVES!

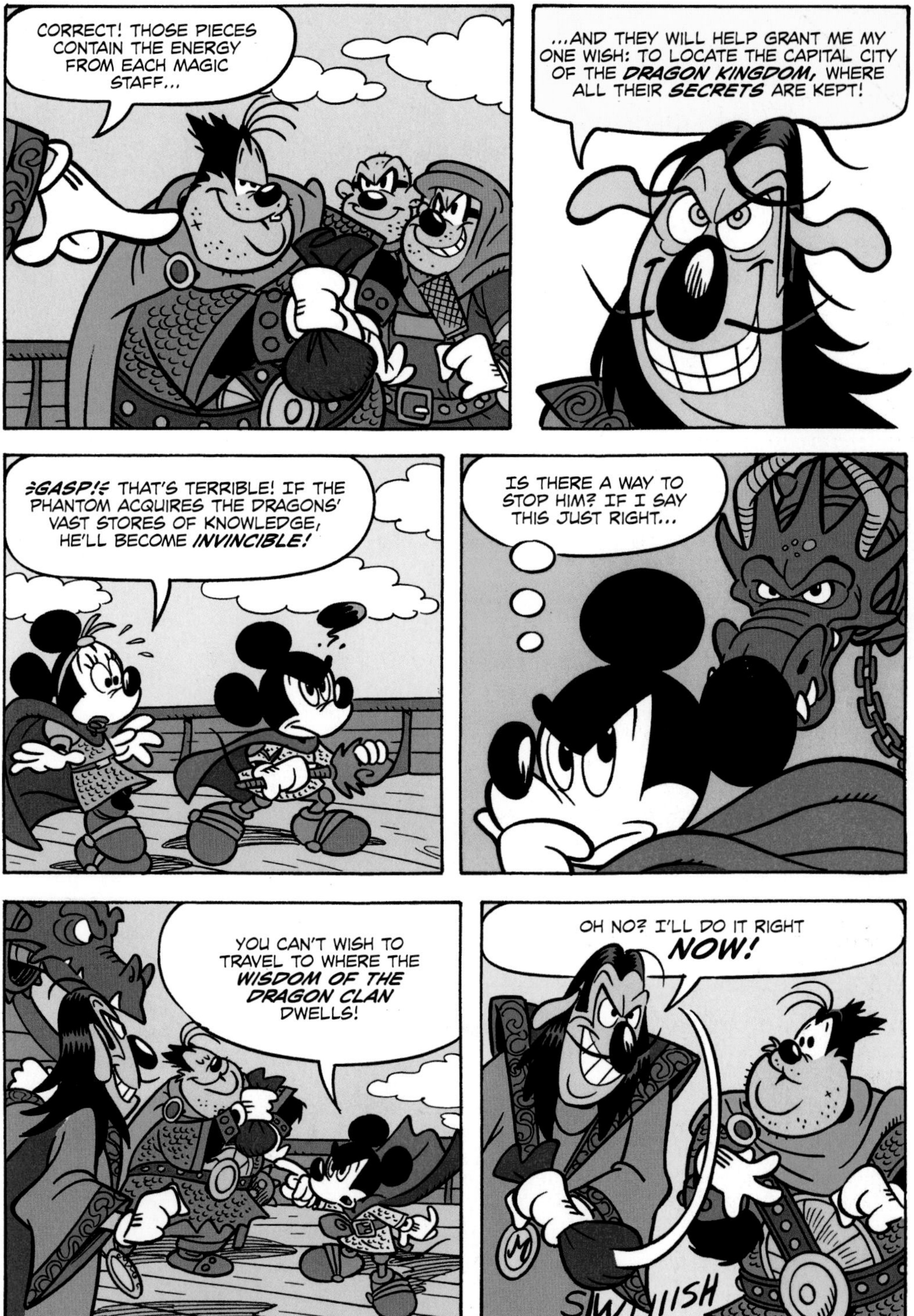
CORRECT! THOSE PIECES CONTAIN THE ENERGY FROM EACH MAGIC STAFF...
...AND THEY WILL HELP GRANT ME MY ONE WISH: TO LOCATE THE CAPITAL CITY OF THE DRAGON KINGDOM, WHERE ALL THEIR SECRETS ARE KEPT!
GASP! THAT'S TERRIBLE! IF THE PHANTOM ACQUIRES THE DRAGONS' VAST STORES OF KNOWLEDGE, HE'LL BECOME INVINCIBLE!
IS THERE A WAY TO STOP HIM? IF I SAY THIS JUST RIGHT...
YOU CAN'T WISH TO TRAVEL TO WHERE THE WISDOM OF THE DRAGON CLAN DWELLS!
OH NO? I'LL DO IT RIGHT NOW!
SWIIISH

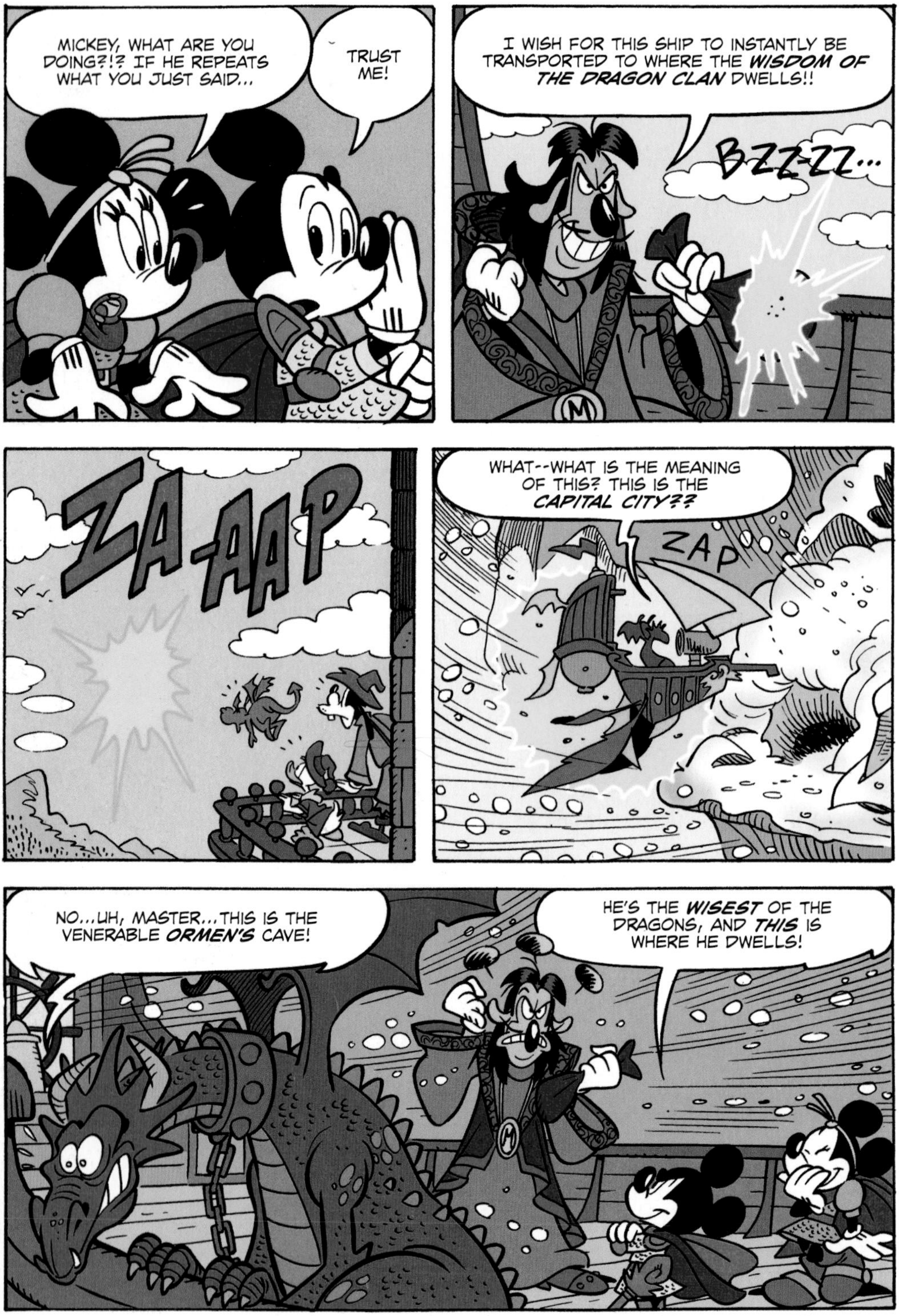

MICKEY, WHAT ARE YOU DOING?!? IF HE REPEATS WHAT YOU JUST SAID...
TRUST ME!
I WISH FOR THIS SHIP TO INSTANTLY BE TRANSPORTED TO WHERE THE WISDOM OF THE DRAGON CLAN DWELLS!!
BZZZZZ...
ZA-AAP
WHAT--WHAT IS THE MEANING OF THIS? THIS IS THE CAPITAL CITY??
ZAP
NO...UH, MASTER...THIS IS THE VENERABLE ORMEN'S CAVE!
HE'S THE WISEST OF THE DRAGONS, AND THIS IS WHERE HE DWELLS!

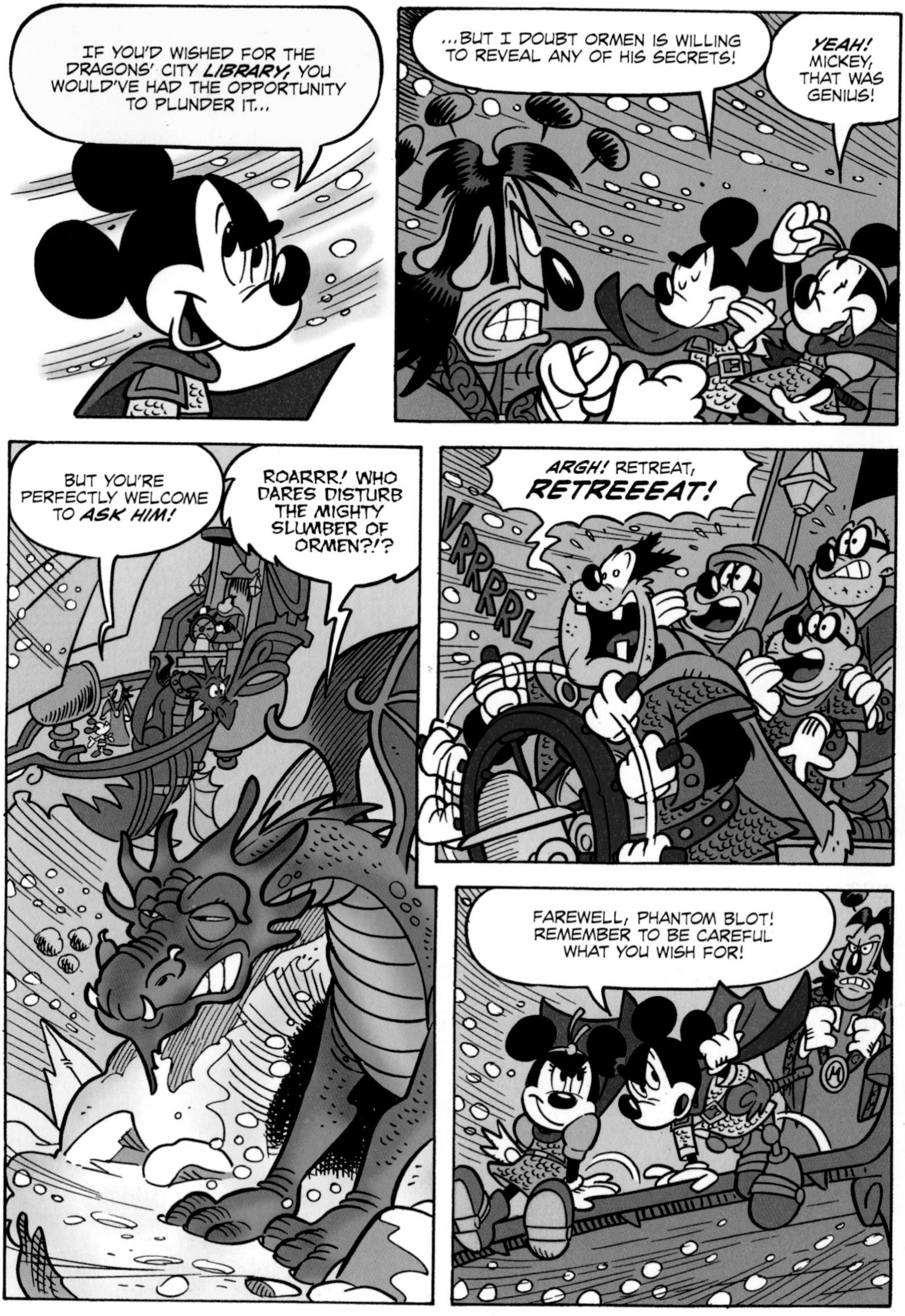
IF YOU'D WISHED FOR THE DRAGONS' CITY LIBRARY, YOU WOULD'VE HAD THE OPPORTUNITY TO PLUNDER IT...
...BUT I DOUBT ORMEN IS WILLING TO REVEAL ANY OF HIS SECRETS!
YEAH! MICKEY, THAT WAS GENIUS!
BUT YOU'RE PERFECTLY WELCOME TO ASK HIM!
ROARRR! WHO DARES DISTURB THE MIGHTY SLUMBER OF ORMEN?!?
ARGH! RETREAT, RETREEEAT!
VRRRRRL
FAREWELL, PHANTOM BLOT! REMEMBER TO BE CAREFUL WHAT YOU WISH FOR!

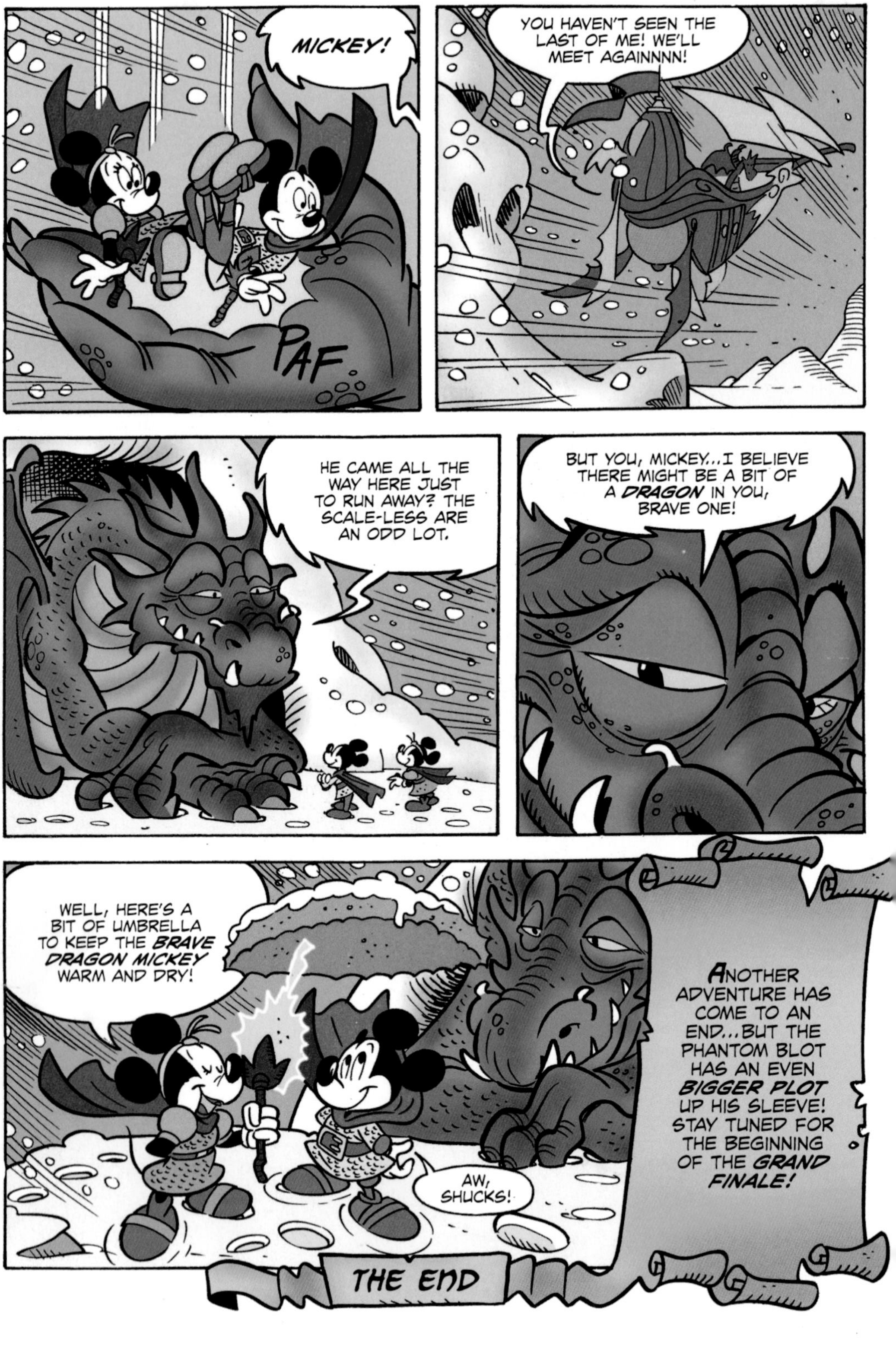
MICKEY!
PAF
YOU HAVEN'T SEEN THE LAST OF ME! WE'LL MEET AGAINNNN!
HE CAME ALL THE WAY HERE JUST TO RUN AWAY? THE SCALE-LESS ARE AN ODD LOT.
BUT YOU, MICKEY...I BELIEVE THERE MIGHT BE A BIT OF A DRAGON IN YOU, BRAVE ONE!
WELL, HERE'S A BIT OF UMBRELLA TO KEEP THE BRAVE DRAGON MICKEY WARM AND DRY!
AW, SHUCKS!
ANOTHER ADVENTURE HAS COME TO AN END...BUT THE PHANTOM BLOT HAS AN EVEN BIGGER PLOT UP HIS SLEEVE! STAY TUNED FOR THE BEGINNING OF THE GRAND FINALE!
THE END

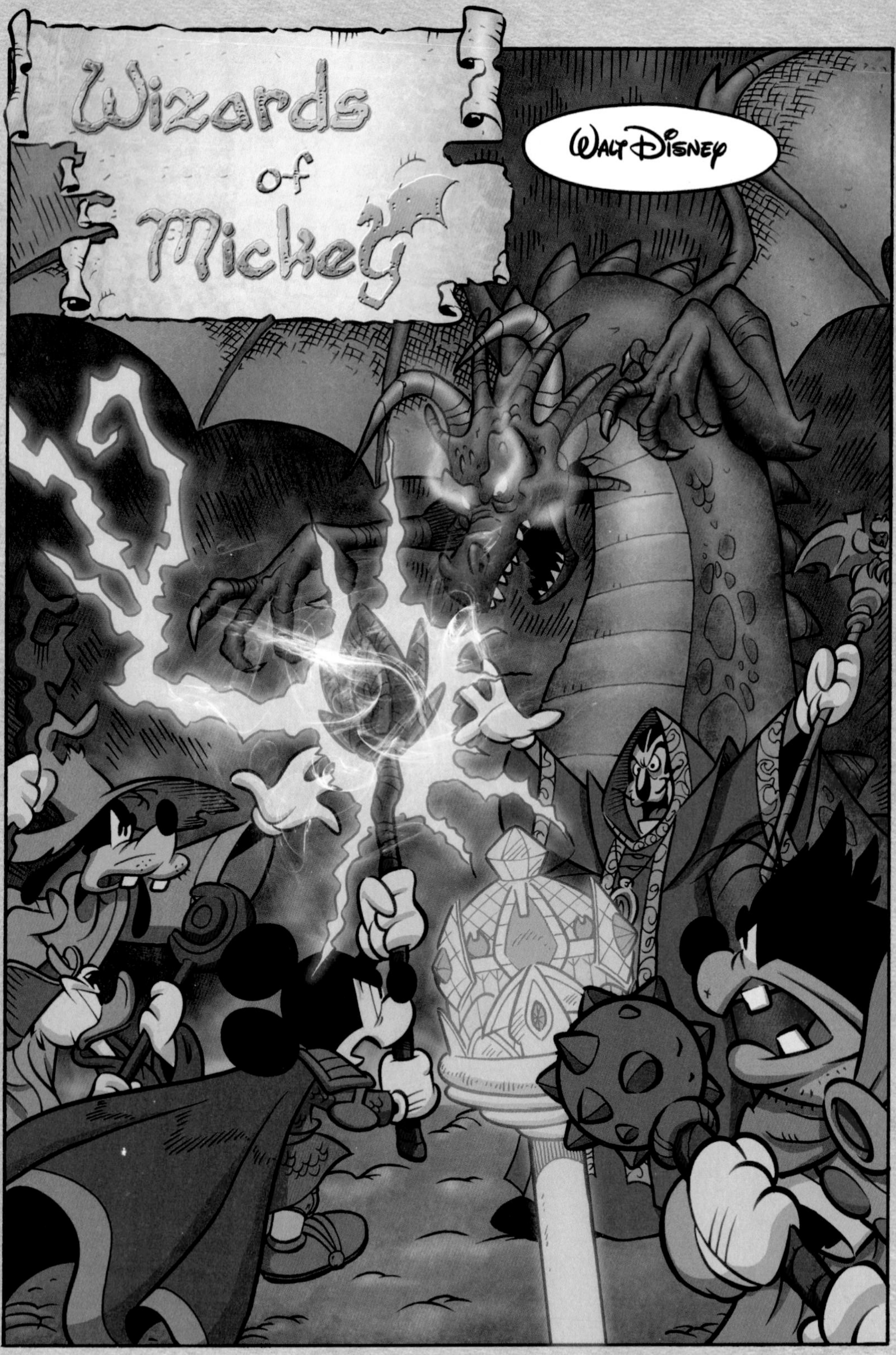
Wizards of Mickey
WALT DISNEY

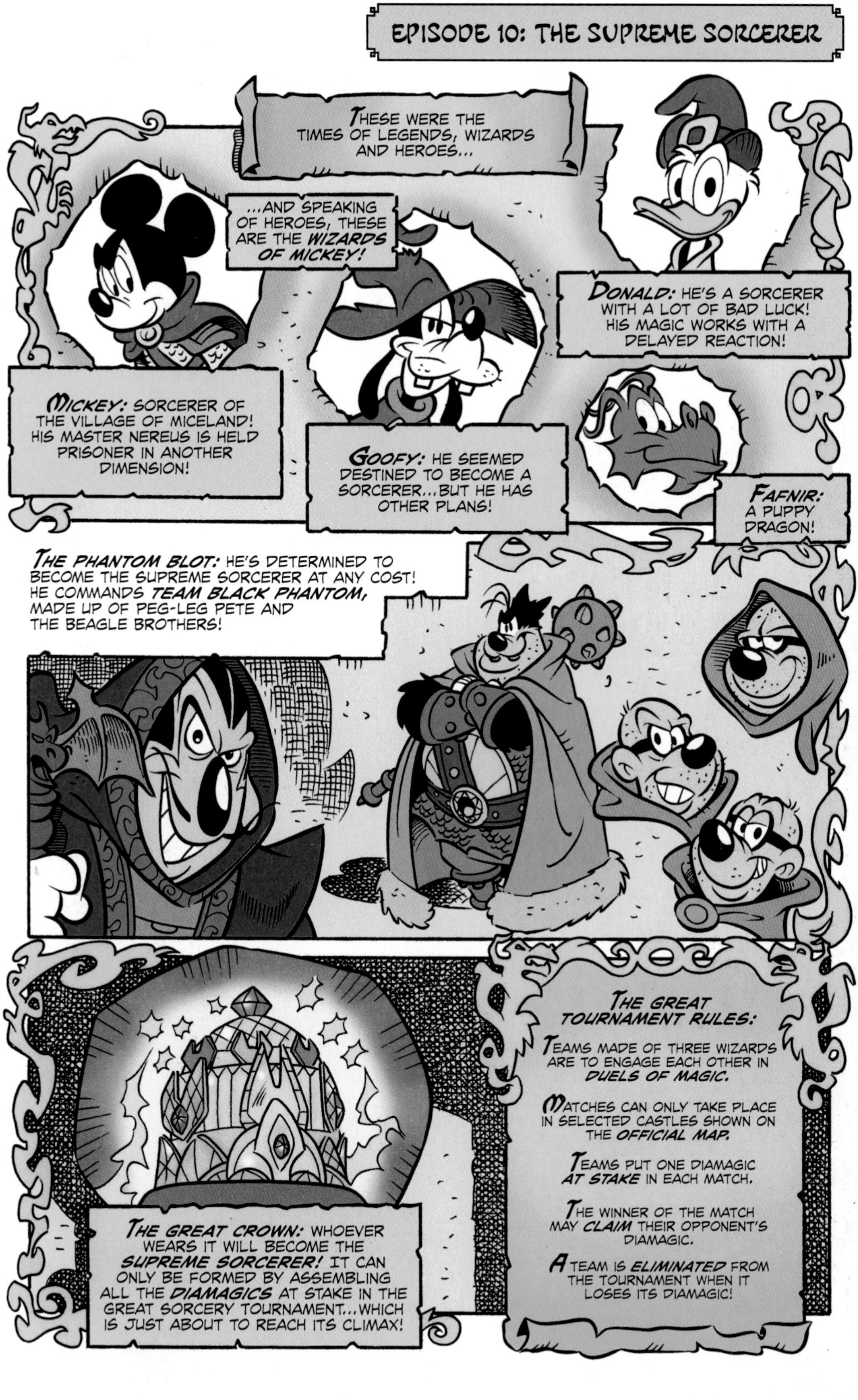
EPISODE 10: THE SUPREME SORCERER
THESE WERE THE TIMES OF LEGENDS, WIZARDS AND HEROES...
...AND SPEAKING OF HEROES, THESE ARE THE WIZARDS OF MICKEY!
DONALD: HE'S A SORCERER WITH A LOT OF BAD LUCK! HIS MAGIC WORKS WITH A DELAYED REACTION!
MICKEY: SORCERER OF THE VILLAGE OF MICELAND! HIS MASTER NEREUS IS HELD PRISONER IN ANOTHER DIMENSION!
GOOFY: HE SEEMED DESTINED TO BECOME A SORCERER...BUT HE HAS OTHER PLANS!
FAFNIR: A PUPPY DRAGON!
THE PHANTOM BLOT: HE'S DETERMINED TO BECOME THE SUPREME SORCERER AT ANY COST! HE COMMANDS TEAM BLACK PHANTOM, MADE UP OF PEG-LEG PETE AND THE BEAGLE BROTHERS!
THE GREAT CROWN: WHOEVER WEARS IT WILL BECOME THE SUPREME SORCERER! IT CAN ONLY BE FORMED BY ASSEMBLING ALL THE DIAMAGICS AT STAKE IN THE GREAT SORCERY TOURNAMENT...WHICH IS JUST ABOUT TO REACH ITS CLIMAX!
THE GREAT TOURNAMENT RULES:
TEAMS MADE OF THREE WIZARDS ARE TO ENGAGE EACH OTHER IN DUELS OF MAGIC.
MATCHES CAN ONLY TAKE PLACE IN SELECTED CASTLES SHOWN ON THE OFFICIAL MAP.
TEAMS PUT ONE DIAMAGIC AT STAKE IN EACH MATCH.
THE WINNER OF THE MATCH MAY CLAIM THEIR OPPONENT'S DIAMAGIC.
A TEAM IS ELIMINATED FROM THE TOURNAMENT WHEN IT LOSES ITS DIAMAGIC!

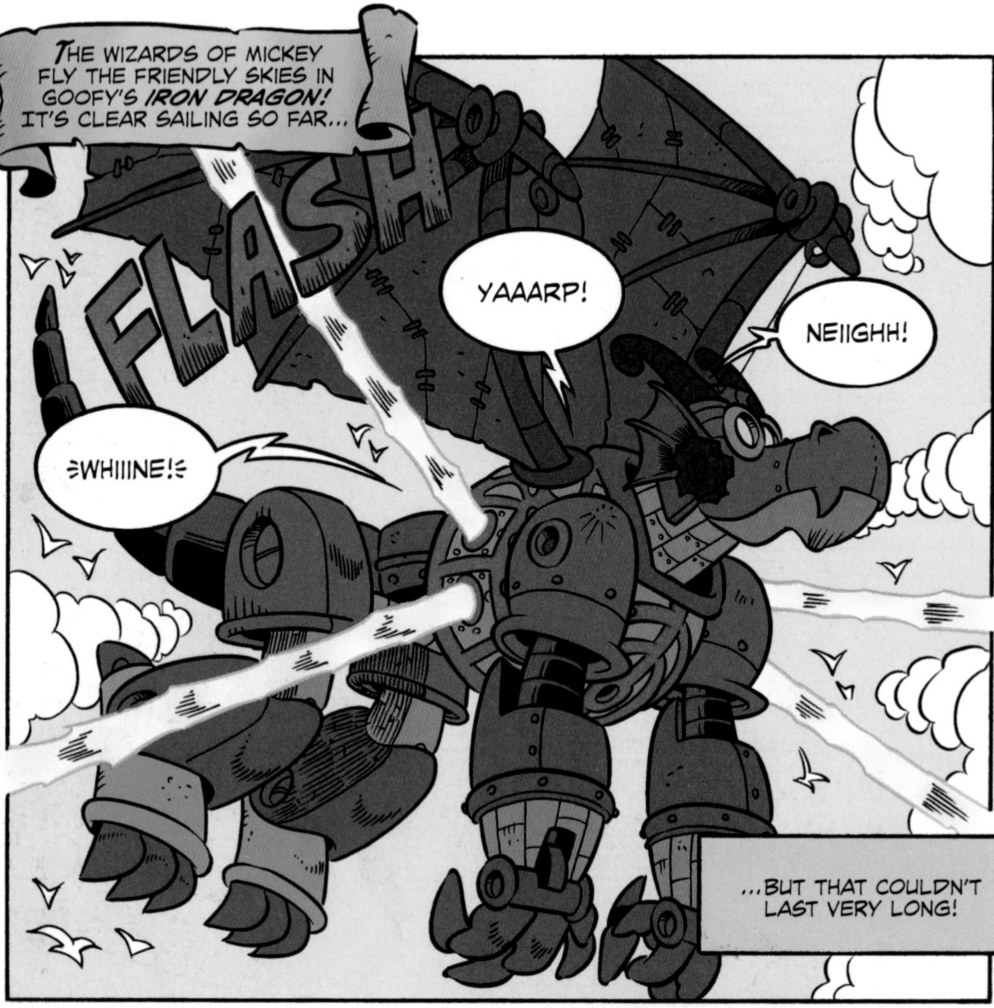
THE WIZARDS OF MICKEY FLY THE FRIENDLY SKIES IN GOOFY'S *IRON DRAGON!* IT'S CLEAR SAILING SO FAR...
FLASH
YAAARP!
NEIIGHH!
≈WHIIINE!≈
...BUT THAT COULDN'T LAST VERY LONG!

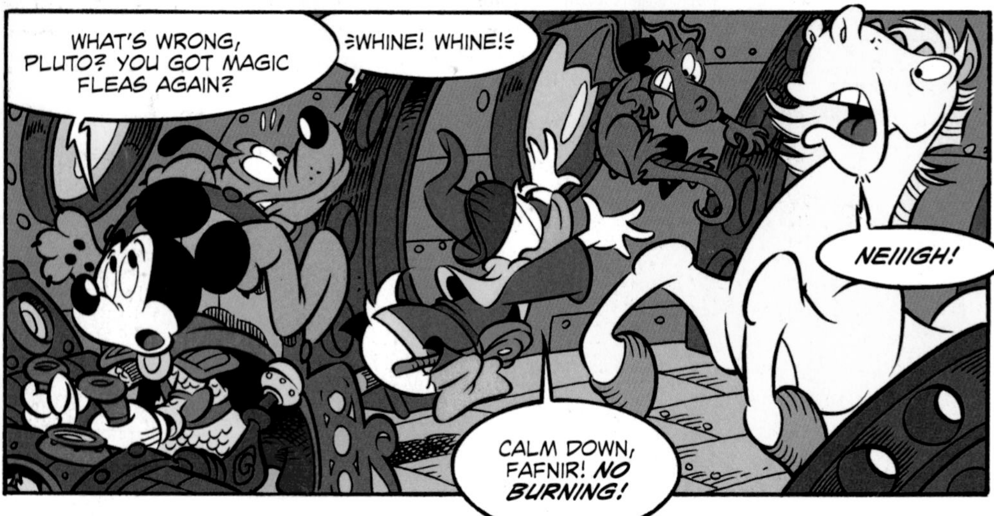
WHAT'S WRONG, PLUTO? YOU GOT MAGIC FLEAS AGAIN?
≈WHINE! WHINE!≈
NEIIIGH!
CALM DOWN, FAFNIR! *NO BURNING!*

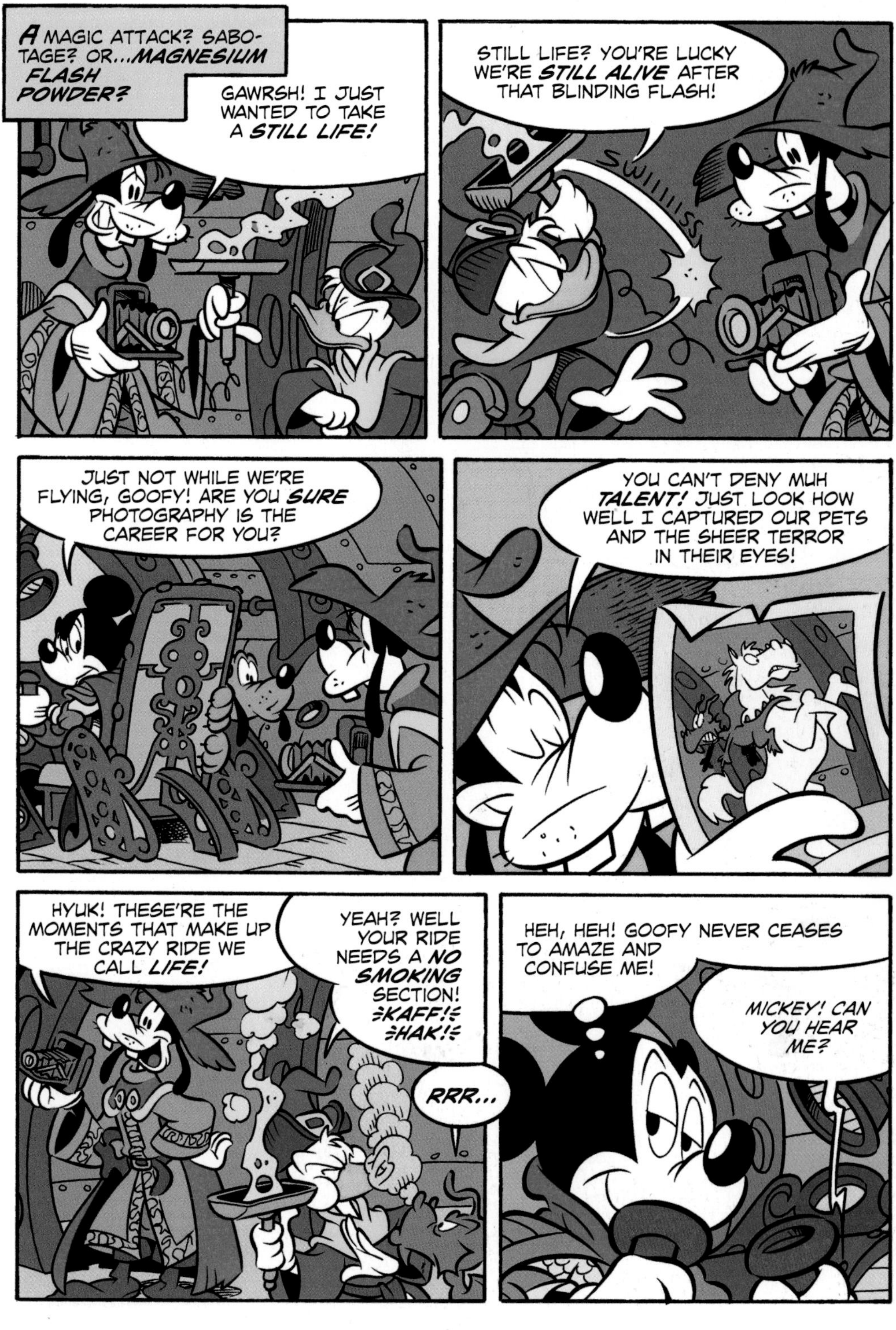
A MAGIC ATTACK? SABO-TAGE? OR...MAGNESIUM FLASH POWDER?
GAWRSH! I JUST WANTED TO TAKE A STILL LIFE!
STILL LIFE? YOU'RE LUCKY WE'RE STILL ALIVE AFTER THAT BLINDING FLASH!
SWIIIIISS
JUST NOT WHILE WE'RE FLYING, GOOFY! ARE YOU SURE PHOTOGRAPHY IS THE CAREER FOR YOU?
YOU CAN'T DENY MUH TALENT! JUST LOOK HOW WELL I CAPTURED OUR PETS AND THE SHEER TERROR IN THEIR EYES!
HYUK! THESE'RE THE MOMENTS THAT MAKE UP THE CRAZY RIDE WE CALL LIFE!
YEAH? WELL YOUR RIDE NEEDS A NO SMOKING SECTION! KAFF! HAK!
RRR...
HEH, HEH! GOOFY NEVER CEASES TO AMAZE AND CONFUSE ME!
MICKEY! CAN YOU HEAR ME?

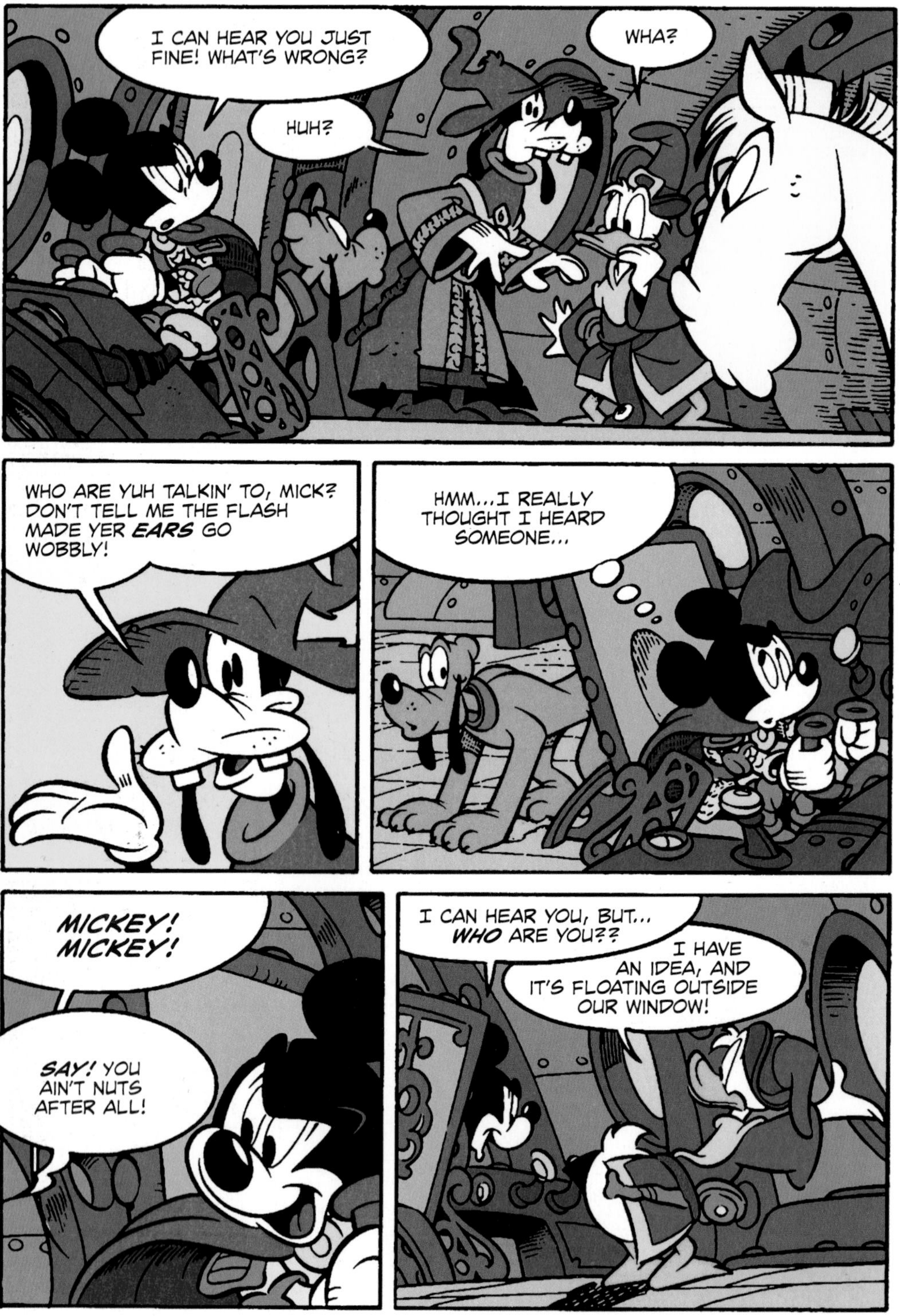
I CAN HEAR YOU JUST FINE! WHAT'S WRONG?
HUH?
WHA?
WHO ARE YUH TALKIN' TO, MICK? DON'T TELL ME THE FLASH MADE YER *EARS* GO WOBBLY!
HMM...I REALLY THOUGHT I HEARD SOMEONE...
MICKEY! MICKEY!
SAY! YOU AIN'T NUTS AFTER ALL!
I CAN HEAR YOU, BUT... *WHO* ARE YOU??
I HAVE AN IDEA, AND IT'S FLOATING OUTSIDE OUR WINDOW!

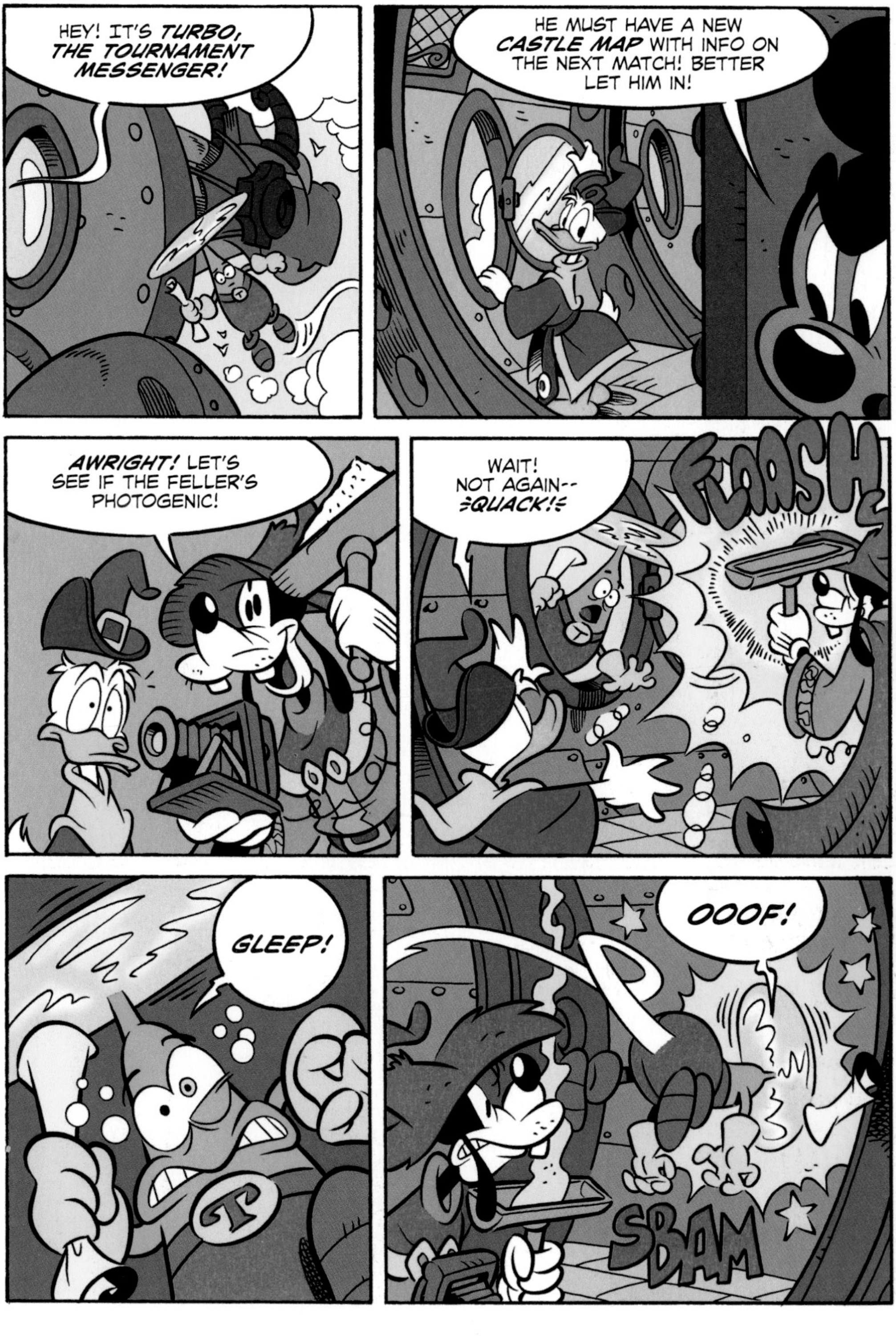
HEY! IT'S TURBO, THE TOURNAMENT MESSENGER!
HE MUST HAVE A NEW CASTLE MAP WITH INFO ON THE NEXT MATCH! BETTER LET HIM IN!
AWRIGHT! LET'S SEE IF THE FELLER'S PHOTOGENIC!
WAIT! NOT AGAIN-- QUACK!
FLAASH
GLEEP!
OOOF!
SBAM

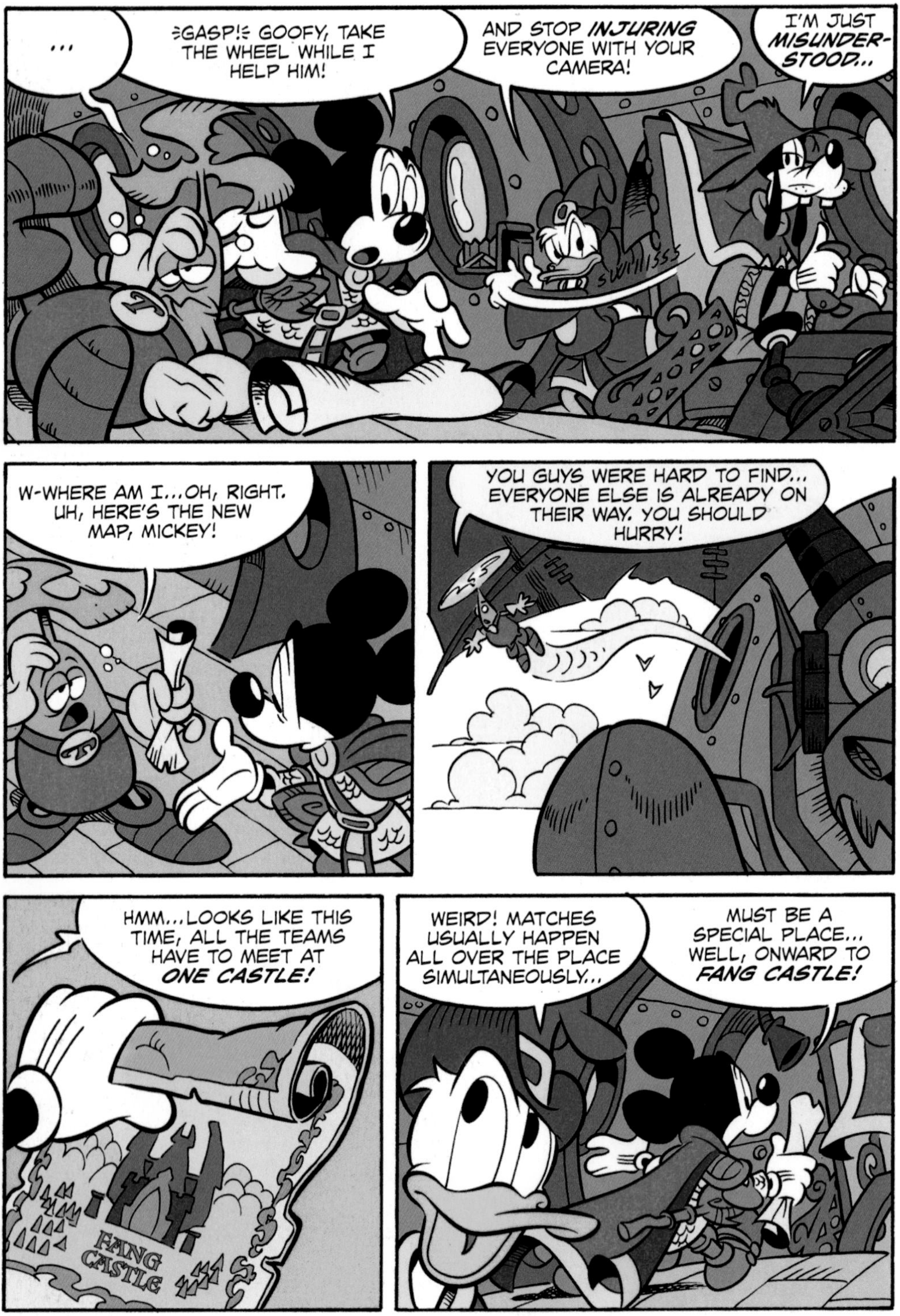
...
≑GASP!≑ GOOFY, TAKE THE WHEEL WHILE I HELP HIM!
AND STOP INJURING EVERYONE WITH YOUR CAMERA!
I'M JUST MISUNDER-STOOD...
SWIIISSS
W-WHERE AM I...OH, RIGHT. UH, HERE'S THE NEW MAP, MICKEY!
YOU GUYS WERE HARD TO FIND... EVERYONE ELSE IS ALREADY ON THEIR WAY. YOU SHOULD HURRY!
HMM...LOOKS LIKE THIS TIME, ALL THE TEAMS HAVE TO MEET AT ONE CASTLE!
FANG CASTLE
WEIRD! MATCHES USUALLY HAPPEN ALL OVER THE PLACE SIMULTANEOUSLY...
MUST BE A SPECIAL PLACE... WELL, ONWARD TO FANG CASTLE!

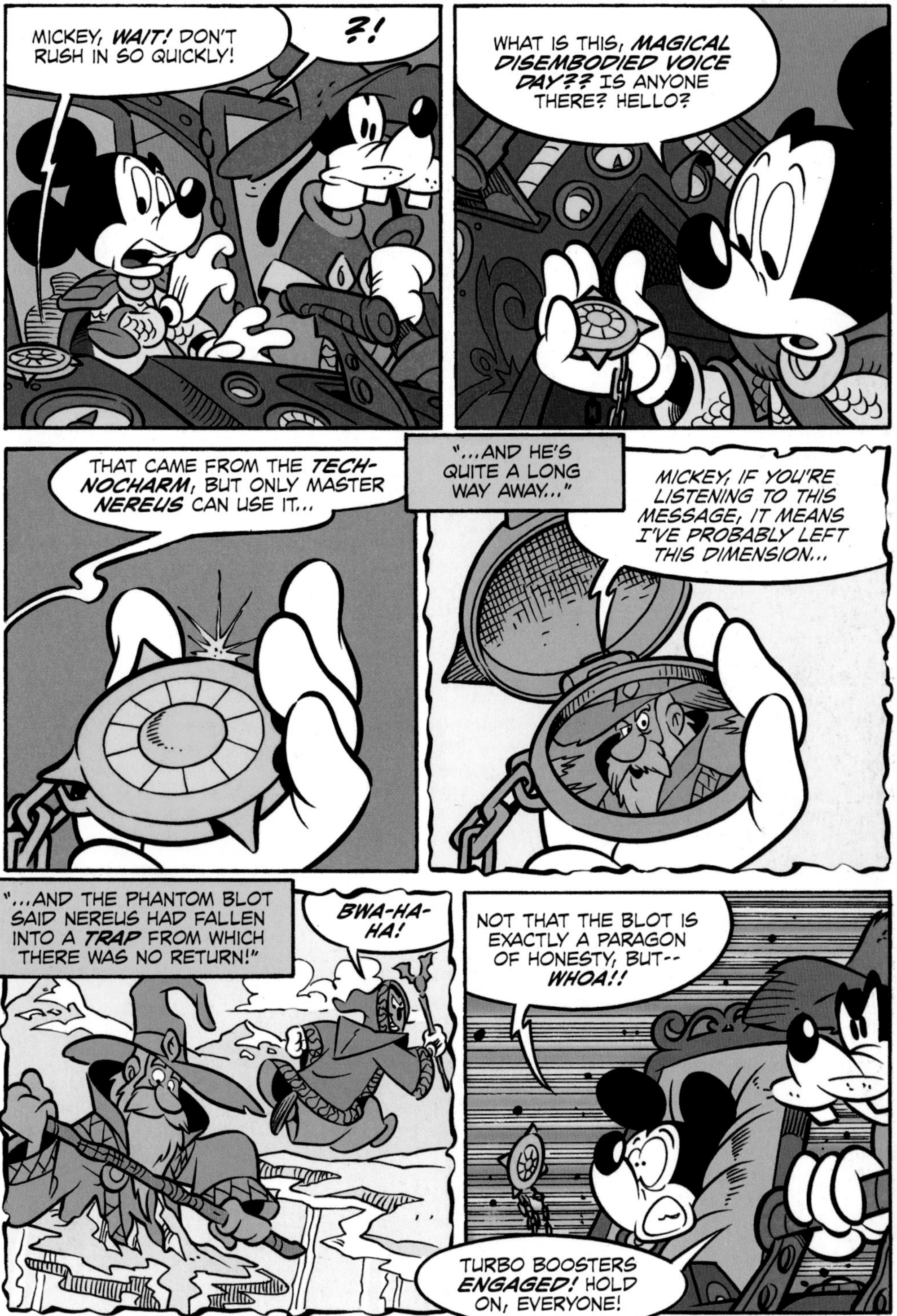
MICKEY, WAIT! DON'T RUSH IN SO QUICKLY!
?!
WHAT IS THIS, MAGICAL DISEMBODIED VOICE DAY?? IS ANYONE THERE? HELLO?
THAT CAME FROM THE TECHNOCHARM, BUT ONLY MASTER NEREUS CAN USE IT...
"...AND HE'S QUITE A LONG WAY AWAY..."
MICKEY, IF YOU'RE LISTENING TO THIS MESSAGE, IT MEANS I'VE PROBABLY LEFT THIS DIMENSION...
"...AND THE PHANTOM BLOT SAID NEREUS HAD FALLEN INTO A TRAP FROM WHICH THERE WAS NO RETURN!"
BWA-HA-HA!
NOT THAT THE BLOT IS EXACTLY A PARAGON OF HONESTY, BUT-- WHOA!!
TURBO BOOSTERS ENGAGED! HOLD ON, EVERYONE!

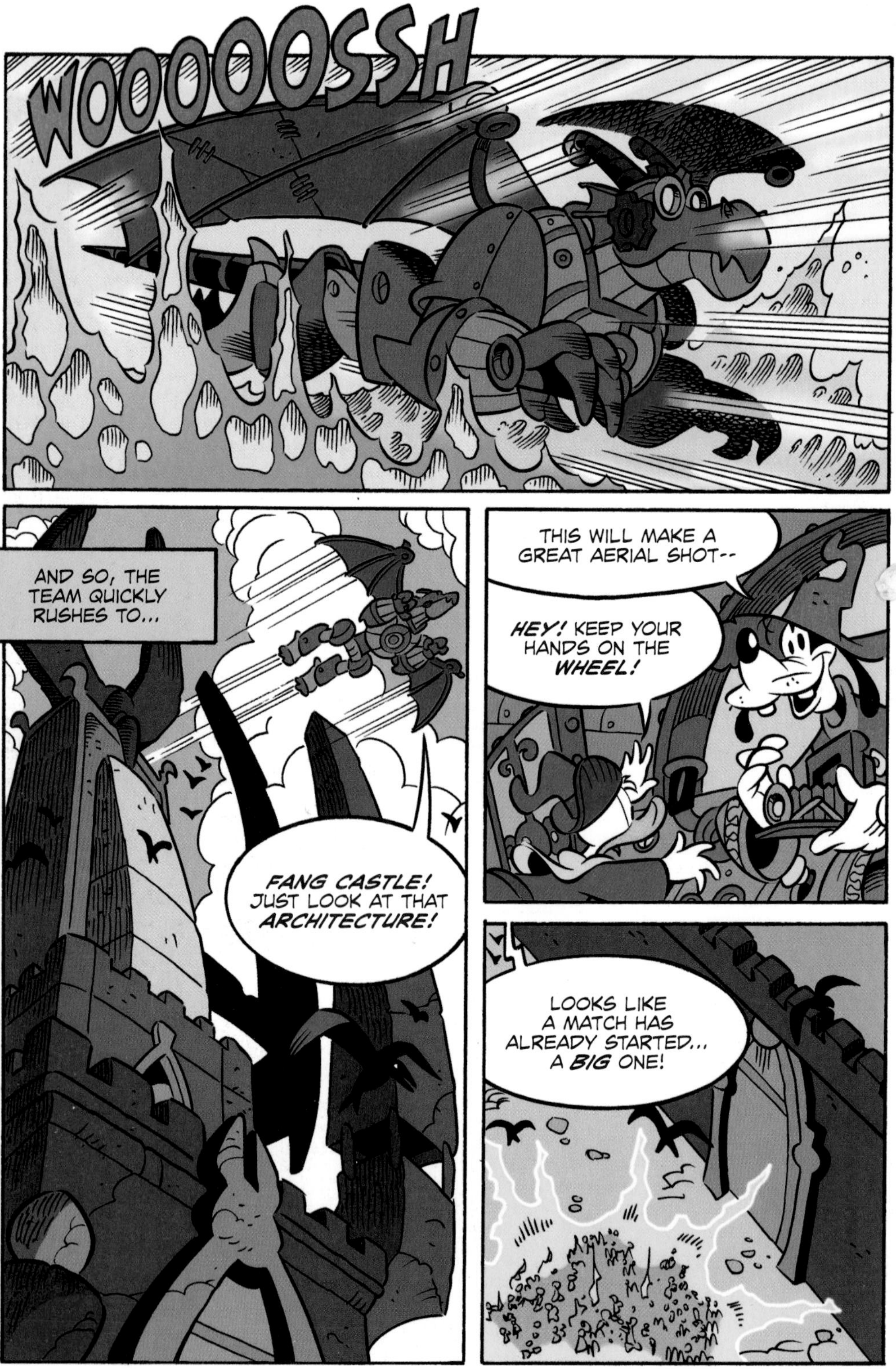
WOOOOOSSH
AND SO, THE TEAM QUICKLY RUSHES TO...
FANG CASTLE! JUST LOOK AT THAT ARCHITECTURE!
THIS WILL MAKE A GREAT AERIAL SHOT--
HEY! KEEP YOUR HANDS ON THE WHEEL!
LOOKS LIKE A MATCH HAS ALREADY STARTED... A BIG ONE!

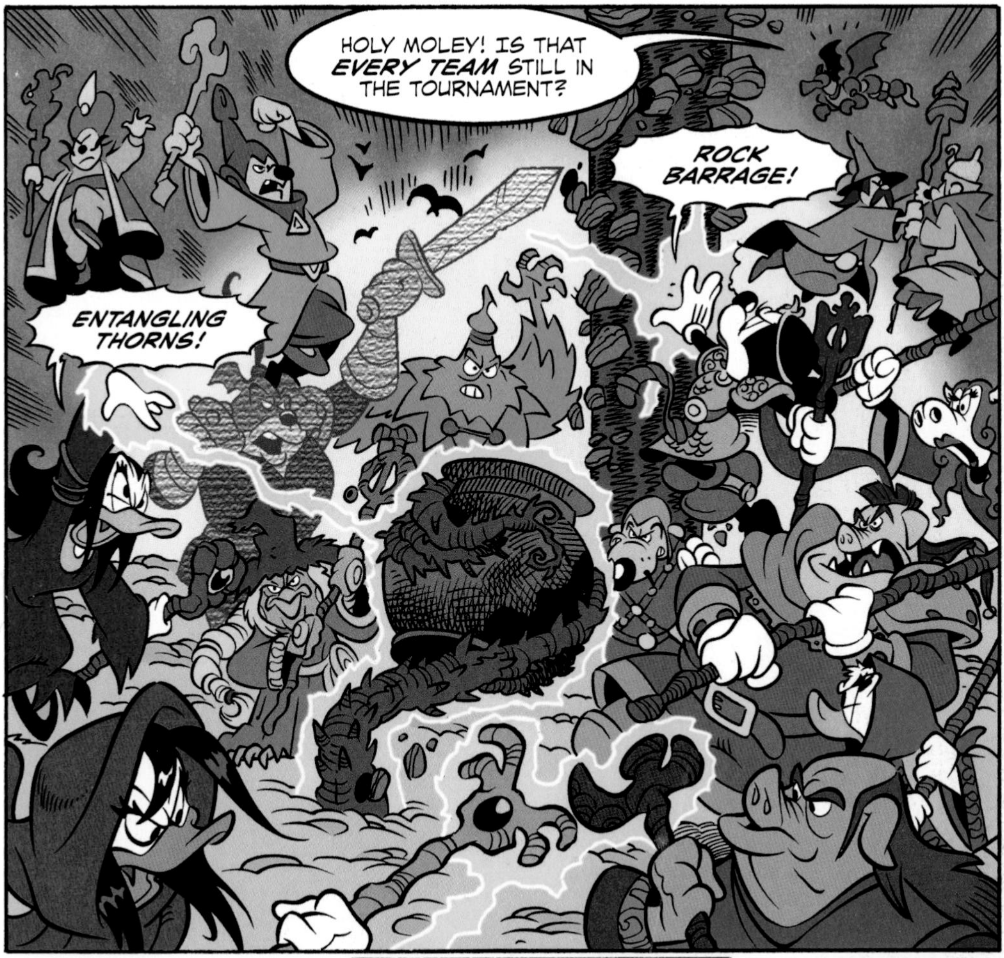
HOLY MOLEY! IS THAT EVERY TEAM STILL IN THE TOURNAMENT?
ROCK BARRAGE!
ENTANGLING THORNS!

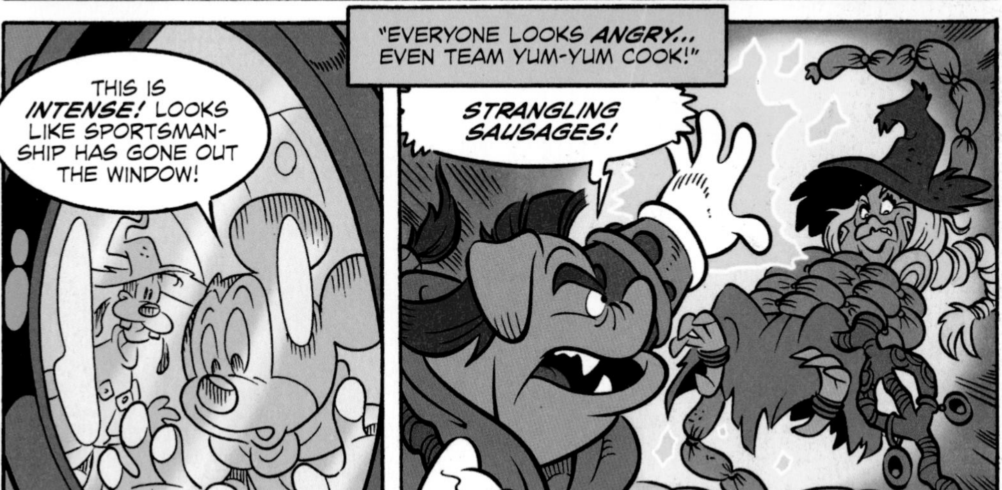
"EVERYONE LOOKS ANGRY... EVEN TEAM YUM-YUM COOK!"
THIS IS INTENSE! LOOKS LIKE SPORTSMAN-SHIP HAS GONE OUT THE WINDOW!
STRANGLING SAUSAGES!

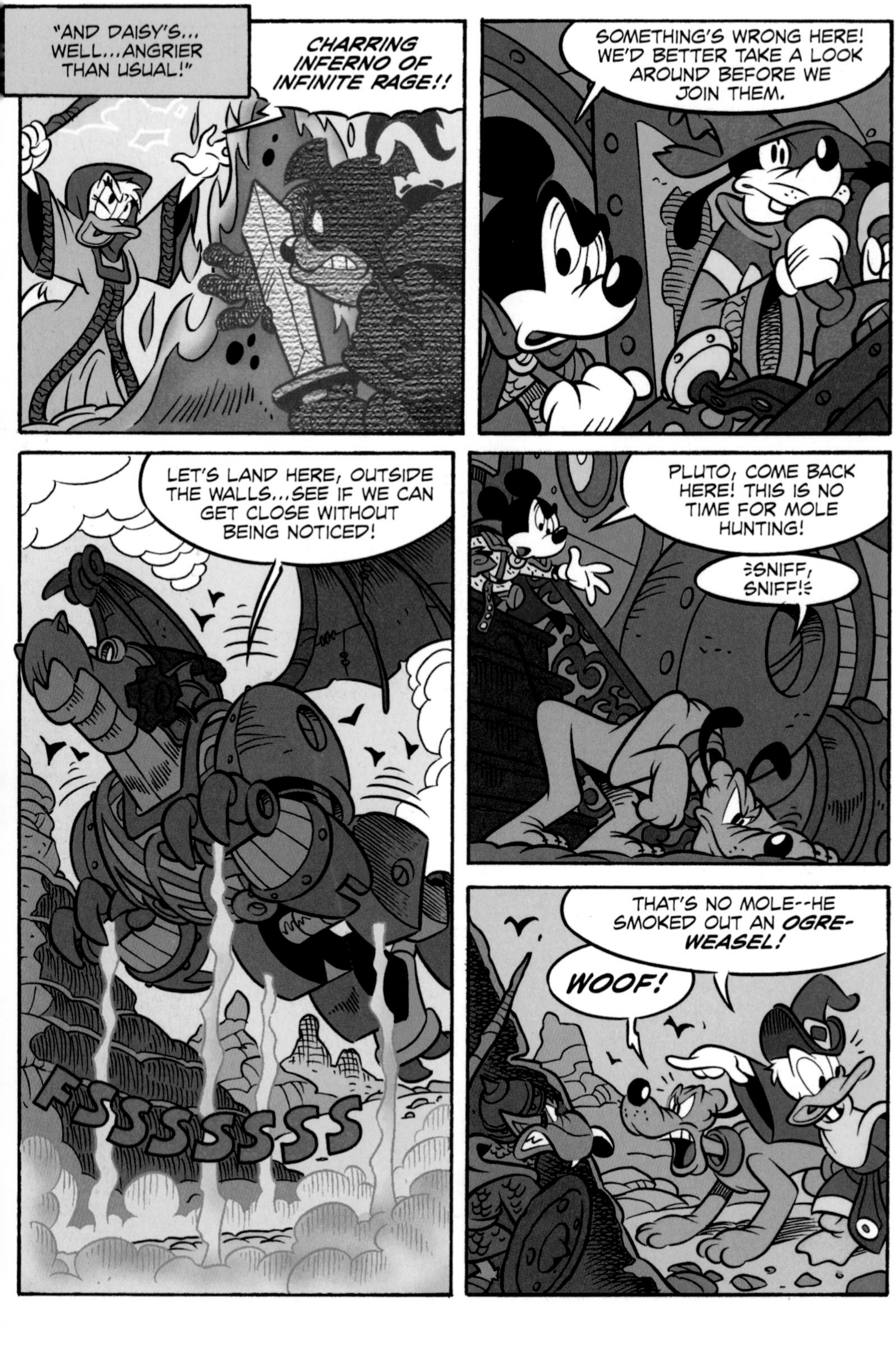
"AND DAISY'S... WELL...ANGRIER THAN USUAL!"
CHARRING INFERNO OF INFINITE RAGE!!
SOMETHING'S WRONG HERE! WE'D BETTER TAKE A LOOK AROUND BEFORE WE JOIN THEM.
LET'S LAND HERE, OUTSIDE THE WALLS...SEE IF WE CAN GET CLOSE WITHOUT BEING NOTICED!
FSSSSSSS
PLUTO, COME BACK HERE! THIS IS NO TIME FOR MOLE HUNTING!
SNIFF, SNIFF!
THAT'S NO MOLE--HE SMOKED OUT AN OGRE-WEASEL!
WOOF!

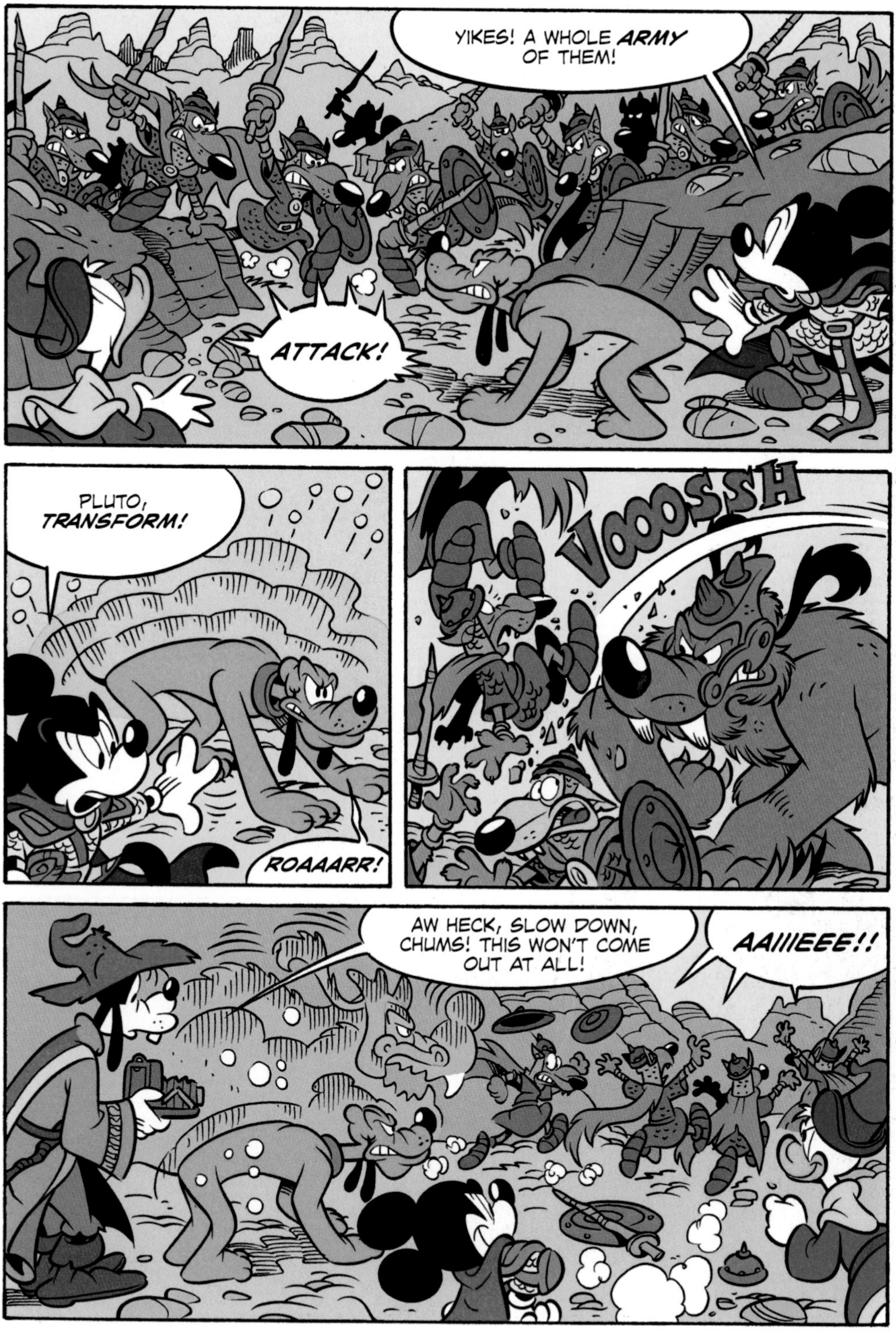
YIKES! A WHOLE ARMY OF THEM!
ATTACK!
PLUTO, TRANSFORM!
ROAAARR!
VOOOSSSH
AW HECK, SLOW DOWN, CHUMS! THIS WON'T COME OUT AT ALL!
AAIIIEEE!!

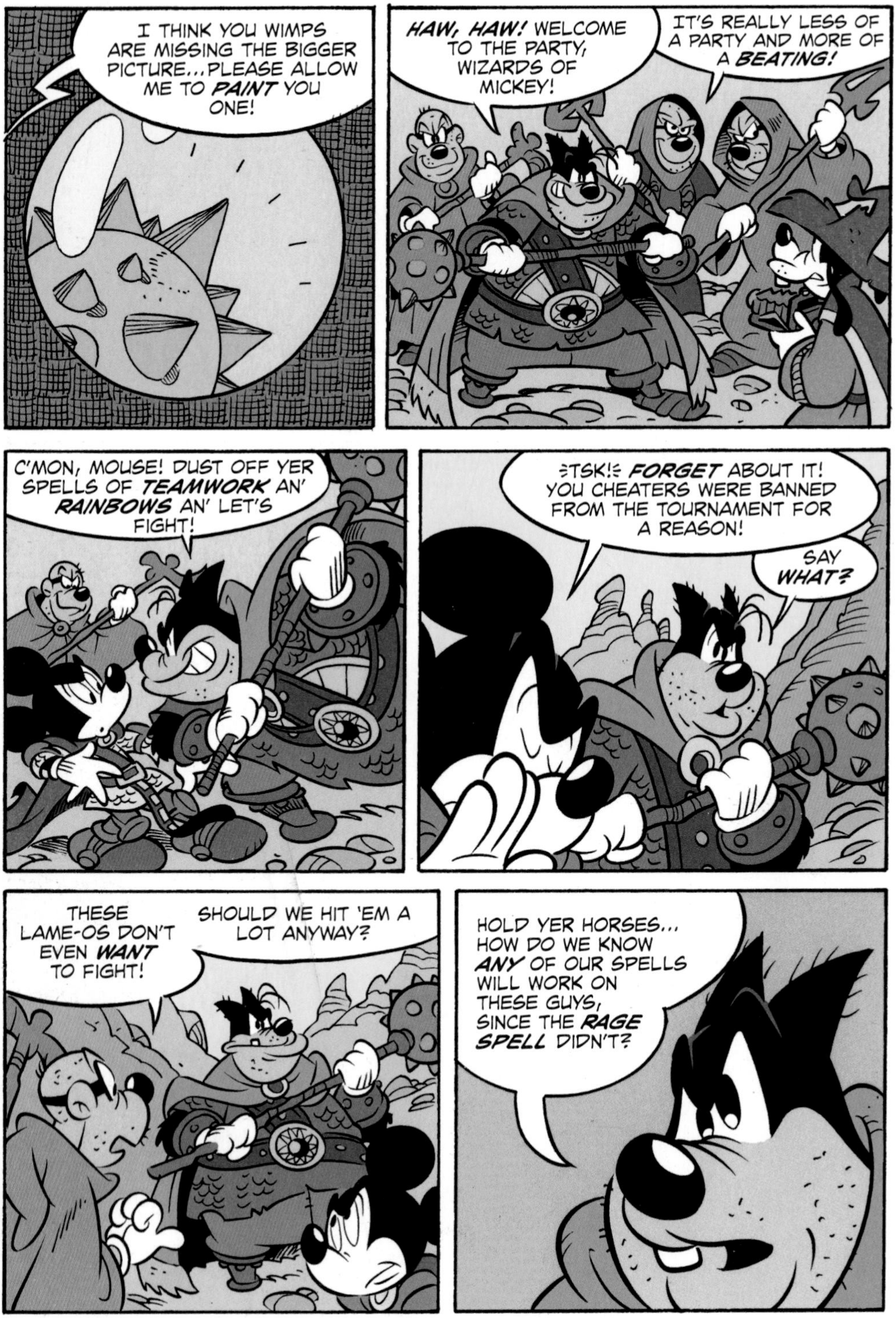

I THINK YOU WIMPS ARE MISSING THE BIGGER PICTURE... PLEASE ALLOW ME TO *PAINT* YOU ONE!
HAW, HAW! WELCOME TO THE PARTY, WIZARDS OF MICKEY!
IT'S REALLY LESS OF A PARTY AND MORE OF A *BEATING!*
C'MON, MOUSE! DUST OFF YER SPELLS OF *TEAMWORK* AN' *RAINBOWS* AN' LET'S FIGHT!
TSK! *FORGET* ABOUT IT! YOU CHEATERS WERE BANNED FROM THE TOURNAMENT FOR A REASON!
SAY *WHAT?*
THESE LAME-OS DON'T EVEN *WANT* TO FIGHT!
SHOULD WE HIT 'EM A LOT ANYWAY?
HOLD YER HORSES... HOW DO WE KNOW *ANY* OF OUR SPELLS WILL WORK ON THESE GUYS, SINCE THE *RAGE SPELL* DIDN'T?

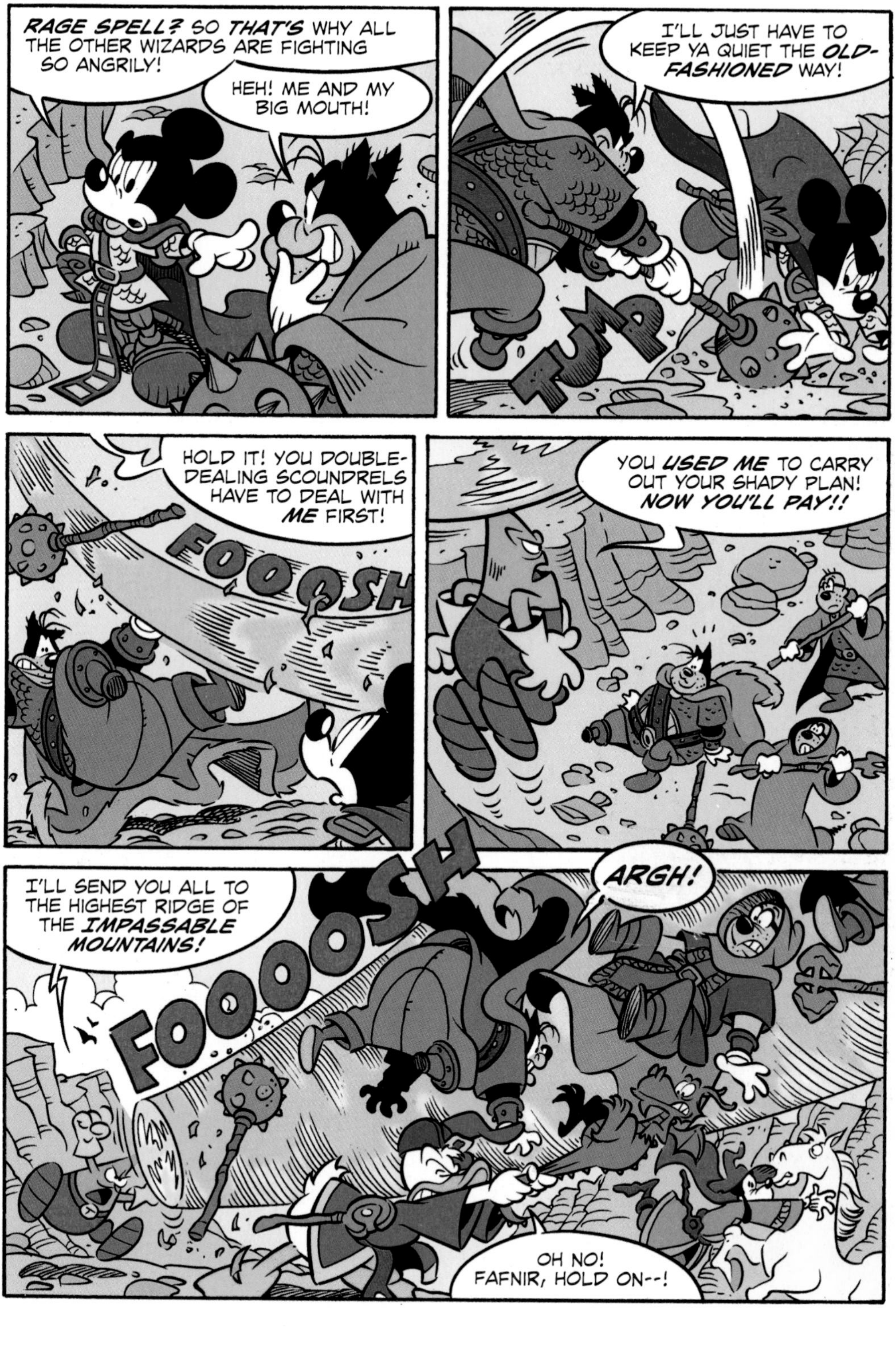
RAGE SPELL? SO THAT'S WHY ALL THE OTHER WIZARDS ARE FIGHTING SO ANGRILY!
HEH! ME AND MY BIG MOUTH!
I'LL JUST HAVE TO KEEP YA QUIET THE OLD-FASHIONED WAY!
TUMP
HOLD IT! YOU DOUBLE-DEALING SCOUNDRELS HAVE TO DEAL WITH ME FIRST!
FOOOSH
YOU USED ME TO CARRY OUT YOUR SHADY PLAN! NOW YOU'LL PAY!!
I'LL SEND YOU ALL TO THE HIGHEST RIDGE OF THE IMPASSABLE MOUNTAINS!
FOOOOOSH
ARGH!
OH NO! FAFNIR, HOLD ON--!

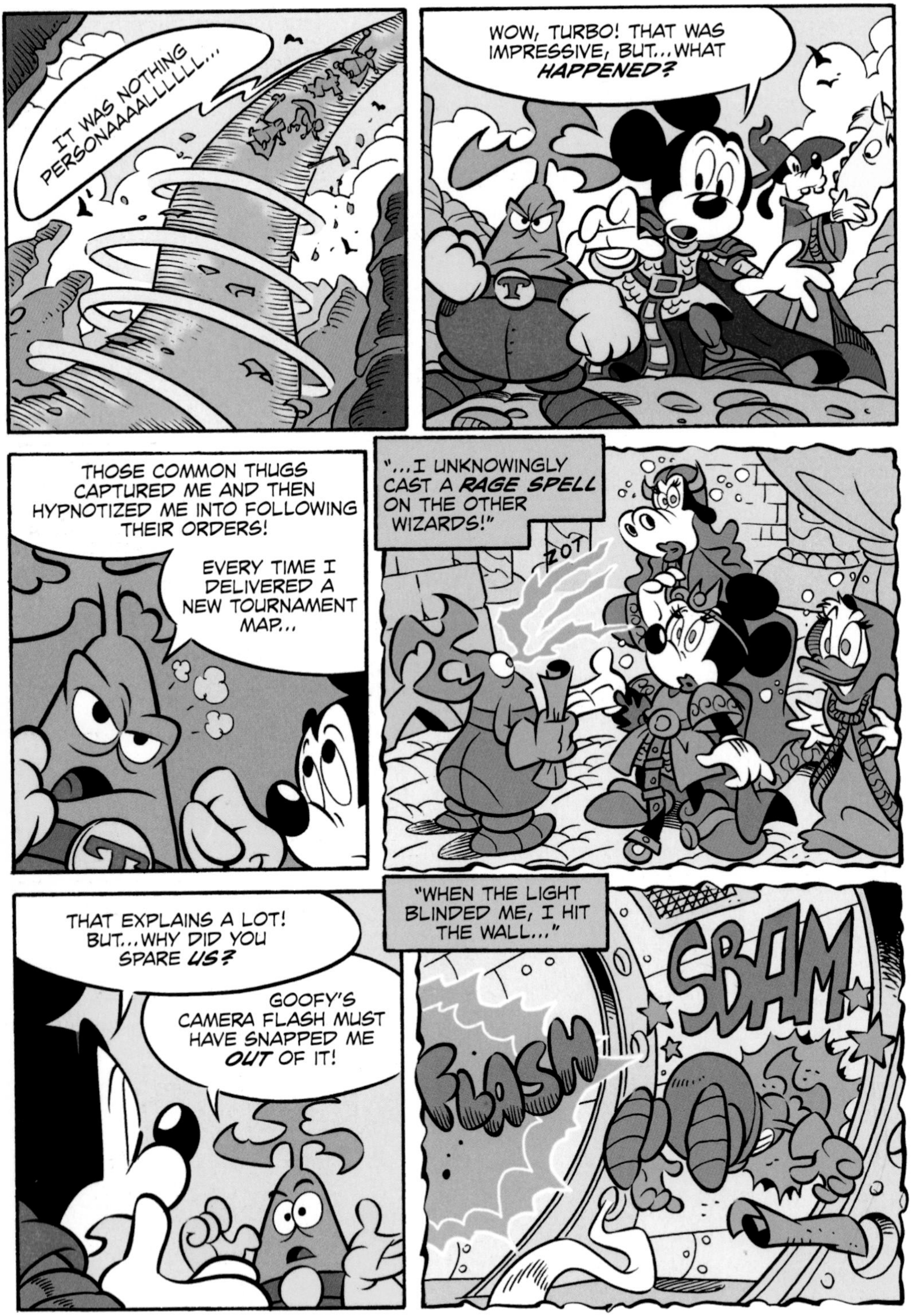
IT WAS NOTHING PERSONAAAALLLLLL...
WOW, TURBO! THAT WAS IMPRESSIVE, BUT...WHAT HAPPENED?
THOSE COMMON THUGS CAPTURED ME AND THEN HYPNOTIZED ME INTO FOLLOWING THEIR ORDERS!
EVERY TIME I DELIVERED A NEW TOURNAMENT MAP...
"...I UNKNOWINGLY CAST A RAGE SPELL ON THE OTHER WIZARDS!"
ZOT
THAT EXPLAINS A LOT! BUT...WHY DID YOU SPARE US?
GOOFY'S CAMERA FLASH MUST HAVE SNAPPED ME OUT OF IT!
"WHEN THE LIGHT BLINDED ME, I HIT THE WALL..."
SBAM
FLASH

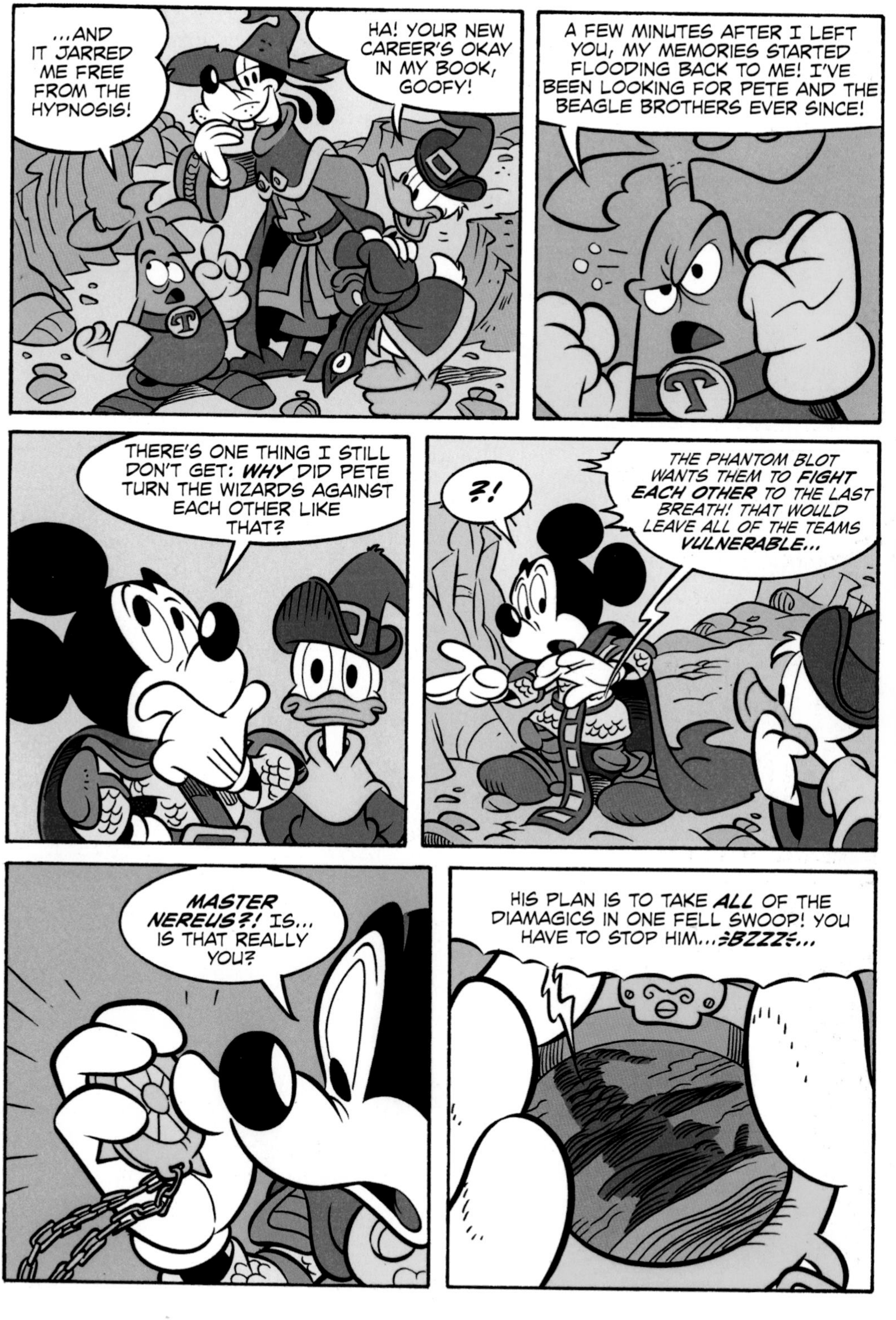
...AND IT JARRED ME FREE FROM THE HYPNOSIS!
HA! YOUR NEW CAREER'S OKAY IN MY BOOK, GOOFY!
A FEW MINUTES AFTER I LEFT YOU, MY MEMORIES STARTED FLOODING BACK TO ME! I'VE BEEN LOOKING FOR PETE AND THE BEAGLE BROTHERS EVER SINCE!
THERE'S ONE THING I STILL DON'T GET: WHY DID PETE TURN THE WIZARDS AGAINST EACH OTHER LIKE THAT?
?!
THE PHANTOM BLOT WANTS THEM TO FIGHT EACH OTHER TO THE LAST BREATH! THAT WOULD LEAVE ALL OF THE TEAMS VULNERABLE...
MASTER NEREUS?! IS... IS THAT REALLY YOU?
HIS PLAN IS TO TAKE ALL OF THE DIAMAGICS IN ONE FELL SWOOP! YOU HAVE TO STOP HIM... BZZZ...

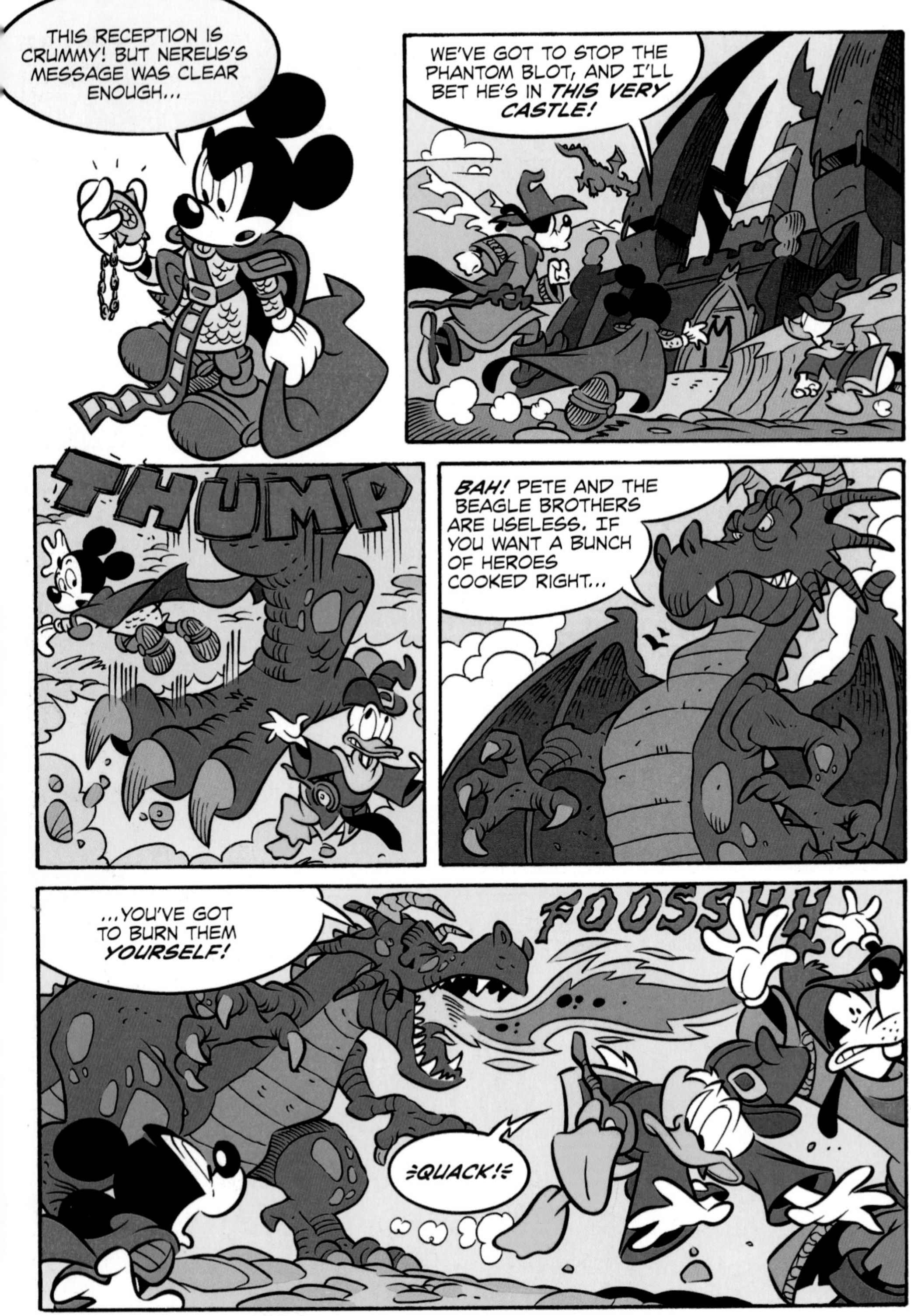
THIS RECEPTION IS CRUMMY! BUT NEREUS'S MESSAGE WAS CLEAR ENOUGH...
WE'VE GOT TO STOP THE PHANTOM BLOT, AND I'LL BET HE'S IN THIS VERY CASTLE!
THUMP
BAH! PETE AND THE BEAGLE BROTHERS ARE USELESS. IF YOU WANT A BUNCH OF HEROES COOKED RIGHT...
...YOU'VE GOT TO BURN THEM YOURSELF!
FOOSSHH
QUACK!

SGNAC

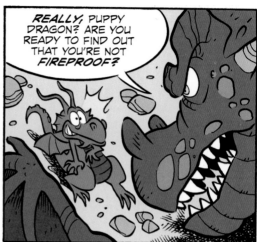

REALLY, PUPPY DRAGON? ARE YOU READY TO FIND OUT THAT YOU'RE NOT FIREPROOF?

FOOSSH

HURRY, YOU TWO, GET IN THE CASTLE! I'LL HANDLE THE DRAGON!

GOOD LUCK...!

GLAD I INSTALLED AN ATTACK MODE AFTER ALL!

GROOOARR

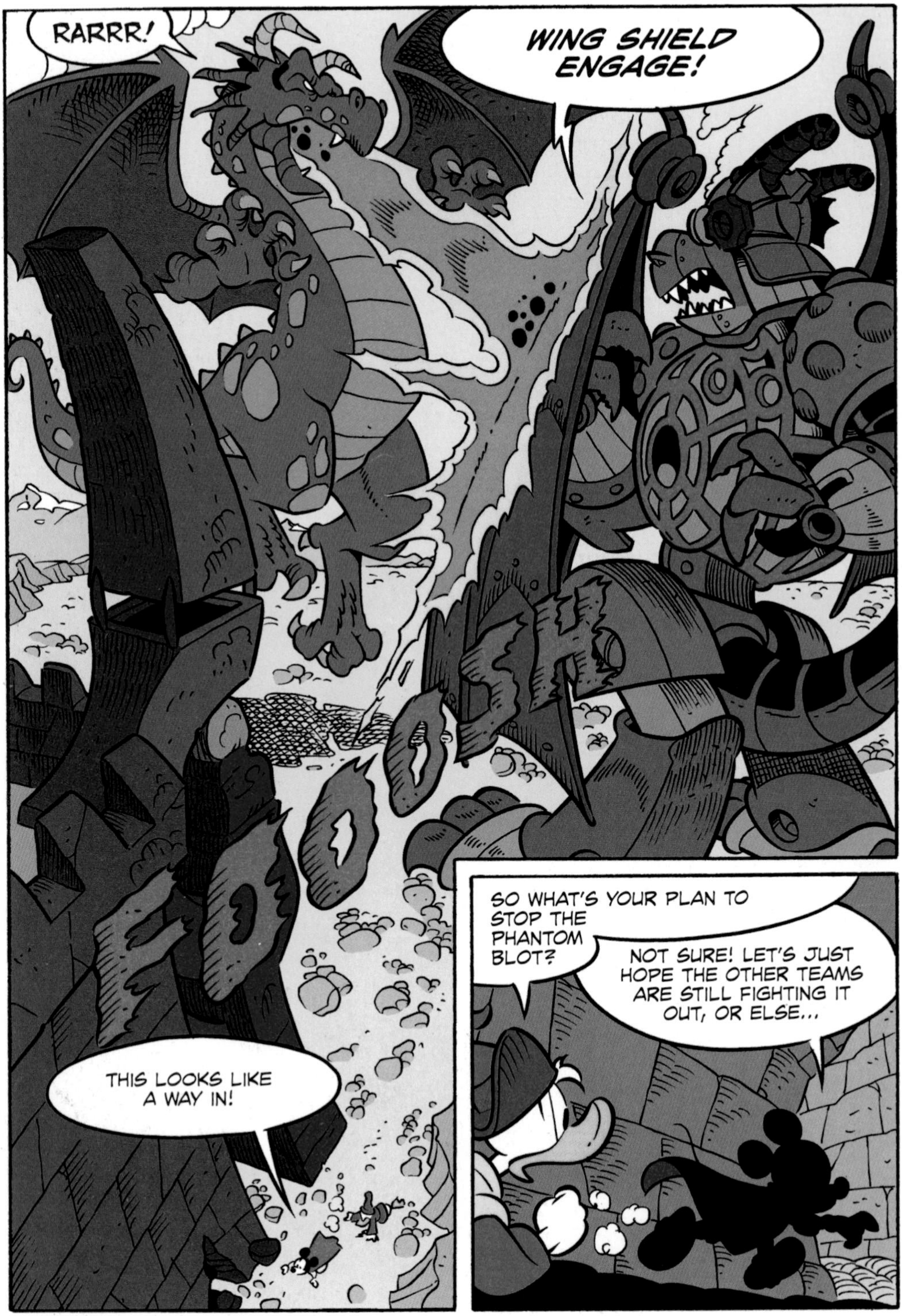
RARRR!
WING SHIELD ENGAGE!
THIS LOOKS LIKE A WAY IN!
SO WHAT'S YOUR PLAN TO STOP THE PHANTOM BLOT?
NOT SURE! LET'S JUST HOPE THE OTHER TEAMS ARE STILL FIGHTING IT OUT, OR ELSE...

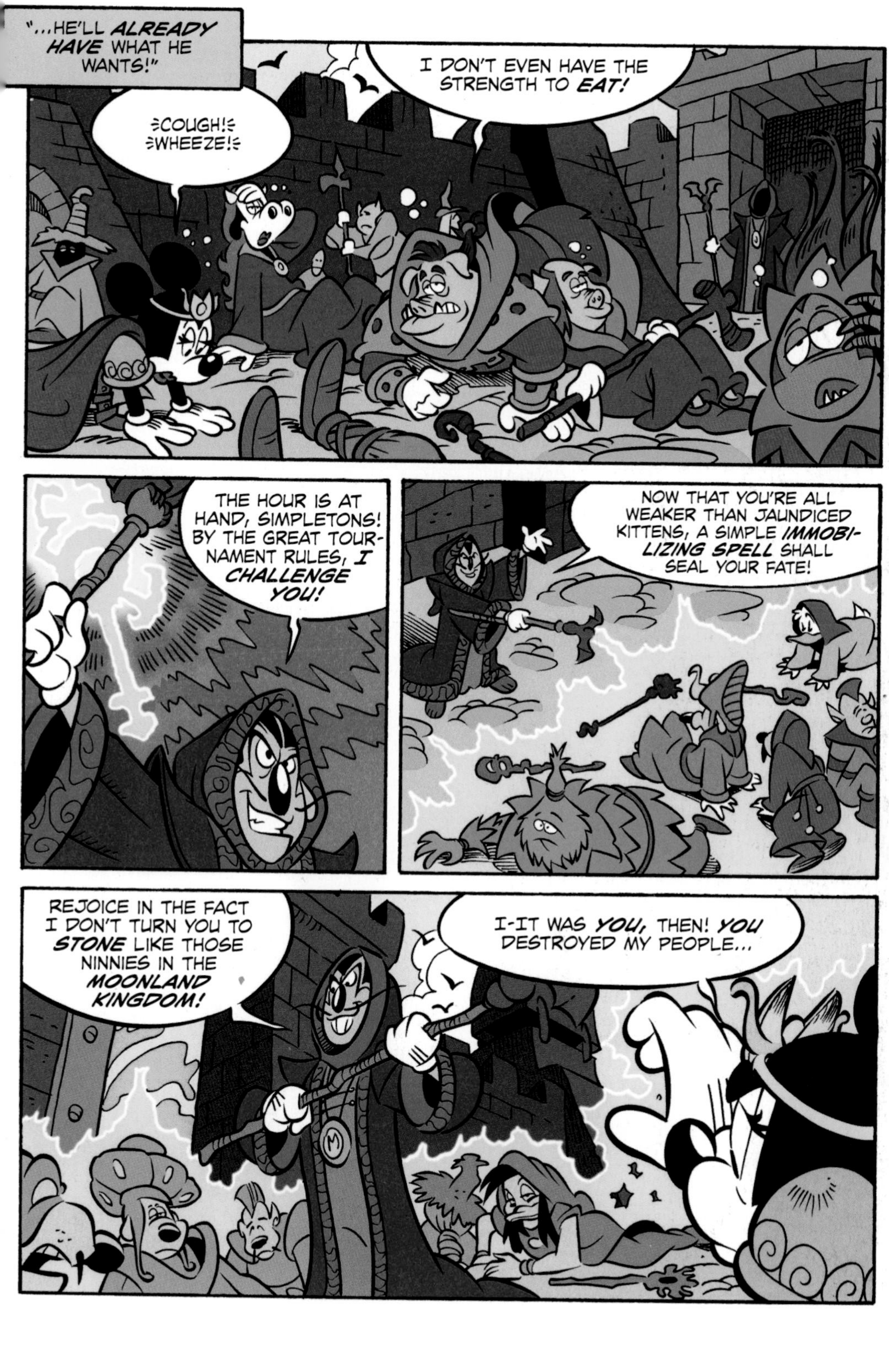
"...HE'LL ALREADY HAVE WHAT HE WANTS!"
I DON'T EVEN HAVE THE STRENGTH TO EAT!
COUGH! WHEEZE!
THE HOUR IS AT HAND, SIMPLETONS! BY THE GREAT TOURNAMENT RULES, I CHALLENGE YOU!
NOW THAT YOU'RE ALL WEAKER THAN JAUNDICED KITTENS, A SIMPLE IMMOBILIZING SPELL SHALL SEAL YOUR FATE!
REJOICE IN THE FACT I DON'T TURN YOU TO STONE LIKE THOSE NINNIES IN THE MOONLAND KINGDOM!
I-IT WAS YOU, THEN! YOU DESTROYED MY PEOPLE...

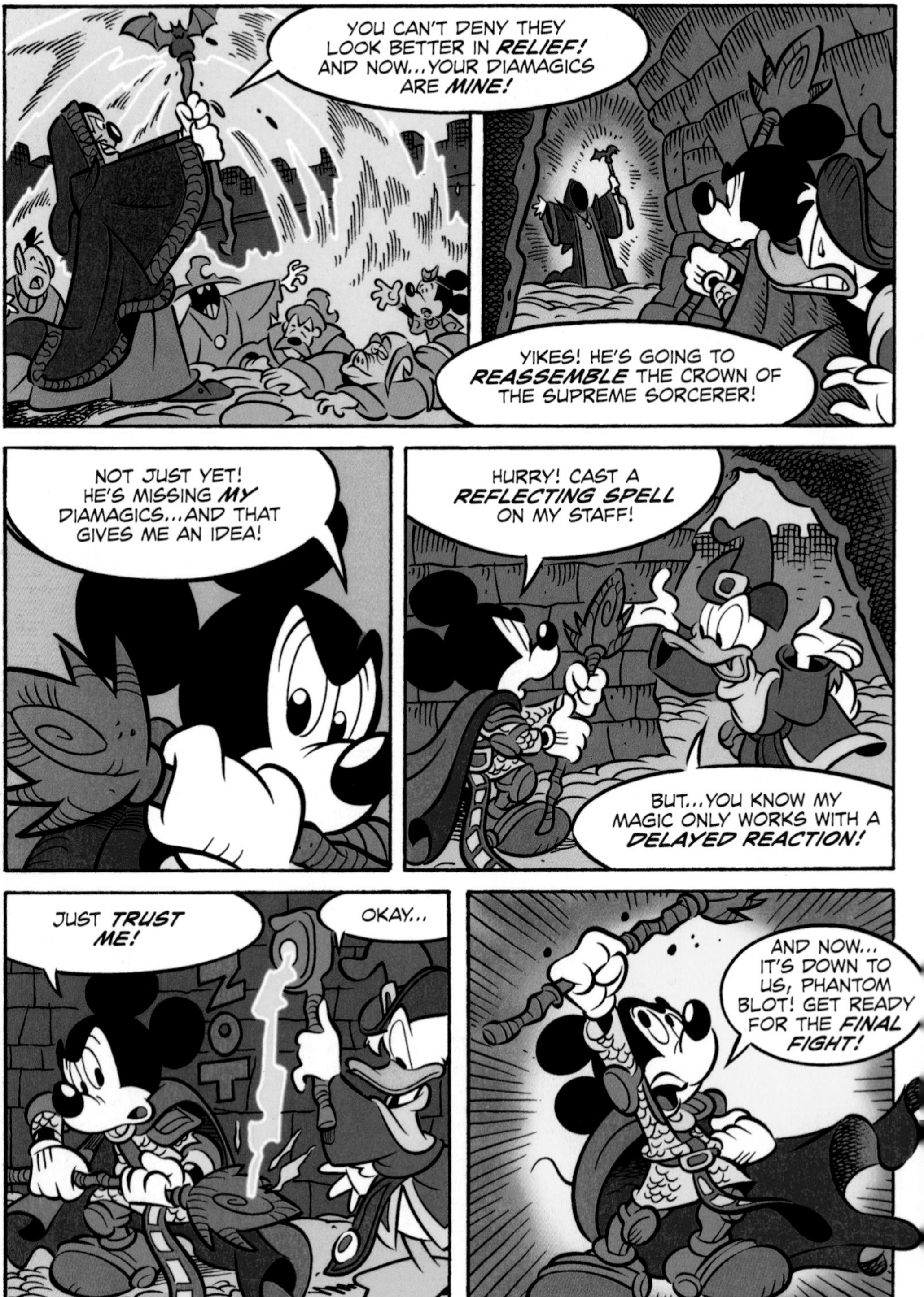
YOU CAN'T DENY THEY LOOK BETTER IN RELIEF! AND NOW...YOUR DIAMAGICS ARE MINE!
YIKES! HE'S GOING TO REASSEMBLE THE CROWN OF THE SUPREME SORCERER!
NOT JUST YET! HE'S MISSING MY DIAMAGICS...AND THAT GIVES ME AN IDEA!
HURRY! CAST A REFLECTING SPELL ON MY STAFF!
BUT...YOU KNOW MY MAGIC ONLY WORKS WITH A DELAYED REACTION!
JUST TRUST ME!
OKAY...
ZOT
AND NOW... IT'S DOWN TO US, PHANTOM BLOT! GET READY FOR THE FINAL FIGHT!

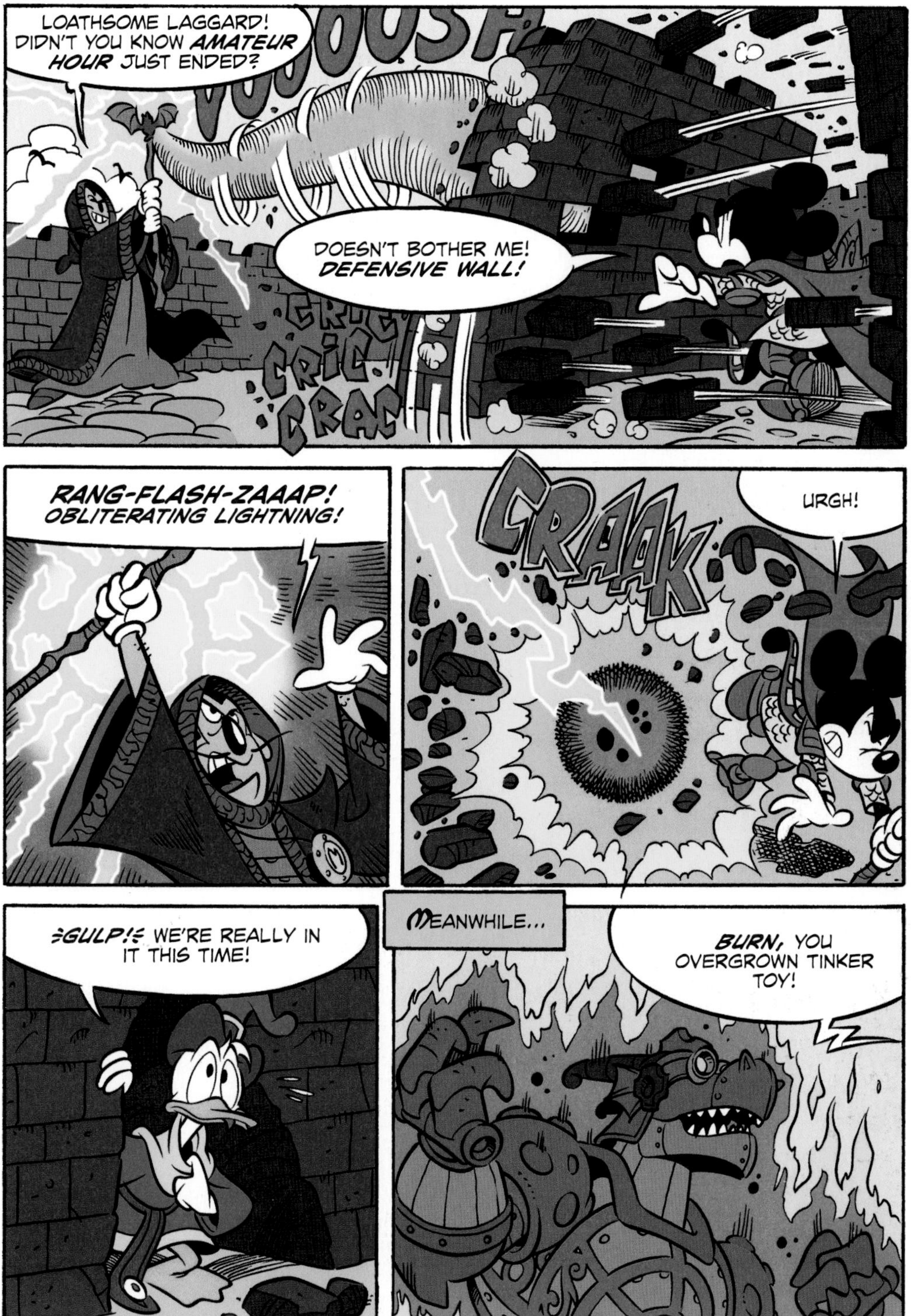
LOATHSOME LAGGARD! DIDN'T YOU KNOW AMATEUR HOUR JUST ENDED?
VOOOOUSH
DOESN'T BOTHER ME! DEFENSIVE WALL!
CRIC CRIC CRAC
RANG-FLASH-ZAAAP! OBLITERATING LIGHTNING!
CRAAK
URGH!
GULP! WE'RE REALLY IN IT THIS TIME!
MEANWHILE...
BURN, YOU OVERGROWN TINKER TOY!

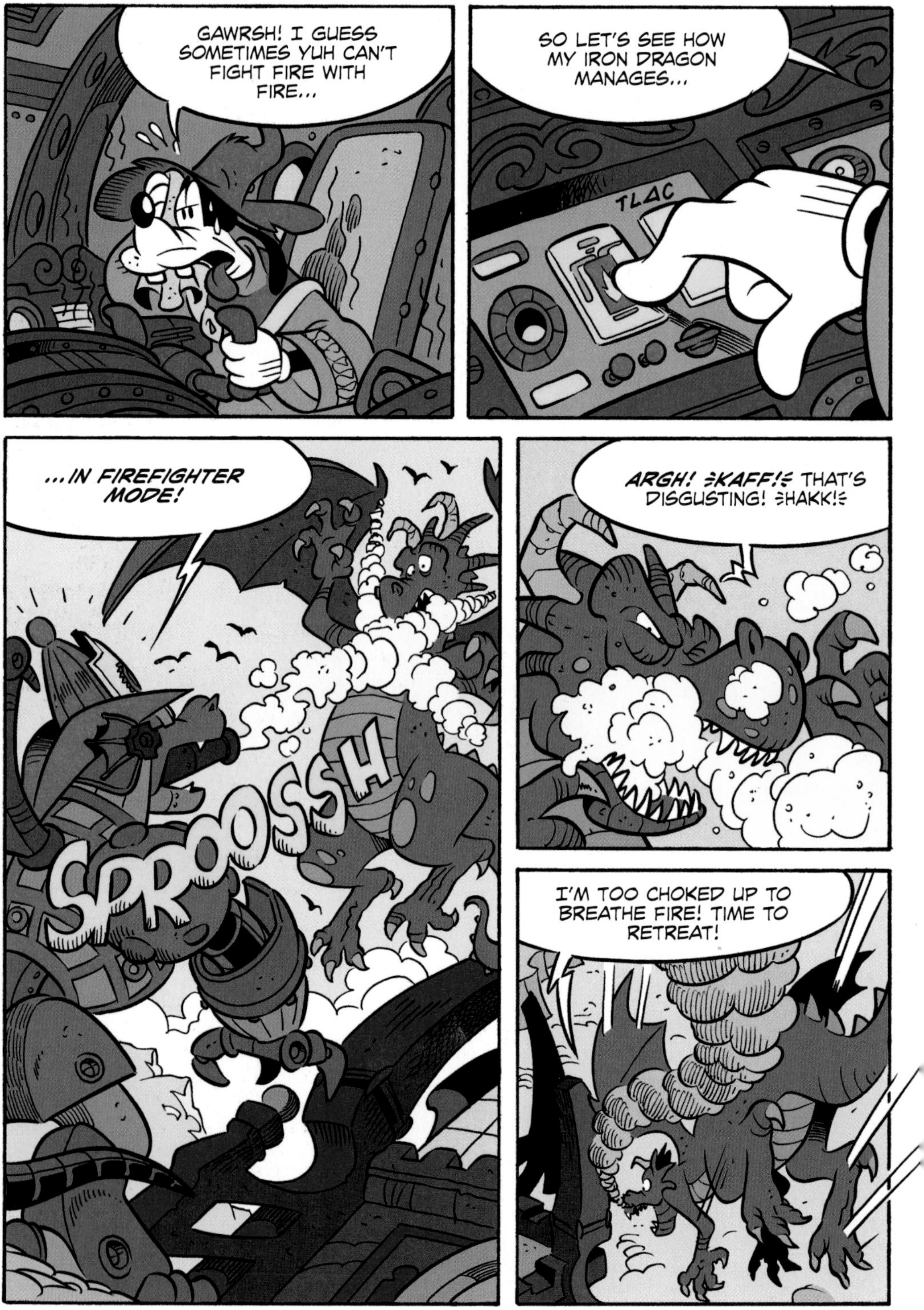
GAWRSH! I GUESS SOMETIMES YUH CAN'T FIGHT FIRE WITH FIRE...
SO LET'S SEE HOW MY IRON DRAGON MANAGES...
TLAC
...IN FIREFIGHTER MODE!
SPROOSSH
ARGH! KAFF! THAT'S DISGUSTING! HAKK!
I'M TOO CHOKED UP TO BREATHE FIRE! TIME TO RETREAT!

YA-HOO! SCORE ONE FER TEAM GOOF!
ER...THE WIZARDS OF MICKEY, I MEAN...
HEY, FELLERS! DID YUH SEE HOW HEROICALLY I--YUH-OH!
"POOR MICKEY! AT LEAST HE CAN STILL SKIP LIKE A CHAMPION!"
ZOT
ZOT
ZOT
SUCH A PITIFUL PERFORMANCE! PREPARE TO SURRENDER YOUR DIAMAGICS, YOU CUT-RATE CONJURER!
WAIT, NO...IT'S TOO SOON! I JUST NEED A LITTLE MORE TIME...!
MORE TIME? MICKEY, IF YOU'RE PLANNING WHAT I THINK YOU ARE, PERHAPS I CAN HELP!

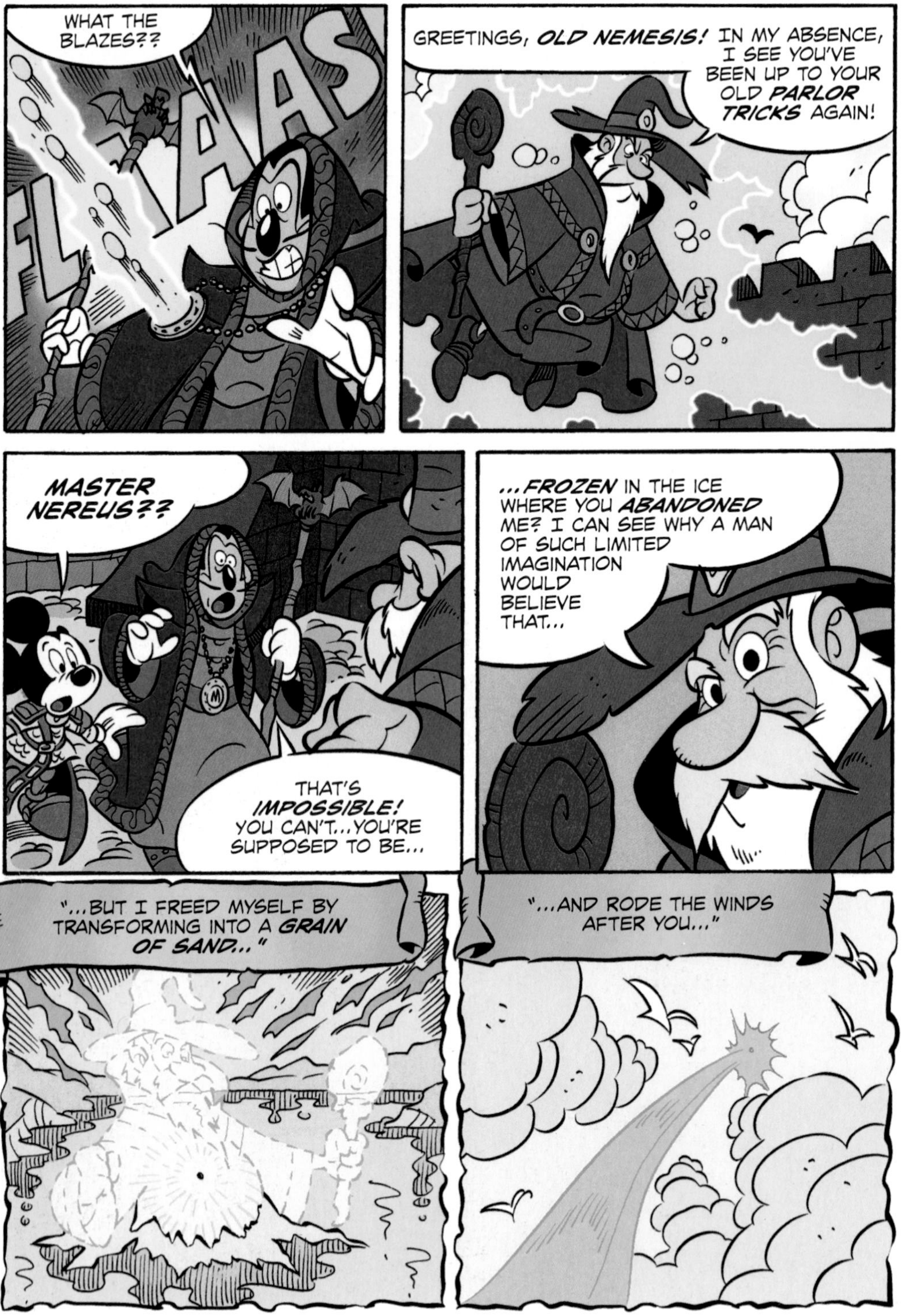
WHAT THE BLAZES??
FLAAAS
GREETINGS, OLD NEMESIS! IN MY ABSENCE, I SEE YOU'VE BEEN UP TO YOUR OLD PARLOR TRICKS AGAIN!
MASTER NEREUS??
THAT'S IMPOSSIBLE! YOU CAN'T... YOU'RE SUPPOSED TO BE...
...FROZEN IN THE ICE WHERE YOU ABANDONED ME? I CAN SEE WHY A MAN OF SUCH LIMITED IMAGINATION WOULD BELIEVE THAT...
"...BUT I FREED MYSELF BY TRANSFORMING INTO A GRAIN OF SAND..."
"...AND RODE THE WINDS AFTER YOU..."

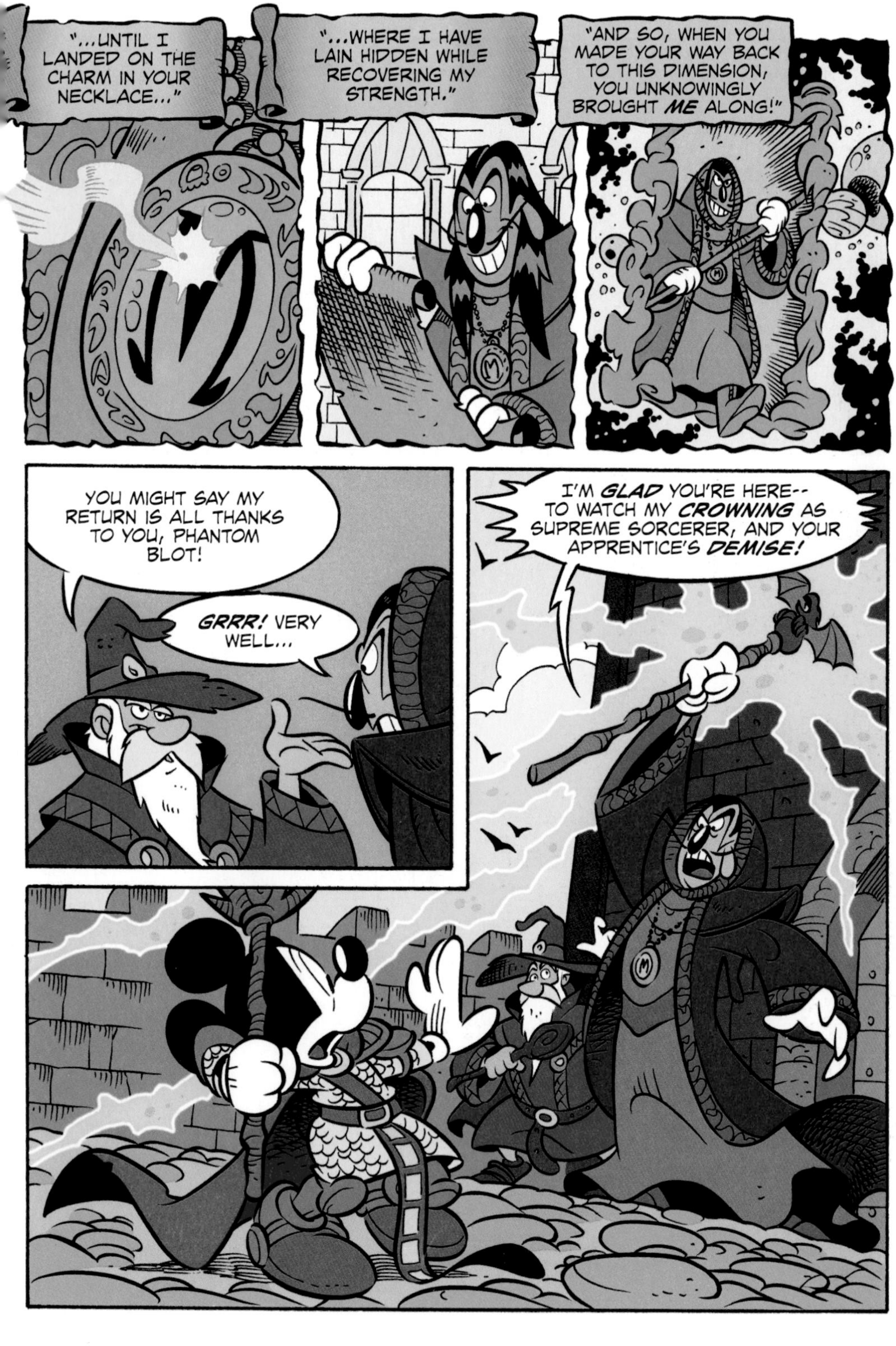
"...UNTIL I LANDED ON THE CHARM IN YOUR NECKLACE..."
"...WHERE I HAVE LAIN HIDDEN WHILE RECOVERING MY STRENGTH."
"AND SO, WHEN YOU MADE YOUR WAY BACK TO THIS DIMENSION, YOU UNKNOWINGLY BROUGHT ME ALONG!"
YOU MIGHT SAY MY RETURN IS ALL THANKS TO YOU, PHANTOM BLOT!
GRRR! VERY WELL...
I'M GLAD YOU'RE HERE-- TO WATCH MY CROWNING AS SUPREME SORCERER, AND YOUR APPRENTICE'S DEMISE!

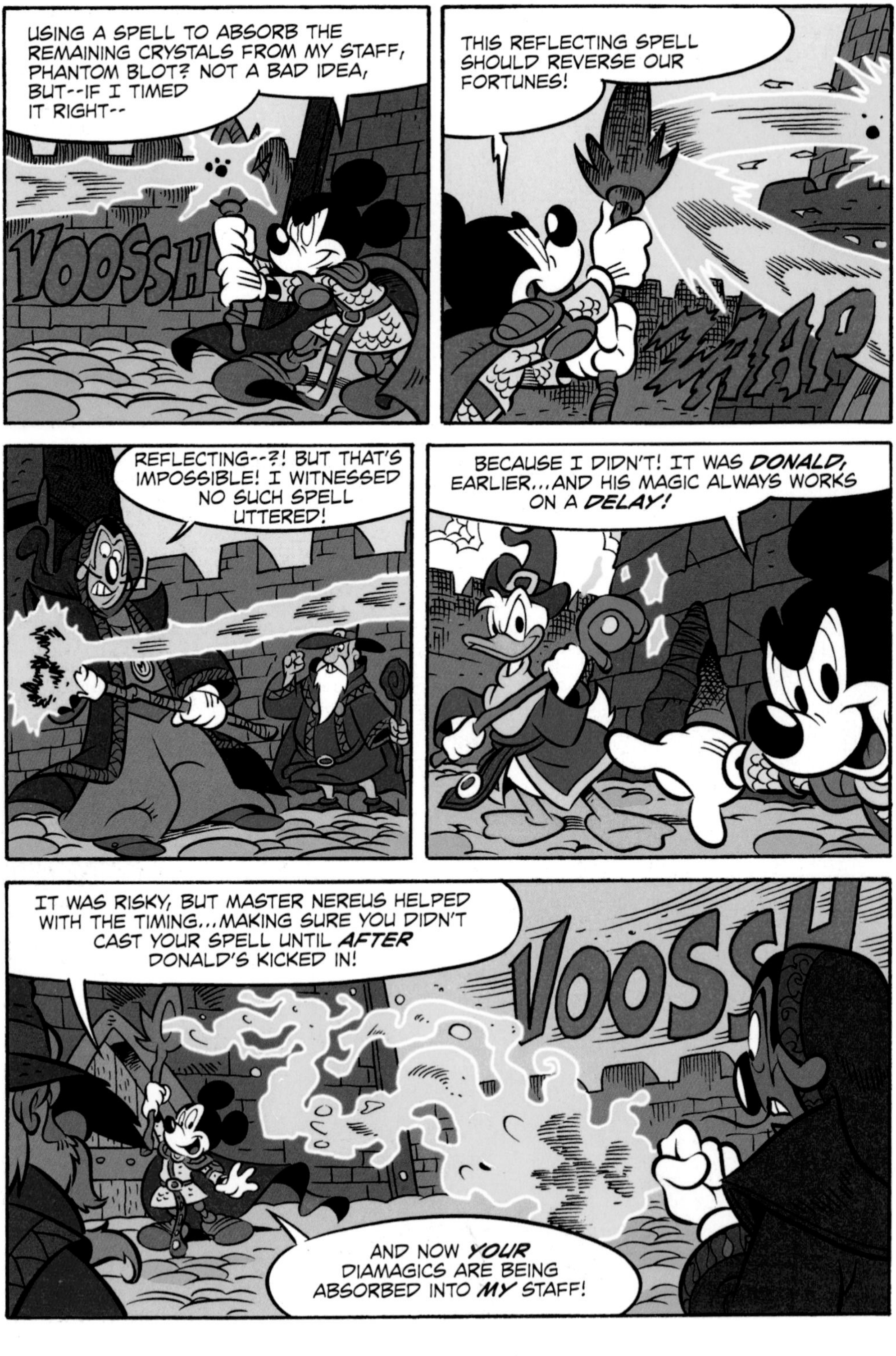
USING A SPELL TO ABSORB THE REMAINING CRYSTALS FROM MY STAFF, PHANTOM BLOT? NOT A BAD IDEA, BUT--IF I TIMED IT RIGHT--
VOOSSH
THIS REFLECTING SPELL SHOULD REVERSE OUR FORTUNES!
ZWAP
REFLECTING--?! BUT THAT'S IMPOSSIBLE! I WITNESSED NO SUCH SPELL UTTERED!
BECAUSE I DIDN'T! IT WAS DONALD, EARLIER...AND HIS MAGIC ALWAYS WORKS ON A DELAY!
IT WAS RISKY, BUT MASTER NEREUS HELPED WITH THE TIMING...MAKING SURE YOU DIDN'T CAST YOUR SPELL UNTIL AFTER DONALD'S KICKED IN!
VOOSSH
AND NOW YOUR DIAMAGICS ARE BEING ABSORBED INTO MY STAFF!

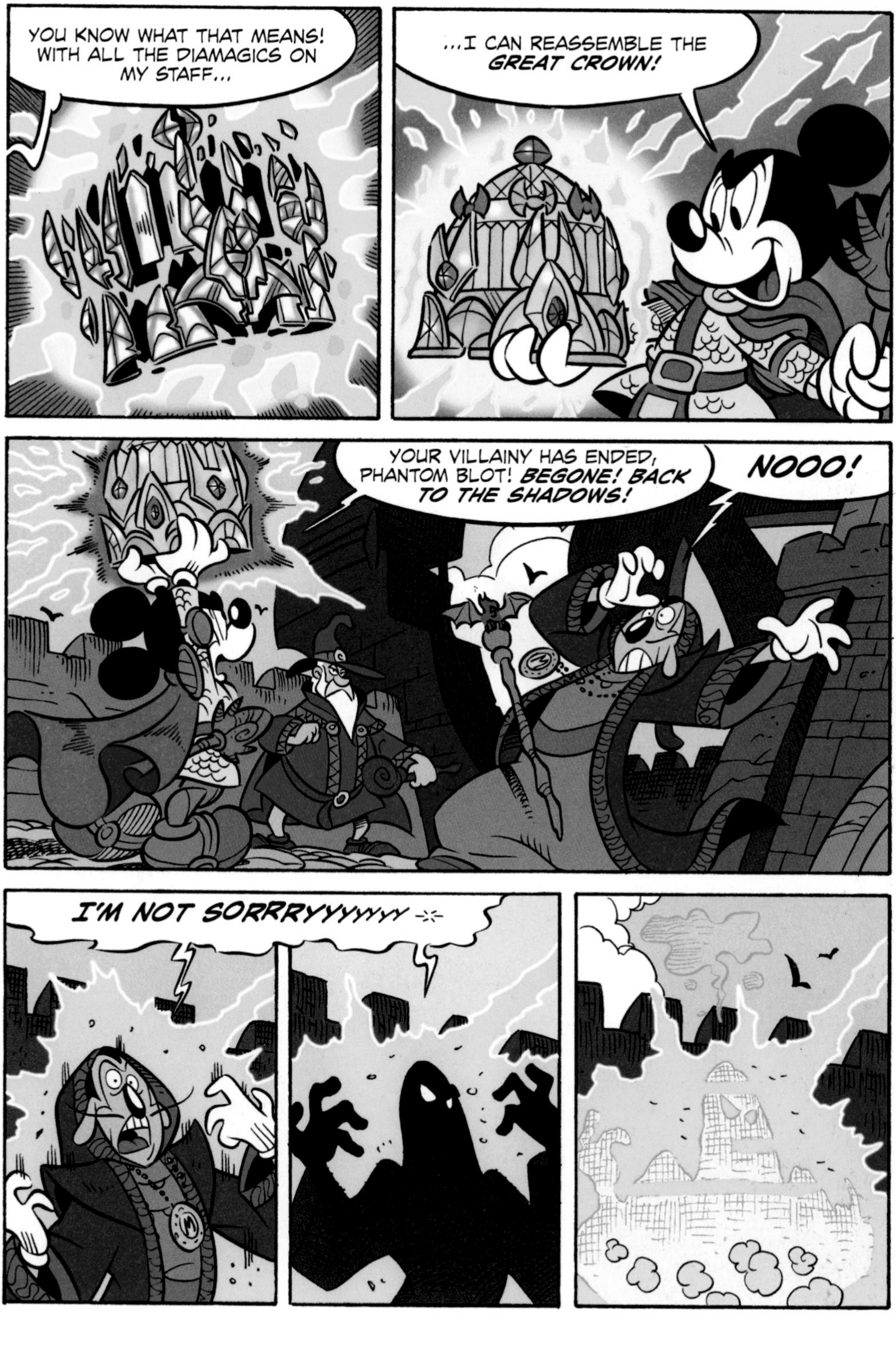
YOU KNOW WHAT THAT MEANS! WITH ALL THE DIAMAGICS ON MY STAFF...
...I CAN REASSEMBLE THE GREAT CROWN!
YOUR VILLAINY HAS ENDED, PHANTOM BLOT! BEGONE! BACK TO THE SHADOWS!
NOOO!
I'M NOT SORRRYYYYYYY

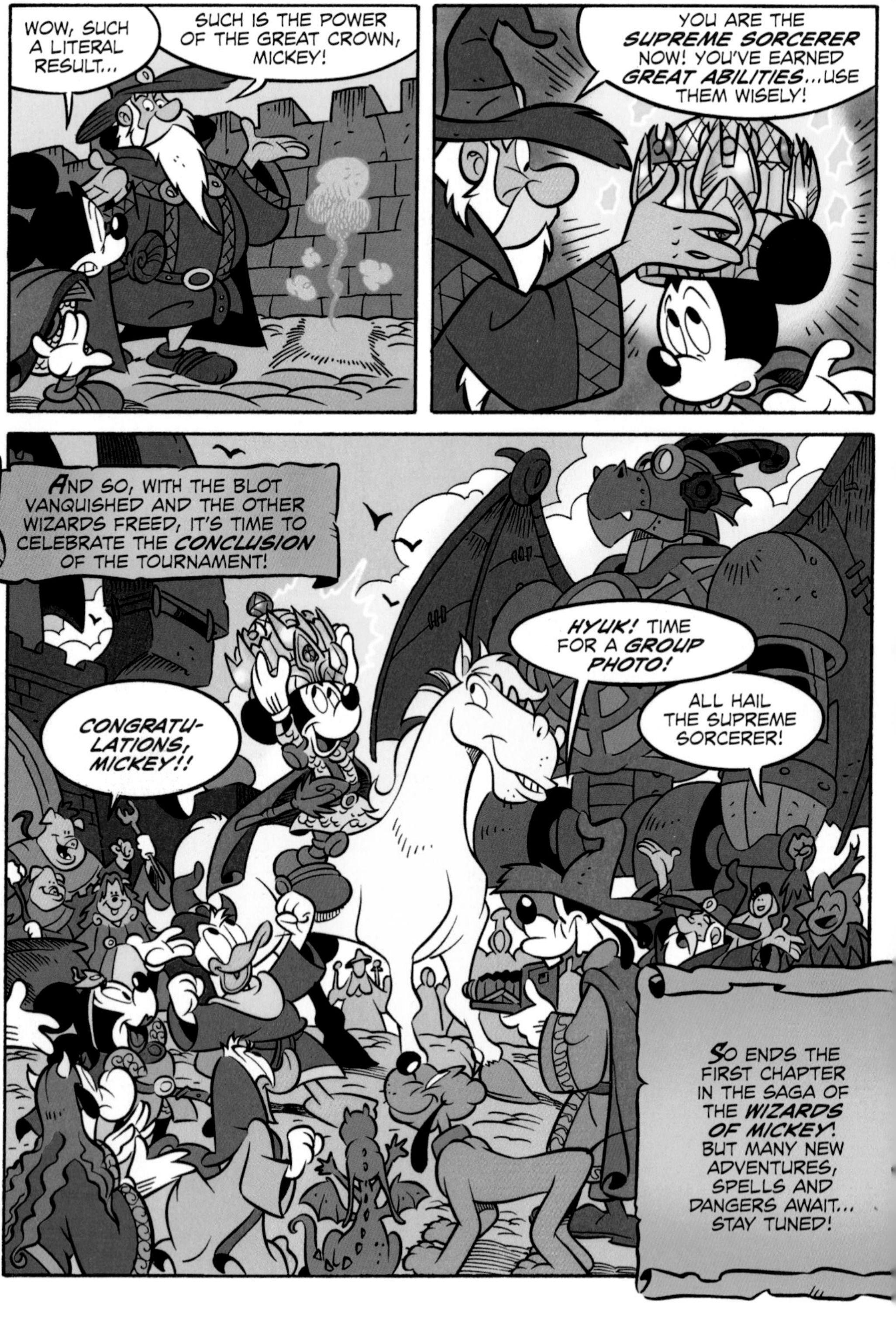
WOW, SUCH A LITERAL RESULT...
SUCH IS THE POWER OF THE GREAT CROWN, MICKEY!
YOU ARE THE SUPREME SORCERER NOW! YOU'VE EARNED GREAT ABILITIES... USE THEM WISELY!
AND SO, WITH THE BLOT VANQUISHED AND THE OTHER WIZARDS FREED, IT'S TIME TO CELEBRATE THE CONCLUSION OF THE TOURNAMENT!
CONGRATU-LATIONS, MICKEY!!
HYUK! TIME FOR A GROUP PHOTO!
ALL HAIL THE SUPREME SORCERER!
SO ENDS THE FIRST CHAPTER IN THE SAGA OF THE WIZARDS OF MICKEY! BUT MANY NEW ADVENTURES, SPELLS AND DANGERS AWAIT... STAY TUNED!

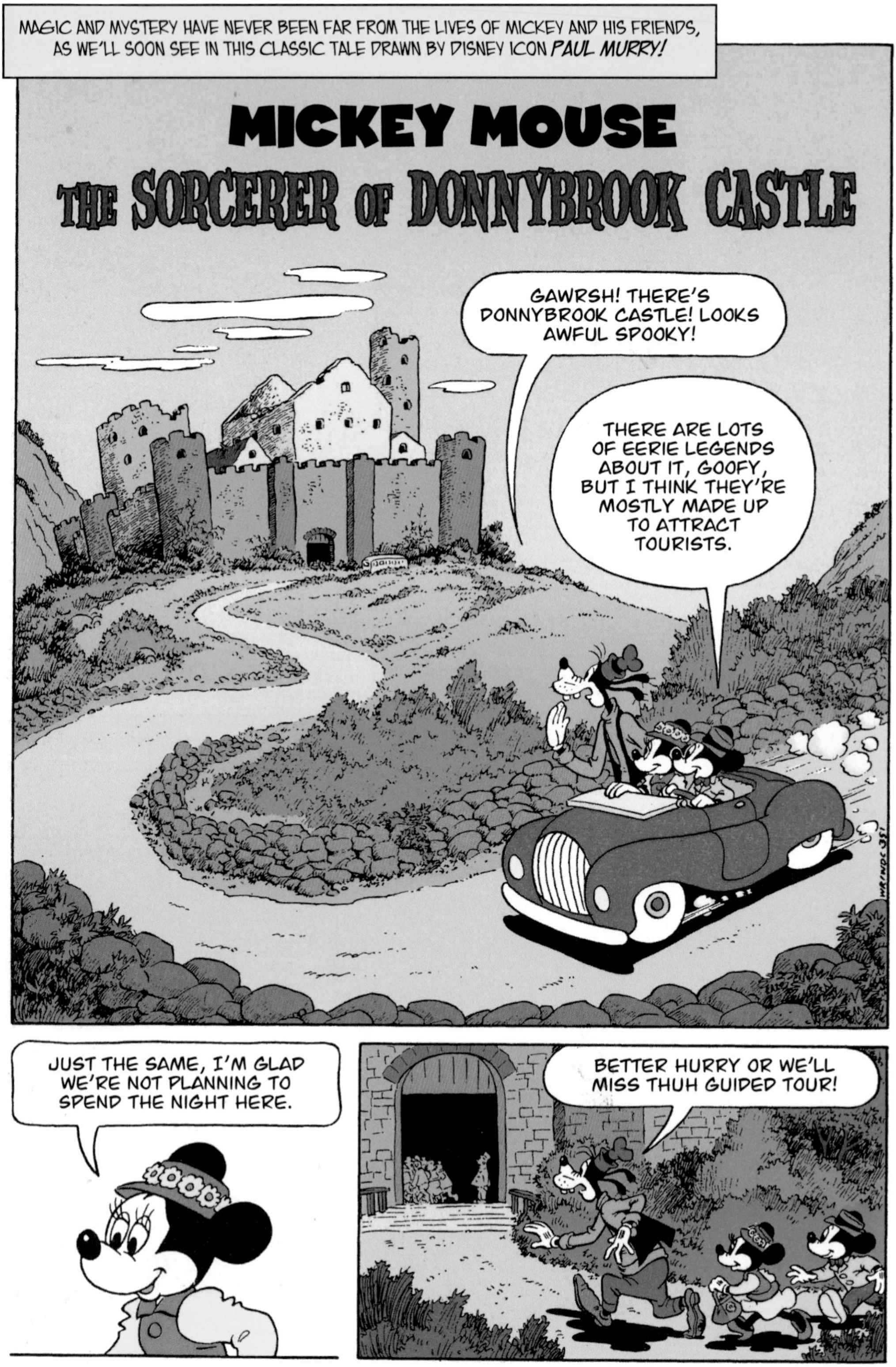
MAGIC AND MYSTERY HAVE NEVER BEEN FAR FROM THE LIVES OF MICKEY AND HIS FRIENDS, AS WE'LL SOON SEE IN THIS CLASSIC TALE DRAWN BY DISNEY ICON PAUL MURRY!
MICKEY MOUSE
THE SORCERER OF DONNYBROOK CASTLE
GAWRSH! THERE'S DONNYBROOK CASTLE! LOOKS AWFUL SPOOKY!
THERE ARE LOTS OF EERIE LEGENDS ABOUT IT, GOOFY, BUT I THINK THEY'RE MOSTLY MADE UP TO ATTRACT TOURISTS.
JUST THE SAME, I'M GLAD WE'RE NOT PLANNING TO SPEND THE NIGHT HERE.
BETTER HURRY OR WE'LL MISS THUH GUIDED TOUR!

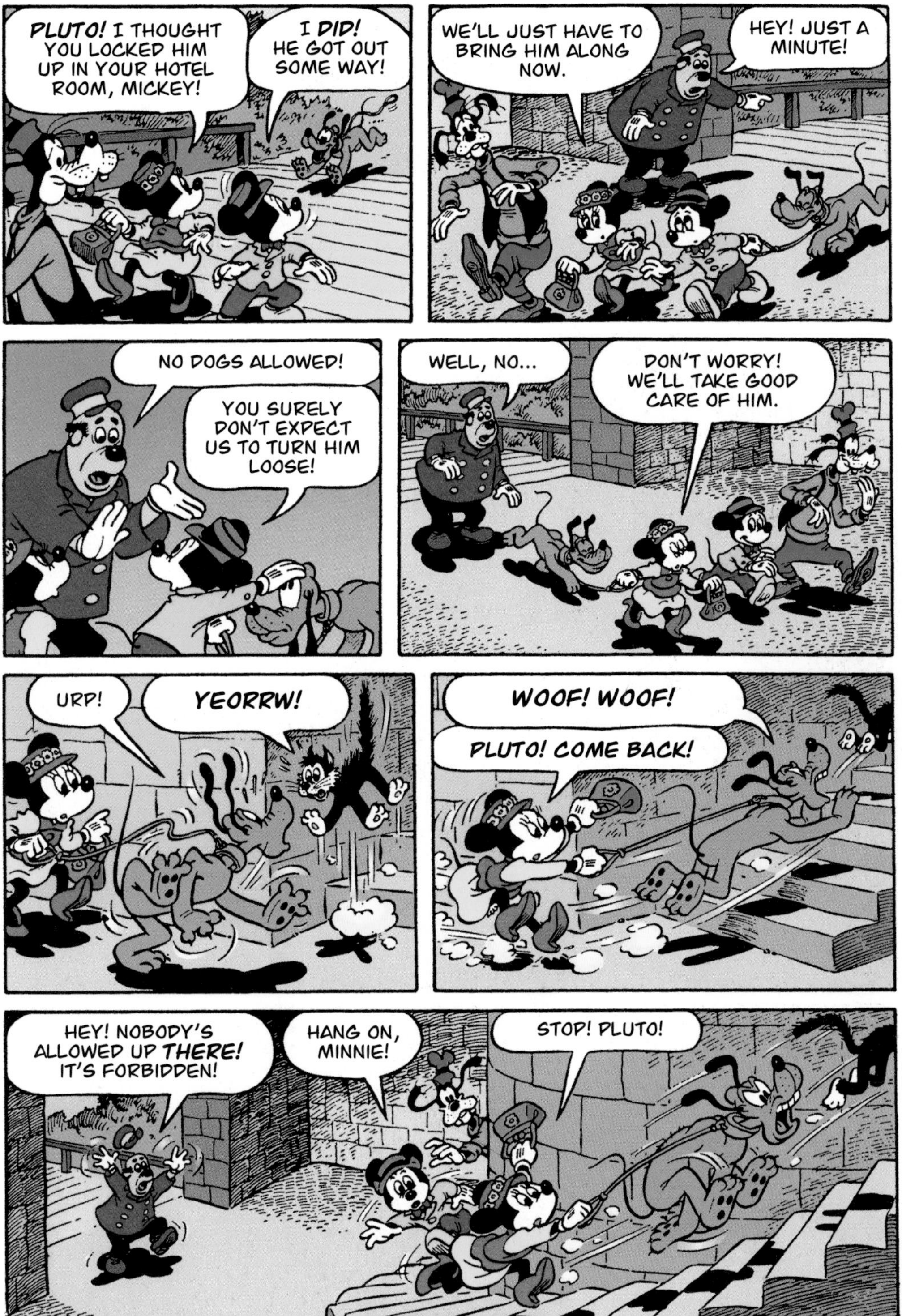
PLUTO! I THOUGHT YOU LOCKED HIM UP IN YOUR HOTEL ROOM, MICKEY!
I DID! HE GOT OUT SOME WAY!
WE'LL JUST HAVE TO BRING HIM ALONG NOW.
HEY! JUST A MINUTE!
NO DOGS ALLOWED!
YOU SURELY DON'T EXPECT US TO TURN HIM LOOSE!
WELL, NO...
DON'T WORRY! WE'LL TAKE GOOD CARE OF HIM.
URP!
YEORRW!
WOOF! WOOF!
PLUTO! COME BACK!
HEY! NOBODY'S ALLOWED UP THERE! IT'S FORBIDDEN!
HANG ON, MINNIE!
STOP! PLUTO!

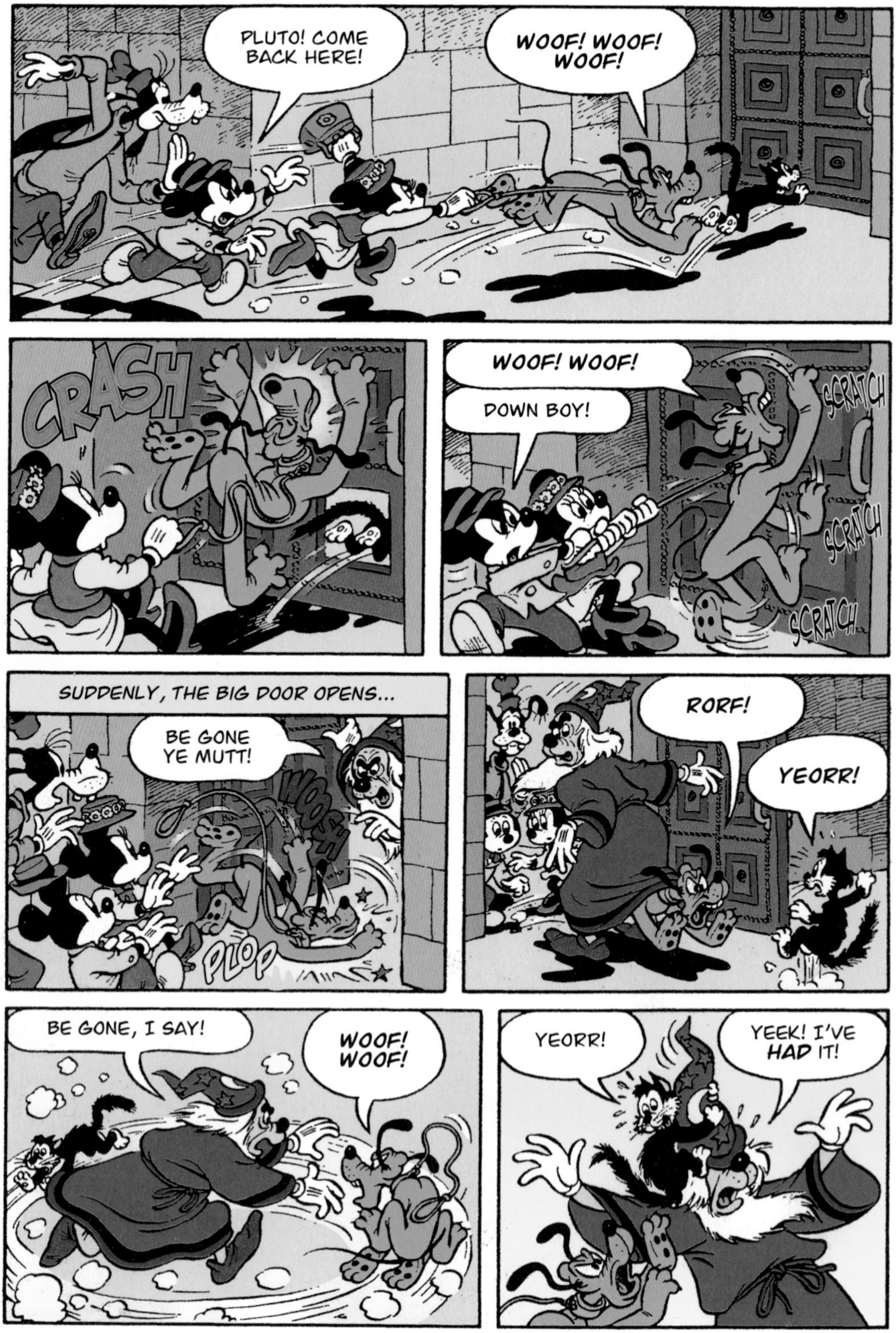
PLUTO! COME BACK HERE!
WOOF! WOOF! WOOF!
CRASH
WOOF! WOOF!
DOWN BOY!
SCRATCH
SCRATCH
SCRATCH
SUDDENLY, THE BIG DOOR OPENS...
BE GONE YE MUTT!
WOOSH
PLOP
RORF!
YEORR!
BE GONE, I SAY!
WOOF! WOOF!
YEORR!
YEEK! I'VE HAD IT!

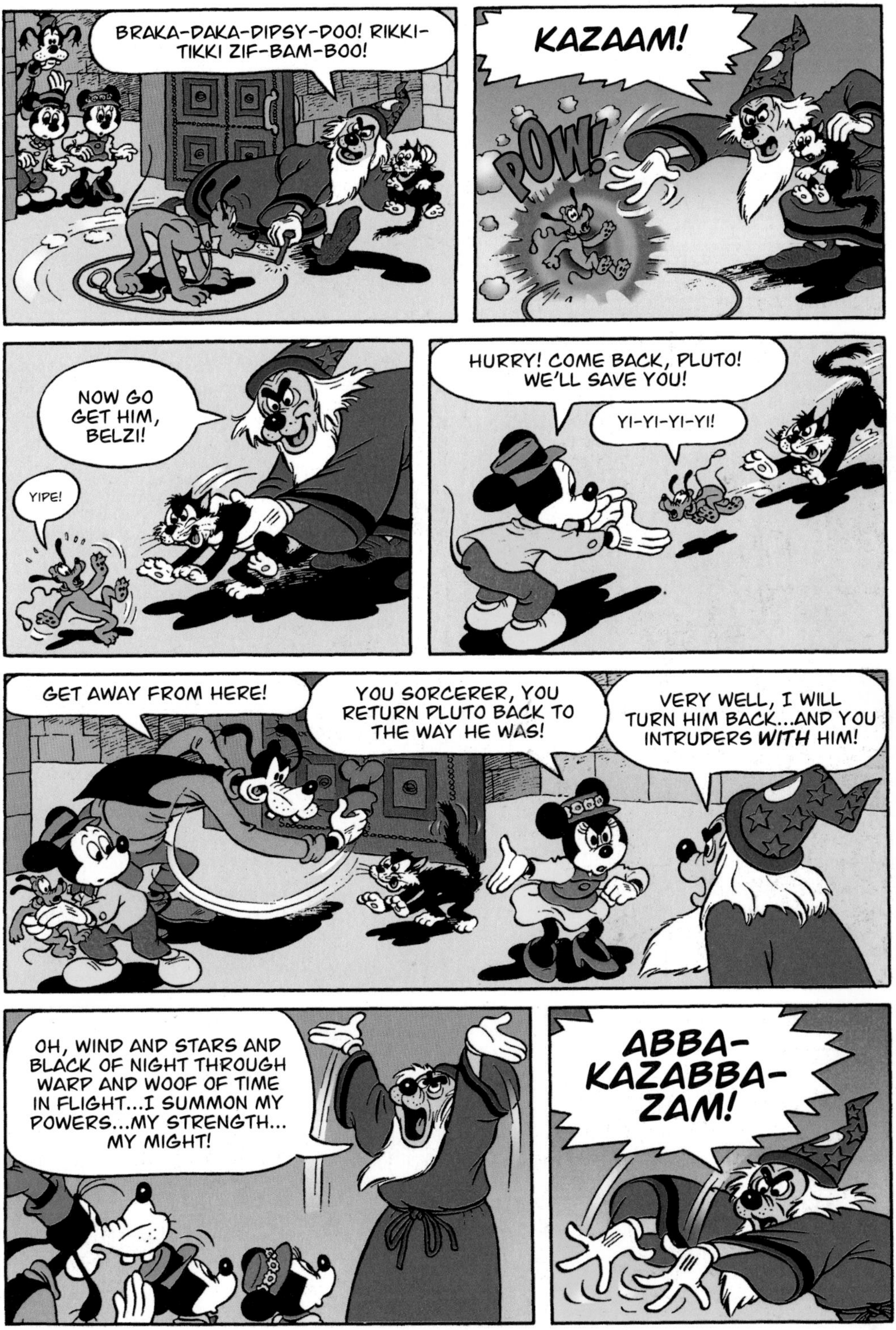
BRAKA-DAKA-DIPSY-DOO! RIKKI-TIKKI ZIF-BAM-BOO!
KAZAAM!
POW!
NOW GO GET HIM, BELZI!
YIPE!
HURRY! COME BACK, PLUTO! WE'LL SAVE YOU!
YI-YI-YI-YI!
GET AWAY FROM HERE!
YOU SORCERER, YOU RETURN PLUTO BACK TO THE WAY HE WAS!
VERY WELL, I WILL TURN HIM BACK...AND YOU INTRUDERS **WITH** HIM!
OH, WIND AND STARS AND BLACK OF NIGHT THROUGH WARP AND WOOF OF TIME IN FLIGHT...I SUMMON MY POWERS...MY STRENGTH... MY MIGHT!
ABBA-KAZABBA-ZAM!

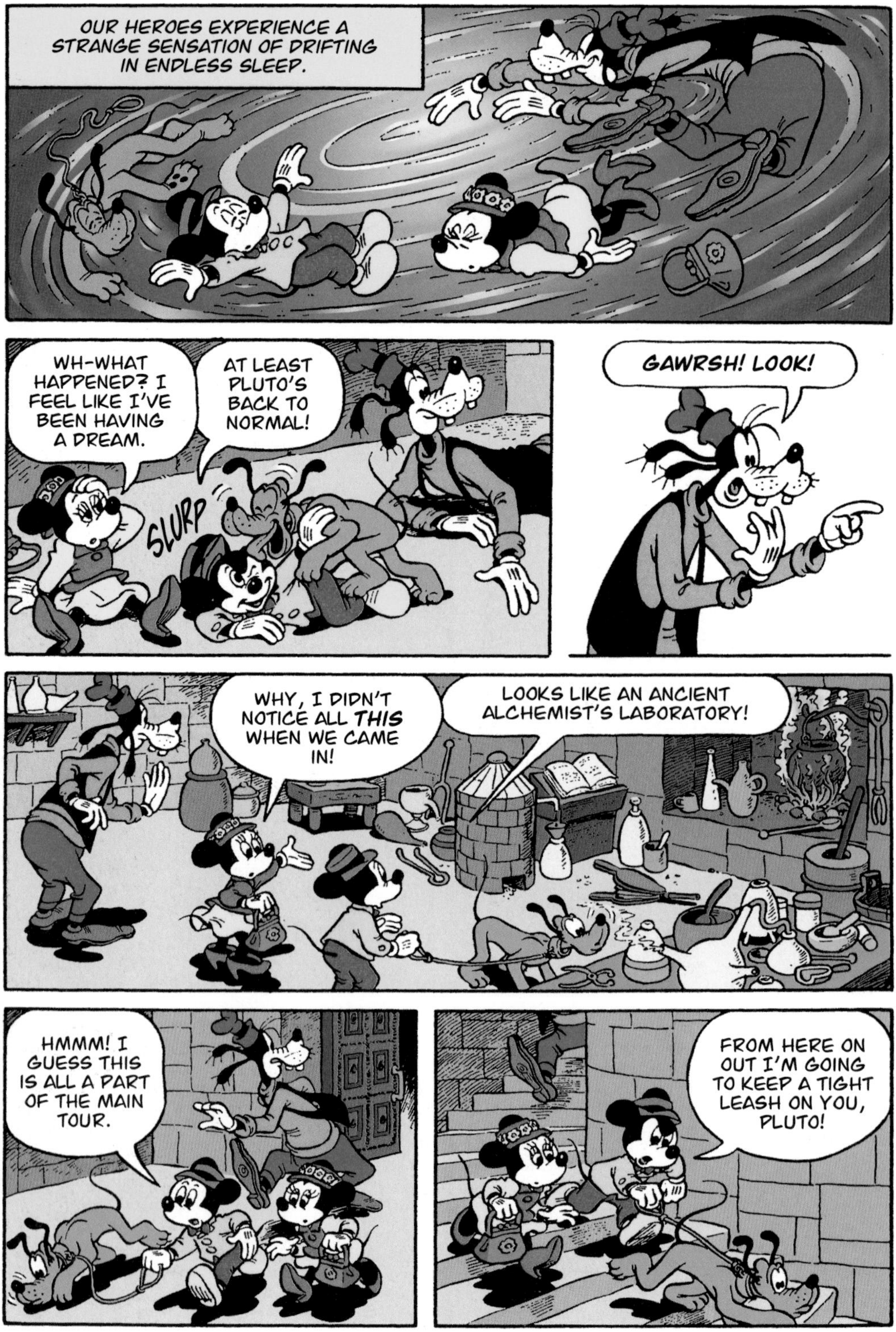
OUR HEROES EXPERIENCE A STRANGE SENSATION OF DRIFTING IN ENDLESS SLEEP.
WH-WHAT HAPPENED? I FEEL LIKE I'VE BEEN HAVING A DREAM.
AT LEAST PLUTO'S BACK TO NORMAL!
SLURP
GAWRSH! LOOK!
WHY, I DIDN'T NOTICE ALL THIS WHEN WE CAME IN!
LOOKS LIKE AN ANCIENT ALCHEMIST'S LABORATORY!
HMMM! I GUESS THIS IS ALL A PART OF THE MAIN TOUR.
FROM HERE ON OUT I'M GOING TO KEEP A TIGHT LEASH ON YOU, PLUTO!

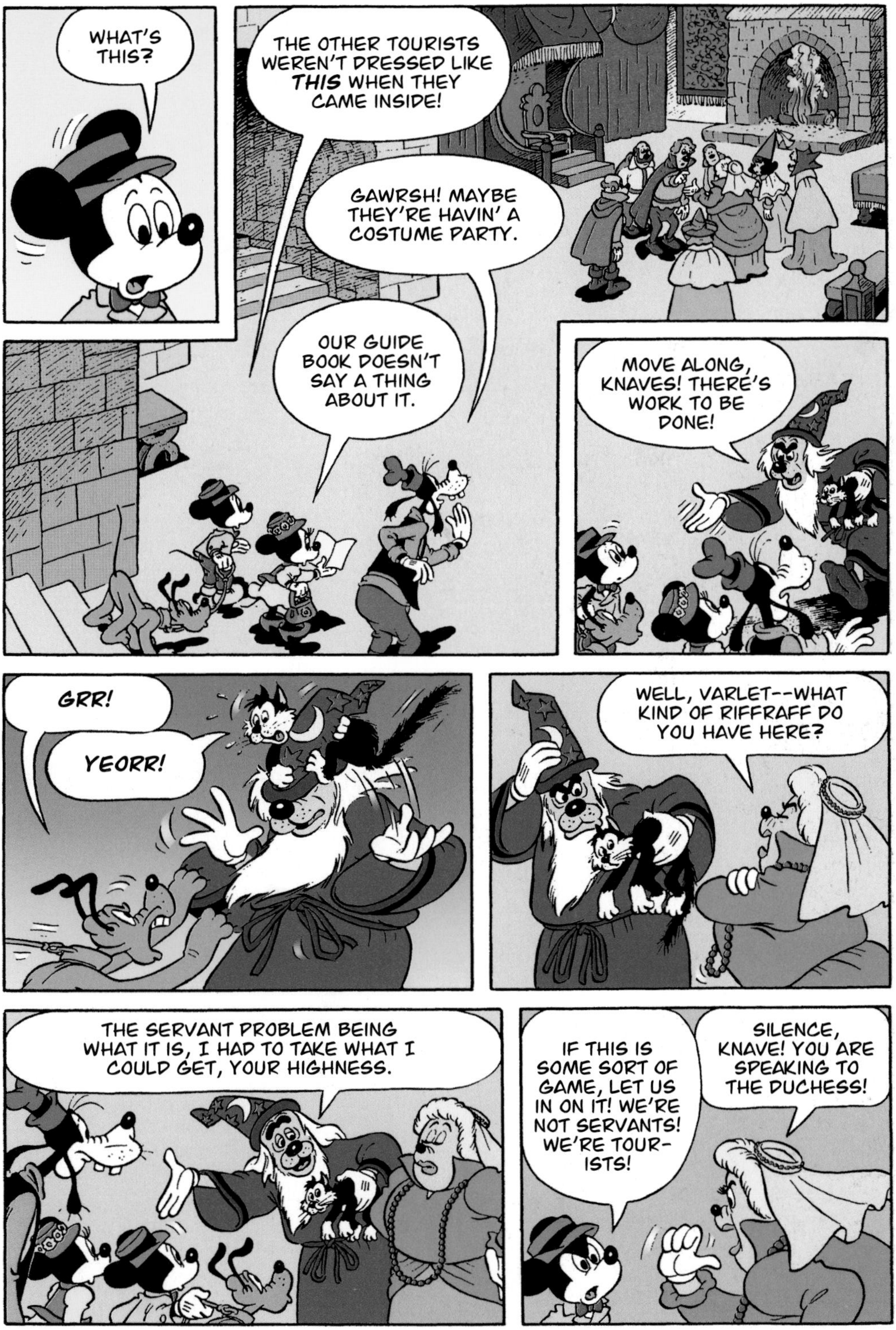
WHAT'S THIS?
THE OTHER TOURISTS WEREN'T DRESSED LIKE *THIS* WHEN THEY CAME INSIDE!
GAWRSH! MAYBE THEY'RE HAVIN' A COSTUME PARTY.
OUR GUIDE BOOK DOESN'T SAY A THING ABOUT IT.
MOVE ALONG, KNAVES! THERE'S WORK TO BE DONE!
GRR!
YEORR!
WELL, VARLET--WHAT KIND OF RIFFRAFF DO YOU HAVE HERE?
THE SERVANT PROBLEM BEING WHAT IT IS, I HAD TO TAKE WHAT I COULD GET, YOUR HIGHNESS.
IF THIS IS SOME SORT OF GAME, LET US IN ON IT! WE'RE NOT SERVANTS! WE'RE TOUR-ISTS!
SILENCE, KNAVE! YOU ARE SPEAKING TO THE DUCHESS!

THIS GIRL WILL DO AS LADY-IN-WAITING FOR OUR PRINCESS.

I'LL BE NO SUCH THING!

KEEP A CIVIL TONGUE OR YOU'LL END UP AS A SCULLERY MAID!!

SAYS WHO?

SSH! PLAY IT COOL, MINNIE. I THINK THIS IS FOR REAL.

HEH! HEH! SORRY YOUR HIGHNESS. I'M JUST TIRED OUT FROM THE TRIP.

THAT'S BETTER! I'LL TAKE YOU TO THE PRINCESS.

AND *YOUR* FIRST CHORE IS TO CUT WOOD FOR THE CASTLE FIRES.

LOWER THE DRAWBRIDGE, GUARD!

CRASH

YOU MAY GATHER TIMBER ON THE OTHER SIDE OF THE MOAT.

BUT DO NOT VENTURE TOO DEEP INTO THE WOODS. WE LOSE MORE WOODCUTTERS THAT WAY!

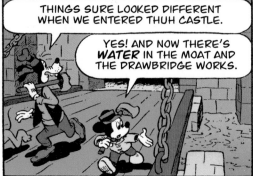

THINGS SURE LOOKED DIFFERENT WHEN WE ENTERED THUH CASTLE.

YES! AND NOW THERE'S *WATER* IN THE MOAT AND THE DRAWBRIDGE WORKS.

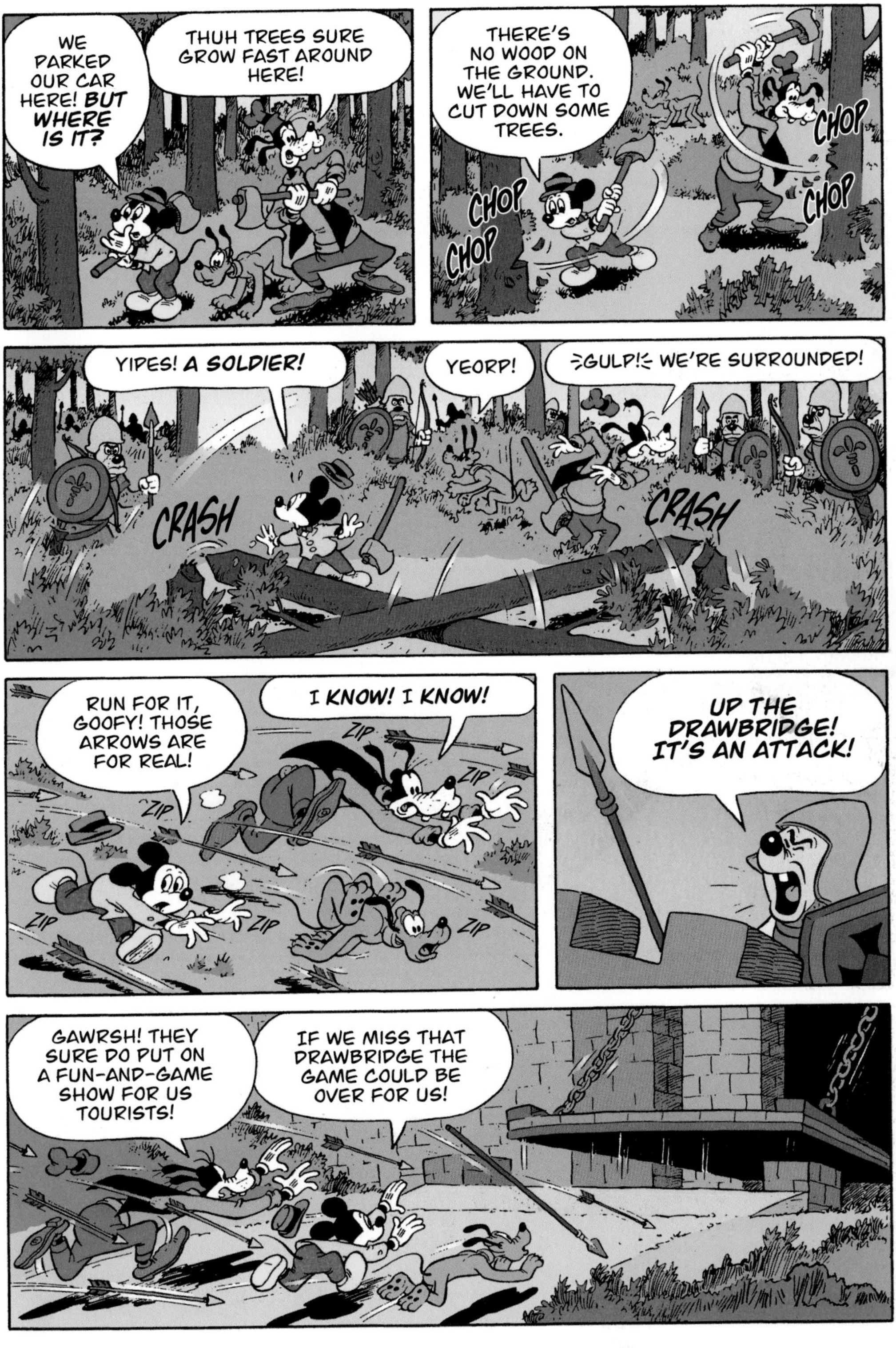
WE PARKED OUR CAR HERE! BUT WHERE IS IT?
THUH TREES SURE GROW FAST AROUND HERE!
THERE'S NO WOOD ON THE GROUND. WE'LL HAVE TO CUT DOWN SOME TREES.
CHOP
CHOP
CHOP
CHOP
YIPES! A SOLDIER!
YEORP!
GULP! WE'RE SURROUNDED!
CRASH
CRASH
RUN FOR IT, GOOFY! THOSE ARROWS ARE FOR REAL!
I KNOW! I KNOW!
ZIP
ZIP
ZIP
ZIP
ZIP
UP THE DRAWBRIDGE! IT'S AN ATTACK!
GAWRSH! THEY SURE DO PUT ON A FUN-AND-GAME SHOW FOR US TOURISTS!
IF WE MISS THAT DRAWBRIDGE THE GAME COULD BE OVER FOR US!

MICKEY MOUSE
THE SORCERER OF DONNYBROOK CASTLE

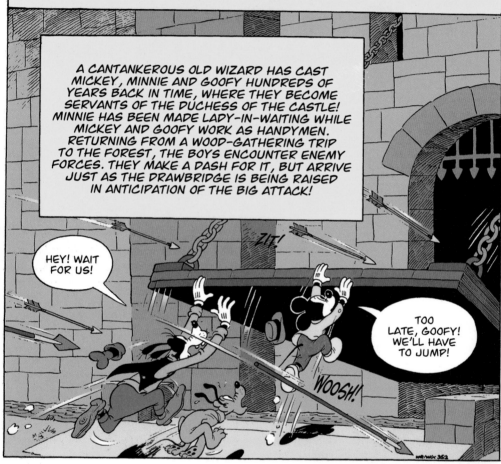

A CANTANKEROUS OLD WIZARD HAS CAST MICKEY, MINNIE AND GOOFY HUNDREDS OF YEARS BACK IN TIME, WHERE THEY BECOME SERVANTS OF THE DUCHESS OF THE CASTLE! MINNIE HAS BEEN MADE LADY-IN-WAITING WHILE MICKEY AND GOOFY WORK AS HANDYMEN. RETURNING FROM A WOOD-GATHERING TRIP TO THE FOREST, THE BOYS ENCOUNTER ENEMY FORCES. THEY MAKE A DASH FOR IT, BUT ARRIVE JUST AS THE DRAWBRIDGE IS BEING RAISED IN ANTICIPATION OF THE BIG ATTACK!

HEY! WAIT FOR US!

ZIT!

TOO LATE, GOOFY! WE'LL HAVE TO JUMP!

WOOSH!

GRROFF!

YAHOO!

ATTA BOY, PLUTO. HANG ON!

HURRY! IT'S ALMOST CLOSED!

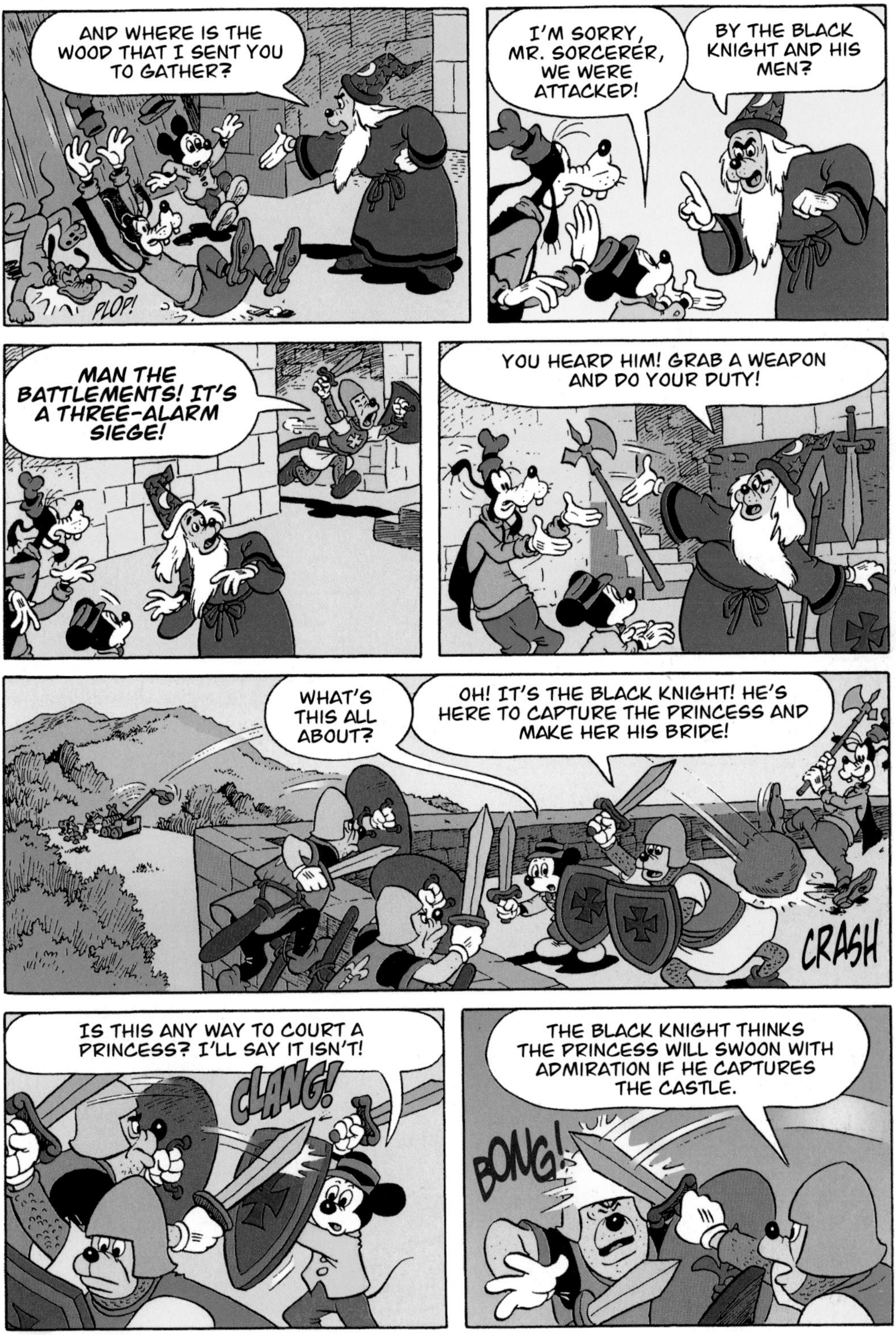
AND WHERE IS THE WOOD THAT I SENT YOU TO GATHER?
PLOP!
I'M SORRY, MR. SORCERER, WE WERE ATTACKED!
BY THE BLACK KNIGHT AND HIS MEN?
MAN THE BATTLEMENTS! IT'S A THREE-ALARM SIEGE!
YOU HEARD HIM! GRAB A WEAPON AND DO YOUR DUTY!
WHAT'S THIS ALL ABOUT?
OH! IT'S THE BLACK KNIGHT! HE'S HERE TO CAPTURE THE PRINCESS AND MAKE HER HIS BRIDE!
CRASH
IS THIS ANY WAY TO COURT A PRINCESS? I'LL SAY IT ISN'T!
CLANG!
THE BLACK KNIGHT THINKS THE PRINCESS WILL SWOON WITH ADMIRATION IF HE CAPTURES THE CASTLE.
BONG!

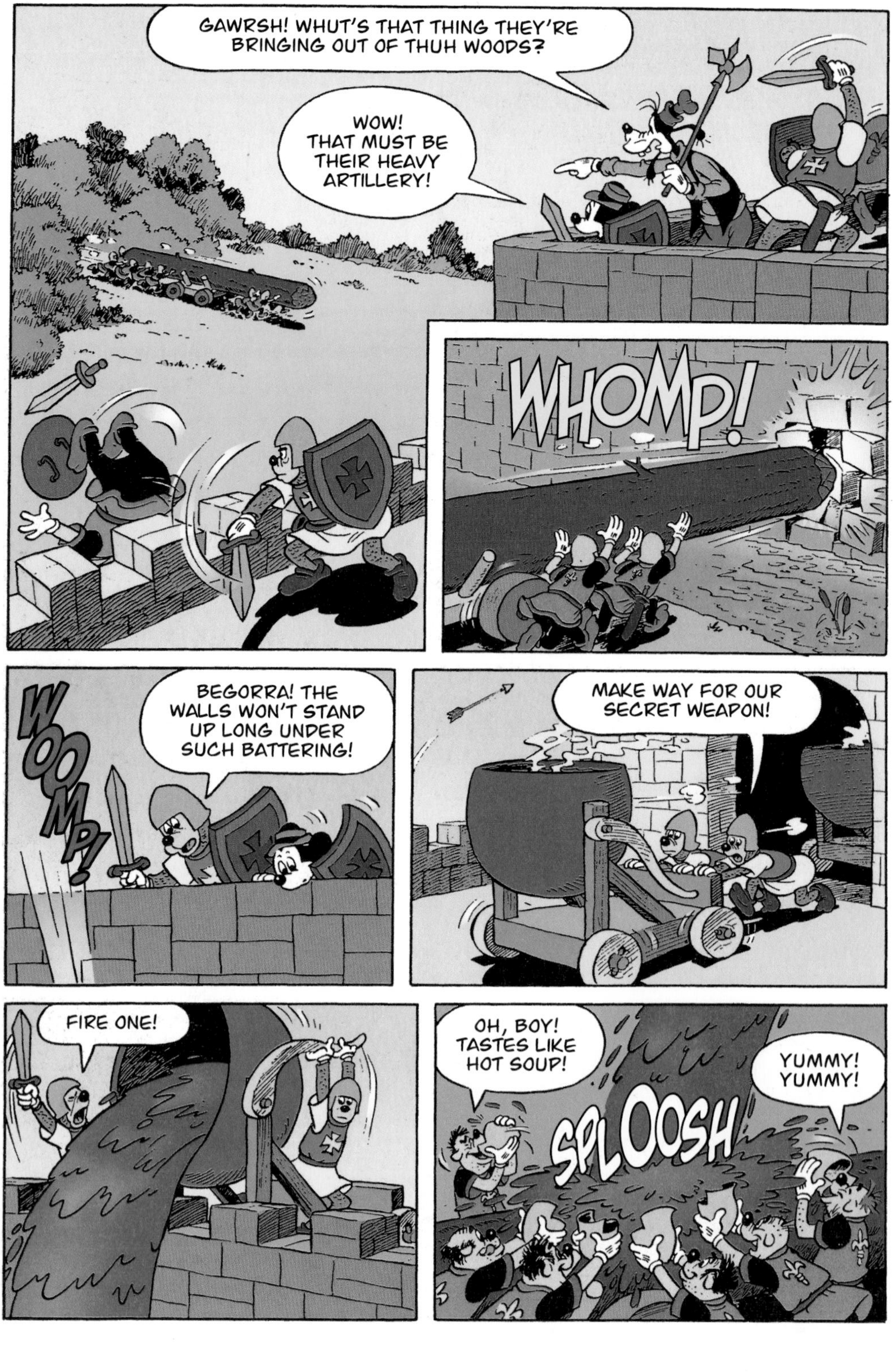
GAWRSH! WHUT'S THAT THING THEY'RE BRINGING OUT OF THUH WOODS?
WOW! THAT MUST BE THEIR HEAVY ARTILLERY!
WHOMP!
WOOMP!
BEGORRA! THE WALLS WON'T STAND UP LONG UNDER SUCH BATTERING!
MAKE WAY FOR OUR SECRET WEAPON!
FIRE ONE!
OH, BOY! TASTES LIKE HOT SOUP!
SPLOOSH
YUMMY! YUMMY!

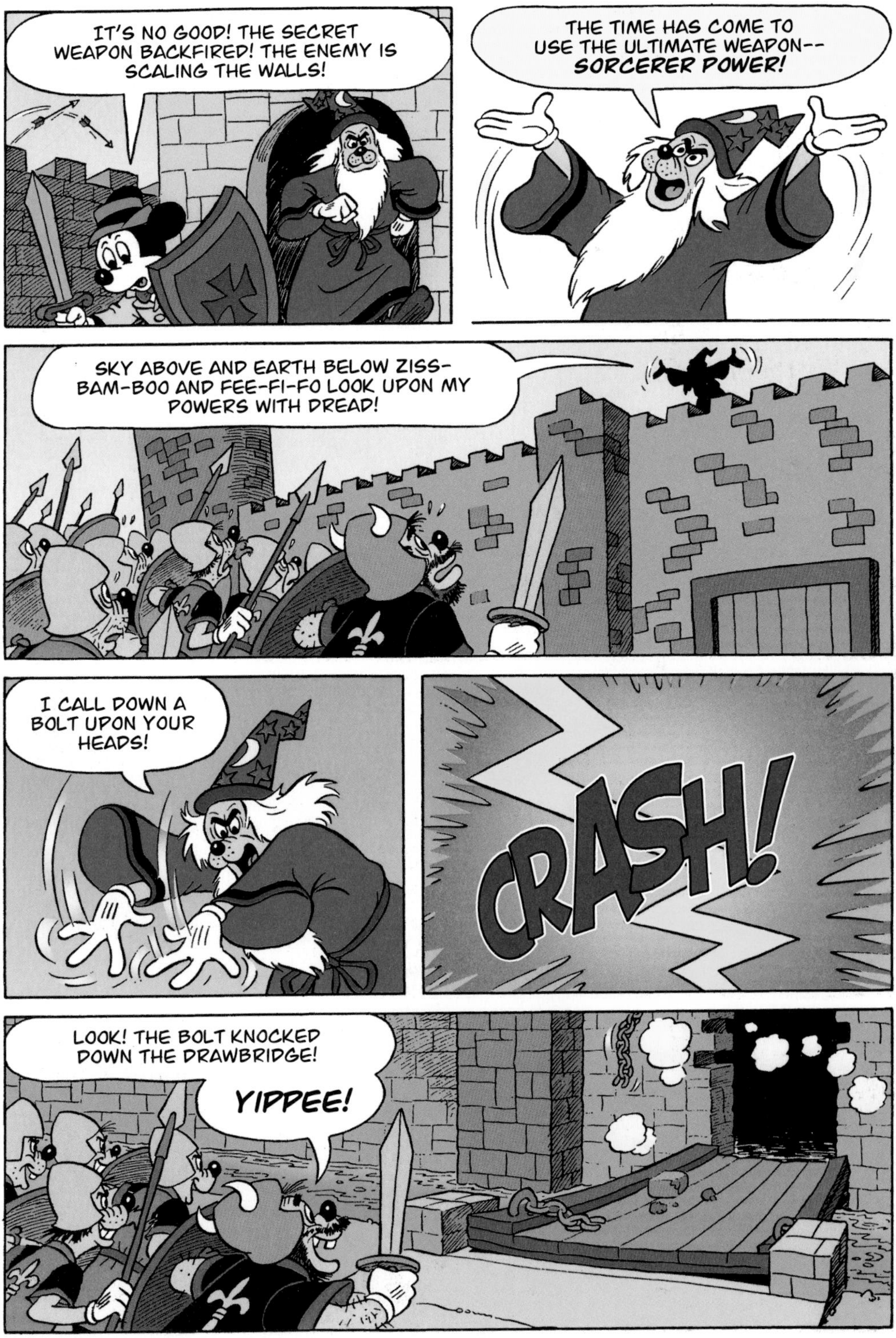

IT'S NO GOOD! THE SECRET WEAPON BACKFIRED! THE ENEMY IS SCALING THE WALLS!
THE TIME HAS COME TO USE THE ULTIMATE WEAPON-- SORCERER POWER!
SKY ABOVE AND EARTH BELOW ZISS-BAM-BOO AND FEE-FI-FO LOOK UPON MY POWERS WITH DREAD!
I CALL DOWN A BOLT UPON YOUR HEADS!
CRASH!
LOOK! THE BOLT KNOCKED DOWN THE DRAWBRIDGE!
YIPPEE!

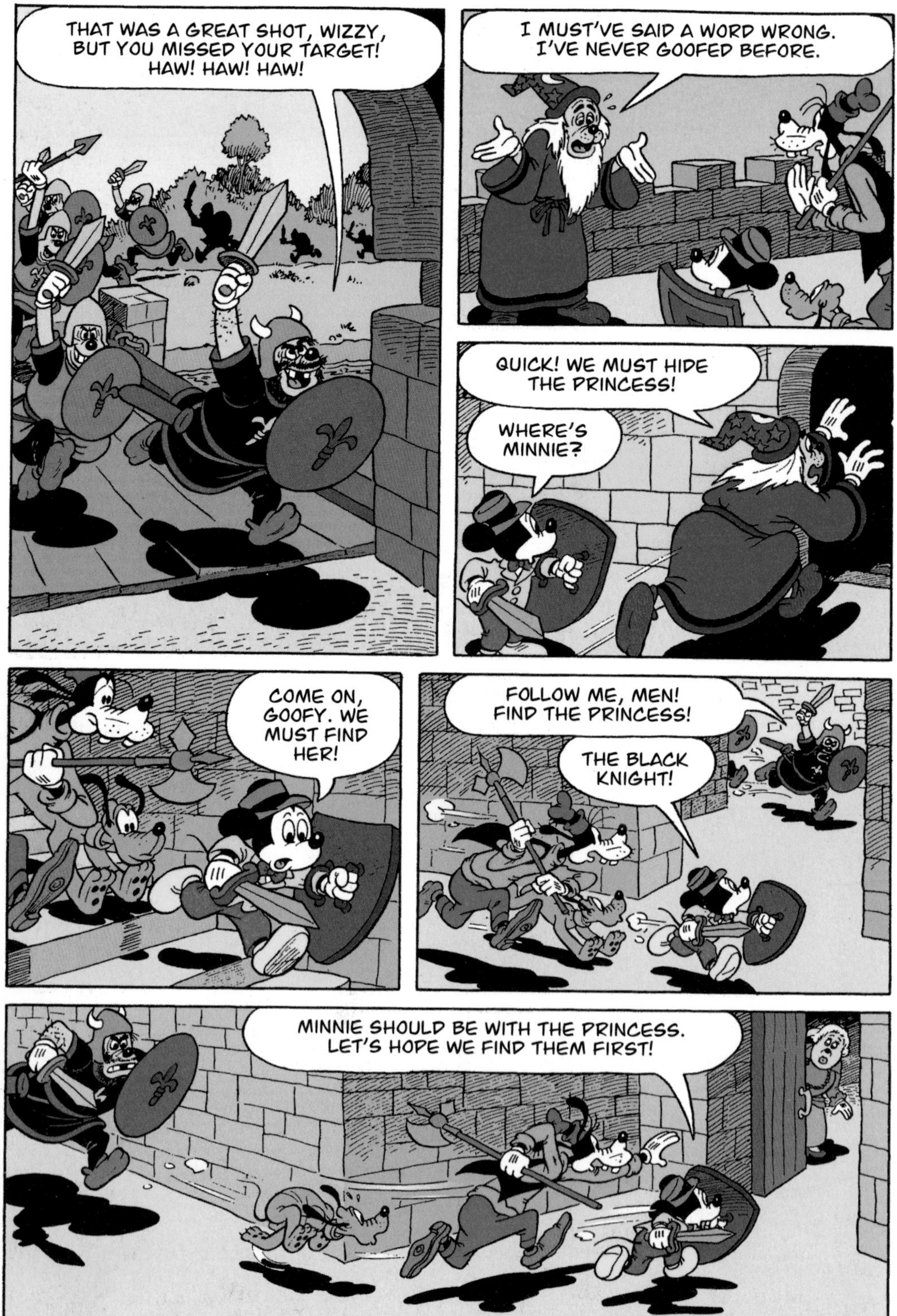
THAT WAS A GREAT SHOT, WIZZY, BUT YOU MISSED YOUR TARGET! HAW! HAW! HAW!
I MUST'VE SAID A WORD WRONG. I'VE NEVER GOOFED BEFORE.
QUICK! WE MUST HIDE THE PRINCESS!
WHERE'S MINNIE?
COME ON, GOOFY. WE MUST FIND HER!
FOLLOW ME, MEN! FIND THE PRINCESS!
THE BLACK KNIGHT!
MINNIE SHOULD BE WITH THE PRINCESS. LET'S HOPE WE FIND THEM FIRST!

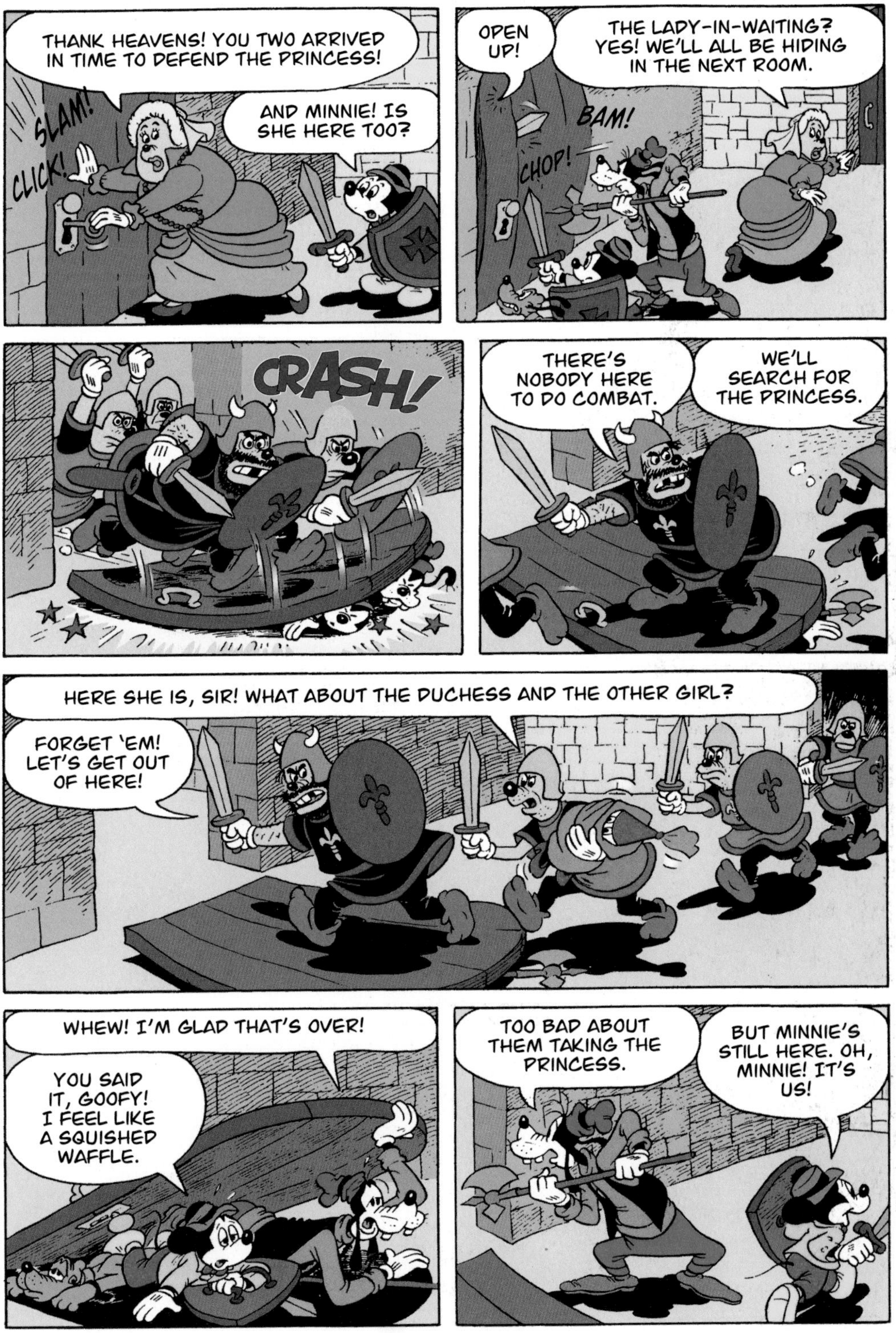
THANK HEAVENS! YOU TWO ARRIVED IN TIME TO DEFEND THE PRINCESS!
SLAM!
CLICK!
AND MINNIE! IS SHE HERE TOO?
OPEN UP!
THE LADY-IN-WAITING? YES! WE'LL ALL BE HIDING IN THE NEXT ROOM.
BAM!
CHOP!
CRASH!
THERE'S NOBODY HERE TO DO COMBAT.
WE'LL SEARCH FOR THE PRINCESS.
HERE SHE IS, SIR! WHAT ABOUT THE DUCHESS AND THE OTHER GIRL?
FORGET 'EM! LET'S GET OUT OF HERE!
WHEW! I'M GLAD THAT'S OVER!
YOU SAID IT, GOOFY! I FEEL LIKE A SQUISHED WAFFLE.
TOO BAD ABOUT THEM TAKING THE PRINCESS.
BUT MINNIE'S STILL HERE. OH, MINNIE! IT'S US!

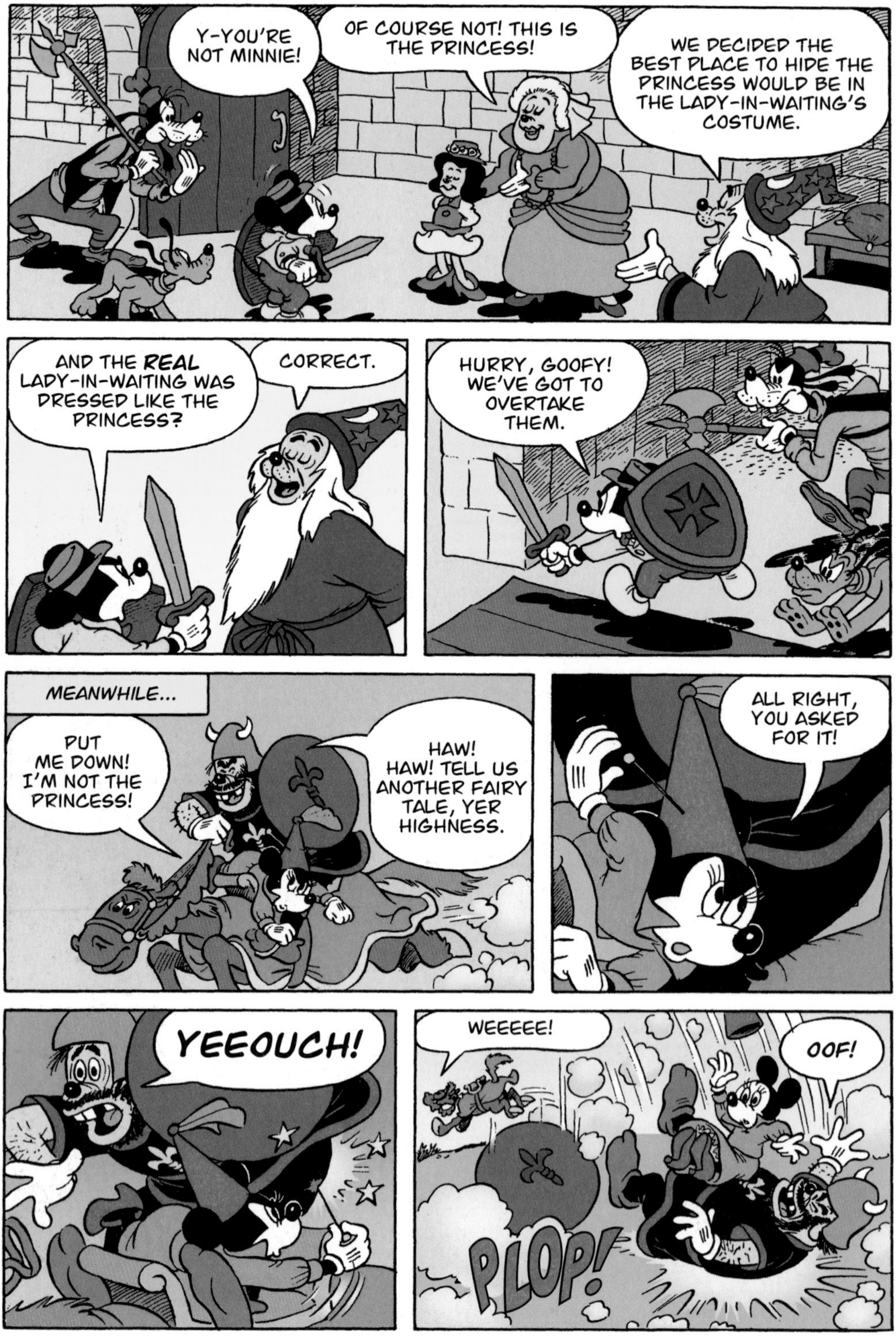

Y-YOU'RE NOT MINNIE!
OF COURSE NOT! THIS IS THE PRINCESS!
WE DECIDED THE BEST PLACE TO HIDE THE PRINCESS WOULD BE IN THE LADY-IN-WAITING'S COSTUME.
AND THE REAL LADY-IN-WAITING WAS DRESSED LIKE THE PRINCESS?
CORRECT.
HURRY, GOOFY! WE'VE GOT TO OVERTAKE THEM.
MEANWHILE...
PUT ME DOWN! I'M NOT THE PRINCESS!
HAW! HAW! TELL US ANOTHER FAIRY TALE, YER HIGHNESS.
ALL RIGHT, YOU ASKED FOR IT!
YEEOUCH!
WEEEEE!
OOF!
PLOP!

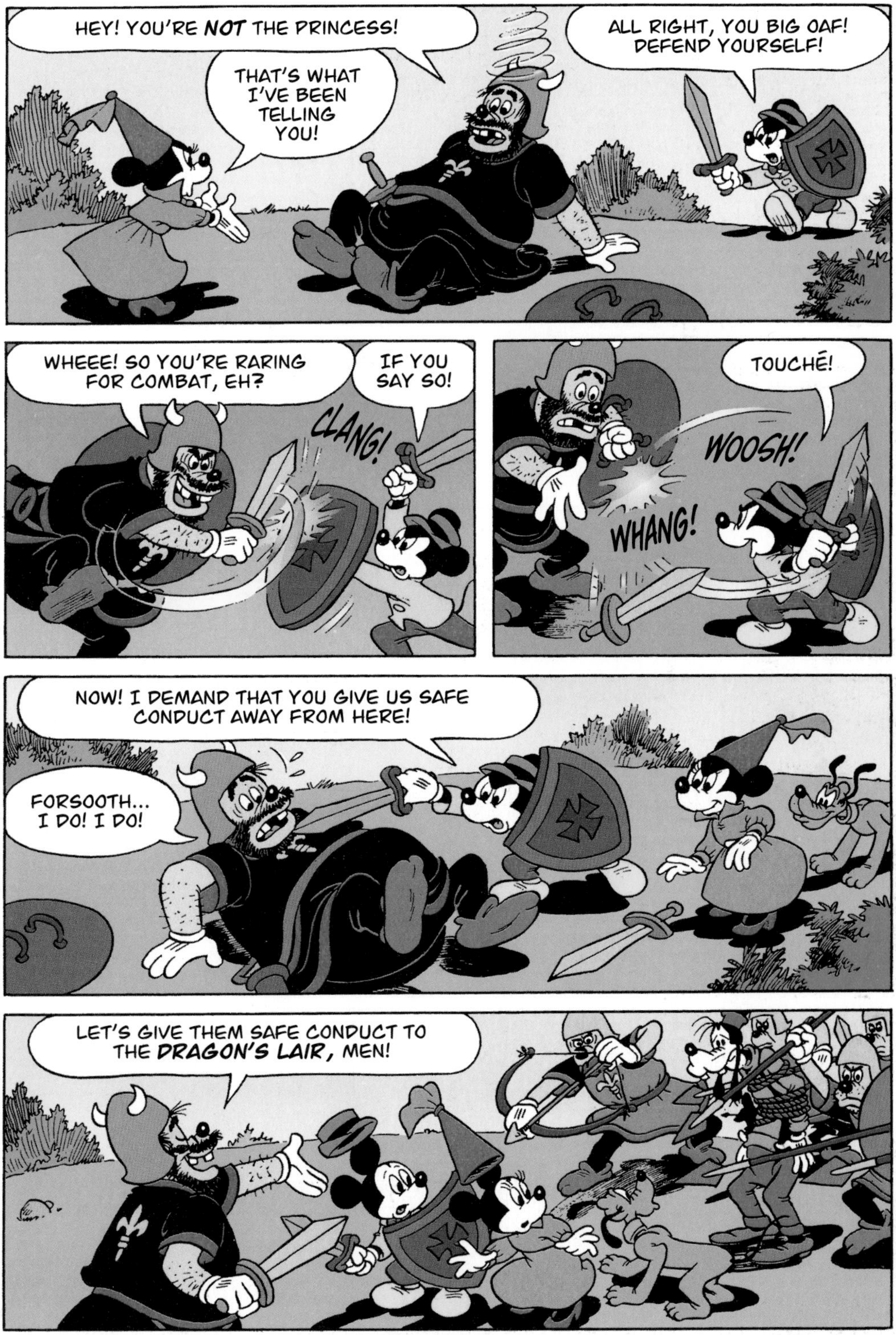
HEY! YOU'RE **NOT** THE PRINCESS!
THAT'S WHAT I'VE BEEN TELLING YOU!
ALL RIGHT, YOU BIG OAF! DEFEND YOURSELF!
WHEEE! SO YOU'RE RARING FOR COMBAT, EH?
IF YOU SAY SO!
CLANG!
TOUCHÉ!
WOOSH!
WHANG!
NOW! I DEMAND THAT YOU GIVE US SAFE CONDUCT AWAY FROM HERE!
FORSOOTH... I DO! I DO!
LET'S GIVE THEM SAFE CONDUCT TO THE **DRAGON'S LAIR,** MEN!

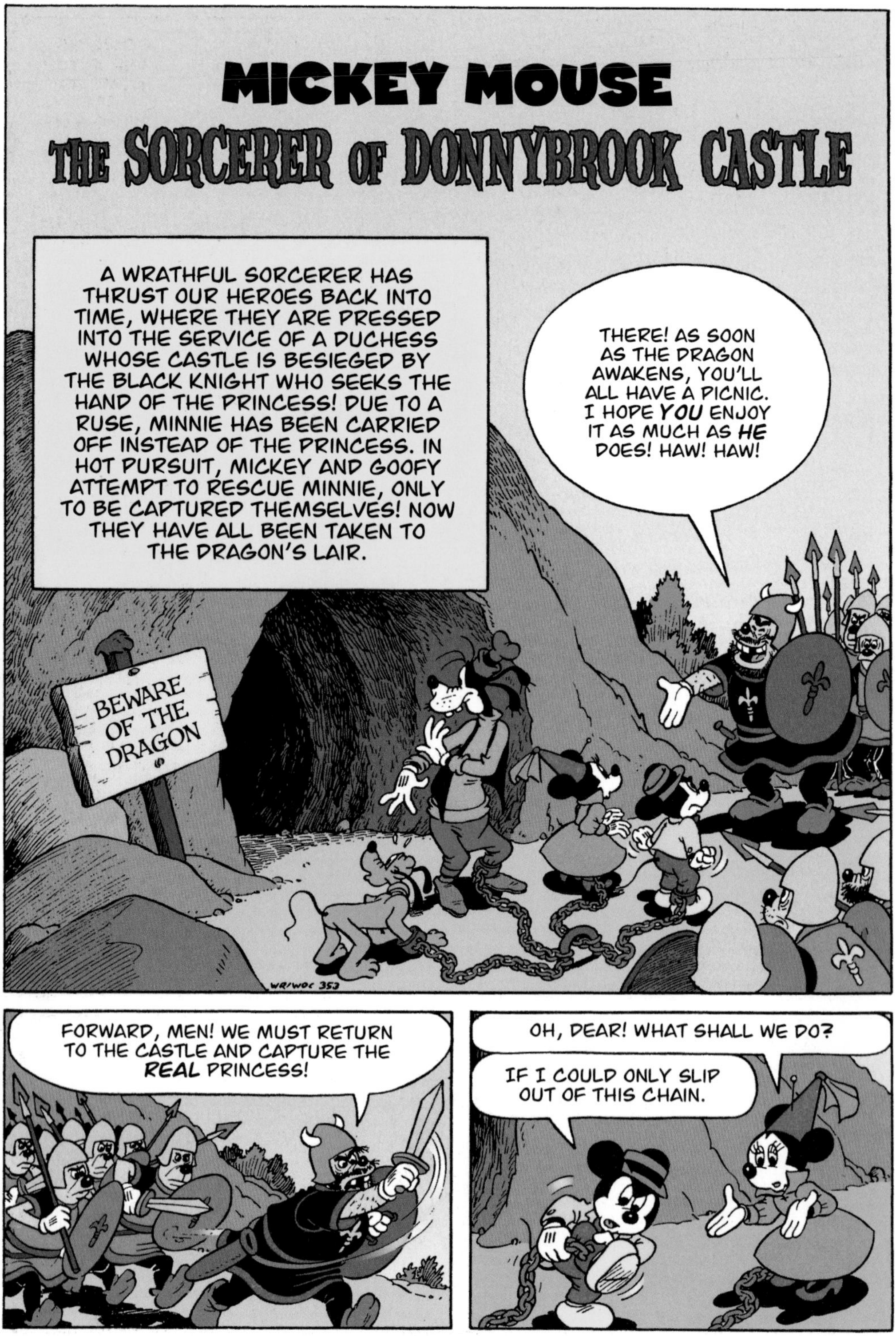
MICKEY MOUSE
THE SORCERER OF DONNYBROOK CASTLE
A WRATHFUL SORCERER HAS THRUST OUR HEROES BACK INTO TIME, WHERE THEY ARE PRESSED INTO THE SERVICE OF A DUCHESS WHOSE CASTLE IS BESIEGED BY THE BLACK KNIGHT WHO SEEKS THE HAND OF THE PRINCESS! DUE TO A RUSE, MINNIE HAS BEEN CARRIED OFF INSTEAD OF THE PRINCESS. IN HOT PURSUIT, MICKEY AND GOOFY ATTEMPT TO RESCUE MINNIE, ONLY TO BE CAPTURED THEMSELVES! NOW THEY HAVE ALL BEEN TAKEN TO THE DRAGON'S LAIR.
THERE! AS SOON AS THE DRAGON AWAKENS, YOU'LL ALL HAVE A PICNIC. I HOPE YOU ENJOY IT AS MUCH AS HE DOES! HAW! HAW!
BEWARE OF THE DRAGON
FORWARD, MEN! WE MUST RETURN TO THE CASTLE AND CAPTURE THE REAL PRINCESS!
OH, DEAR! WHAT SHALL WE DO?
IF I COULD ONLY SLIP OUT OF THIS CHAIN.

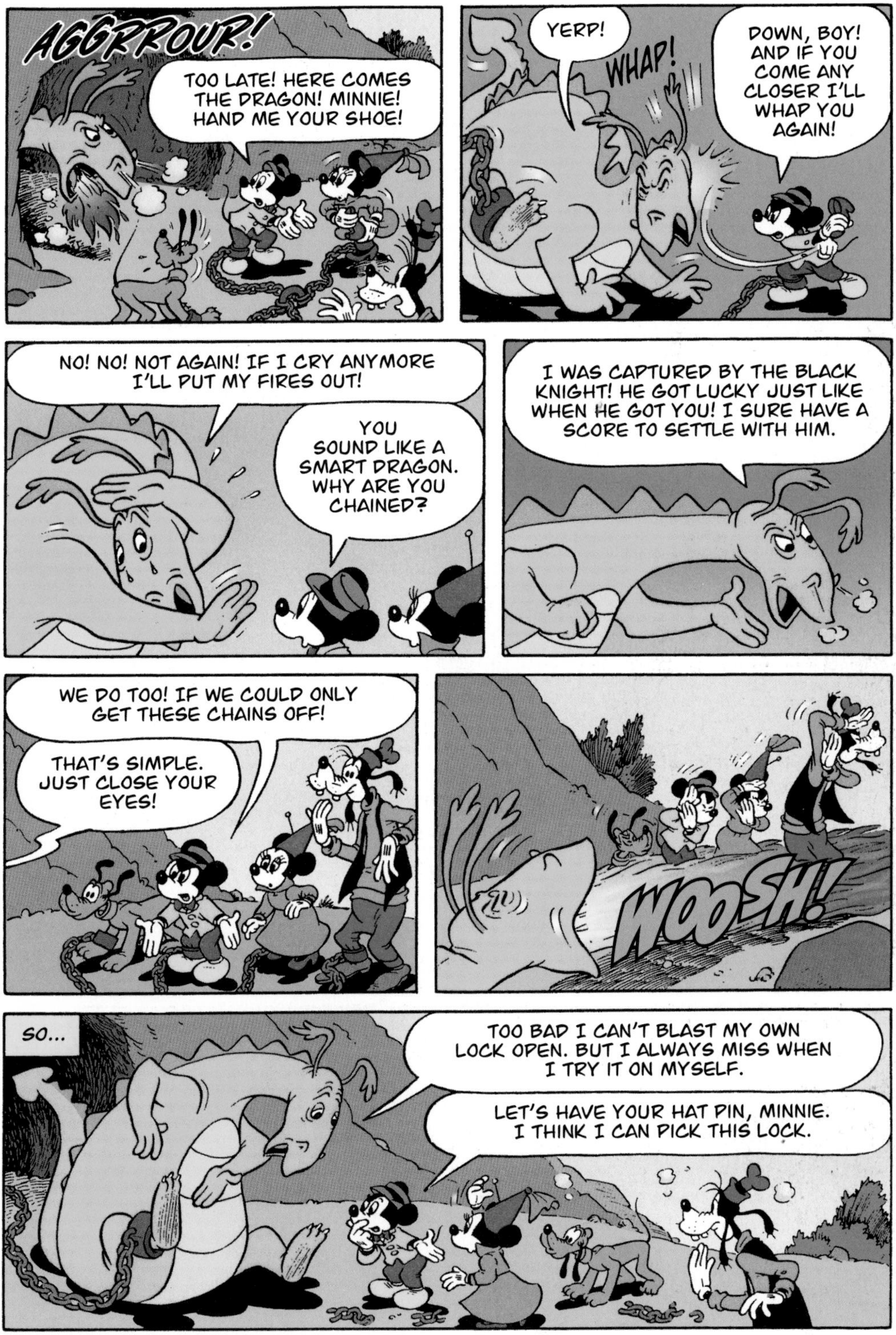
AGGRROUR!
TOO LATE! HERE COMES THE DRAGON! MINNIE! HAND ME YOUR SHOE!
YERP!
WHAP!
DOWN, BOY! AND IF YOU COME ANY CLOSER I'LL WHAP YOU AGAIN!
NO! NO! NOT AGAIN! IF I CRY ANYMORE I'LL PUT MY FIRES OUT!
YOU SOUND LIKE A SMART DRAGON. WHY ARE YOU CHAINED?
I WAS CAPTURED BY THE BLACK KNIGHT! HE GOT LUCKY JUST LIKE WHEN HE GOT YOU! I SURE HAVE A SCORE TO SETTLE WITH HIM.
WE DO TOO! IF WE COULD ONLY GET THESE CHAINS OFF!
THAT'S SIMPLE. JUST CLOSE YOUR EYES!
WOOSH!
SO...
TOO BAD I CAN'T BLAST MY OWN LOCK OPEN. BUT I ALWAYS MISS WHEN I TRY IT ON MYSELF.
LET'S HAVE YOUR HAT PIN, MINNIE. I THINK I CAN PICK THIS LOCK.

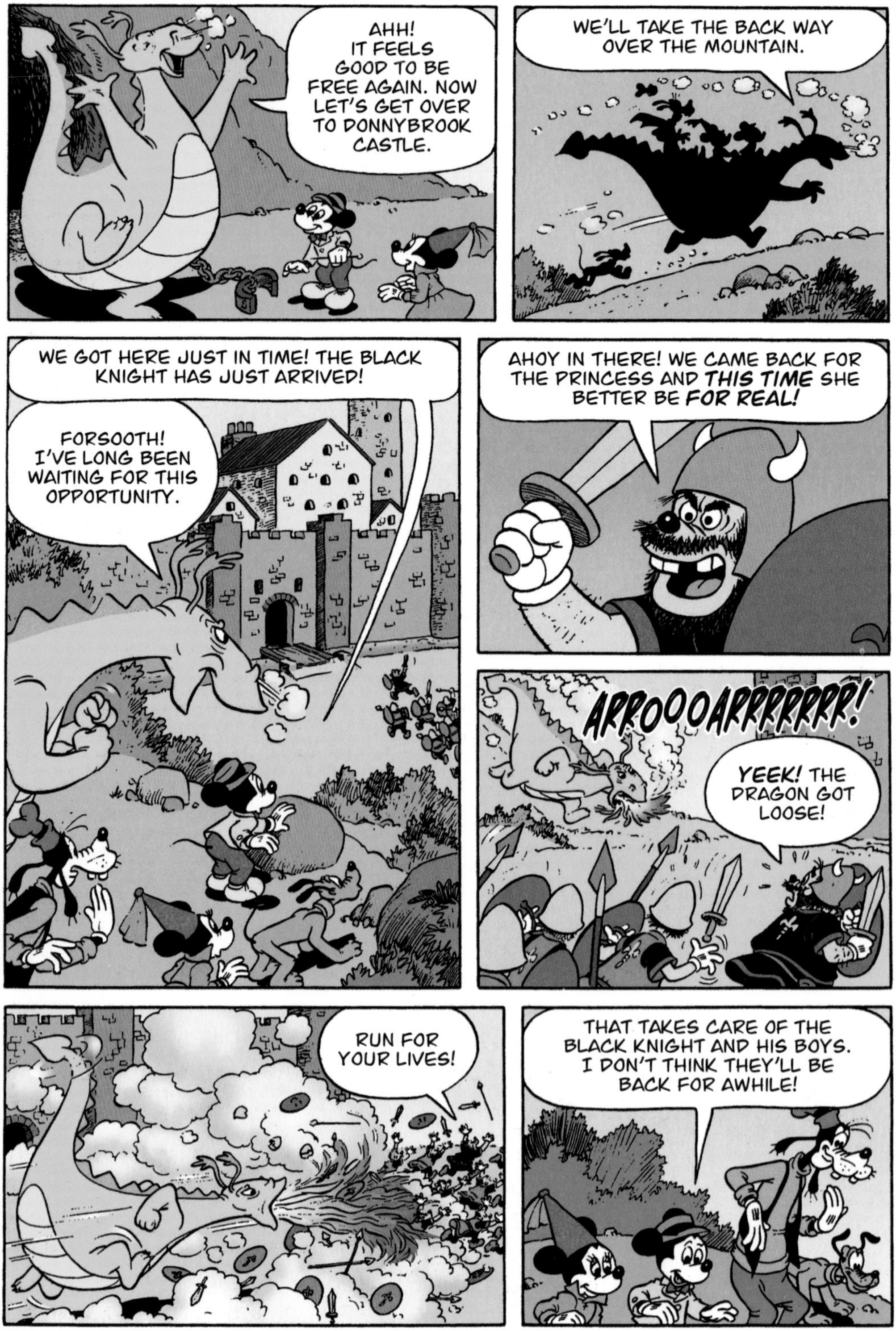
AHH! IT FEELS GOOD TO BE FREE AGAIN. NOW LET'S GET OVER TO DONNYBROOK CASTLE.
WE'LL TAKE THE BACK WAY OVER THE MOUNTAIN.
WE GOT HERE JUST IN TIME! THE BLACK KNIGHT HAS JUST ARRIVED!
FORSOOTH! I'VE LONG BEEN WAITING FOR THIS OPPORTUNITY.
AHOY IN THERE! WE CAME BACK FOR THE PRINCESS AND THIS TIME SHE BETTER BE FOR REAL!
ARROOOARRRRRRR!
YEEK! THE DRAGON GOT LOOSE!
RUN FOR YOUR LIVES!
THAT TAKES CARE OF THE BLACK KNIGHT AND HIS BOYS. I DON'T THINK THEY'LL BE BACK FOR AWHILE!

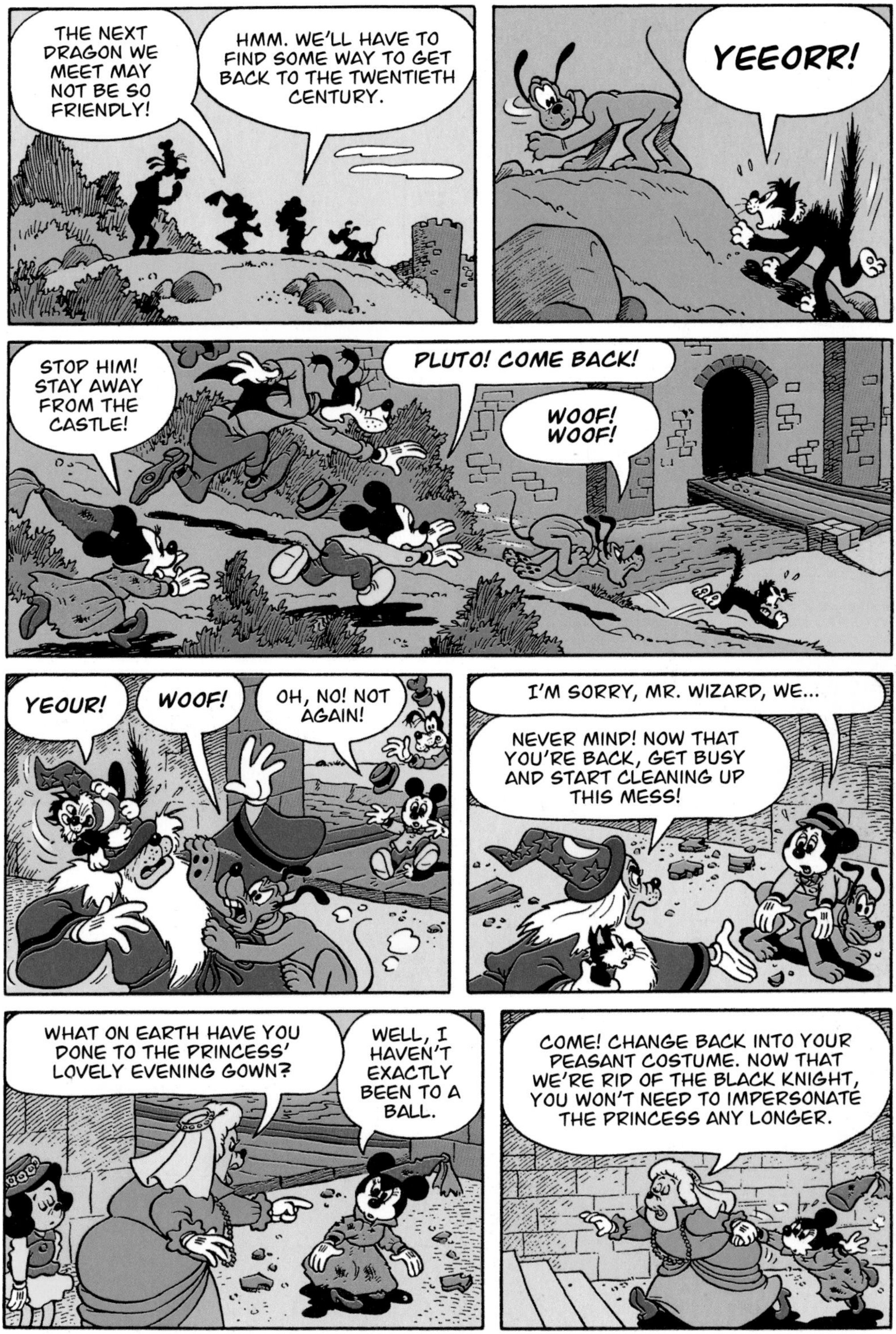
THE NEXT DRAGON WE MEET MAY NOT BE SO FRIENDLY!
HMM. WE'LL HAVE TO FIND SOME WAY TO GET BACK TO THE TWENTIETH CENTURY.
YEEORR!
STOP HIM! STAY AWAY FROM THE CASTLE!
PLUTO! COME BACK!
WOOF! WOOF!
YEOUR!
WOOF!
OH, NO! NOT AGAIN!
I'M SORRY, MR. WIZARD, WE...
NEVER MIND! NOW THAT YOU'RE BACK, GET BUSY AND START CLEANING UP THIS MESS!
WHAT ON EARTH HAVE YOU DONE TO THE PRINCESS' LOVELY EVENING GOWN?
WELL, I HAVEN'T EXACTLY BEEN TO A BALL.
COME! CHANGE BACK INTO YOUR PEASANT COSTUME. NOW THAT WE'RE RID OF THE BLACK KNIGHT, YOU WON'T NEED TO IMPERSONATE THE PRINCESS ANY LONGER.

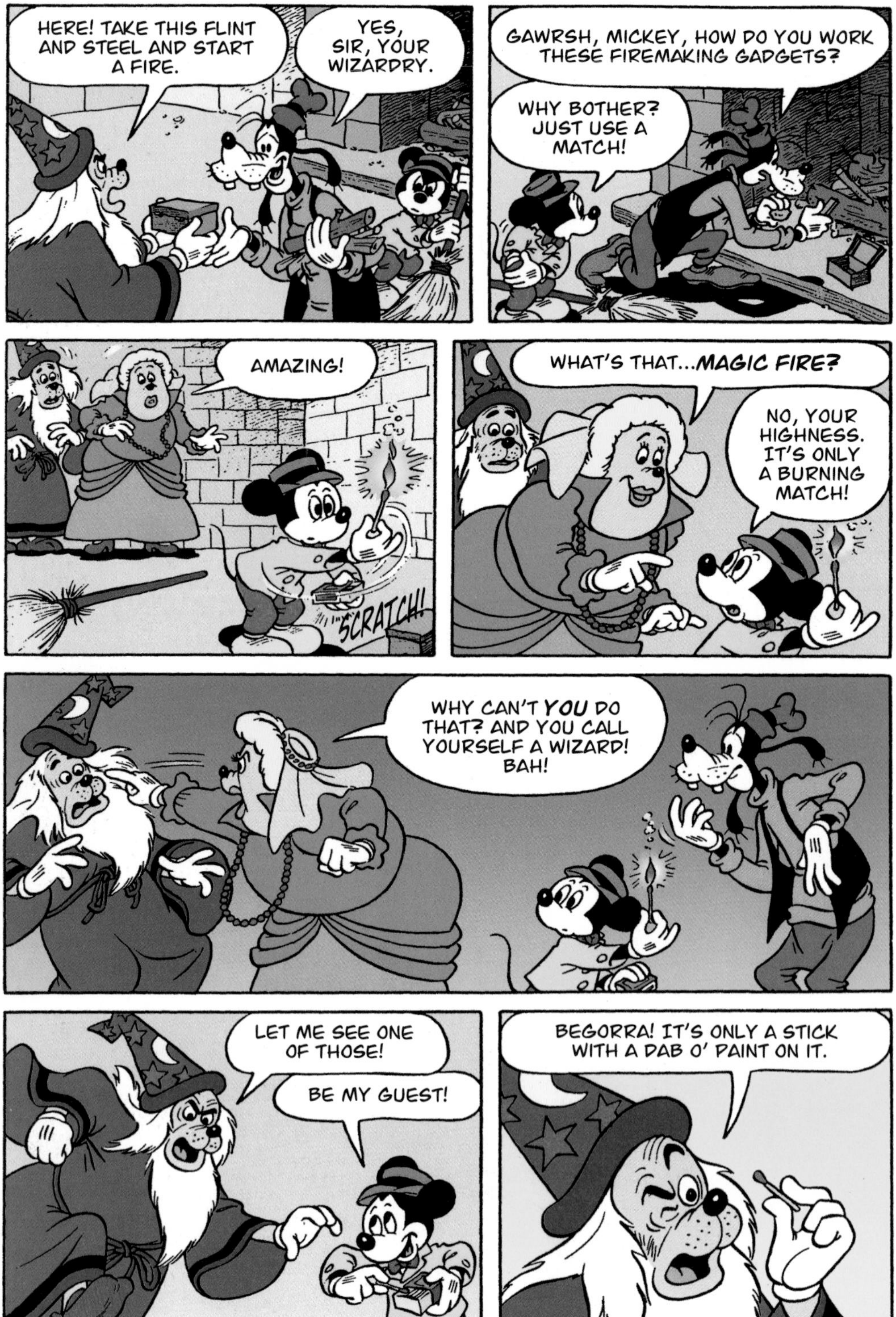
HERE! TAKE THIS FLINT AND STEEL AND START A FIRE.
YES, SIR, YOUR WIZARDRY.
GAWRSH, MICKEY, HOW DO YOU WORK THESE FIREMAKING GADGETS?
WHY BOTHER? JUST USE A MATCH!
AMAZING!
SCRATCH!
WHAT'S THAT... *MAGIC FIRE?*
NO, YOUR HIGHNESS. IT'S ONLY A BURNING MATCH!
WHY CAN'T *YOU* DO THAT? AND YOU CALL YOURSELF A WIZARD! BAH!
LET ME SEE ONE OF THOSE!
BE MY GUEST!
BEGORRA! IT'S ONLY A STICK WITH A DAB O' PAINT ON IT.

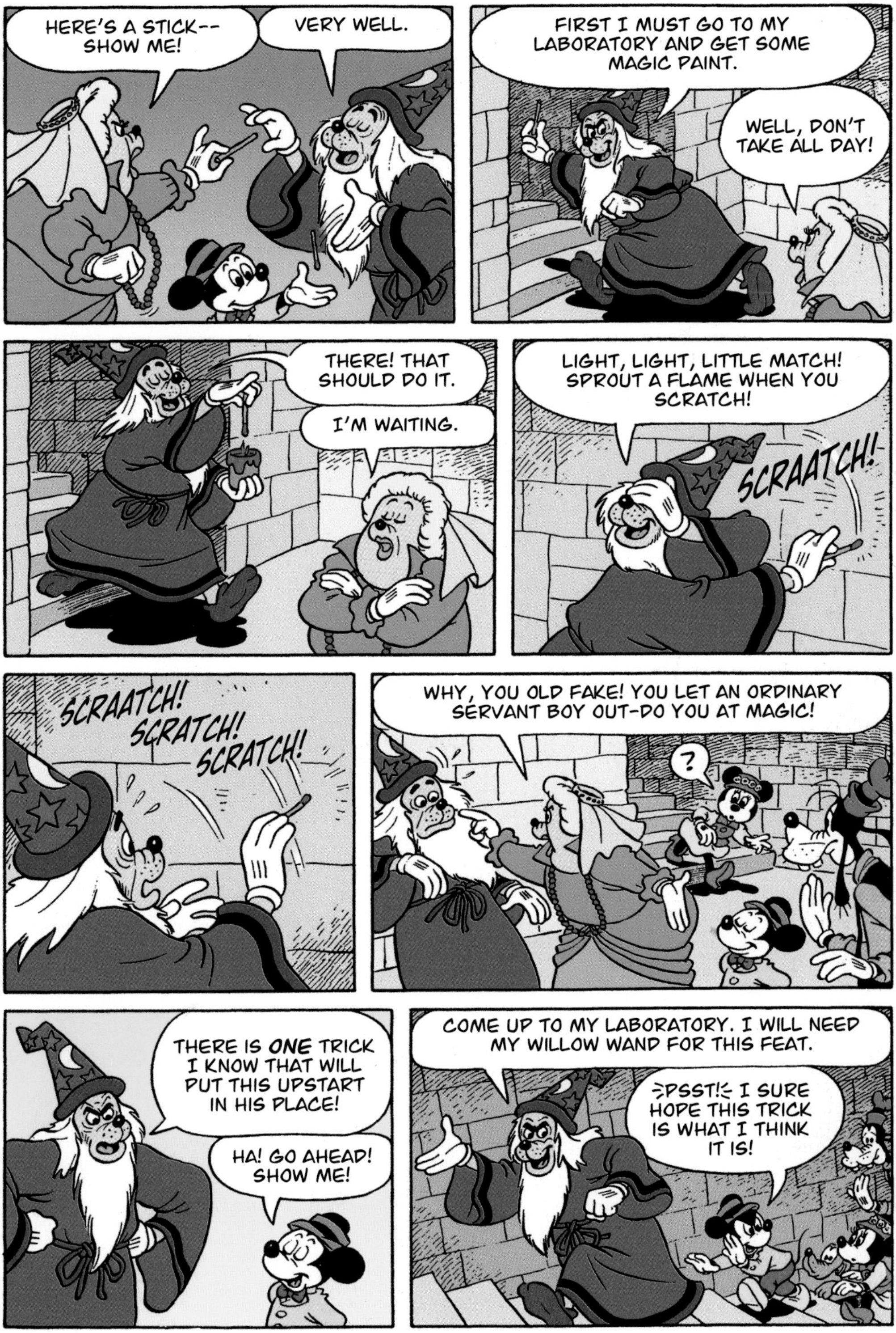
HERE'S A STICK-- SHOW ME!
VERY WELL.
FIRST I MUST GO TO MY LABORATORY AND GET SOME MAGIC PAINT.
WELL, DON'T TAKE ALL DAY!
THERE! THAT SHOULD DO IT.
I'M WAITING.
LIGHT, LIGHT, LITTLE MATCH! SPROUT A FLAME WHEN YOU SCRATCH!
SCRAATCH!
SCRAATCH!
SCRATCH!
SCRATCH!
WHY, YOU OLD FAKE! YOU LET AN ORDINARY SERVANT BOY OUT-DO YOU AT MAGIC!
?
THERE IS ONE TRICK I KNOW THAT WILL PUT THIS UPSTART IN HIS PLACE!
HA! GO AHEAD! SHOW ME!
COME UP TO MY LABORATORY. I WILL NEED MY WILLOW WAND FOR THIS FEAT.
PSST! I SURE HOPE THIS TRICK IS WHAT I THINK IT IS!

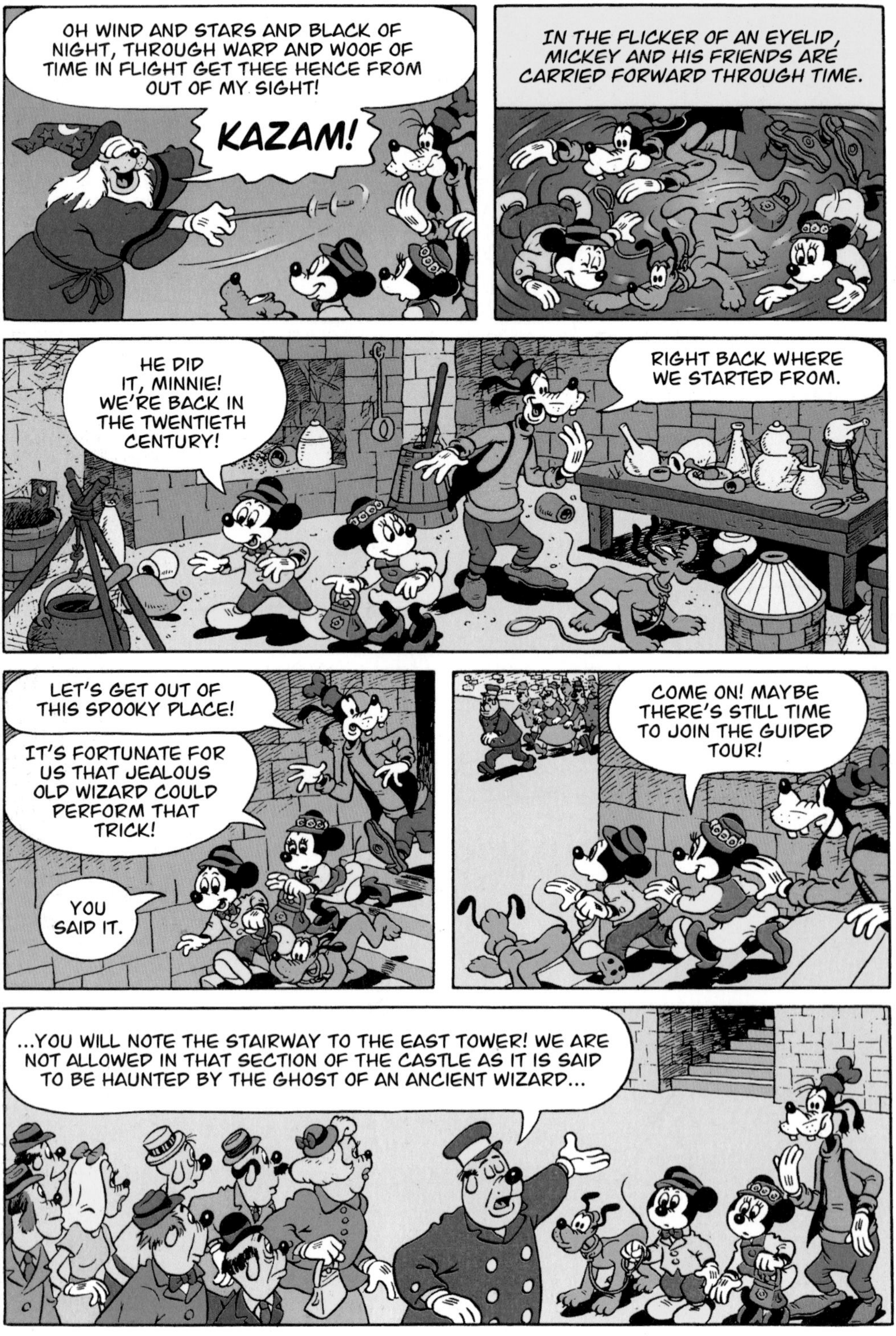
OH WIND AND STARS AND BLACK OF NIGHT, THROUGH WARP AND WOOF OF TIME IN FLIGHT GET THEE HENCE FROM OUT OF MY SIGHT!
KAZAM!
IN THE FLICKER OF AN EYELID, MICKEY AND HIS FRIENDS ARE CARRIED FORWARD THROUGH TIME.
HE DID IT, MINNIE! WE'RE BACK IN THE TWENTIETH CENTURY!
RIGHT BACK WHERE WE STARTED FROM.
LET'S GET OUT OF THIS SPOOKY PLACE!
IT'S FORTUNATE FOR US THAT JEALOUS OLD WIZARD COULD PERFORM THAT TRICK!
YOU SAID IT.
COME ON! MAYBE THERE'S STILL TIME TO JOIN THE GUIDED TOUR!
...YOU WILL NOTE THE STAIRWAY TO THE EAST TOWER! WE ARE NOT ALLOWED IN THAT SECTION OF THE CASTLE AS IT IS SAID TO BE HAUNTED BY THE GHOST OF AN ANCIENT WIZARD...

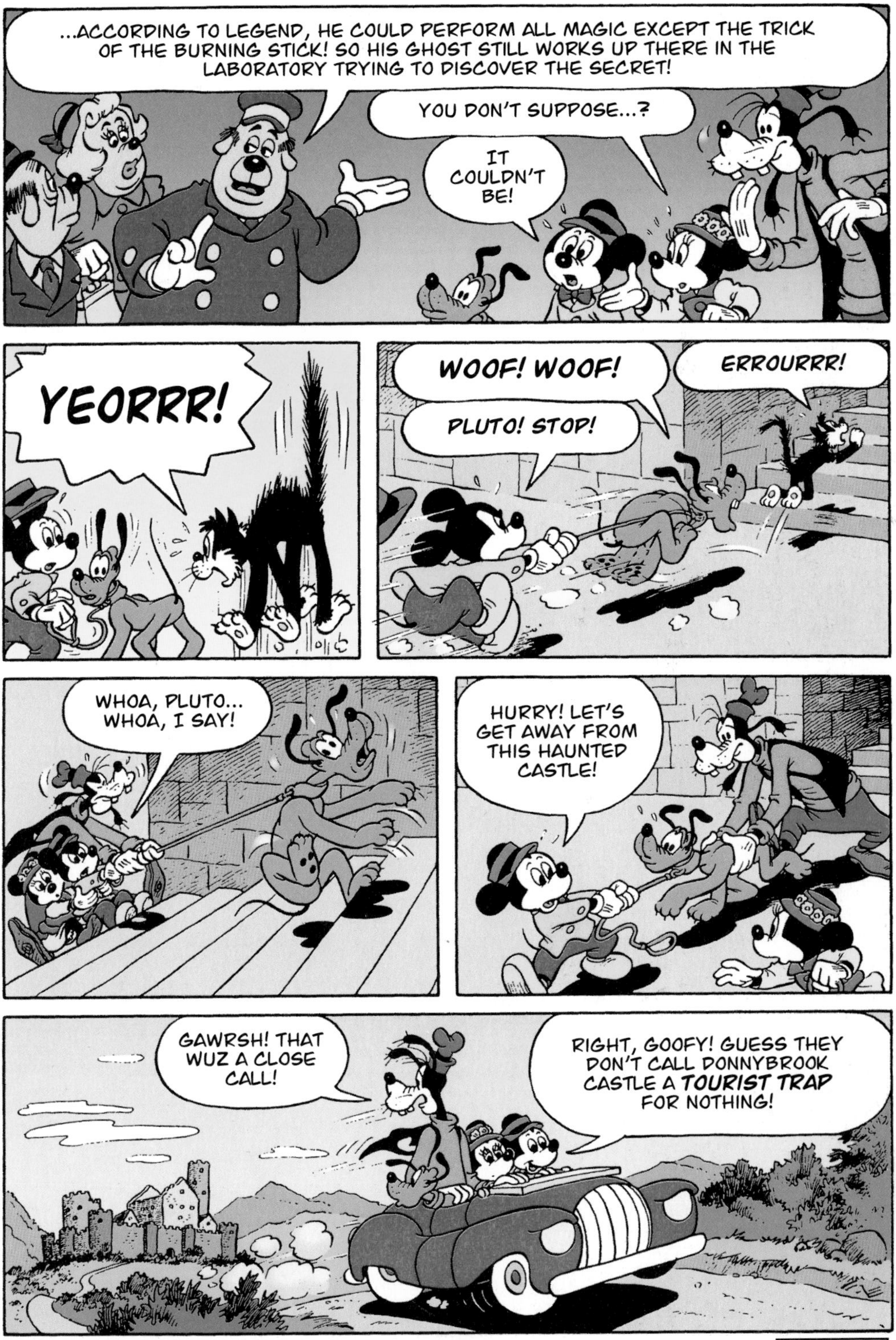
...ACCORDING TO LEGEND, HE COULD PERFORM ALL MAGIC EXCEPT THE TRICK OF THE BURNING STICK! SO HIS GHOST STILL WORKS UP THERE IN THE LABORATORY TRYING TO DISCOVER THE SECRET!
YOU DON'T SUPPOSE...?
IT COULDN'T BE!
YEORRR!
WOOF! WOOF!
ERROURRR!
PLUTO! STOP!
WHOA, PLUTO... WHOA, I SAY!
HURRY! LET'S GET AWAY FROM THIS HAUNTED CASTLE!
GAWRSH! THAT WUZ A CLOSE CALL!
RIGHT, GOOFY! GUESS THEY DON'T CALL DONNYBROOK CASTLE A *TOURIST TRAP* FOR NOTHING!

THE END

LOOKING FOR MORE FUN WITH YOUR FAVORITE CHARACTERS?

CHECK OUT THESE EXCLUSIVE PREVIEWS OF OTHER GREAT TITLES NOW AVAILABLE FROM

BOOM KIDS!

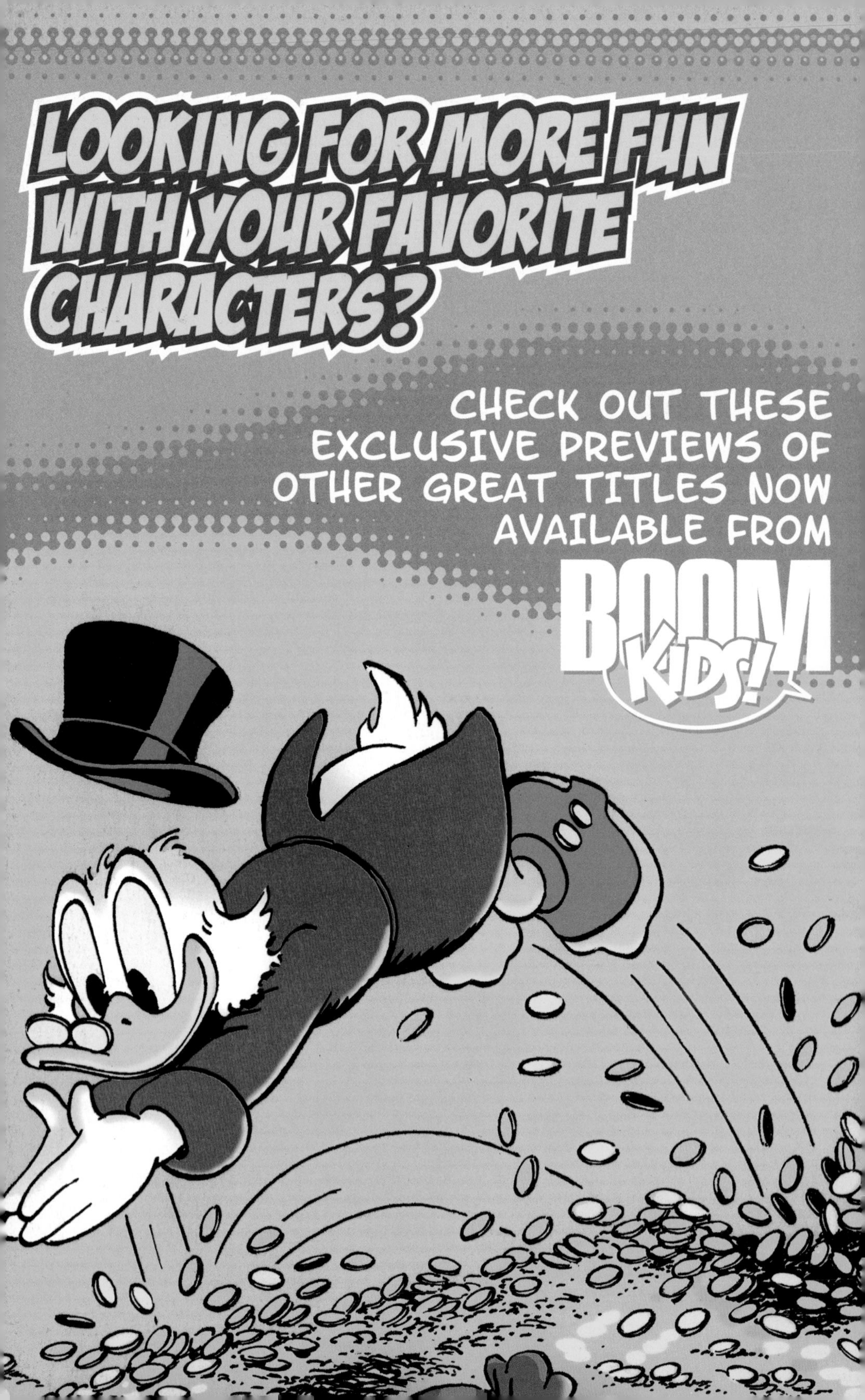

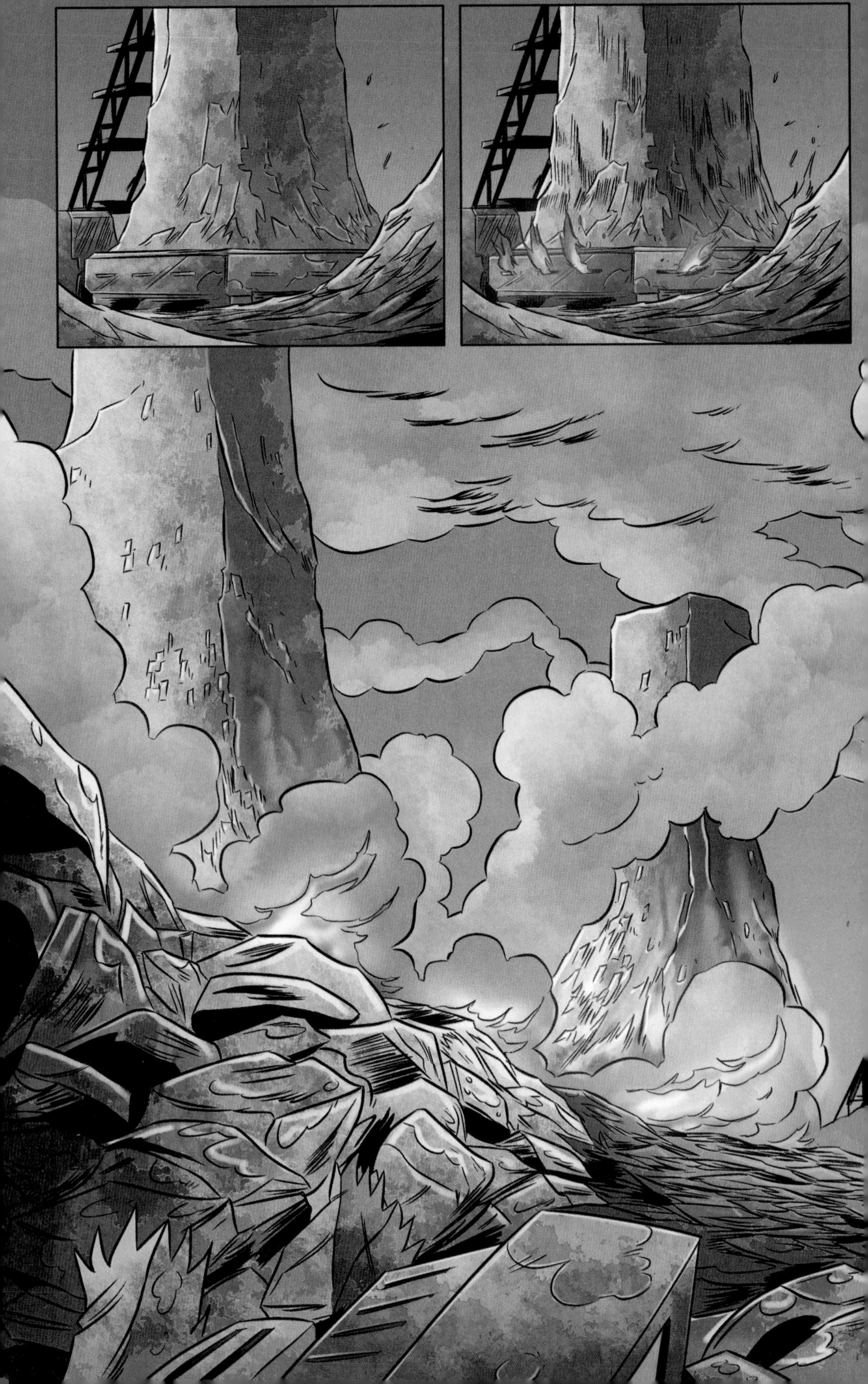

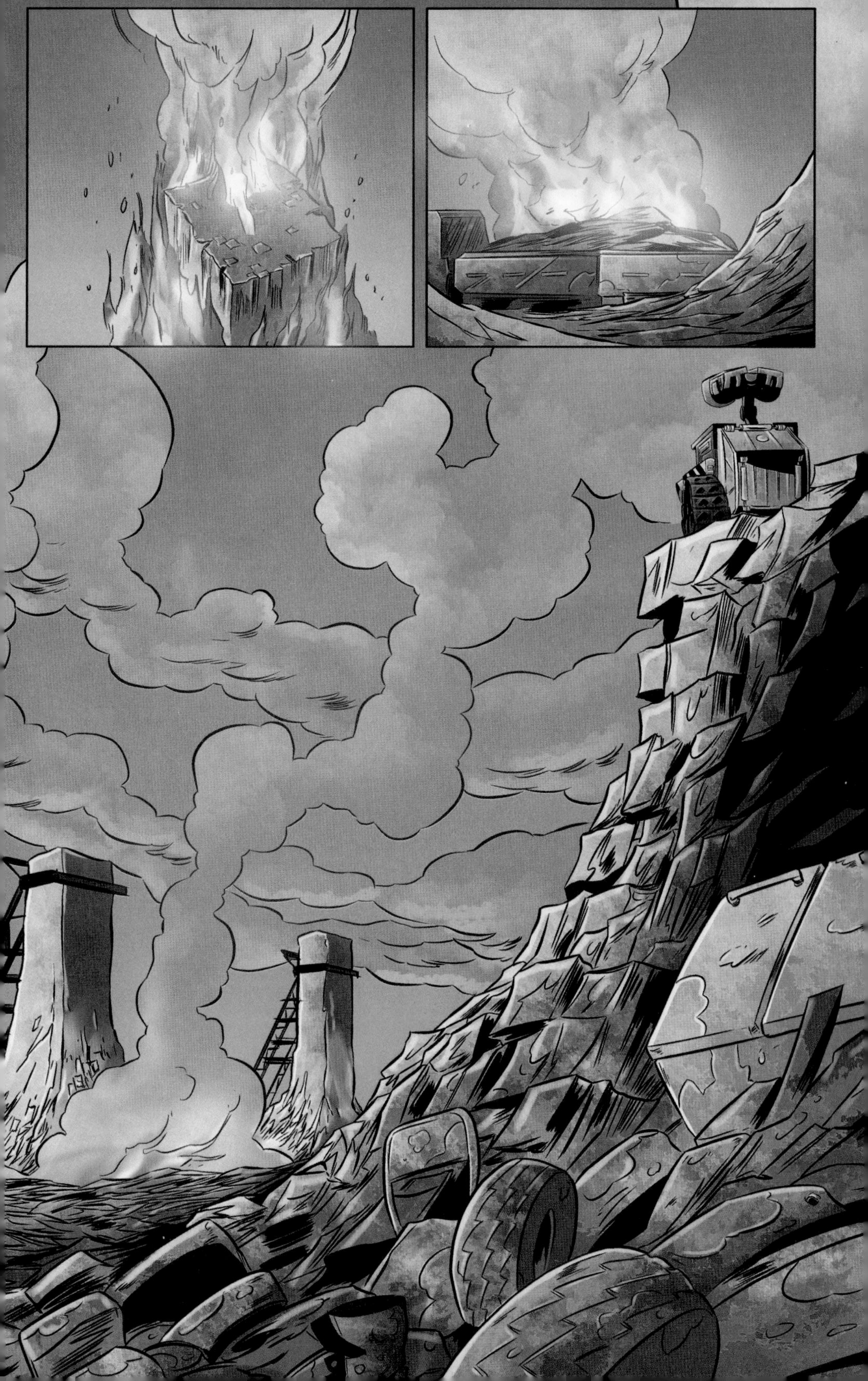

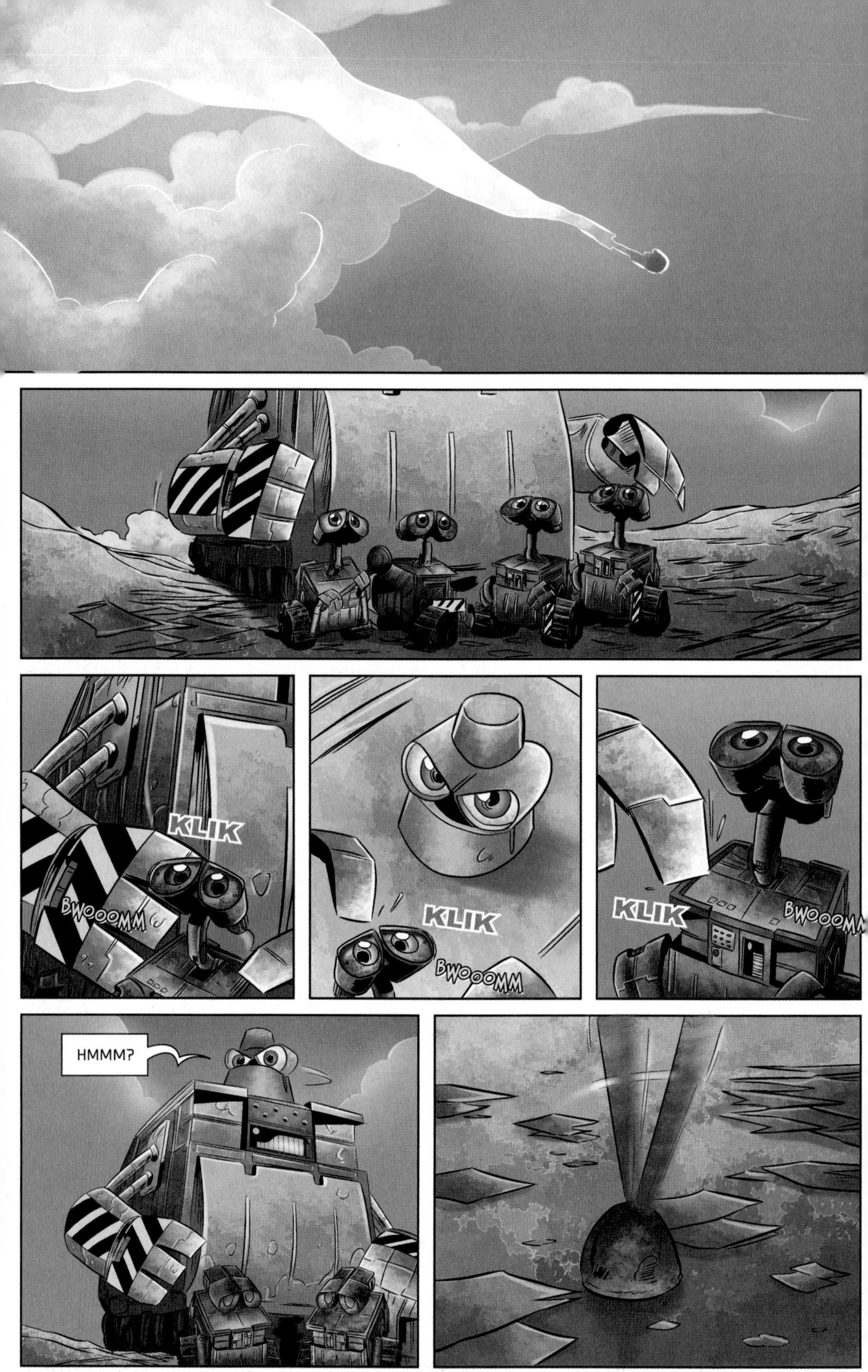
KLIK
BWOOOMM
KLIK
BWOOOMM
KLIK
BWOOOM
HMMM?

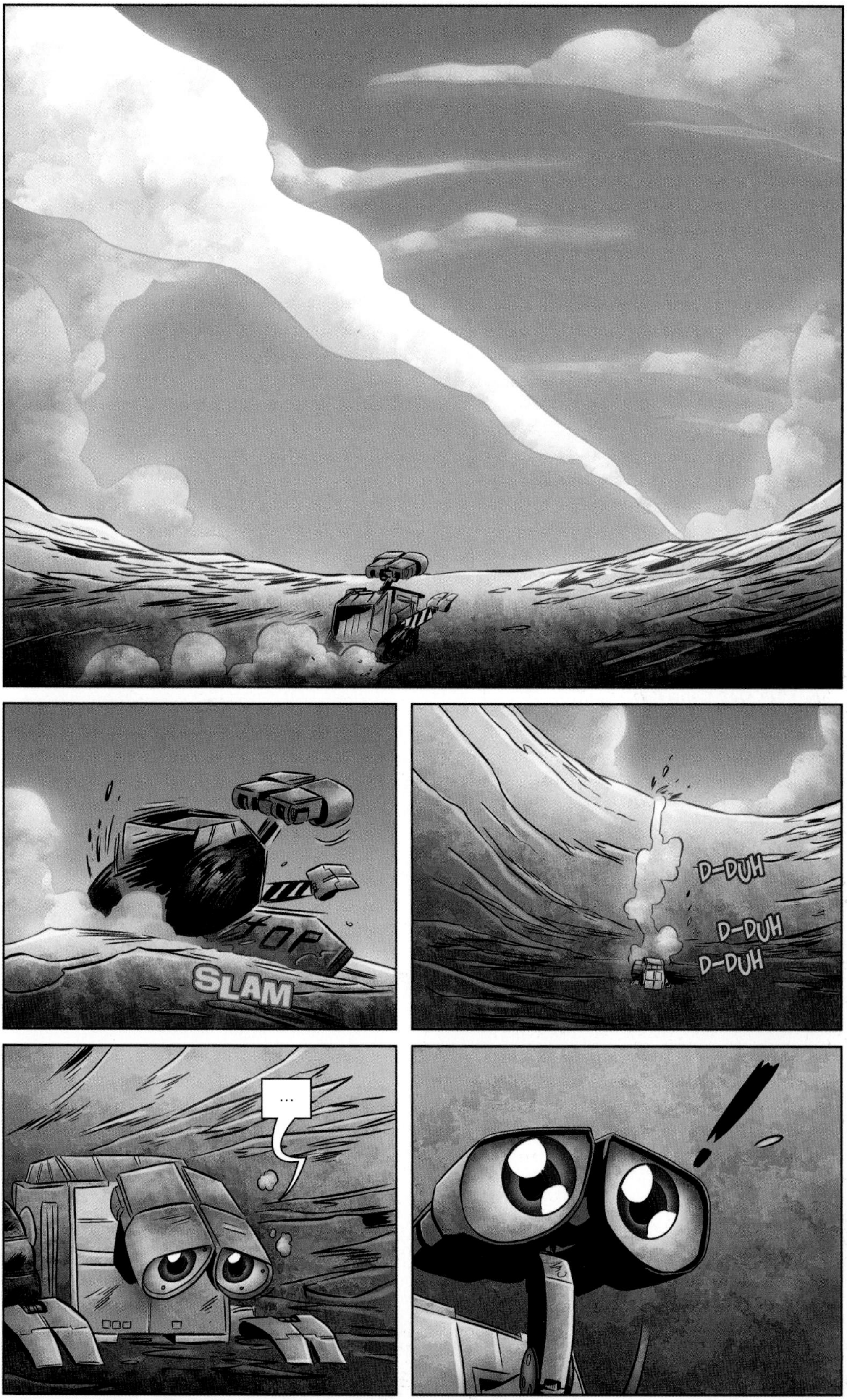
SLAM
D-DUH
D-DUH
D-DUH
...
!

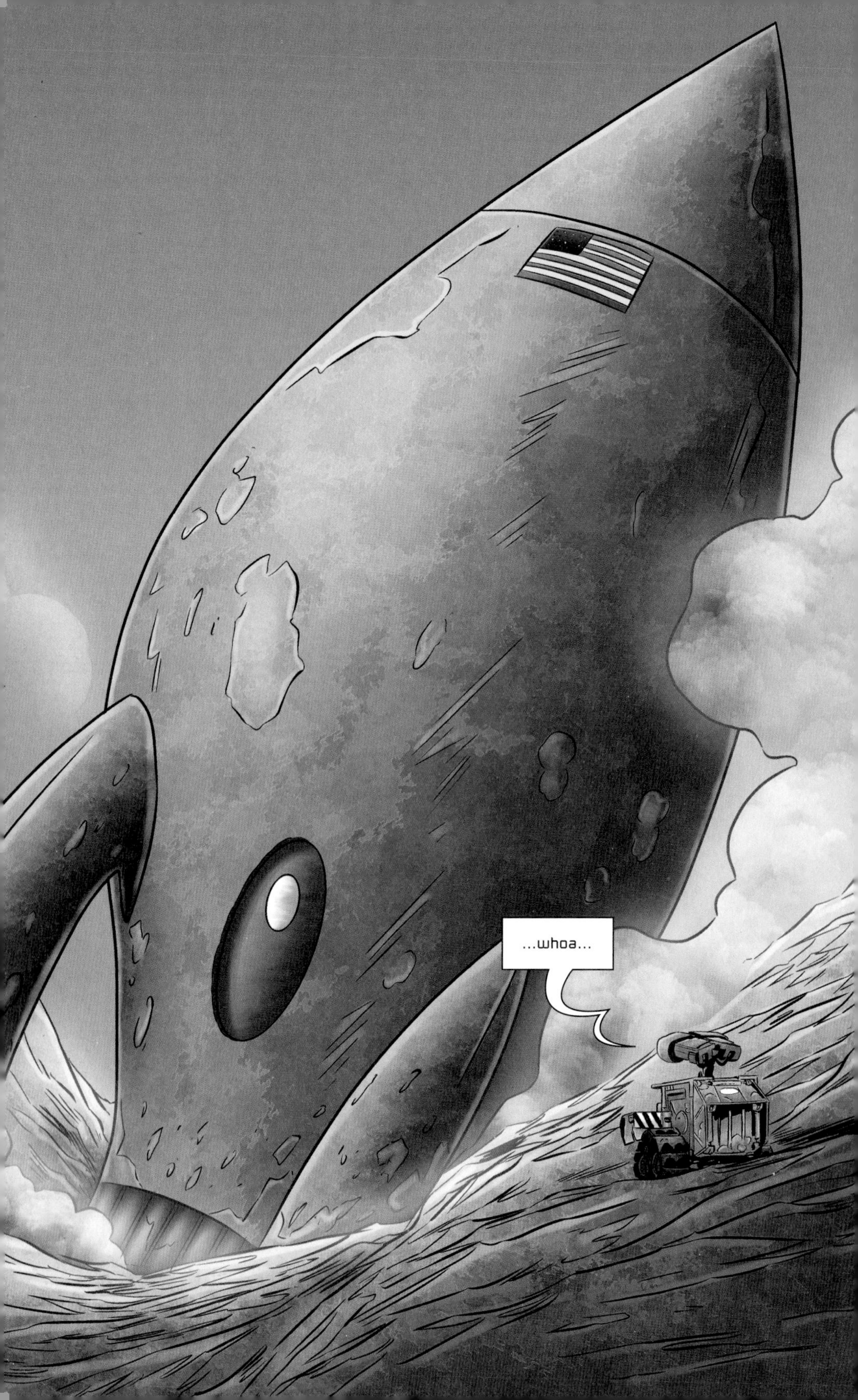
...whoa...

The greatest team of Disney super-heroes ever
assembled combats Emil Eagle and the Sinister 7!
It's a tremendous tug-of-war for control over the
earth-shattering Ultramachine!

DISNEY'S HERO SQUAD: ULTRAHEROES VOL. 2:
RACE FOR THE ULTRAPODS
DIAMOND CODE: MAR100809
SC $9.99 ISBN 9781608865604

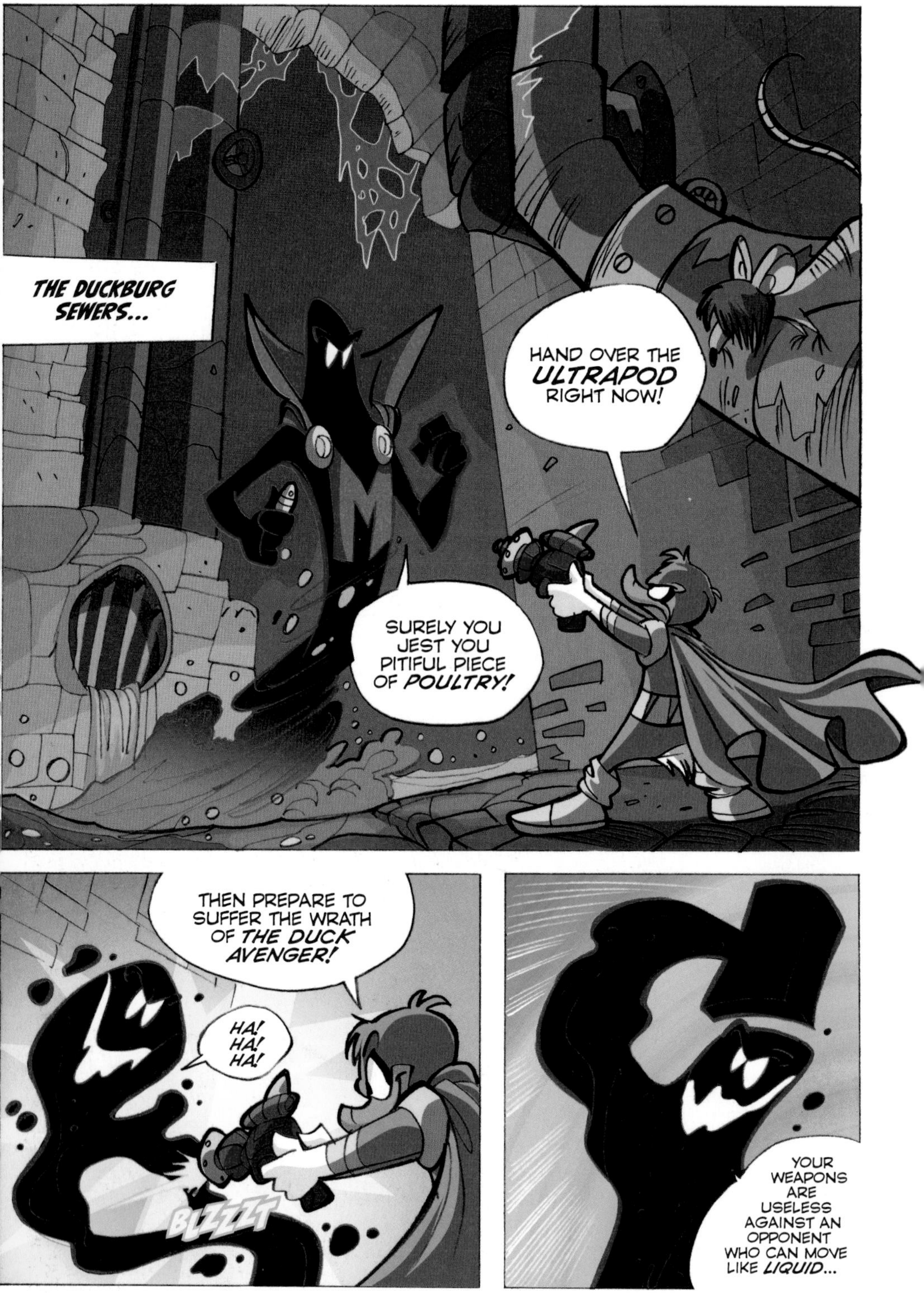
THE DUCKBURG SEWERS...
HAND OVER THE ULTRAPOD RIGHT NOW!
SURELY YOU JEST YOU PITIFUL PIECE OF POULTRY!
THEN PREPARE TO SUFFER THE WRATH OF THE DUCK AVENGER!
HA! HA! HA!
BLZZZT
YOUR WEAPONS ARE USELESS AGAINST AN OPPONENT WHO CAN MOVE LIKE LIQUID...

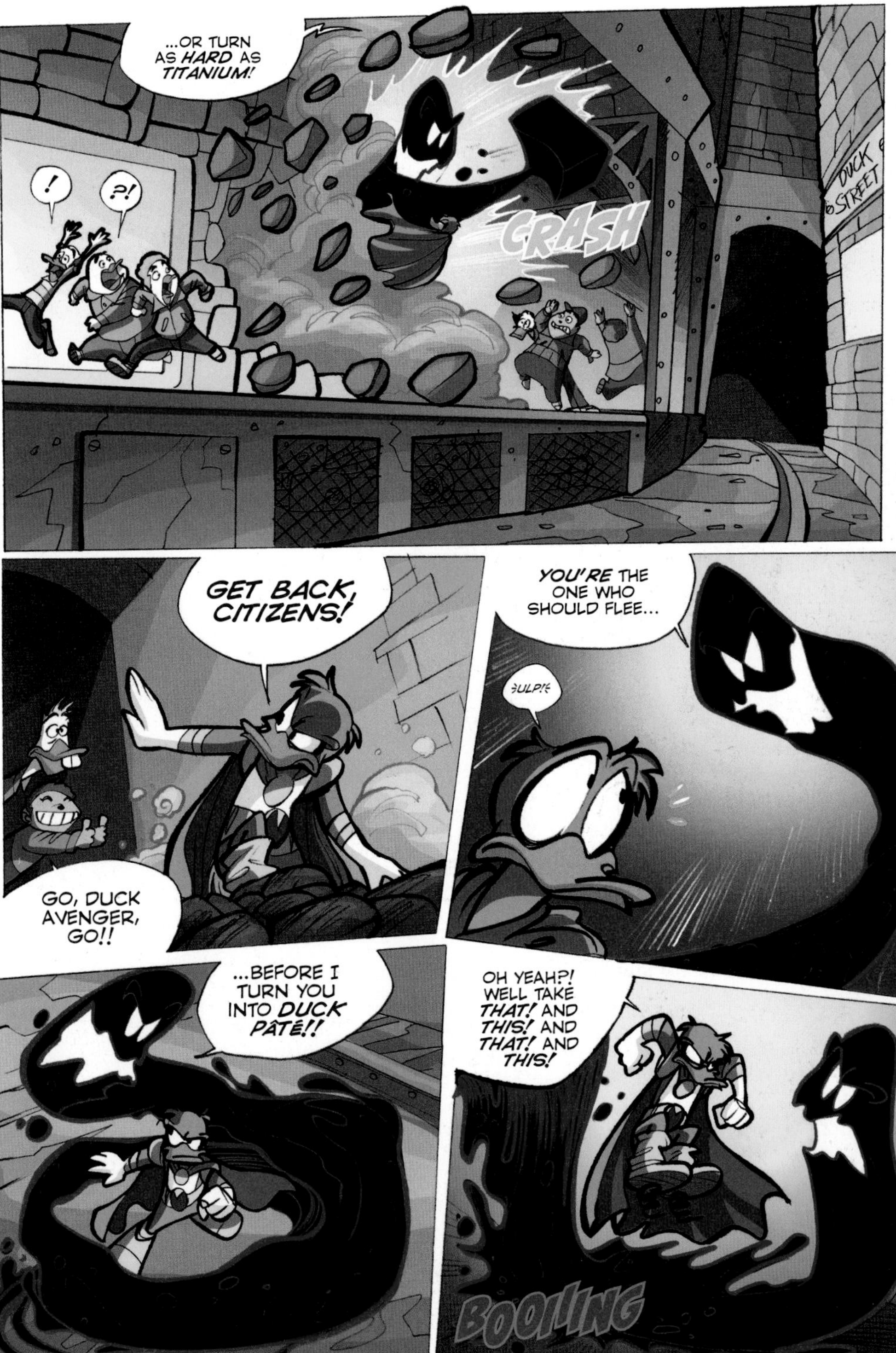

...OR TURN AS HARD AS TITANIUM!
!
?!
CRASH
DUCK STREET
GET BACK, CITIZENS!
GO, DUCK AVENGER, GO!!
YOU'RE THE ONE WHO SHOULD FLEE...
GULP!
...BEFORE I TURN YOU INTO DUCK PÂTÉ!!
OH YEAH?! WELL TAKE THAT! AND THIS! AND THAT! AND THIS!
BOOING

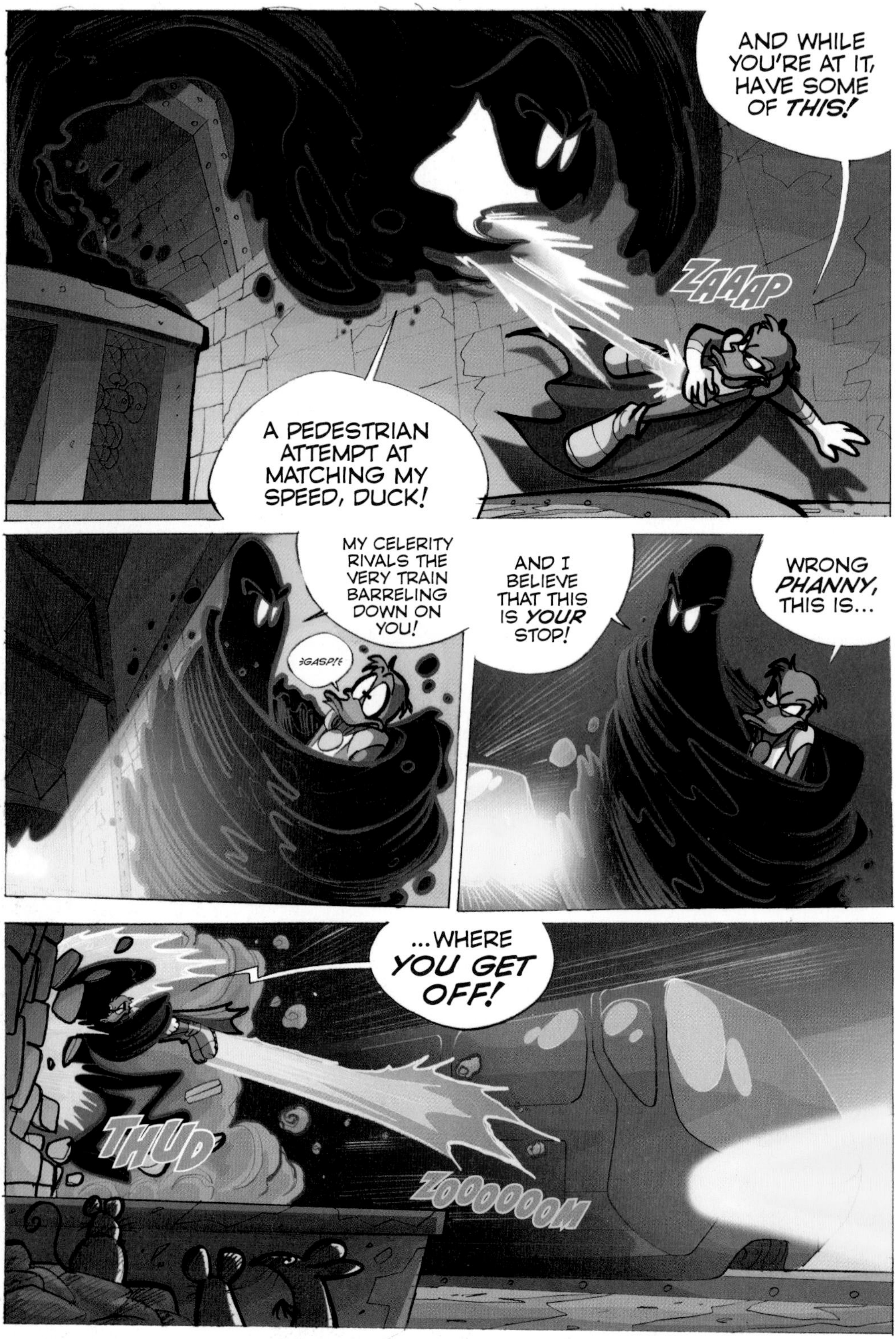
AND WHILE YOU'RE AT IT, HAVE SOME OF THIS!
ZAAAP
A PEDESTRIAN ATTEMPT AT MATCHING MY SPEED, DUCK!
MY CELERITY RIVALS THE VERY TRAIN BARRELING DOWN ON YOU!
GASP!
AND I BELIEVE THAT THIS IS YOUR STOP!
WRONG PHANNY, THIS IS...
...WHERE YOU GET OFF!
THUD
ZOOOOOOOM

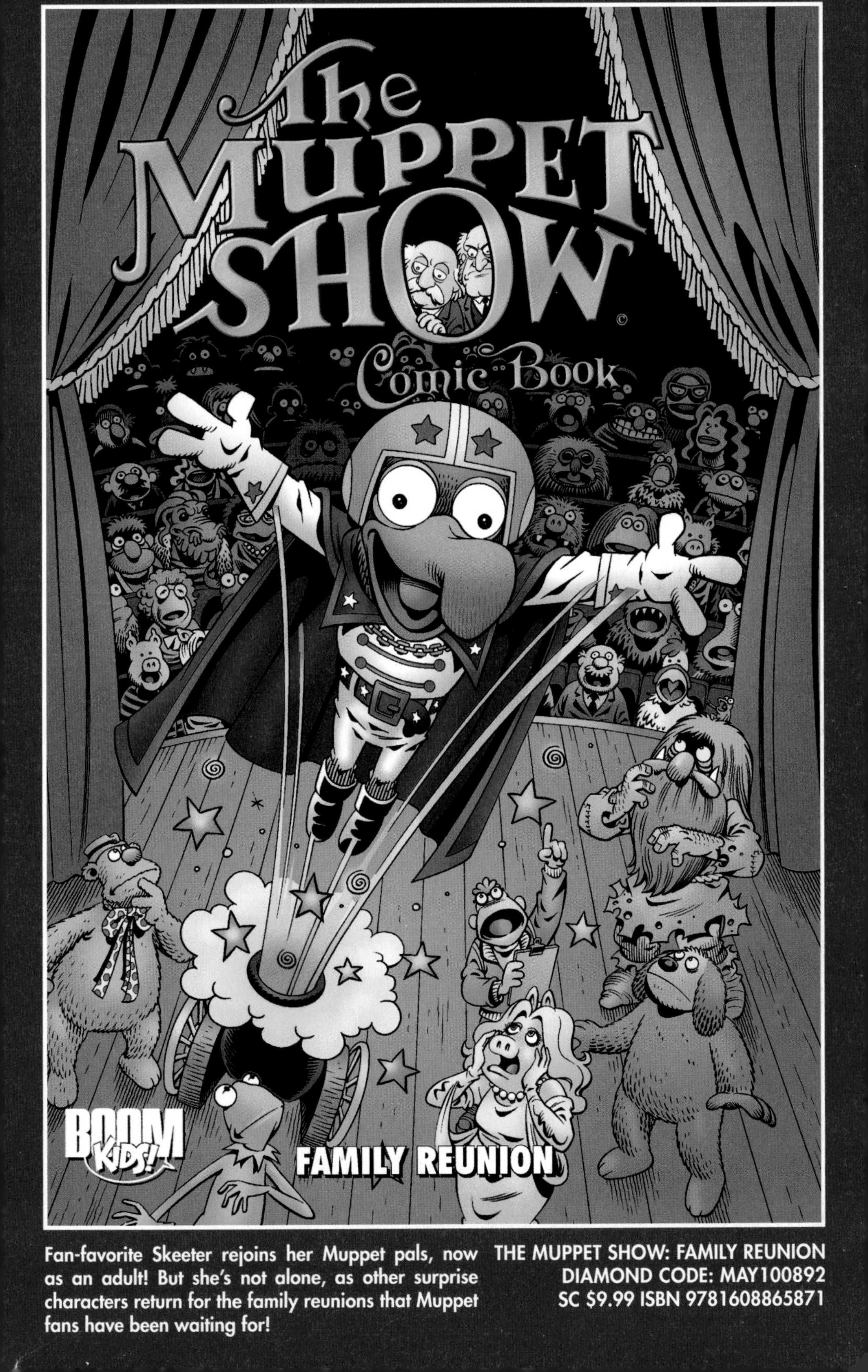
The Muppet Show
Comic Book
FAMILY REUNION

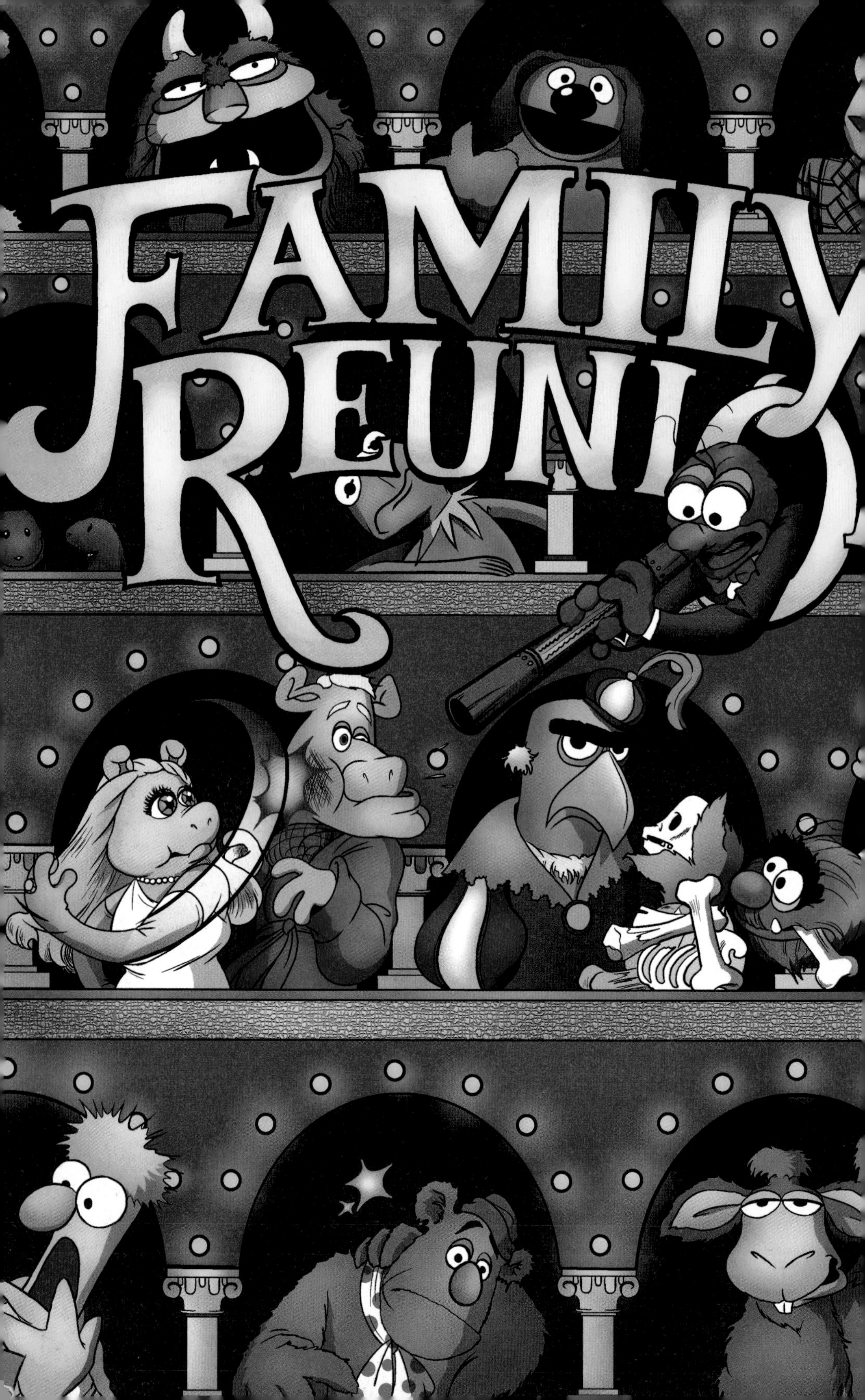
FAMILY
REUNI

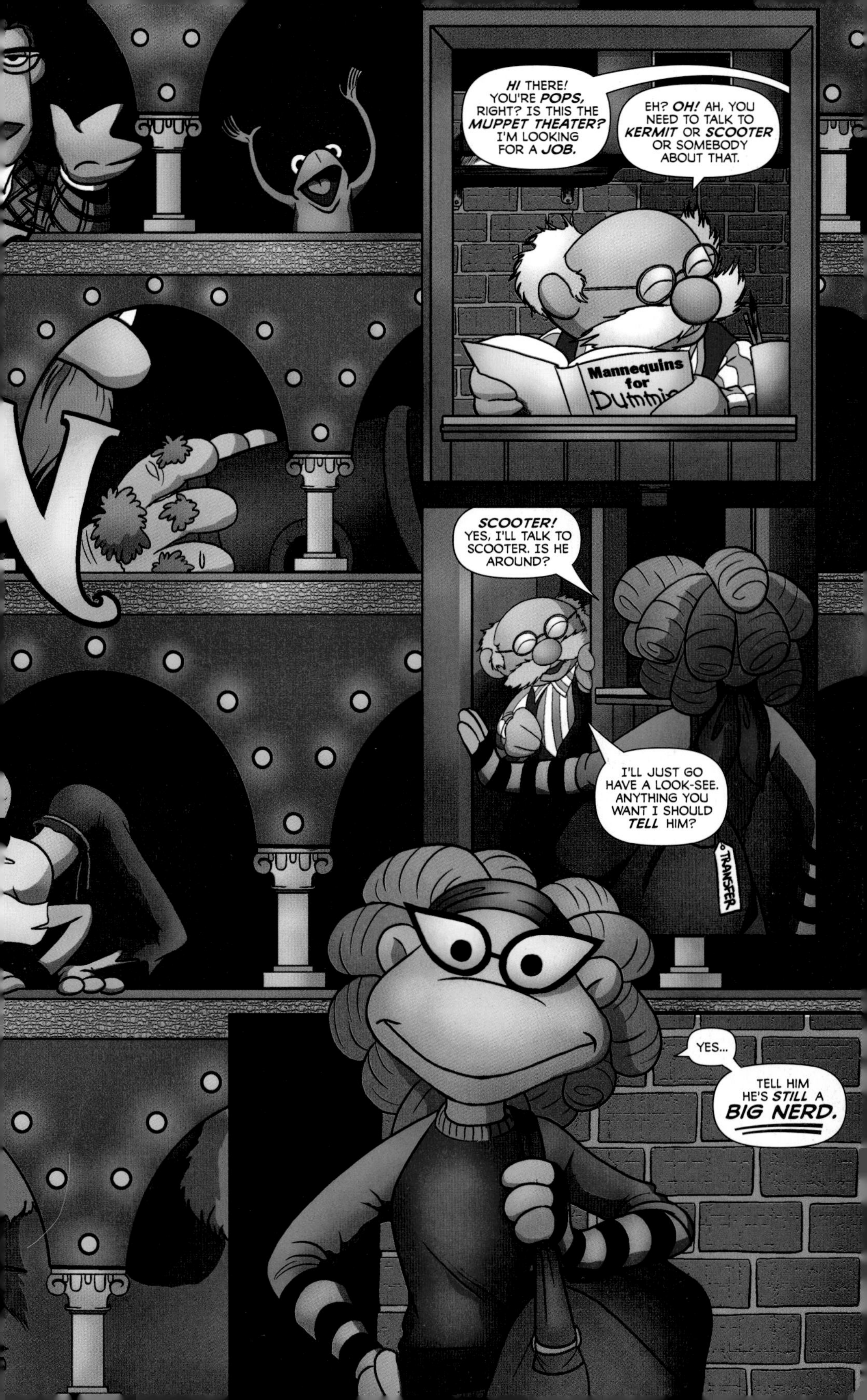
HI THERE! YOU'RE POPS, RIGHT? IS THIS THE MUPPET THEATER? I'M LOOKING FOR A JOB.
EH? OH! AH, YOU NEED TO TALK TO KERMIT OR SCOOTER OR SOMEBODY ABOUT THAT.
Mannequins for Dummies
SCOOTER! YES, I'LL TALK TO SCOOTER. IS HE AROUND?
I'LL JUST GO HAVE A LOOK-SEE. ANYTHING YOU WANT I SHOULD TELL HIM?
TRANSFER
YES...
TELL HIM HE'S STILL A BIG NERD.

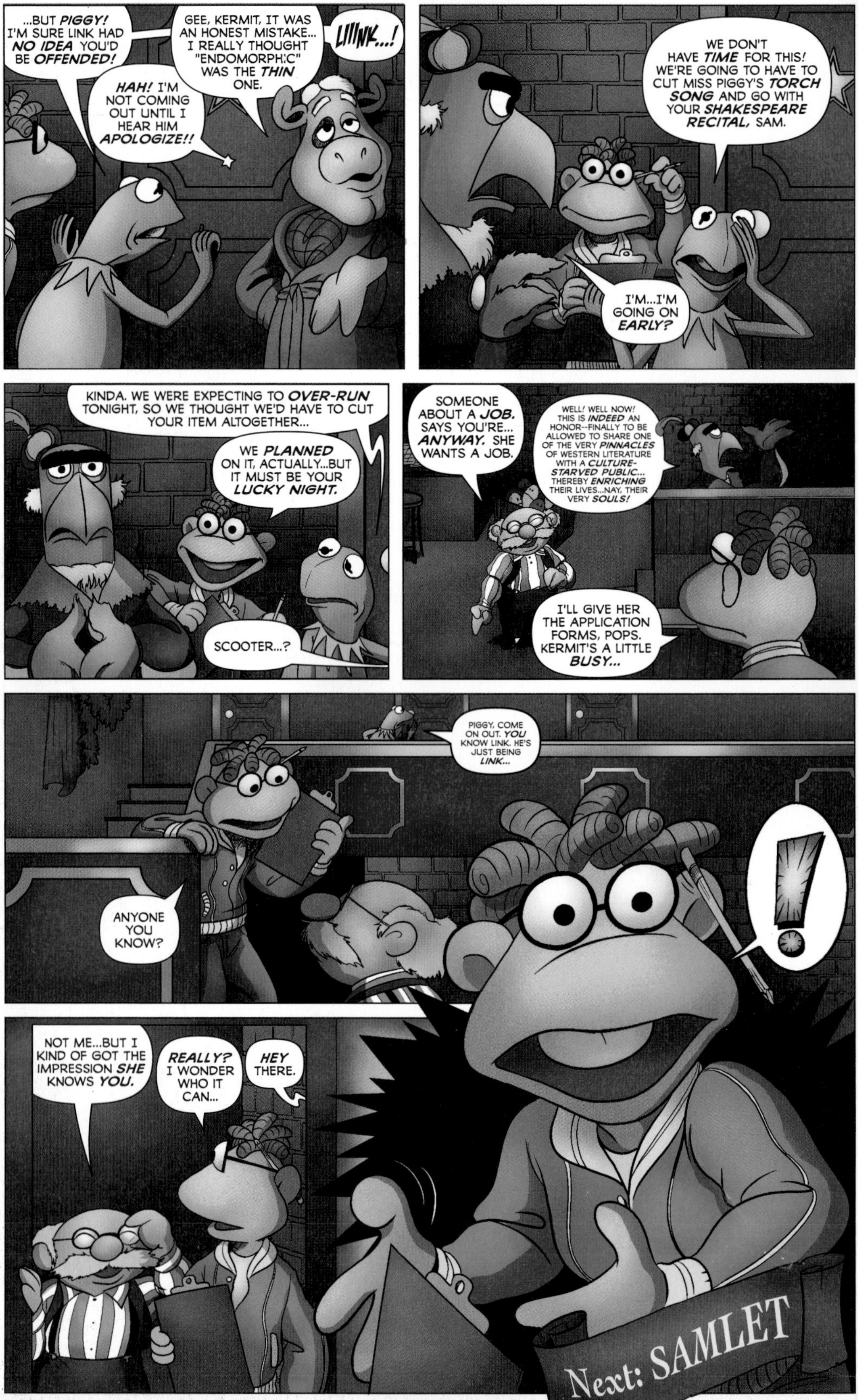
...BUT PIGGY! I'M SURE LINK HAD NO IDEA YOU'D BE OFFENDED!
GEE, KERMIT, IT WAS AN HONEST MISTAKE... I REALLY THOUGHT "ENDOMORPHIC" WAS THE THIN ONE.
LIIINK...!
HAH! I'M NOT COMING OUT UNTIL I HEAR HIM APOLOGIZE!!
WE DON'T HAVE TIME FOR THIS! WE'RE GOING TO HAVE TO CUT MISS PIGGY'S TORCH SONG AND GO WITH YOUR SHAKESPEARE RECITAL, SAM.
I'M...I'M GOING ON EARLY?
KINDA. WE WERE EXPECTING TO OVER-RUN TONIGHT, SO WE THOUGHT WE'D HAVE TO CUT YOUR ITEM ALTOGETHER...
WE PLANNED ON IT, ACTUALLY...BUT IT MUST BE YOUR LUCKY NIGHT.
SCOOTER...?
SOMEONE ABOUT A JOB. SAYS YOU'RE... ANYWAY. SHE WANTS A JOB.
WELL! WELL NOW! THIS IS INDEED AN HONOR--FINALLY TO BE ALLOWED TO SHARE ONE OF THE VERY PINNACLES OF WESTERN LITERATURE WITH A CULTURE-STARVED PUBLIC... THEREBY ENRICHING THEIR LIVES...NAY, THEIR VERY SOULS!
I'LL GIVE HER THE APPLICATION FORMS, POPS. KERMIT'S A LITTLE BUSY...
PIGGY, COME ON OUT. YOU KNOW LINK. HE'S JUST BEING LINK...
ANYONE YOU KNOW?
!
NOT ME...BUT I KIND OF GOT THE IMPRESSION SHE KNOWS YOU.
REALLY? I WONDER WHO IT CAN...
HEY THERE.
Next: SAMLET

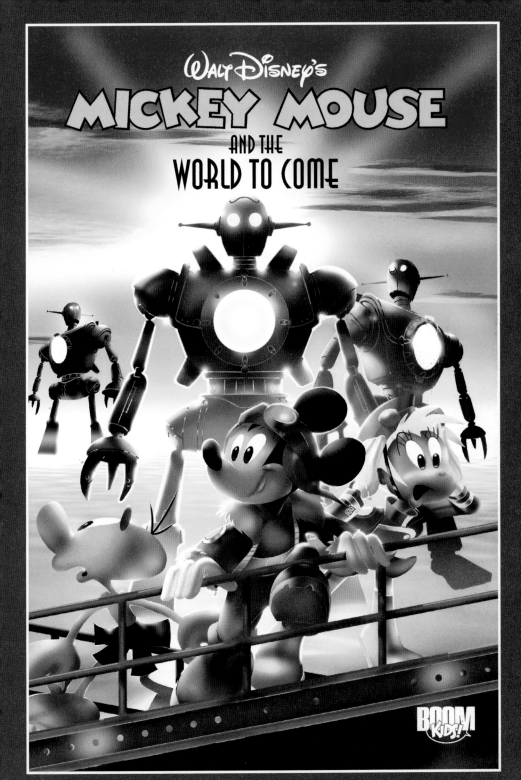

Join Mickey Mouse, Minnie and Eega Beeva on a
high-flying adventure to stop a terrifying possible
future from coming true!

MICKEY MOUSE AND THE
WORLD TO COME
DIAMOND CODE: MAR100814
SC $9.99 ISBN 9781608865628

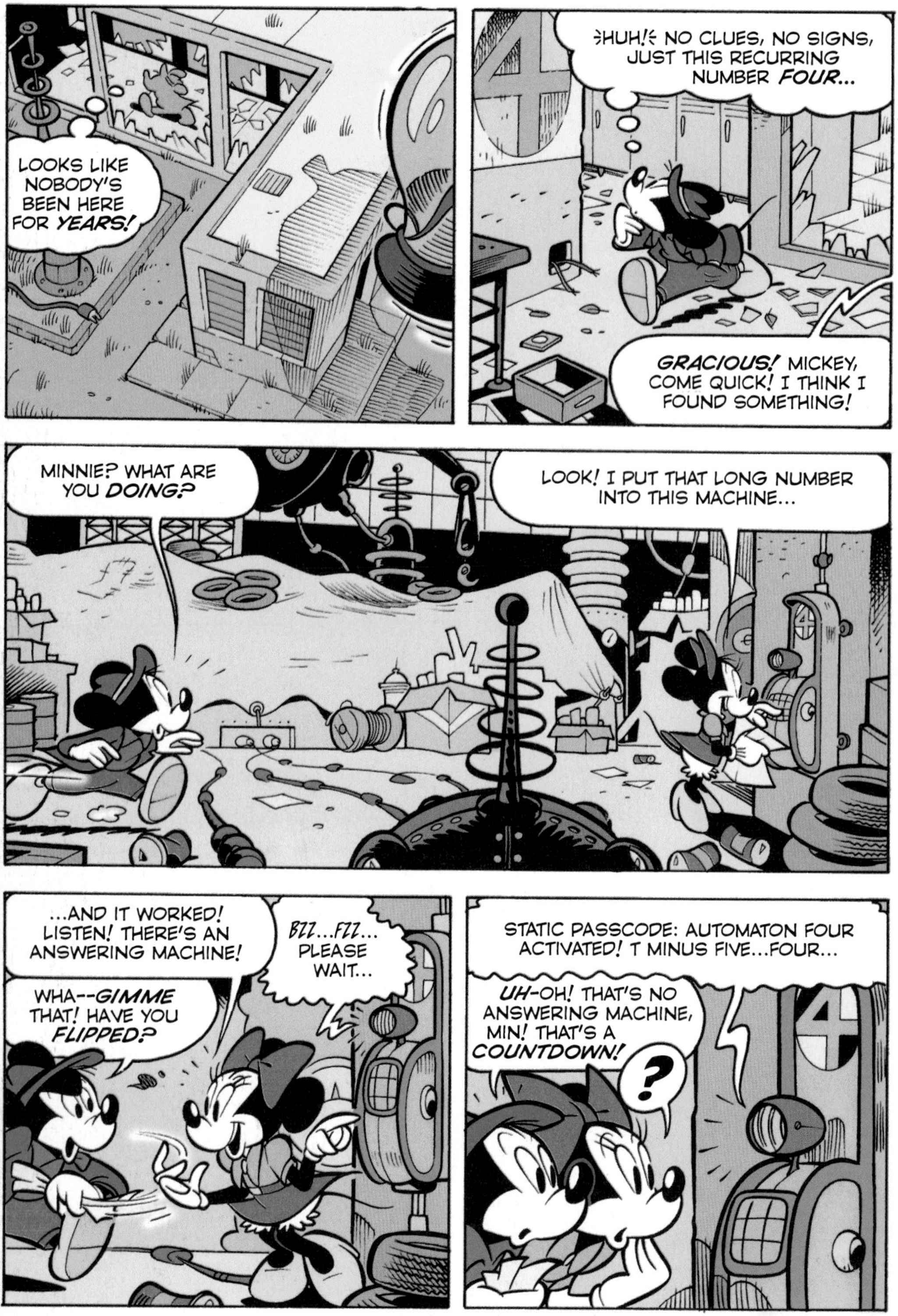
LOOKS LIKE NOBODY'S BEEN HERE FOR *YEARS!*
HUH! NO CLUES, NO SIGNS, JUST THIS RECURRING NUMBER *FOUR...*
GRACIOUS! MICKEY, COME QUICK! I THINK I FOUND SOMETHING!
MINNIE? WHAT ARE YOU *DOING?*
LOOK! I PUT THAT LONG NUMBER INTO THIS MACHINE...
...AND IT WORKED! LISTEN! THERE'S AN ANSWERING MACHINE!
BZZ...FZZ... PLEASE WAIT...
WHA--*GIMME* THAT! HAVE YOU *FLIPPED?*
STATIC PASSCODE: AUTOMATON FOUR ACTIVATED! T MINUS FIVE...FOUR...
UH-OH! THAT'S NO ANSWERING MACHINE, MIN! THAT'S A *COUNTDOWN!*
?

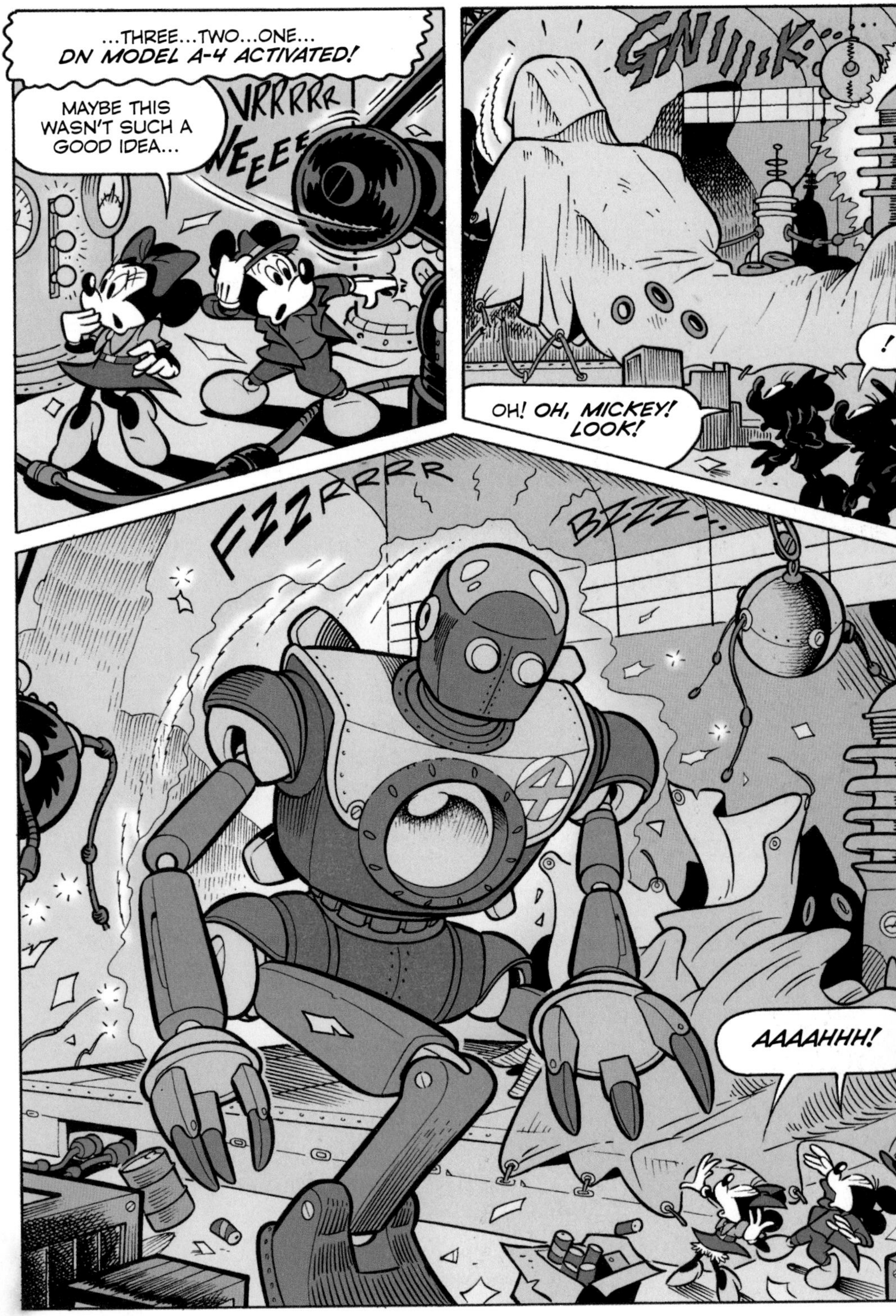
...THREE...TWO...ONE...
DN MODEL A-4 ACTIVATED!
MAYBE THIS WASN'T SUCH A GOOD IDEA...
VRRRRR
WEEEE
GNIIIIK
!
OH! OH, MICKEY! LOOK!
FZZRRRRR
BZZZ
AAAAHHH!

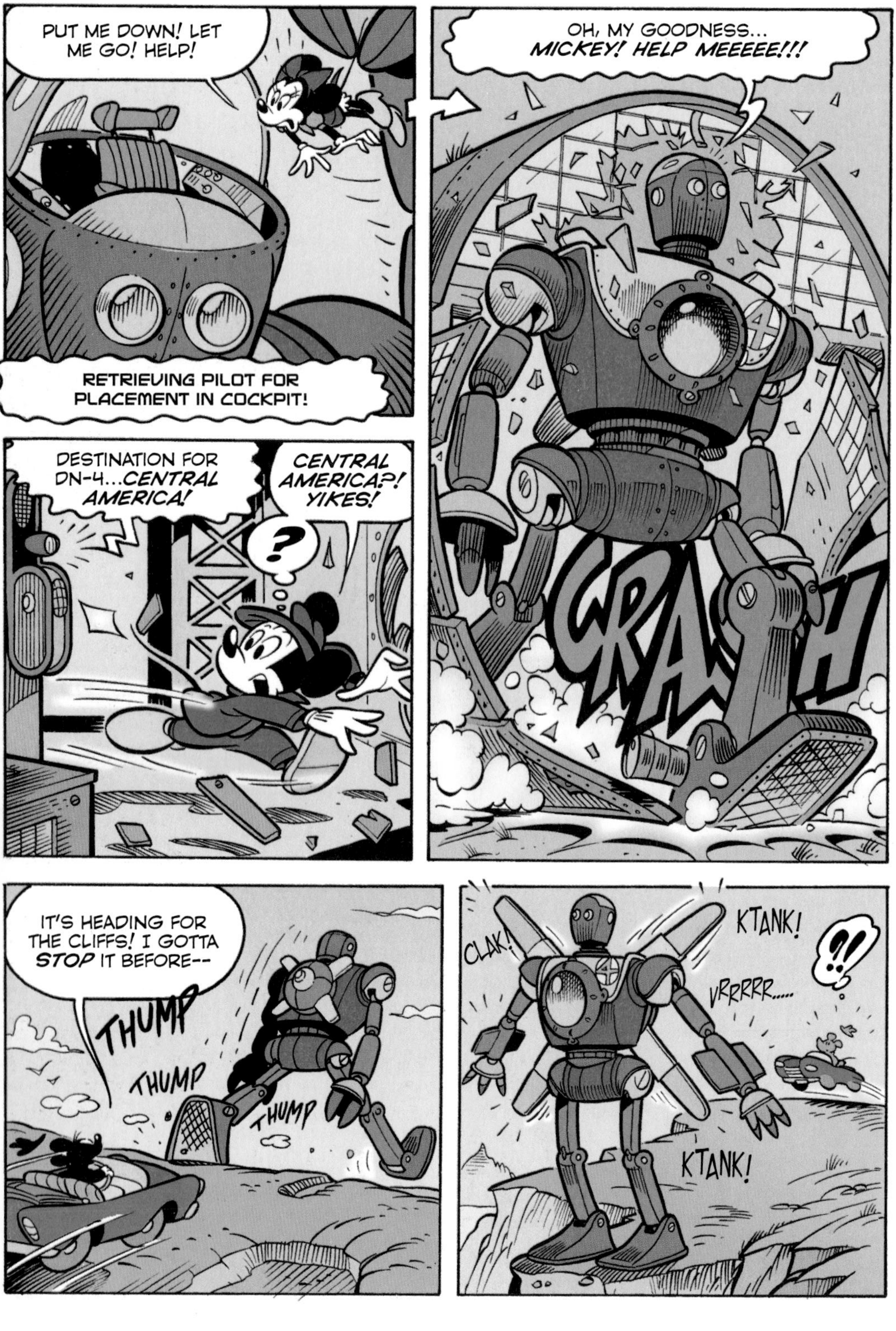
PUT ME DOWN! LET ME GO! HELP!
RETRIEVING PILOT FOR PLACEMENT IN COCKPIT!
OH, MY GOODNESS... MICKEY! HELP MEEEEE!!!
DESTINATION FOR DN-4...CENTRAL AMERICA!
CENTRAL AMERICA?! YIKES!
?
CRASH
IT'S HEADING FOR THE CLIFFS! I GOTTA STOP IT BEFORE--
THUMP
THUMP
THUMP
CLAK!
KTANK!
?!
VRRRRR.....
KTANK!

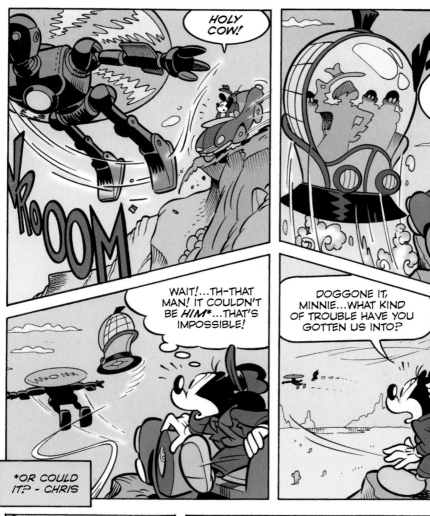

HOLY COW!

VZRRR

WHAT IN THE WORLD IS— *HEY!*

!

WAIT!...TH-THAT MAN! IT COULDN'T BE *HIM**...THAT'S IMPOSSIBLE!

DOGGONE IT, MINNIE...WHAT KIND OF TROUBLE HAVE YOU GOTTEN US INTO?

*OR COULD IT? - CHRIS

BIG TROUBLE, RODENT! BIG, *BIG* TROUBLE!

SKREEEEEE

!!

DON'T MOVE!

HANDS IN THE AIR!

DON'T EVEN BREATHE OR YOU'RE TOAST!

!!!

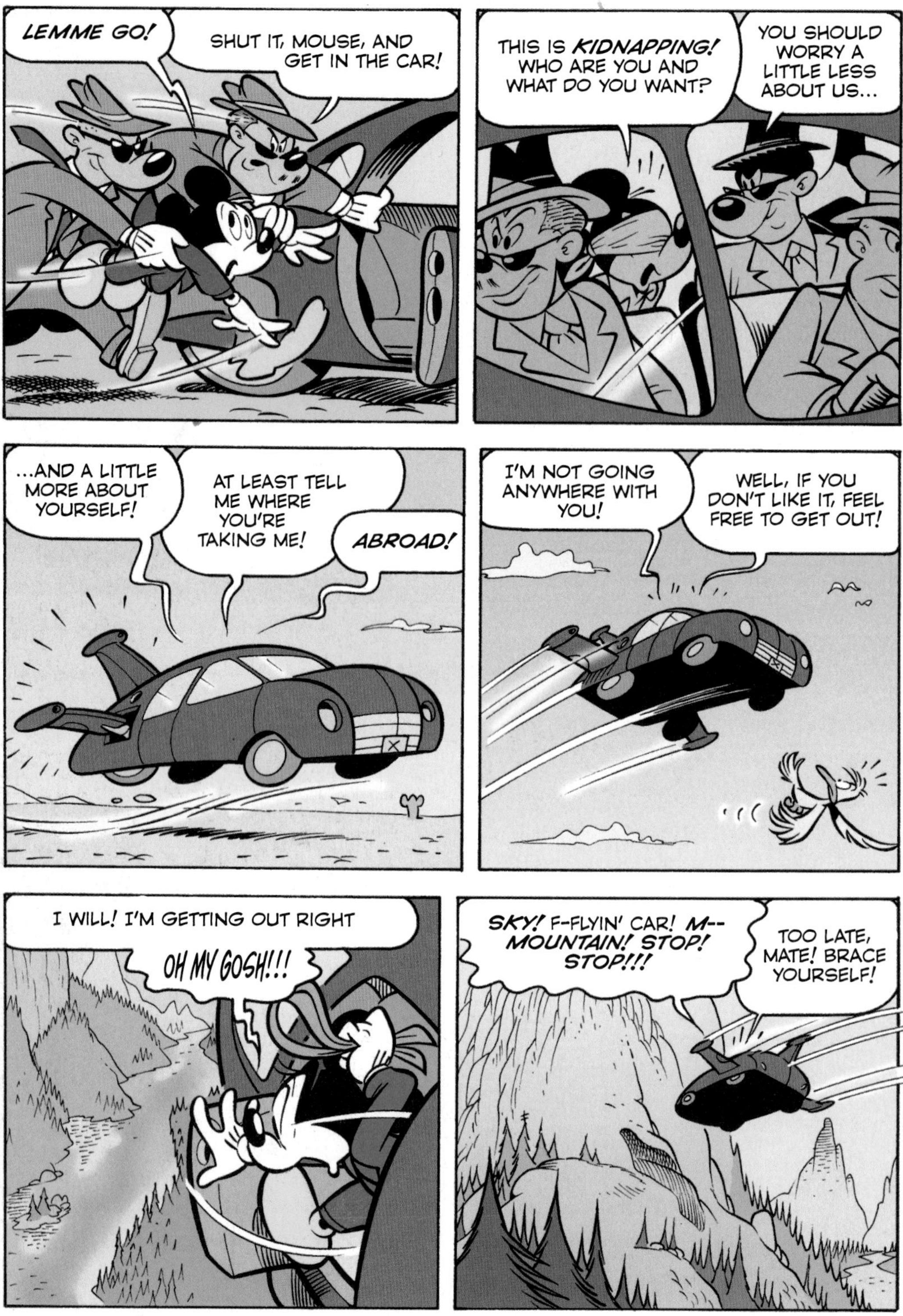
LEMME GO!
SHUT IT, MOUSE, AND GET IN THE CAR!
THIS IS KIDNAPPING! WHO ARE YOU AND WHAT DO YOU WANT?
YOU SHOULD WORRY A LITTLE LESS ABOUT US...
...AND A LITTLE MORE ABOUT YOURSELF!
AT LEAST TELL ME WHERE YOU'RE TAKING ME!
ABROAD!
I'M NOT GOING ANYWHERE WITH YOU!
WELL, IF YOU DON'T LIKE IT, FEEL FREE TO GET OUT!
I WILL! I'M GETTING OUT RIGHT
OH MY GOSH!!!
SKY! F--FLYIN' CAR! M--MOUNTAIN! STOP! STOP!!!
TOO LATE, MATE! BRACE YOURSELF!

Someone is stealing comedy props from the other employees, making it hard for them to harvest the laughter they need to power Monstropolis...and all evidence points to Sulley's best friend, Mike Wazowski!

MONSTERS, INC.: LAUGH FACTORY
DIAMOND CODE: OCT090801
SC $9.99 ISBN 9781608865086
HC $24.99 ISBN 9781608865338

SORRY, BOO. FUN'S OVER. TIME TO GET YOU BACK TO YOUR ROOM.

KITTY! WHAAAAH!

ZZT!! FFZZT!!

KIIIITTY!

SEE WHAT YOU'VE DONE, MIKE?!

GET HER HOME BEFORE SHE SHORTS OUT THE WHOLE POWER PLANT!

YEAH, LISTEN TO THE BOSS, KID. WOULDN'T WANT TO HURT HIS PRECIOUS COMPANY, WOULD WE?

MMMM MRR!

HELLO, ROZ? LISTEN, THERE'S SOMETHING FISHY GOING ON HERE AT THE FACTORY. I JUST FOUND ALL THESE STOLEN PROPS SHOVED INTO MIKE'S LOCKER AND--

--DON'T WORRY, SULLIVAN. I'LL TAKE CARE OF IT.

BUT WAIT, I--

DIALLING: ROZ

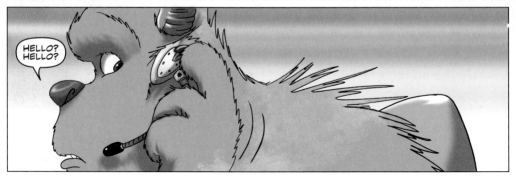

HELLO? HELLO?

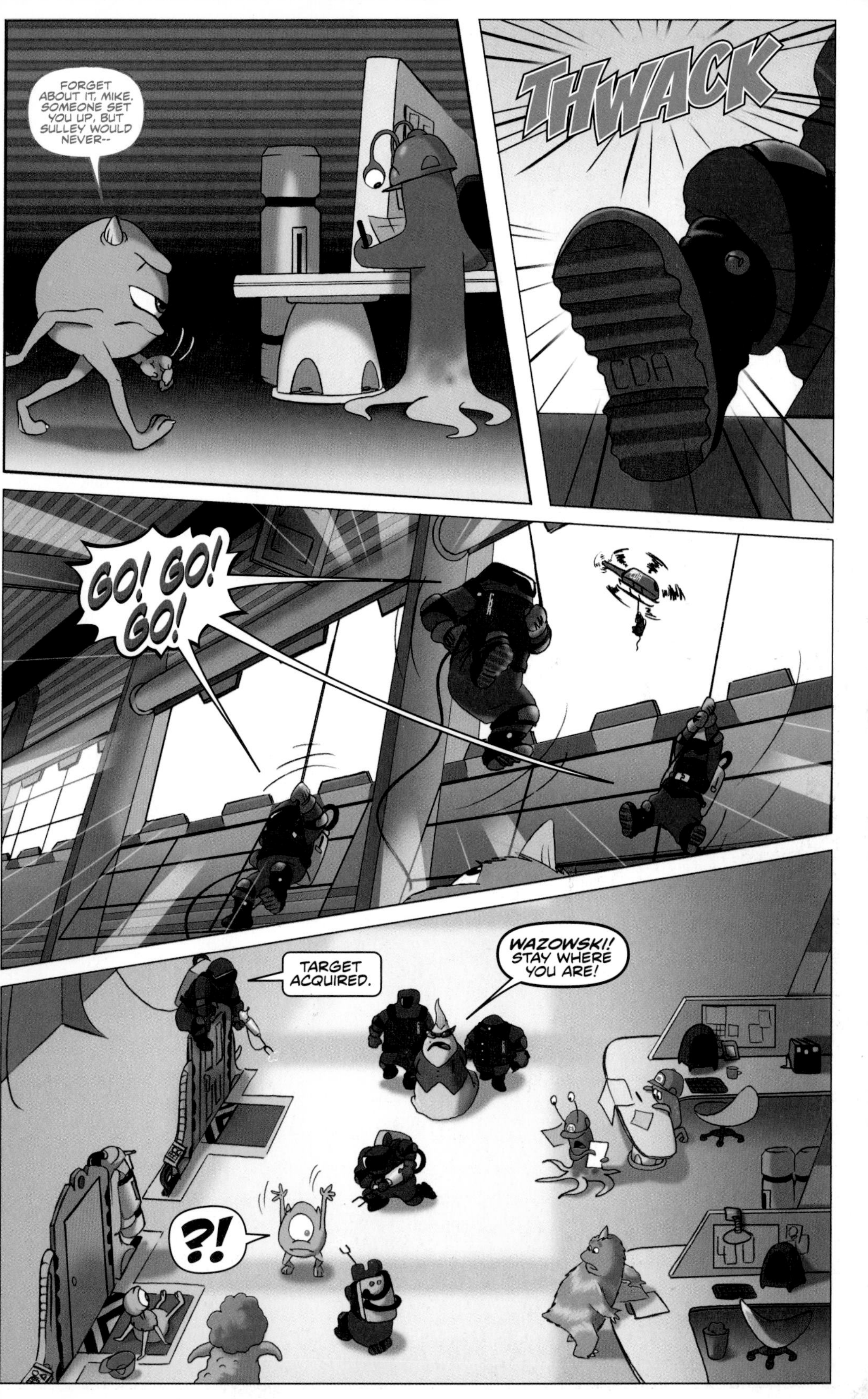
FORGET ABOUT IT, MIKE. SOMEONE SET YOU UP, BUT SULLEY WOULD NEVER--
THWACK
GO! GO! GO!
TARGET ACQUIRED.
WAZOWSKI! STAY WHERE YOU ARE!
?!

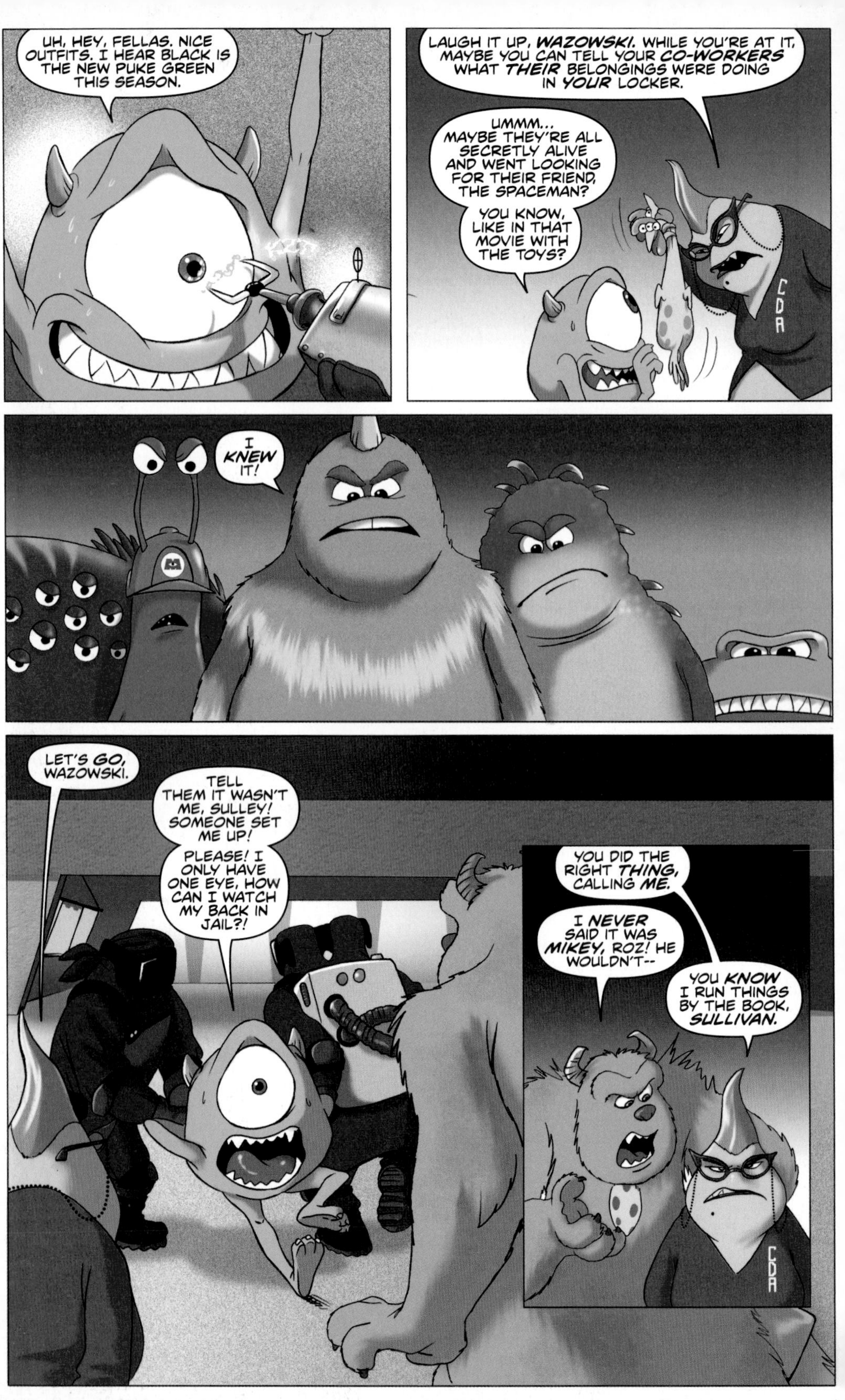
UH, HEY, FELLAS. NICE OUTFITS. I HEAR BLACK IS THE NEW PUKE GREEN THIS SEASON.
LAUGH IT UP, WAZOWSKI. WHILE YOU'RE AT IT, MAYBE YOU CAN TELL YOUR CO-WORKERS WHAT THEIR BELONGINGS WERE DOING IN YOUR LOCKER.
UMMM... MAYBE THEY'RE ALL SECRETLY ALIVE AND WENT LOOKING FOR THEIR FRIEND, THE SPACEMAN?
YOU KNOW, LIKE IN THAT MOVIE WITH THE TOYS?
CDA
I KNEW IT!
LET'S GO, WAZOWSKI.
TELL THEM IT WASN'T ME, SULLEY! SOMEONE SET ME UP!
PLEASE! I ONLY HAVE ONE EYE, HOW CAN I WATCH MY BACK IN JAIL?!
YOU DID THE RIGHT THING, CALLING ME.
I NEVER SAID IT WAS MIKEY, ROZ! HE WOULDN'T--
YOU KNOW I RUN THINGS BY THE BOOK, SULLIVAN.
CDA

GRAPHIC NOVELS AVAILABLE NOW!

BOOM KIDS!

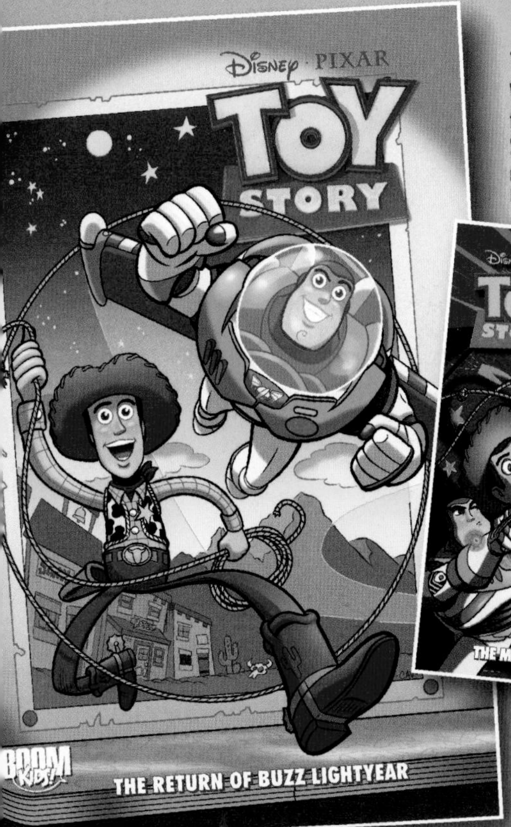

DISNEY · PIXAR
TOY STORY
BOOM KIDS!
THE RETURN OF BUZZ LIGHTYEAR

TOY STORY: THE RETURN OF BUZZ LIGHTYEAR

When Andy is given a surprise gift, no one is more surprised than the toys in his room...it's a second Buzz Lightyear! The stage is set for a Star Command showdown when only one Buzz can stay!

SC $9.99 ISBN 9781608865574
HC $24.99 ISBN 9781608865581

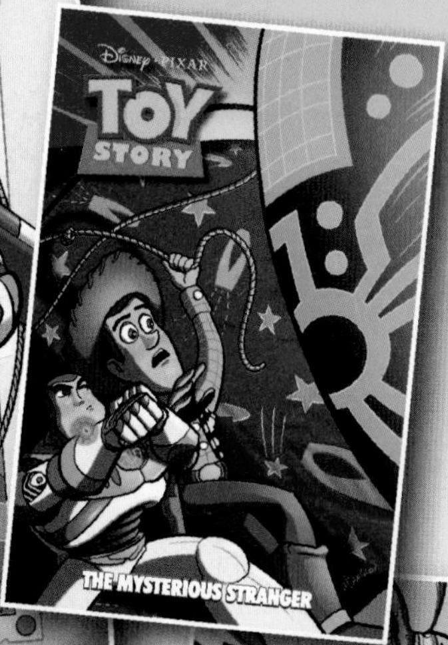

DISNEY · PIXAR
TOY STORY
THE MYSTERIOUS STRANGER

TOY STORY: THE MYSTERIOUS STRANGER

Andy has a new addition to his room—a circuit-laden egg. Is this new gizmo a friend or foe? This adventure kicks off the first of four self-contained stories featuring all your favorite characters from the TOY STORY movies – Woody, Buzz and the gang!

SC $9.99 ISBN 9781934506912
HC $24.99 ISBN 9781608865239

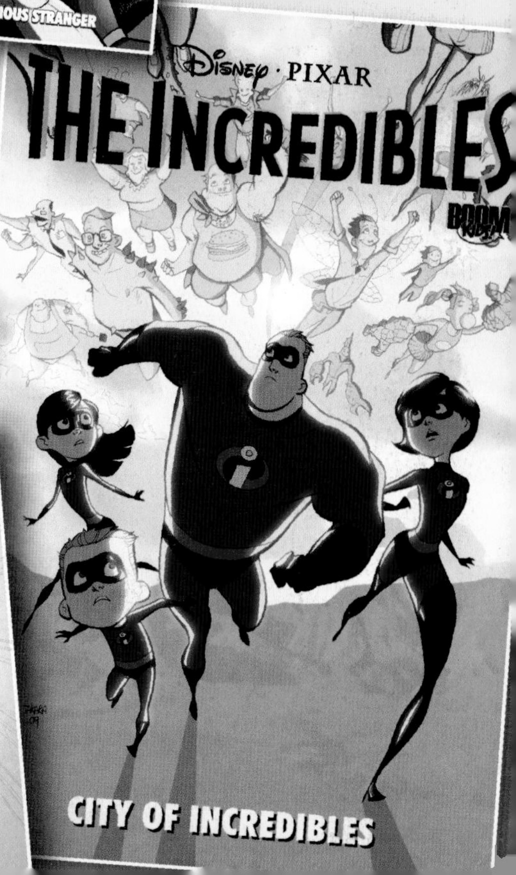

DISNEY · PIXAR
THE INCREDIBLES
BOOM KIDS!
CITY OF INCREDIBLES

THE INCREDIBLES: CITY OF INCREDIBLES

Baby Jack-Jack, everyone's favorite super-powered toddler, battles...a nasty cold! Hopefully the rest of the Parr family can stay healthy, because the henchmen of super villains are rapidly starting to exhibit superpowers!

SC $9.99 ISBN 9781608865031
HC $24.99 ISBN 9781608865291

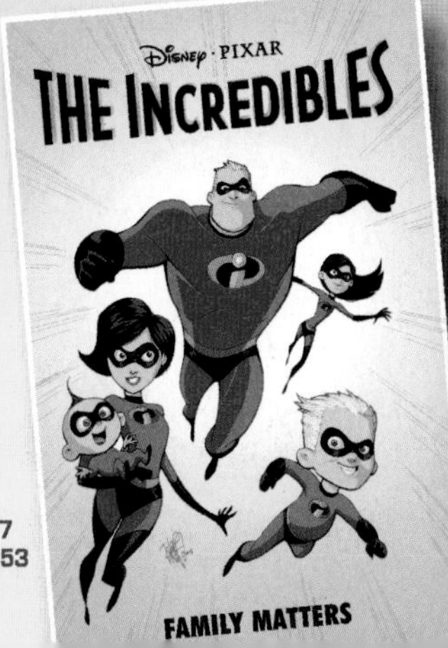

DISNEY · PIXAR
THE INCREDIBLES
FAMILY MATTERS

THE INCREDIBLES: FAMILY MATTERS

Acclaimed scribe Mark Waid has written the perfect INCREDIBLES story! What happens when Mr. Incredible's super-abilities start to wane...and how long can he keep his powerlessness a secret from his wife and kids?

SC $9.99 ISBN 9781934506837
HC $24.99 ISBN 9781608865253

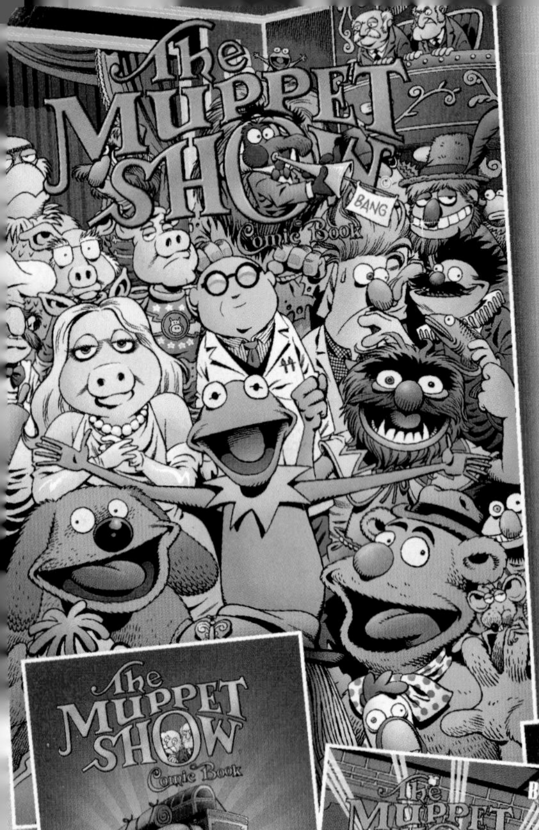
The Muppet Show
Comic Book
BANG

THE MUPPET SHOW COMIC BOOK: MEET THE MUPPETS

Collecting the first four issues of the Eisner Award-nominated THE MUPPET SHOW COMIC BOOK, written and drawn by the incomparable Roger Langridge! Packed full of madcap skits and gags, this trade is certain to please old and new fans alike!

SC $9.99 ISBN 9781934506851
HC $24.99 ISBN 9781608865277

THE MUPPET SHOW COMIC BOOK: THE TREASURE OF PEG-LEG WILSON

Scooter discovers old documents which reveal that a cache of treasure is hidden somewhere within the Muppet Theater...and when Rizzo the Rat overhears this, the news spreads like wildfire! Can Kermit keep everyone from tearing the theater apart?

SC $9.99 ISBN 9781608865048
HC $24.99 ISBN 9781608865307

THE MUPPET SHOW COMIC BOOK: ON THE ROAD

With the Muppet Theater destroyed, the Muppets take their act on the road...but with two very familiar hecklers in every town, will the show be a hit, or will our Muppet minstrels be run out of town in tar and feathers? Also: PIGS IN SPACE!

SC $9.99 ISBN 9781608865161

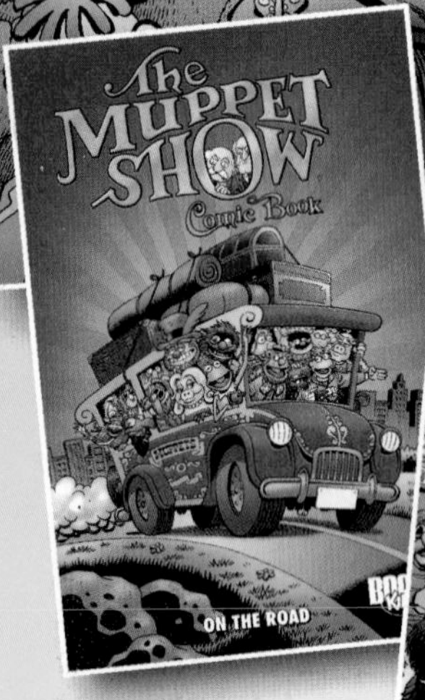
The Muppet Show
Comic Book
ON THE ROAD

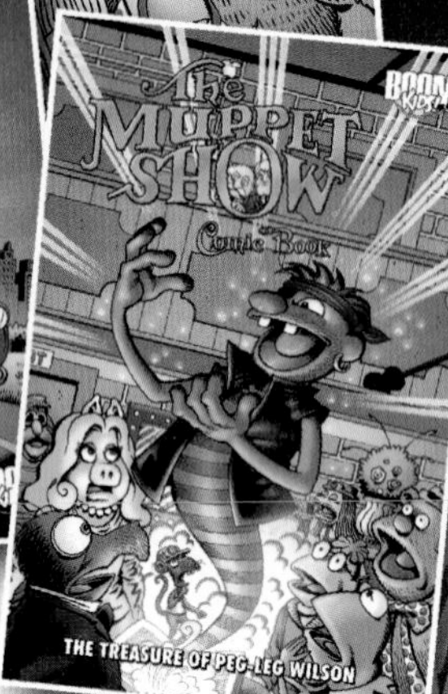
The Muppet Show
Comic Book
BOOM Kids!
THE TREASURE OF PEG-LEG WILSON

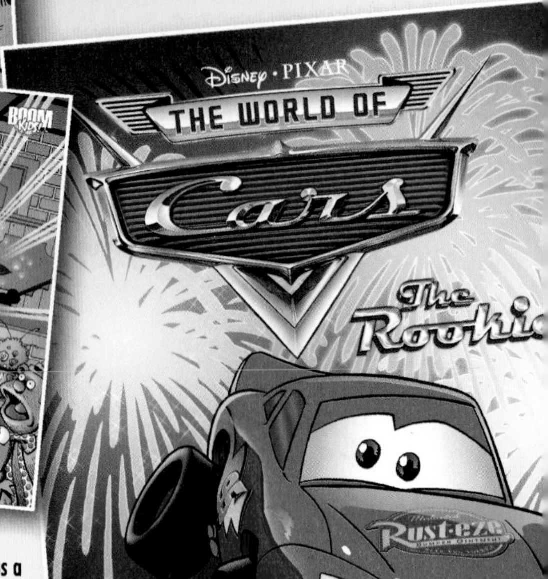
Disney · PIXAR
THE WORLD OF
Cars
The Rookie
Rust-eze
95

CARS: THE ROOKIE

See how Lightning McQueen became a Piston Cup sensation! CARS: THE ROOKIE reveals Lightning McQueen's scrappy origins as a local short track racer who dreams of the big time... and recklessly plows his way through the competition to get there!

SC $9.99 ISBN 9781934506844
HC $24.99 ISBN 9781608865222

CARS: RADIATOR SPRINGS

Lightning McQueen is hanging out with his friends at Flo's V8 Café when he realizes that everyone knows his story...but he doesn't know anyone else's! Lightning wants to know how his friends ended up in Radiator Springs...and more importantly, why they decided to stay!

SC $9.99 ISBN 9781608865024
HC $24.99 ISBN 9781608865284

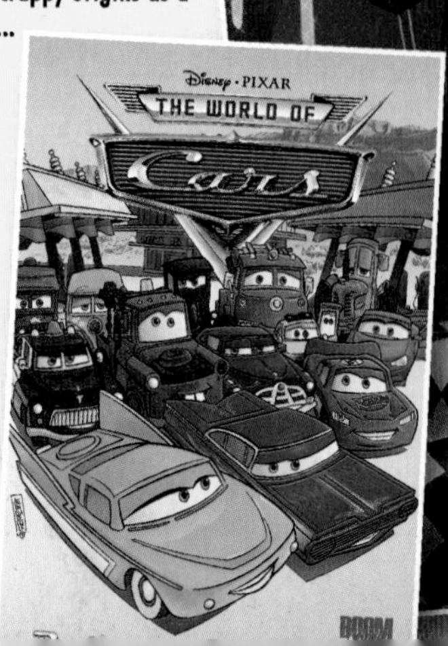
Disney · PIXAR
THE WORLD OF
Cars
BOOM

WALL•E: RECHARGE

Before WALL•E becomes the hardworking robot we know and love, he lets the few remaining robots take care of the trash compacting while he collects interesting junk. But when these robots start breaking down, WALL•E must adjust his priorities...or else Earth is doomed!

SC $9.99 ISBN 9781608865123
HC $24.99 ISBN 9781608865543

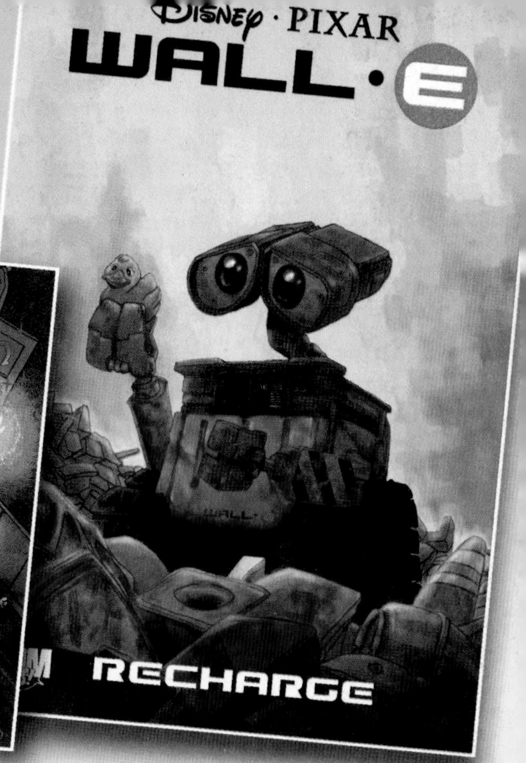
DISNEY · PIXAR
WALL·E
RECHARGE

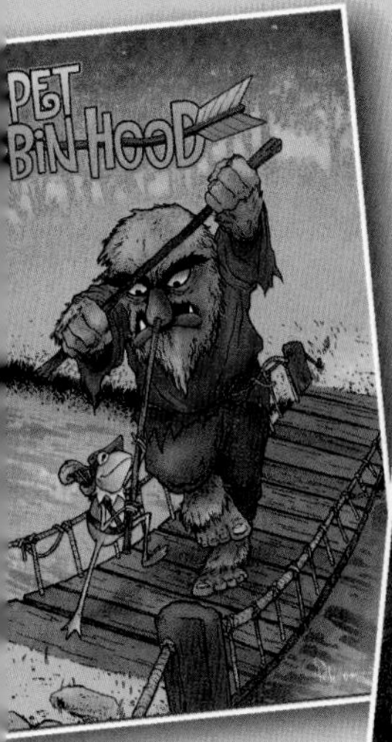

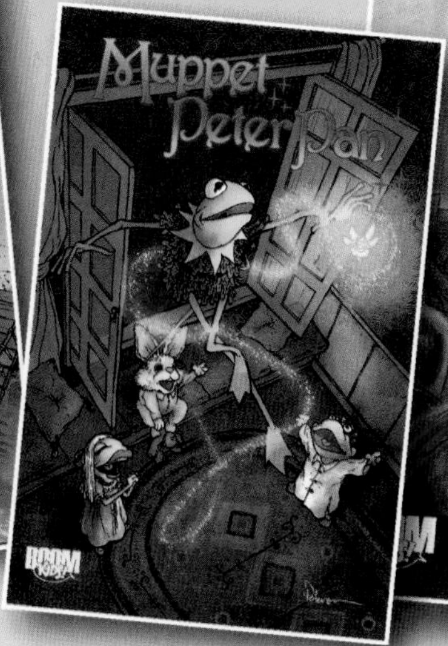
Muppet Peter Pan

MUPPET ROBIN HOOD

The Muppets tell the Robin Hood legend for laughs, and it's the reader who will be merry! Robin Hood (Kermit the Frog) joins with the Merry Men, Sherwood Forest's infamous gang of misfit outlaws, to take on the Sheriff of Nottingham (Sam the Eagle)!

SC $9.99 ISBN 9781934506790
HC $24.99 ISBN 9781608865260

MUPPET PETER PAN

When Peter Pan (Kermit) whisks Wendy (Janice) and her brothers to Neverswamp, the adventure begins! With Captain Hook (Gonzo) out for revenge for the loss of his hand, can even the magic of Piggytink (Miss Piggy) save Wendy and her brothers?

SC $9.99 ISBN 9781608865079
HC $24.99 ISBN 9781608865314

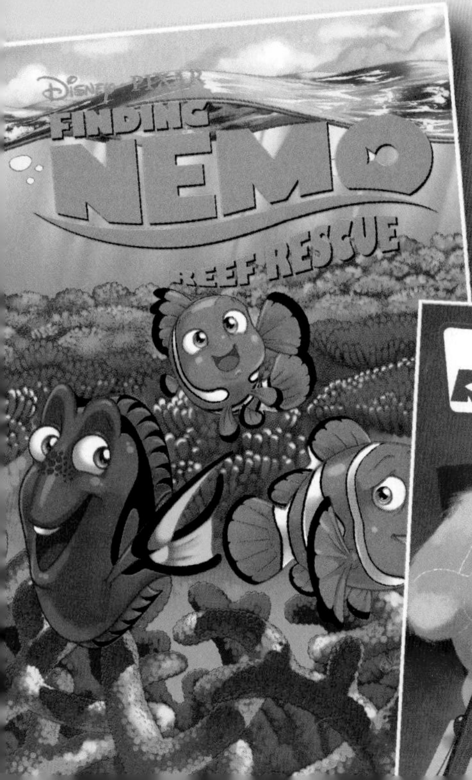
FINDING NEMO
REEF RESCUE

FINDING NEMO: REEF RESCUE

Nemo, Dory and Marlin have become local heroes, and are recruited to embark on an all-new adventure in this exciting collection! The reef is mysteriously dying and no one knows why. So Nemo and his friends must travel the great blue sea to save their home!

SC $9.99 ISBN 9781934506882
HC $24.99 ISBN 9781608865246

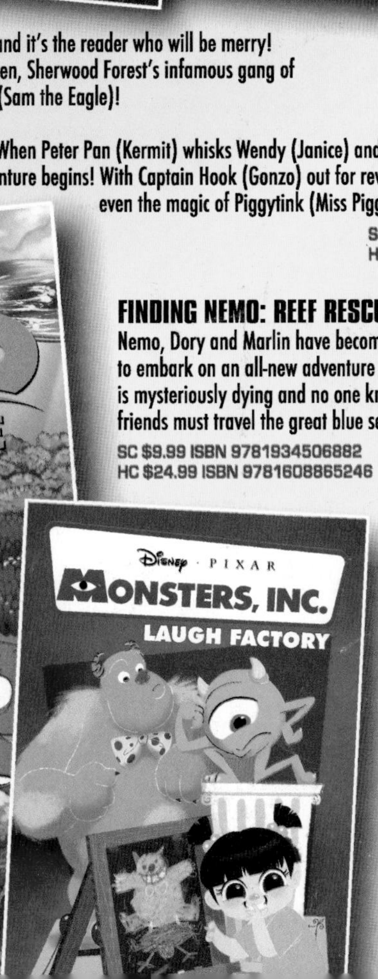
DISNEY · PIXAR
MONSTERS, INC.
LAUGH FACTORY

MONSTERS, INC.: LAUGH FACTORY

Someone is stealing comedy props from the other employees, making it difficult for them to harvest the laughter they need to power Monstropolis...and all evidence points to Sulley's best friend Mike Wazowski!

SC $9.99 ISBN 9781608865086
HC $24.99 ISBN 9781608865338

DISNEY'S HERO SQUAD: ULTRAHEROES
VOL. 1: SAVE THE WORLD

It's an all-star cast of your favorite Disney characters, as you have never seen them before. Join Donald Duck, Goofy, Daisy, and even Mickey himself as they defend the fate of the planet as the one and only Ultraheroes!

SC $9.99 ISBN 9781608865437
HC $24.99 ISBN 9781608865529

UNCLE SCROOGE:
THE HUNT FOR THE OLD
NUMBER ONE

Join Donald Duck's favorite penny-pinching Uncle Scrooge as he, Donald himself and Huey, Dewey, and Louie embark on a globe-spanning trek to recover treasure and save Scrooge's "number one dime" from the treacherous Magica De Spell.

SC $9.99 ISBN 9781608865475
HC $24.99 ISBN 9781608865536

WIZARDS OF MICKEY VOL. 1: MOUSE MAGIC

Your favorite Disney characters star in this magical fantasy epic! Student of the great wizard Nereus, Mickey allies himself with Donald and teammate Goofy, in a quest to find a magical crown that will give him mastery over all spells!

SC $9.99 ISBN 9781608865413
HC $24.99 ISBN 9781608865505

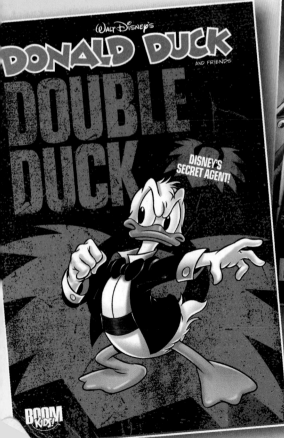

DONALD DUCK AND FRIENDS:
DOUBLE DUCK VOL. 1

Donald Duck as a secret agent? Villainous fiends beware as the world of super sleuthing and espionage will never be the same! This is Donald Duck like you've never seen him!

SC $9.99 ISBN 9781608865451
HC $24.99 ISBN 9781608865512

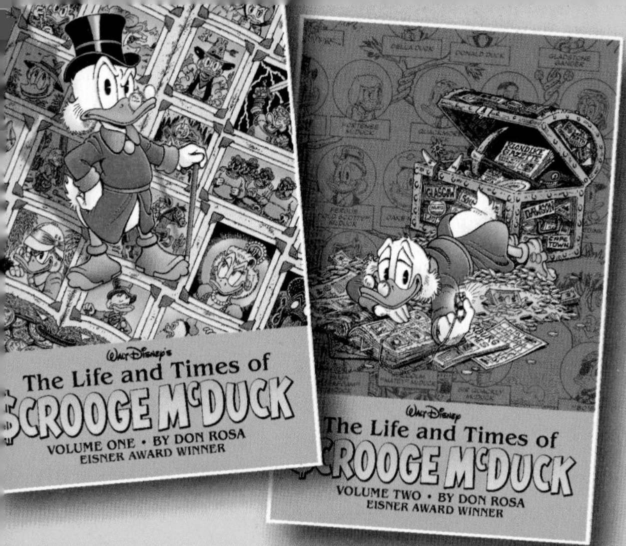
Walt Disney's
The Life and Times of
Scrooge McDuck
Volume One • By Don Rosa
Eisner Award Winner
Walt Disney
The Life and Times of
Scrooge McDuck
Volume Two • By Don Rosa
Eisner Award Winner

THE LIFE AND TIMES OF SCROOGE McDUCK VOL. 1

BOOM Kids! proudly collects the first half of THE LIFE AND TIMES OF SCROOGE MCDUCK in a gorgeous hardcover collection – featuring smyth sewn binding, a gold-on-gold foil-stamped case wrap, and a bookmark ribbon! These stories, written and drawn by legendary cartoonist Don Rosa, chronicle Scrooge McDuck's fascinating life.

HC $24.99 ISBN 9781608865383

THE LIFE AND TIMES OF SCROOGE McDUCK VOL. 2

BOOM Kids! proudly presents volume two of THE LIFE AND TIMES OF SCROOGE MCDUCK in a gorgeous hardcover collection in a beautiful, deluxe package featuring smyth sewn binding and a foil-stamped case wrap! These stories, written and drawn by legendary cartoonist Don Rosa, chronicle Scrooge McDuck's fascinating life.

HC $24.99 ISBN 9781608865420

MICKEY MOUSE CLASSICS: MOUSE TAILS

See Mickey Mouse as he was meant to be seen! Solving mysteries, fighting off pirates, and generally saving the day! These classic stories comprise a "Greatest Hits" series for the mouse, including a story produced by seminal Disney creator Carl Barks!

HC $24.99 ISBN 9781608865390

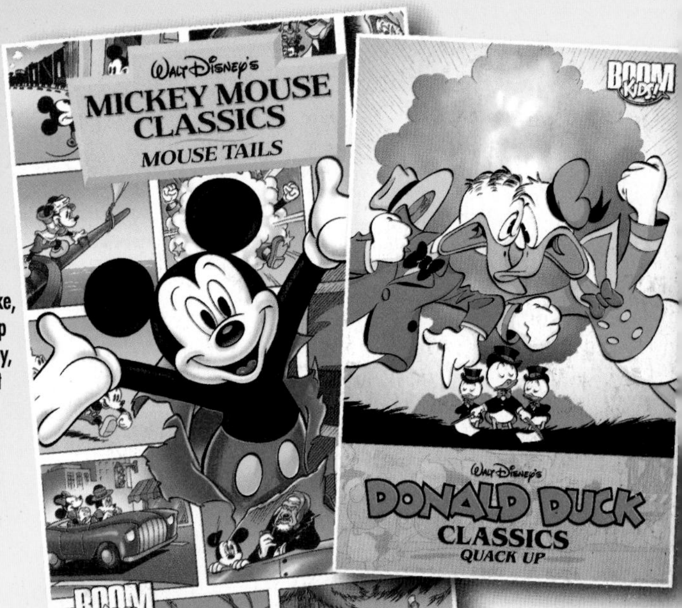
Walt Disney's
Mickey Mouse Classics
Mouse Tails
BOOM Kids!
BOOM Kids!
Walt Disney's
Donald Duck
Classics
Quack Up

DONALD DUCK CLASSICS: QUACK UP

Whether it's finding gold, journeying to the Klondike, or fighting ghosts, Donald will always have the help of his much more prepared nephews – Huey, Dewey, and Louie – by his side. Featuring some of the best Donald Duck stories Carl Barks ever produced!

HC $24.99 ISBN 9781608865406

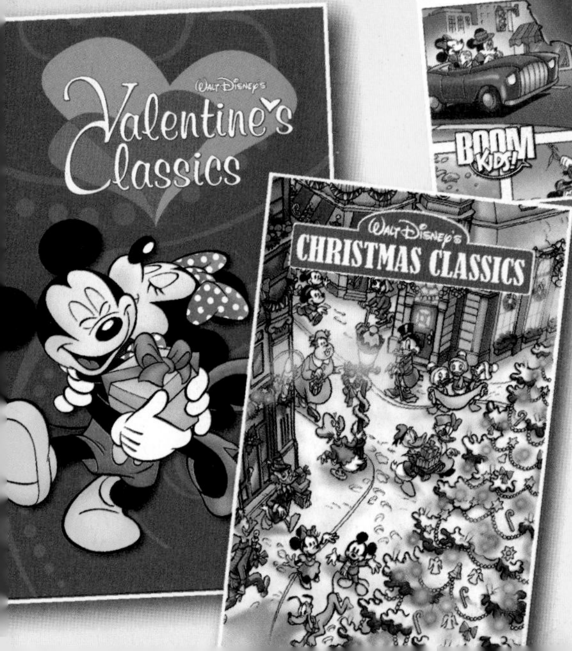
Walt Disney's
Valentine's Classics
Walt Disney's
Christmas Classics

WALT DISNEY'S VALENTINE'S CLASSICS

Love is in the air for Mickey Mouse, Donald Duck and the rest of the gang. But will Cupid's arrows cause happiness or heartache? Find out in this collection of classic stories featuring work by Carl Barks, Floyd Gottfredson, Daan Jippes, Romano Scarpa and Al Taliaferro.

HC $24.99 ISBN 9781608865499

WALT DISNEY'S CHRISTMAS CLASSICS

BOOM Kids! has raided the Disney publishing archives and searched every nook and cranny to find the best and the greatest Christmas stories from Disney's vast comic book publishing history for this "best of" compilation.

HC $24.99 ISBN 9781608865482

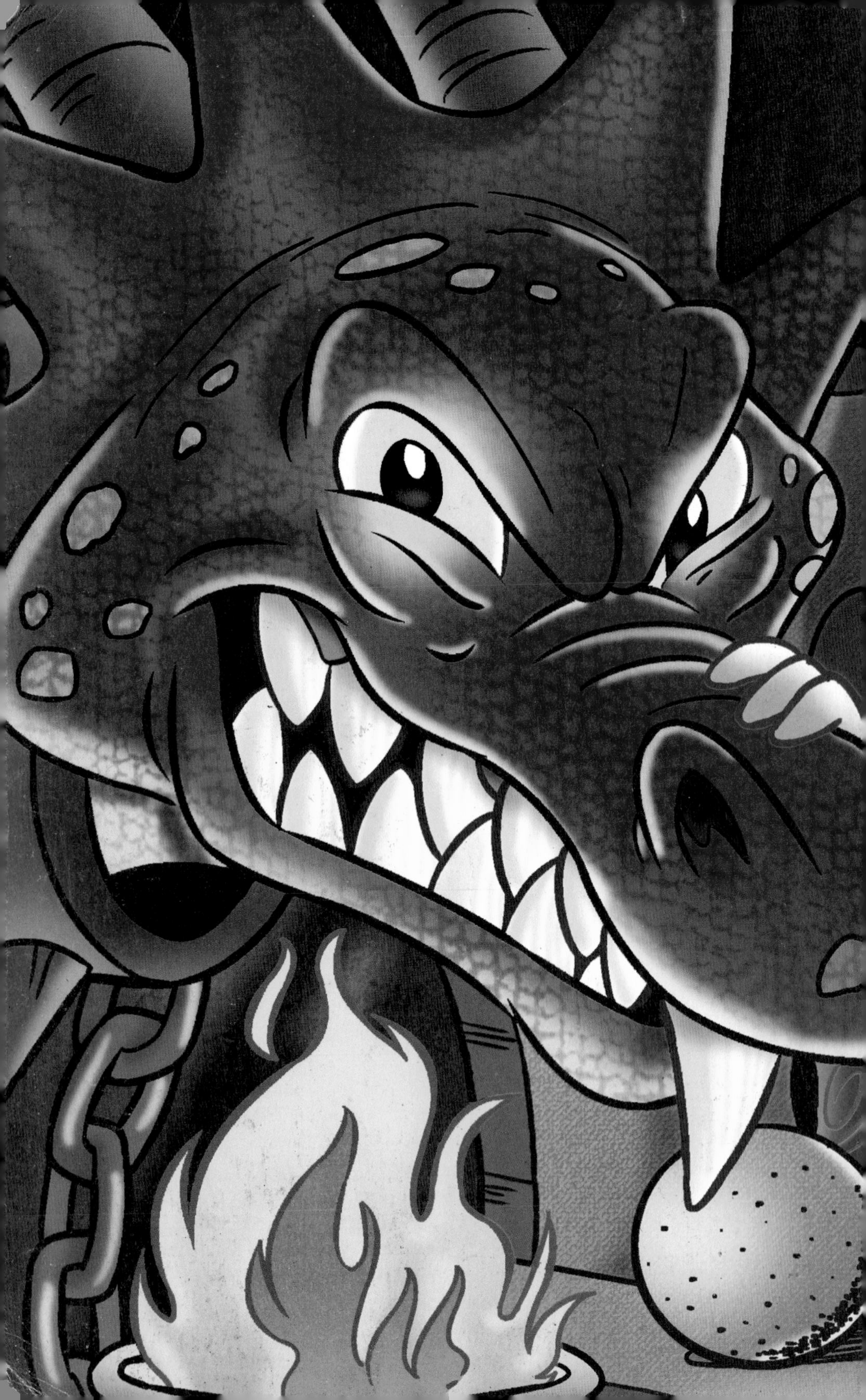